YES, SERGEANT VICTOR

By CONNIE TEAL

Volume two of 'Threads'

The story continues September 1915

Also in this series.

Threads. Volume one.

The Other Arf. Volume thre

Polladras Publishers
Penrose Farm
Trew, Breage,
 Helston. Cornwall.
 England.
TR13 9QN
writerconnieteal@mail.com

Published 2011

Connie Teal asserts the moral right to be identified as the
author of this work.

A catalogue record of this book is available from The British
Library.

ISBN 978-0-9562599-3-6

Printed and bound by the MPG Books Group Ltd

Cover by Knight Design
www.knightdesign.co.uk

CHAPTER ONE

"What's up wi' me mam?"

A tough looking lad in his early teens, fixed his eyes on Annie as she looked up from the floor where she knelt in front of Evelyn Barnicoat. An infant sat on a pot by the window where another child, a girl of nine or ten, waited alongside, to attend her younger sibling.

The infant whimpered, "Come on, you said you wanted to go," the girl spoke impatiently, "have you done it yet?" Her hand reached down to pull on the little boy's vest, the hasty inspection revealed the desired result and with ability beyond her years she cleaned her young brother's bottom and hurried out through the back door with the pot.

Annie held the woman's hand tightly between her own and spoke urgently but quietly, "Jake is back from Wrenshaws Evelyn," this produced another heart rending wail of grief, the infant rubbed one eye with a grubby little hand as tears rolled down his face, transferring the grime and dappling his cheeks with the tear soaked solution.

"It's me dad innit?" Said Jake, "It wer' Tommy's dad yesterday and Charlie's the week afore, I can tell it's me dad, mam cried the same when grandma died."

The girl crossed the room and prised open her mother's clenched hands, then placed her little brother's comforter in one palm. "E's split it again, 'e wont stop cryin 'til we give 'im a new one."

Evelyn rose to her feet, walked to the scullery and from a drawer in the dresser she took a child's dummy. Returning to the living room she picked up the infant, gathered him to her and carried him up the stairs. The bed in the room above creaked as Evelyn lay her weight over it, the child's crying ceased and just a gentle sound of the bed spring as mother and baby rocked in each others arms told Annie what she must do.

The girl's eyes followed her mother, eyes of the deepest blue Annie had ever seen. In any other circumstance they would have radiated well being but this day their sparkle was hidden, nervous, afraid to shine.

"Go to your mam Ida, tell her it will be alright, I need to speak with Jake then I will come up." Annie smiled as reassuringly as she could before turning to the lad. "Who could sit with your mam Jake," she asked, "where is your other grandma?"

" Aven't got another grandma, me dad's mam buggered off when 'e wer' just a kid. There's aunty Mavis but me mam and 'er don't get on, not since grandad snuffed it an' she kept the lot. Me dad fancied the brass fender but aunt Mavis told 'im that if 'e thought that much of it, 'e should 'ave spent more time sittin' by it listenin' to grandad spittin' an' cussin' his gammy leg instead of leavin' 'er to do it all."

Annie sighed, Jake sensed her dismay, he liked Annie Eddowes so he quickly suggested an alternative.

"Ethel Crabtree, she'd be alright, 'er ol' man works down pit an' they never 'ad kids, summat to do wi' 'er aviaries, I'll fetch 'er."

He was gone through the door before Annie had chance to utter a single word. If Jake listens as intently at his work as he obviously listens in to conversation at home, then his knowledge will know no bounds, thought Annie. She was still musing over Ethel's 'aviaries' as she checked the pantry. It revealed sufficient food and the coal bunker held fuel for several days. She put a kettle of water on the range and found the tea and milk. As Annie climbed the stairs with a mug of sugary tea, she could hear Evelyn humming softly, Annie recognised the tune, 'Love's old sweet song'. All three lay on the bed, huddled together, late afternoon sun bathed one half of the room in a curious light, filtering through the net curtain which stirred gently with the breeze from the open window. A framed photograph of Stanley lay underneath the sun's beam, it appeared strangely animated as the light flickered across the glass. Annie felt compelled to smile at the image.

"You need to drink something Evelyn," said Annie. She placed the tea on the table by the bed and carefully lifted the little boy into her arms, at once offering a biscuit to distract his mind from tears.

Ida sat up and pleaded, "Let's go downstairs Mam," the girl's eyes were reddened from crying, her fingers pulled at her mother's apron, " please Mam," her voice wavered from anxiety. The appeal reached Evelyn's motherliness, she too sat up, turned, put her feet to the floor before raising her face to Annie and with a look which begged for comfort said, "Where's Jake?"

" Drink the tea, Jake will be back at any minute, he has gone to fetch Mrs.Crabtree," replied Annie with a smile of hope. A shaky hand reached for the mug and the sweet warm beverage delivered that first dose of fortitude which Annie had come to know as being crucial. This was not the first time she had found herself amid such emotion, indeed it happened all too often. This war took casualties far beyond the battlefields, wounds that mutilated and scarred a regiment of total innocents. It made no sense, achieved no gain and pained with a most brutal hurt which no application of honour could ease or cure.

A door rattled below. " Mam, Mam," Jake's urgent voice travelled up the stairs. Evelyn's feet responded, she took the little boy from Annie's arms, bid Ida follow and hurried to her elder son. Annie picked the mug from the table, retrieved the forgotten dummy from the bedcover and with a glance around the room which filled her heart with compassion, she went downstairs, inwardly asking God to bless Stanley Barnicoat and to give strength to his family.

As Annie walked along Sherwood Road her thoughts tormented her, why did mankind behave so, why couldn't he be content, what did Sherwood Road, Mitchell Street, Hood Street and even more questionable Peverell Street, possibly have that the rest of the world might covet. No gold, no gems, perhaps it was the seams of coal which undermined these streets. Did the world really envy those men whose days were spent sweating in tunnels of blackness fit only for a life form naturally blind. Could the great wide world possibly crave the rag n' bone man's cart with its booty of leaking saucepans, old flock mattresses and chipped chamber pots and could it ever justify the inhuman outcome. When a woman did not turn up at her work, the reason seemed always to be the very worst of mankind's deeds. Evelyn had not arrived at the workshop this morning, as soon as Charles had told Annie she had taken John and Hilda to Edna's and made her way to the Barnicoat's house. William, Freddy and George were old enough to be left alone for a little while. Annie had brought them up to be sensible, boyish pranks and games were just as likely at the Eddowes' household as they were at any other but the certain grasp of good and bad ever prevailed.

" If you pull that damn sheep under my feet just once more our Liza, I'll turn it into firewood." Edna's frustrated tone could be heard coming from the scullery of No. 24 as Annie entered the yard. Liza, Edna and Billy's youngest daughter, appeared dragging a wooden sheep on wheels.

" It won't work on the cobbles aunty Annie, it only goes on the flags."

Annie produced a peardrop from her pocket and kissed the pretty little girl's cheek. Liza immediately abandoned the troublesome toy, running inside to her sisters, Annie and Susie and to John and Hilda, calling out excitedly "aunty Annie's got sweets."

At least this army advanced with nothing but love, albeit with the intent of securing the 'treats' and all five youngsters besieged her. "You spoil 'em" said Edna with a huff of pretend disapproval.

"Oh yes," replied Annie " so you won't want this then?" She held out a sherbet bon-bon, Edna's favourite and grinned at her friend's perplexed expression.

"God help us, me only vice, sherbet." Edna popped it into her mouth, smacked her lips and contorted her hips as though in a state of ecstasy. Then looking down at the scullery table she declared.

"It's all very well sendin' the best to the men, but what about us women. We're supposed to keep the 'ome front goin' on summat that's been on the bloody 'oof since it stepped off the Ark." She prodded the piece of 'scrag end' which sat on a plate in front of her. "There's bugger all of anythin' these days," she said despairingly. "I'm fed up to the back teeth wi' mutton, I'm goin' to treat us all on Sunday and roast a duck egg, we'll 'ave it 'ot wi' batter puddin', then Monday we'll eat it cold wi' bubble an' squeak and Tuesday I'll make what's left of it into faggots."

Annie smiled and tried to inspire hope in Edna by saying, "It won't last for ever."

Edna fully understood the meaning in Annie's remark but roguishly replied, "I know, but I'll 'ave to make it do three days." Both women burst into laughter until a feeling of guilt at allowing themselves a moment of merriment subdued their mood. "How is poor Evelyn?" Asked Edna, looking over her shoulder at her own brood.

"I left her with Ethel Crabtree," Annie swallowed hard. "Jake will grow up overnight, I see it regularly, the eldest boy still grieving for his father yet donning dad's cap and boots and in the space of just a few hours, filling their spare size with nothing but sheer determination."

Annie's words sent Edna's hand into the pocket of her apron. "What about girls Annie, what do they do, I often wonder. I tell 'em their dad's got that many pints lined up for 'im at The Nelson 'e won't waste them. All the old blokes down there promised Billy afore 'e left 'we'll get 'em in ready for yer lad'. That'll bring 'im back if anythin' will." She took an envelope from her pocket and passed it to Annie.

"Billy loves you and the girls with every fibre of his being Edna, you know he does," said Annie.

Edna sniffed and wiped the tears which had welled in her eyes. "Go on, read it, there's nothin' soppy in it." Edna's voice trembled. Annie prayed each night for Billy and Frank. They had volunteered after the bombardment of Scarborough. Both joined The Sherwood Foresters and were now somewhere in France. 'The Western Front', those three words carried the threat of deepest despair for so many women. Annie opened the folds of paper, she felt a real presence of Billy but the written word was Edna's only substitute for that wonderful embrace, his kiss, that big heart and his utter loyalty. Annie hesitated, it felt wrong to be sharing the letter.

" 'E knows I'd give it to you to read an'all, go on, read it, don't be daft," said Edna firmly, " 'e don't mention Frank, 'is Battalion must be some place else."

Dear Edna,

Me writin's bloody awful but I'm not drunk so don't get all airiated. Me fingers won't hold the soddin' pencil, none of us lads could hold a pint mug if it fell down from the sky in front of us ready filled an' ready paid for, our hands are allus locked around our rifles til we can't alter the shape of 'em, even wipin' our own arses is near bloody impossible. When I wer' a kid at school there wer' this lad, we used to call im sixfeet because his father wer' grave digger at St. Andrews an' Witford cemetery, his proper name wer' Alfie Cresswell. Poor little bugger, one day he had this almighty guts ache, a real exploder, he couldn't help it. When he got home he said to his mam, Billy Dodds been an' messed my pants, I spose he had to blame somebody poor sod. I reckon that's what this war's all about, the world's been an' shit its pants an' all us lads are gettin' the blame. I think of Harold, all them times he went on about seein' the world, I used to listen and think to meself, aye, I reckon Billy Dodds could fancy that an'all. Well Harold didn't miss nothin' the world don't like folks gawpin at it. It bloody well messed itself but we all stink to high heaven because of it. Alfie Cresswell's most likely over here somewhere, wonder if he ever thinks about it all. When you go out into our back yard tomorrow, wrap your arms around our clothes post, tell it Billy says it's bloody beautiful, use our Annie's chalks to write paradise on our front door. When I shut me eyes I can see Winchester Street, every cracked cobble, every sooted chimney pot, all them weathered old doors, that wonky drain pipe that pisses water all over the step at Nellie Drapers, I shut me eyes a lot. We got 2 days to sit an' twitch then we go in again. I heard you sayin' goodnight to our girls last night, I say goodnight to 'em an'all, every night, all through the night. Tell 'em their dad loves 'em and mind they behave thesels. Keep me dinner hot an' give our mam me best.

Love yer, God knows, I love yer.

    Billy.   XXXX

Annie could feel a lump in her throat, it made her breathing tight. Billy's longing for his family grew more and more with every word he wrote. Edna had not once asked why Charles was still at home. His insistence that keeping their own small industry alive and his continued presence in doing so were paramount in order to maintain a living for the others to return to, somehow lacked genuine sentiment. Annie held no desire whatsoever for Charles to be placed in peril, for him to exchange his home for a desperate field of battle and in the name of a peace which day on day demanded too great a price. However, a man must have respect, firstly for himself and then for his peers. The snide remarks, the disparaging looks, Annie herself had not been entirely spared. She felt Charles' reluctance of late to spend time outside the workshops and the house must surely confirm an even greater condemnation must have been shown to him. Their marriage appeared in all respects decent. John had been born five years ago and Hilda was now two. Their relationship was orderly, neither raised voice in anger nor spirit in passion. It was staid, accepted. Anyone viewing from a distance would imagine a serenity, indeed there was but Annie had ever sensed an event in waiting, a dormancy. It brought no actual influence to her days but was never far from Annie's mind. The children were her absolute joy, they thrived well and through them she embraced the future.

"I must be going Edna," she held her dearest friend tightly,
" write a cheerful letter to Billy, write it very soon, any word from home will strengthen him, tell him we all send our love as always."
Annie called to John and Hilda, "Now say thank-you to aunty Edna, we must go home to your brothers."
The farewells echoed about the small back yard, Annie hoped Billy would hear their voices now just as he had heard his wife say goodnight to their little girls.

Dear Frank, she would call on Davina, Ivy and the children before the end of the week. Whilst everyone sought news, human nature created a hesitancy before the lips were able to form the enquiry 'have you heard from'?

And such a measure of relief at good news that for a few precious moments, all enemies were cut down.

"What's for tea Mam?" Asked John as they passed a house where the savoury aroma of onions being cooked drifted through the entry to the street.

"Macaroni cheese and jam roly poly." The answer obviously pleased him and he skipped ahead for several yards before stopping to wait for his mother and sister to catch up. He thrust his hand into Annie's.

"Love you Mam," he said. Hilda's fingers squeezed more tightly around her mother's in unspoken accord. The three walked hand in hand towards Hood Street. The greater world might lack unity but their world held no division.

John began to sing, " Roly-poly pudding and pie, kissed the girls and made them cry." Before they reached the corner, all three voices blended together as one, very soon three more would be added. William, Freddy and George waved from the open door of home, all were smiling, all were safe. Annie thanked God it was so.

CHAPTER TWO

"Hannibal has really done us proud this time Annie, look in here." Catherine Appleyard gazed into a large box as though it held the secret of life itself, which in many ways , it did.

Annie put down the jar of malt which was destined for the Oconnells and turned around to see what Burton's had donated this week. Oats, flour, butter, cheese, dried apple rings, some tins of sardines and several loaves at varying stages of staleness but all entirely edible.

"We must consult the list Annie, decide the order of most need and despatch the parcels immediately."

"I believe two families on Forest Road have been bereaved," replied Annie, "I can take to them if you could go to the Oconnells and the Spooners. Don't forget Mrs.Spooner is very hard of hearing."

"I do remember," Catherine chuckled, "Edith Spooner could call 'order' at any multitudinous gathering with no need of a megaphone, I could quite easily imagine that when she summons her free range brood for tea, she might be converged upon by the entire neighbourhood."

Catherine Appleyard possessed the remarkable ability to persuade Hannibal Burton to relieve his store of all items which would perish or otherwise become stale on the shelves if not sold. Equally, she could charm and inspire her more wealthy friends and acquaintances to shop avidly at Burton's Department store for those luxury goods common to them but of little or no use to ordinary households. Achieving a remarkable balance in trade and funds which enabled Hannibal Burton to exhibit a most generous, philanthropic nature to the city elite, thus endearing himself and perpetuating a loyal customer base, at the same time, putting help and hope on the tables of the much less fortunate.

Catherine Appleyard took no credit herself, declaring that it simply made good sense to keep all wheels turning. She and Annie would sort and pack whatever they had available and with a pram each, deliver a parcel to the families most in need. Catherine had told Annie 'This is not charity, the men folk engage the enemy, women must engage tribulation. To do so requires us all to remain strong, to keep body and mind from defeat'. She made a curious sight, this elegant woman of considerable years, Annie could only guess at her actual age, travelling purposefully along the streets, pushing a child's pram filled with her very own war effort.

"You should try again to persuade Charles to join the 'Lodge' Annie, Robert would be delighted to put him forward," said Catherine as she squeezed a large bloomer loaf, " uhm, not of the best but it will make bread pudding." The loaf was wrapped and placed in a box along with arrowroot, cheese and apple rings. "Mrs. Spooner is very enterprising in her kitchen, I have observed her at her work, making wholesome nourishing food from the most diverse ingredients. 'If it's 'ot an' got jam on it, they'll eat anythin'." Catherine Appleyard laughed as she repeated at full volume, Edith Spooner's words.

Annie and Catherine had become good friends over the years. The difference in their ages seemed unimportant, as with Davina, it was their shared beliefs, the comfortable understanding which existed between them that created a firm bond. It was a strange coincidence that the Appleyard's elder son, Norman, taught at Redmonds, a public school in Durham where Davina's young cousin, Lawrence Hardwick was also a master. They had another son Philip, currently serving as a junior officer with the Lancashire Regiment in the Dardanelles. Their daughter, the youngest, when in her early twenties had abandoned the Anglican Church and converted to Catholicism, joining an order of Nuns and entering a convent. When Catherine had told Annie of this, she had spoken of her daughter Margaret with deep disappointment and a totally unmasked resentment.

Annie had found the moment awkward and responded by saying, 'I can imagine a tremendous peace within the convent'.

Catherine's reply had been immediate and quite caustic, 'death is peaceful Annie but we should at least have the patience to await it'. The subject had not been spoken of since.

The two women went their separate ways, Annie towards home via Forest Road and Catherine to Alfreton Road in the opposite direction.

Her pram now emptied, Annie collected Hilda from Edna's and hurried to Hood Street before the boys arrived home from school. William grew so fast, he would be thirteen in just a few weeks. He was a bright boy with a friendly disposition, yet at times he displayed that harsh judgemental attitude which his mother had so often shown. The tragedy of Enid's early death had wiped away all those biting remarks she seemed always to inflict on her nearest and dearest. In recent weeks Annie had nevertheless recognised a similar trait in William. It worried her, some children could be cruel if given even the slightest incitement, it was likely that the conversations between other mothers and fathers had been overheard by their offspring and the resentment of Charles' continued presence in their midst had fuelled the tongues of the youngsters also. William was doubtless suffering their insensitive prodding and goading.

It had become late so Annie had fed the boys. Charles had been coming home in good time over recent weeks, it was unusual for him to be still not back from the workshop at such an hour. The youngest were in bed when Charles finally arrived. Only William and Freddy sat reading in the living room and they too would soon need to go upstairs. Charles held his jacket over his arm, he hesitated before putting it down on the scullery table. Annie thought it strange, he would usually hang it on the hook behind the back door. Her instinct told her there was a problem, she could see in Charles' manner the evidence of trouble.

"Your meal is prepared, William and Freddy are just about to get ready for bed, say goodnight to your dad, he must be tired and hungry."

Annie had thrown Charles a lifeline, whatever had happened he would not want his sons to know, of that she felt sure.

Charles smiled nervously at the two boys who now stood in the scullery doorway. "A long, busy day Son," Charles looked from one to the other, "your dad's going to eat and sit down for a while, before it all begins again tomorrow, big order for the ministry, urgent and all that."

Freddy's innocent mind accepted it readily. Nothing threatened his immediate situation, he was aware of the war, the subdued atmosphere in the streets, the absence of certain children from school when word came of casualties but all these things Freddy could cope with while ever they remained outside his domain. For William it was far more involved, he looked beyond his father to the jacket, its appearance, bundled inside out on the table aroused his suspicions.

Annie spoke firmly "Come on now, only one more day of school and then it is the weekend, we shall do something interesting on Saturday, go to bed and think about it, tell me in the morning what you would like to do."

Both boys climbed the stairs and disappeared through their bedroom doorway, Annie heard the click of the latch as the door closed.

"Sit down, I'll bring our meal." Charles pulled out a chair from around the table and sat with his eyes fixed on the jacket. Annie put a plate of food in front of him and fetched her own. He made no attempt to eat and sat in silence. "What has happened Charles?" She asked.

He spoke slowly. "I stayed at Basford for a while, there was a problem with one of the machines, I managed to fix it, the spool was jammed. I decided to tally the women's time sheets, to save doing it tomorrow. Making up the wages is never straight forward anymore, some are called away to look after the children of........" he paused and drew a deep breath before continuing, "the children of a friend or relative who has received word from the war office. Some don't come to work at all. Anyway, by the time I had finished, it was getting dim. As I walked past the 'cut' to the canal, two men jumped out and grabbed my arms, one pulled my jacket off while the other held my arm behind my back, I couldn't make out in the darkness what he was doing with the jacket but I could smell tar. They pulled the jacket back on, both spat at my face, then they let go and left. They were men from the pit, their eyes were the only recognisable feature, the rest was black from coal dust, I didn't know them. When I reached our corner, I took my jacket off and held it under the lamp. They took nothing from the pockets."

Annie stood and lifted the bundle from the table, she lay it on the floor by the back door. In crude lettering, written with what looked likely to have been a stick coated with tar, were the letters, 'UNUK'.

They may not have been able to spell thought Annie but they nevertheless conveyed their opinion unequivocally. She bundled it up again and went out to the yard where she put it in the shed with the coal, she would burn it in the morning.

Annie washed her hands and returned to the table. "Whatever happens Charles we must eat, to keep body and mind from defeat."

If he could not engage the enemy, then like the women he must engage tribulation. Annie took up her knife and fork, she knew it could be only a matter of time before the decision was made for him. Unbeknown to both of them, William had tiptoed down the stairs and sat on the bottom tread, listening to all that was said. His adolescent mind should not have been exposed to such a tormenting account. William's very own battle now raged in his head, it kept him from sleep until the early hours. Freddy dreamed of a visit to the cattle market on Saturday, where he could see the multi coloured poultry and spotted pigs. His sleep was sweet. William was blessed with no such comfort, he chewed on the corner of his pillowcase, a habit he had taken up following his mother's death but abandoned by the time he began school. Now it returned to him, that forgotten taste of starch, the dryness on his tongue relieved only by the tears which ran down his cheeks, finding the corners of his mouth. The release of that salty solution which vent his pain. Yet another wounding of the innocent.

The next day Annie and Hilda set off to visit Davina. It would be George's birthday in ten days time. Annie knew it would not pass without the usual family 'get-together'. Now that Frank and Ivy had two children and Annie's family having grown, for the past three years the birthday meal had been held at Davina's house. Sarah, Samuel and the girls brought with them such fun and laughter, however Annie could not help thinking that this year would be very different. With Frank at the Western Front, it was difficult for his mam and dad to find any mirth. Samuel's usual glorious laughter had lost its might, previously capable of rousing the saddest of souls from their melancholy, his own anxieties and dreads now bowed his shoulders and cast his eyes to the ground. Losing Harold had torn at his heart terribly, he had forced himself to look at brightness above and about him for Sarah's sake and to protect his young daughters from the bleakness of misery. The fear of losing his second son trapped his spirit, Annie felt it would take much more than George's birthday to set it free. Only the sight of Frank, with life in his eyes could raise Samuel's own from their downcast gaze.

At the end of Sherwood Road Annie could catch the tram to take her to Market Square, from there it was only a short distance to The Park and Hilda's little legs coped admirably with the walk at either side of the tram ride.

"Look, it's coming, we must hurry," she took Hilda's hand and together they ran to the stop. Annie lifted the little girl onto the foot plate and handed the fare to the conductor. "One and a half to the square please," she said.

He was a good humoured man and winked at Hilda. "Prettiest young lady I've had on my tram today." The child beamed, the man melted under her charm and returned some change to Annie. "No charge for Princesses," he said.

"Thank-you, that's very kind, if the Princess should ever become Queen, then she will surely make you her consort," said Annie.
The conductor was still chuckling as the tram pulled away.

Market Square fascinated young Hilda, the big stone lions in front of the Council House, the domed roof, the elegant Arcade, where Hilda's eager voice echoed under the archways when she called out in excitement at a window display. "Say Bye-Bye, wave to the kind man," said Annie as they turned to watch the tram. The pigeons wandered around their feet, there was a general bustle of activity.

"We'll look quickly to see if Jean is in the window today shall we?" Said Annie. Hilda agreed with a vigorous nod of the head. Jean still attended classes at the school of art. She had shown considerable ability and was encouraged by her tutor to apply for the position of window dresser at Burton's store. A trial period had proved beyond doubt her artistic flair and

Jean now worked full time for Hannibal Burton, not only creating the window displays but also as an assistant in the millinery department. Jean had once said to her mam, 'If you put one of them posh hats on, you'd look like Louisa Burton herself'. Sarah had replied, 'If I were to put one o' them plumed creations atop my head, your father 'ould expect me to lay an egg an' hatch it, I've been broody enough times already'.

Hilda began to wave and jump up and down. There in a window at the far end of the Arcade, Jean was positioning some very fine china, silver and glassware. She caught sight of Hilda's frantic waving and in typical Jean fashion, picked up a long handled brush and with a large decorative silver salver held in front of her and the brush held up like a trident, Jean pretended to be Britannia. Annie giggled, Jean shared the ability to mimic with Frank, both could be roguish and perform such comedy. The two women mouthed a silent exchange. "Are you coming on Sunday."

Annie read Jean's lips and replied, "yes, see you then."
Jean acknowledged her understanding and blew her niece a kiss.

Annie led Hilda across the pavings, a woman in Salvation Army uniform stood at the top of the steps as they walked from the square, she smiled and offered a collection tin. Annie took her purse from her pocket and gave Hilda the coins to drop through the slot, smiling back at the woman Annie said, "That is from a kindly conductor also."

The walk along the roads in The Park was always a pleasure. So many splendid trees and the gardens which surrounded the large houses held flowers of every hue and such delicate perfume. Sometimes an elegant peony or a radiant rhododendron would escape through the railings. Today it was the turn of a sweet scented late rose and the robust cotoneaster with its vibrant red berries to venture beyond their confines. The leaves were just beginning to fall and the foliage of the deciduous trees had been gilded, as if to create one last brilliant display before they relinquished life. Nature glorifies her simple leaves to honour them before they are lost to time, thought Annie, yet man allows his own kind to fall while still in bud, not ever having lived their intended span under blue sky and sunshine. Their gilding came too late, it was all futile when already they lay on the ground, crumpled and trodden. Annie hoped so very much that Ivy would have heard from Frank. She would soon know, they had reached the gate to Davina's . Hilda skipped along the path and up to the side door, she stood on the step waiting for Annie, knowing that her mother would lift her up so that she might reach the big brass knocker. Ivy came to the door with that look of concern which she had carried since waving goodbye to Frank but her face broke to a genuine smile at the sight of Hilda and Annie, it was reassuring and Annie felt relieved.

Davina's home had embraced the arrival of two children with sheer joy. The arrangement of a separate sitting room for the young family had long since been abandoned. When Annie, Ivy and Hilda entered the room, Davina looked up from her concentration on a jigsaw and young Molly Boucher immediately jumped down from her chair and ran across the room to her cousin, taking Hilda by the hand and introducing her to the puzzle.

"We need to find that piece, look," her finger pointed to the picture of two ponies, where one more piece would complete the biggest of the animals.

Ivy's elder child Harold was now six years old and at school, little Molly was four.

"Annie my dear I was hoping you would come, we have plans to make, tell me, how is George and his brothers too of course. I told Sarah only last week, it is almost time for our annual get-together. I will not allow The Kaiser to interfere with that. I would beat him about the head with that Jardinière, Aspidistra and all if he so much as tried."

Annie could not contain her laughter. Davina was so forthright and yet to imagine this gentle, elderly lady, single-handedly putting down The Kaiser with nothing but passion and an Aspidistra brought a moment of light heartedness to them all. Over a cup of tea and buttered malt loaf, news of Frank through his recent letter and Annie's report of Billy strengthened the three women. The children playing happily together were a welcome distraction and Davina's determination in planning George's birthday moved the time along so swiftly, Annie looked up at the clock and declared it to be well past the hour they should have left.

"If we hurry we will catch the tram in time to be home before the boys," said Annie, encouraging Hilda's young legs to cover the ground more quickly. They reached Market Square as the big clock on the Town Hall struck a quarter past the hour, 2-15. No one stood at the stop, perhaps it had gone. Hilda's face fell. They were just about to set off towards the next stop when the green and white tram appeared travelling along Parliament Street.

"It's alright ,see, perhaps we shall meet that kind conductor again."

The tram pulled up and several people got off. It was not their friendly conductor, indeed it was a most unfriendly man who snapped his impatience as Annie felt in her purse for the right money and cautioned poor Hilda not to drop any wrapper on the tram floor or she'd be told off! Hilda clutched a bar of chocolate, given her by Davina. Annie frowned at his unnecessary ill manner as she handed over the coins. However she thanked him politely for the tickets, his response was a gruff, "get to a seat we're late as it is."

Annie was still despairing at such an appalling lack of courtesy, when the tram passed the rear gates of the arboretum. A figure sat huddled on the low wall at the base of the railings, it was William. He should have been in school at this hour.

Annie took Hilda's hand and getting to her feet said anxiously,

"We must get off at the next stop." If they walked back quickly William might still be there.

The conductor muttered, "You paid up to Sherwood Road."

"Yes," replied Annie, "but our plans have been forced to change as I can only hope your manners may, good afternoon."

She helped Hilda to the pavement and walked away, leaving the man to do as he would with the remark. There was within Annie, so much of Aunt Bella though Annie herself was barely aware, so naturally did it show itself through her brightness and competence. Annie felt dismay when, on reaching the arboretum, there was no sign of William. These were the rear gates, if he had cut through the grounds to the front and then towards Hood Street, they might still catch up.

Annie scanned the grassy banks, the benches and the laurel hedges, they hurried along the pathways. Hilda was getting tired, "Not long now, we will soon be home." When they drew level with the bandstand, Annie spotted the boy sitting alone, clutching his bag. He looked up, his face pale from lack of sleep, his boots scuffed and grubby from hours of shuffling up and down the streets.

"Have you been in school at all today?" Asked Annie, she did not raise her voice. He shook his head, she sat down beside him and lifted Hilda onto her knee.

"Chocolate William." The tiny hand pushed the chocolate bar into her brother's lap and tapped his shoulder. Only two years old thought Annie and yet more aware of William's unhappiness than their father.
Within minutes Hilda had nestled into Annie's chest and closed her eyes.

Annie must talk to William, find a way of consoling him, give him something to cling to. The boy needed to feel only good about his father,
she herself had tried to be everything a mother should be but Charles was his flesh and blood, his example.

Annie sighed and began her task. "I know how hard it is for you William, people can be very callous and often it is because they do not understand the real circumstances, they make their own judgments in spite of not knowing the facts. Provided we know, then their foolish, misguided actions we can ignore for what they are. You see William, it is a long time since I worked at the sewing machines and kept the books in order for the workshops. Your father is aware that when he goes away like uncle Frank and Billy, I shall have to run the business. He is determined to have everything as orderly as possible so as to make it easier for me. When he has prepared everything he will join the other men. It is for my sake he endures the insults of such thoughtless people. Strength isn't always shown in the most obvious ways. Hold your head high William, make allowance for others' weaknesses but always be proud of your own strengths."

He looked intently into Annie's eyes. "Will you tell Mr. Dunn I had a belly ache today?"

"Yes, I'll tell him you had a bad ache. Now shall we go home to your brothers?"

William picked up his bag and unwrapped a piece of chocolate. "What are we doing tomorrow?" He asked, "perhaps we could walk to the embankment after we have been to see the pigs."

They chatted as they made their way, Annie telling him of Davina's plans for their get together on the 28th, the Sunday after next. Mavis and Maggie would be there. William's head was relieved of its troubles, he accepted Annie's explanation, she could only hope that Charles would somehow make his son proud. Fate could deal a tough hand, Charles she knew was a master at cards, but this opponent did not play fair. Charles would need to draw on every bit of his acquired skill if he was to win. 14 Hood Street came into view, Annie would be thankful to reach it. Hilda still slept in her arms and the weight pulled at her back relentlessly.

Saturday passed pleasantly, Freddy saw his animals, in fact they all enjoyed the cattle market. Several sows had litters alongside and the piglets' antics caused much amusement.

"Look, that one's feeling cold," cried George at the sight of a large litter which had just finished suckling and now bedded down in a heap, one, particularly small, franticly trying to prise a gap between his siblings, desperate to squeeze into the mass and not to be left uncovered at the top. The poor creature's legs worked so hard, Annie could tell it began to tire. "Oh dear, let him in," she thought aloud and the children laughed at her motherly concern. Then at last, the heap of 'infant pig' yielded and the tiny scrap of life slipped down among his brothers and sisters, almost immediately their entire number, which Freddy had declared to be, 'blimey, sixteen of 'em' slept soundly. Now relaxed the rows of tiny tails fell straight. Annie smiled to herself at the thought, so, all those piglets would have their tails wound up like a clockwork toy to set them in motion again. The sow had cast a watchful eye from where she lay on the other side of the pen, her teats swollen from the piglets' feeding frenzy.

William seemed pensive, Annie worried he may be drifting back to his anxieties. She need not have concerned herself, his mind travelled in a perfectly natural direction.

"I'd like to see her standing upright on her hind legs," said William, his eyes firmly fixed on the sow's undercarriage.

Annie had observed his quickening development, William was growing up fast, that subtle transition from boy to man now waiting somewhere very closeby, ready to move in unnoticed one day when everyone's attentions were diverted.

"She'd fall over and hurt herself," cried John, he thought William was being mean.

"Come on," said Annie, "lets go see the chickens." The array of bantams and hens, ducks and geese, all promoting themselves as 'Best Bird' with noisy crowing, clucking, quacking and honking made for an almighty racket. In one pen squatted a huge grey turkey cock with wattles that swung from side to side with the slightest movement of his head. It reminded Annie of a judge, he definitely presided over the proceedings at this poultry section and that obnoxious hen intent on picking bald the rear end of her neighbour will find herself charged and suitably punished, thought Annie.

"Could we have some chickens Mam?" Asked Freddy.

"That would be good, grandad would make us a coop," agreed George, "you'd have plenty of eggs then Mam."

Indeed it made sense, since Byron had died, they had not asked for another dog or any other pet. The tears and heartache had been immense. Annie herself, still talked to him every day at the corner of the garden where they had buried him. The boys had laid a ring of large stones around the grave and spelled 'Byron' in small gravels across the centre. To Annie it represented so much more, that peaceful corner of ground, away from the noise of the street, safe from the world and all its troubles. She would tell Harold and Bella all about the children's latest deeds, speak to Saul about the workshop and reaffirm her promise to Enid that she would always love William and Freddy. So much love lay there that Annie could scarce' swallow from the emotion which welled up inside her as she knelt beside their memory.

Chickens, yes they seemed very different somehow. Perhaps it was time for the children to have the responsibility of caring for another creature, or in this case several. She would speak with Charles and if he agreed then they would ask Samuel if he could make the necessary coop. Tomorrow they would go to Mitchell Street and see all the family, even Gertie was often there on a Sunday with Steve. Gertie had been married just over a year, Steve Wainwright worked at the pit face, a strong young man from a large family, he had two older brothers in the army. Gertie had continued to work for Charles and now took on considerable responsibility at the Basford workshop. Annie began to think that Nora might never marry. She worked as cook for the Hymers in The Park. It was a live in position, Nora seemed happy enough and showed no inclination to wed. Mavis was now eighteen and engaged to Eddie, he worked in the office at the colliery. Maggie, dear Maggie, still as full of life as she had been in those days when Frank carried her in the basket of Lovatt's bike, up and down Mitchell Street, bouncing over the cobbles, those bright red cheeks glowing with delight. Both Mavis and Maggie had taken work at the munitions factory, it was hard work and dangerous but a determination to 'help our lads' drove their legs as they pedalled to and from Brassington and powered their slight fingers to produce that vital ammunition for the troops.

The thought of having poultry in the back yard inspired the children and the distance from the cattle market to the embankment was covered almost before they realised. William had always liked the side of the river and the embankment displayed such a spectacle for a young lad. Elegant ladies in wonderful fashion, wealthy looking gentlemen parading their success. The ice cream sellers in summer and braziers of roast chestnuts in winter. The swans and his favourites the moorhens, such busy little birds, seemingly taking advantage of the graceful swans' ability to draw all the attention, whilst they, the humble moorhens, sieved the water for the pieces of stale bread and scraps which floated downstream, momentarily unnoticed by the pretentious, preening aristocrats of the bird world. Tomorrow they would have to walk to Sarah's so Annie saved their young legs just a little and caught a tram back to Sherwood Road.

Charles was at home, he seemed edgy. Before the happy mood could be spoiled Annie broached the subject of chickens. It might just give Charles an opportunity to involve himself in his family's eager designs.

"Samuel I'm sure would make a coop, perhaps you might offer to help him, we could all go there tomorrow, you haven't gone with us for weeks," said Annie.

Charles' face revealed his awkwardness at the thought of being in Samuel's company and more than likely the company of Steve Wainwright too. He knew what they must think of him.

Annie spoke quickly, "They know you have been busy Charles, no one would make you feel unwelcome."

Of that she could be certain, regardless of the situation, it was not in Samuel's character to be snide or remotely aggressive, nor would he permit anyone else to show such a nature while under his roof. Away from the women and children possibly but certainly not in front of his dear Sarah and daughters. William, with a perception that might elude a much older man and he still a youth, nevertheless said, "There's no reason why you shouldn't go with us Dad, is there Mam?"

Annie smiled at Charles, partly to reassure William but also to encourage his father. If you refuse the boy Charles you may never win him back, she spoke the words silently to herself, willing him to do the right thing.

"We'll see, poultry can encourage vermin," was Charles response. Annie despaired at his lack of wit and felt for his son's longing.

Sunday arrived with a clear blue sky and mild air. Annie busily set about her chores and cooked their Sunday dinner in good time so as to enable them to leave for Mitchell Street by early afternoon. Charles spent much of the morning reading a newspaper while the older boys planned for the arrival of chickens, clearing a patch of garden in readiness for the coop and seeking out an old enamel bowl for corn and a badly dented milk churn lid to hold water.

John and Hilda had picked dandelions and arranged them for Byron.

John was too young to remember him and Hilda had been born long after losing Byron but they decorated the grave with no less care, so often was the animal spoken of and with so much affection by their brothers.

Charles had not mentioned the subject of poultry since his hapless remark yesterday. Annie had cautioned the boys to leave him think on it, if they pestered he would almost certainly announce his opposition to their plans. She was clearing away the last of the dishes and about to take off her apron to call the children when Charles finally announced his intent.

"They can have chickens if it means that much to them but you don't need me to go today. Sarah has enough going on around her as it is. I would simply be another mouth to feed with tea and cake. I shall stay here and chop wood, the nights will be colder soon, we shall need more fire. Give them my regards." He turned away and took himself to the privy.

Annie sighed, the sooner she acquired a coop and some chickens the better. It would occupy William to some degree but she would need to think of other ways to bolster the boy's confidence. His father gave him little to live up to. Uncle Frank and Billy were real men, they were fighting for their country. The image that brought to a young lad's mind was of daring heroism, excitement. He didn't think of death or pain, of cruel maiming and disfigurement but only of glory in victory. My dad, the soldier, William wanted to be like the other boys, looking after their mam and younger siblings until dad came home. Writing letters to the front and signing them, 'Your proud son'.

"Come on, now we're going to Mitchell Street," she called to the children, all rushed to her in their eagerness.

"Dad isn't out of the privy yet," the voice was William's.

"Dad says he needs to chop wood so he will stay here," said Annie, "but the good news is, you can have chickens so we must ask grandad's help."

As they walked the chatter between George, Freddy, John and little Hilda was incessant, their excitement bubbled over, only William remained quiet. Annie put her hand on his shoulder, she spoke softly, so as not to let the others hear.

"When your mother died the pain and hurt would have crushed a man of less strength than your father. You and Freddy, so young. He endured and survived more desperate times than anything this war could inflict upon him. Enid was very beautiful, I'm sure she could have married almost any man so fine were her features and so elegant her figure but she chose your father. That makes him special doesn't it?"

William looked into Annie's eyes. "Would mother have wanted him to go to war?"

"No wife wants her husband to fight a war, she wants only for him to be safe at home. It is the men themselves who feel the need to stand against the enemy, to protect their families from the aggressor. Charles will go when he is ready, we must leave the time to him and be strong at heart when that time comes. In the meantime William, I need you to help me organise the arrival of our poultry."

Her smile won a smile in return. He ran to catch up the others who had just reached the corner of Mitchell Street, pulling Freddy's cap off in fun as he drew level. Freddy picked up the cap and walloped William across the backside with it. This time both boys laughed and Annie called out.

"Wait for me," she knew as they were now so close to Samuel's gate this would send them racing ahead crying, 'slow coach'. When she finally reached No.69, Sarah's hearth seemed like a good place to be, Annie needed Harold's family around her before she, like William, gave in to doubt. Samuel greeted them all warmly and hugged Annie as only he could, within minutes they were safely surrounded by the 'Boucher Brigade', as Edna always called them.

"Ere you are lass," it was Samuel's habit to pop a mint into Annie's mouth. She knew it was his way of staying close to Harold, "that'll do yer good," and it always did.

CHAPTER THREE

The atmosphere in the streets was a fine balance of childhood excitement, cautious optimism that men would have leave, the ever present need to be thrifty and the desolation of those who must face this Christmas with heart rending absence from their hearths. The women were driven all the more to protect and nurture their offspring, to give them a Christmas to take their young minds from shocking news and predictions of even worse to come. Yet gladness and sadness proved hard to mix, the days were challenging for everyone.

Both Edna and Ivy had received word from the men. They would be home for Christmas, ten days leave.

"Billy reckons 'e should be 'ome by the 23rd 'an' I don't know what to get 'im Annie. I don't s'pose e'll be able to take much back wi' 'im," said Edna.

"The girls have grown a lot since Billy went away, I thought I would take the boys and Hilda to have a photograph taken, in case Charles has to go away with little notice. Why don't you come too and have one done of the girls for Billy," suggested Annie.

"I bet that costs, it'll 'ave to be summat cheap, I want to feed 'im up a bit while 'e's 'ere. All them lads must 'ave lost tallow, I know they send all the bully beef over there but my Billy loves a good plate o' dinner and a bowl o' rich puddin' at Christmas, not to mention a bottle or two o' stout an' some smokes." Edna sighed in her frustration.

"I don't believe the photographer is all that expensive, come on Edna, let's take all the children on Saturday and have a really nice photograph done." Annie's appeal won the day and it was agreed they would dress the children in their best clothes and go to 'Askew's' on the following Saturday.

"I wish I could get our Susie's hair to curl like Annie's and Liza's. I've tried rags at night and the 'ot poker but it makes no difference, it still 'angs straight as a pound o' candles," said Edna.

"Then simply put a pretty ribbon in her hair and let her lovely face do the rest. Ivy is expecting Frank back around the 23rd as well. I would think he and Billy might be on the same troop ship. Little Harold is bubbling up like a bottle of pop and Molly has drawn so many pictures for her dad that Davina has brought another roll of lining paper for her and a bigger box of crayons. I am glad for you Edna, I know ten days isn't long but for Billy it will go even faster. Make sure he has chance to go fishing, you should all go with him," said Annie.

"Me fanny 'ould freeze over if I wer' to go down by the Trent wi' Billy this time o' year. 'E sits there for 'ours watchin' that bloody float thing bobbin' up and down. Me an' the girls 'ould end up blue wi' cold an' stiff as buckram."

Annie laughed, "I can remember when you used to enjoy going fishing on a Sunday with Billy."

"Well I wer' a lot younger then, stayin' cool wer' more the problem," she giggled girlishly. "Sometimes sittin' there wi' Billy, I used to feel like me bits wer' on fire. I could 'ave ripped that soddin' rod right out of 'is 'and an' ravished 'im til all them 'orrible maggots 'ad turned into bloody blowflies 'an 'e didn't know 'is perch from 'is pike." She gave a wicked laugh and blew a kiss at a picture of Billy which stood on the mantelpiece. "Look at 'im, silly sod , what's 'e got to be over in France for, why isn't 'e 'ere wi' us." Now Edna's hand trembled as she reached for her coat. "I'll walk along wi' you, they'll be out o' school soon an' I need to go to the shop for spuds before I meet 'em."

Annie put her arm through Edna's and called to Hilda, who had sat quietly playing with her doll, dressing and undressing it over and over and happily singing to herself. "Let's put your coat on," said Annie. The child obliged then promptly gathered up the doll, wrapping it once more in the makeshift shawl, which had been given her by Davina. It was in fact an old fringed table cloth which had suffered an unfortunate incident with a hot iron. The large brown mark was of no importance to Hilda and she carried the bundle on her arm, telling the doll, "Hush, go sleepy," as they walked along.

"I've been thinkin' Annie, now Liza's in school, I ought to be doin' some hours at a machine. Do you think Charles might 'ave some work for me after Christmas."

"I'm sure he will, sometimes events mean a machine is idle for days, you know how it is," said Annie.

Edna shivered, "Yes I know 'ow it is."

Annie squeezed her arm, "Come on Mrs. Dodds, you've a man coming home in just a few days, we can think about work in the new year."

Annie had already decided that the ideal gift from herself to Edna would be the photograph, not just of Billy's three girls but of Edna too. She must do up her hair, put on her best and sit by their daughters so Billy could take all his girls with him in his pocket.

Annie was busily preparing the meal, Freddy had picked up the eggs, which today numbered four, and latched the coop door for the night.

"Look at this one Mam, it wouldn't fit on an egg cup," he held up a very large egg.

"That one will have two yolks in it," said Annie.

"Like Mrs.Sowerby's twins you mean," said Freddy. Observing Annie's puzzled expression he went on with the explanation. "Jimmy Sowerby's got twin brothers, they're only babies. Well he told me it was because his mam had a double yolker and Jimmy's dad says it takes a lot longer to poach them. Jimmy's dad reckons it took him that long to poach hers that his steam ran out."

Annie did her best to stifle laughter and to appear appropriately edified at this revelation.

Charles arrived home in his usual remote state of mind. His children's brightness and eagerness in the approach to Christmas seemed to have no effect on him. He had withdrawn to a place of safety, keeping his head down and barely uttering a sound, Charles had managed to convince himself that from this position he might weather the storm. William's mood had become even more difficult. Annie sensed his reasoning swung like a pendulum from, 'father with no mettle', to 'mother with no art', and to whichever it pointed, William thought himself let down.

Freddy's acceptance of all things without question only achieved to create a distance, albeit unwittingly between the two brothers, this troubled

Annie more than anything.

"Carol singers at the door Mam." George's voice called out from the hallway. Annie opened the front door and looked out on a group of children, she recognised Tommy Spooner, Elsie Madley and Ida Baines. In the dim light it was difficult to identify them all but she knew most of them and all of them had lost their fathers since last Christmas.

"Come inside for a moment," said Annie. She led them through to the living room. "Now stand by the fire," Charles sat in his chair, hidden behind the 'Evening Post'. "Now there are seven of you and here there are five more," said Annie pointing to her own. "That makes the right number for the twelve days of Christmas." Annie's eyes scanned the gathering. "Do you know it?"

"Not sure missus," said Tommy Spooner.

"Well have a go anyway," said Annie, "ready?" She began to sing, prompting all the children to follow her. If they faltered, she sang out louder to encourage them, keeping a smile on her face throughout Annie succeeded in bringing out their boldness and now, shyness gone, by the time they reached the twelve drummers drumming, the volume was impressive and the satisfaction it gave them all was evident in their clapping and cries of delight at the end. Even Charles had lowered his paper and smiled at the young choristers. Annie went through to the kitchen returning with a bourbon biscuit for each of them. She was about to reach into her pocket for the pennies she had quickly gathered up from her purse, when Charles put aside his paper and rose to his feet. He glanced at Annie before handing each of the carol singers a sixpence. It seemed like a fortune to them, anything silver had to be a lot!

"Thanks mister," said Tommy, his young voice too innocent to disguise his astonishment.

"When each of you gets home mind you give that to your mam," said Charles.

Right away Annie's eyes travelled across the room to William. It was obvious that his father had, to some measure, redeemed himself. The boy's manner was easier, he exchanged banter with Tommy Spooner. The goodbyes and best wishes at the door as they left gave Annie a good feeling. Aunt Bella would have approved of the children's efforts she felt sure.

The smell of hot pot on the range now diverted her attentions to the kitchen but it was with a greater optimism she now stirred the pot and fed her family.

Saturday was dry but bitingly cold, Charles had gone to Basford and Annie bustled through her chores. The chickens fed and watered, it was time to put on tidy clothes for Askew's. She inspected them in a line, the boys handsome, Hilda pretty as a picture, a little adjustment was required of John's collar.

"Now you all look very smart," said Annie. "We will walk to aunty Edna's then all of us will go to Sherwood Road for a tram to town.

When they turned into Winchester Street, Winnie Bacon was cleaning her windows.

"Cooo-ee." The hand began to wave the shammy like a flag. Annie felt they were being ordered to advance and quickened her step.

"My word," said Winnie, "I 'aven't seen folk looking so grand since me uncle Cuth' married into the Wrenshaws, that wer' a day that wer'. All them suits an' posh 'ats on their side an' none of 'em out o' pawn. When their women stood up, from the back o' church it looked like a flock o' parrots takin' off. So where are you all goin' then?"

"We are meeting Edna and the girls and then we are all going into town to have photographs done for the men," said Annie.

"Well bless me, Elsie took 'er lot for the same thing only last week, but when she seen the picture she wer' that mad, she cuffed Jack 'ard around 'is ear. She paid good money for that an' there 'e were, wi' 'is finger 'arf way up 'is nose. The others looked lovely. Still, like I said to 'er, tis no use frettin' over it. Ted's nearly seventy, it took 'im donkeys years to grow out th'abit but when we 'ad our 40th 'do' I only seen 'im forget 'isself once. They eventually move on to summat else but men 'ave allus got to be fiddling wi' a bit o' their anatomy. Well, best get on wi me windows, I 'aven't done round the back yet and Elsie's comin' to cut me hair after dinner." She looked at the children and shook her hand, the shammy seemed to emphasise her words as it swung towards their faces. "Now don't forget, no spring cleanin' yer nose when the man's ready wi' that camera thing. Byee."

Edna must have been watching for them, the door opened as they reached No.24. The girls stood behind her, all dressed up in their best and Susie's little face beamed out between two huge pink bows.

Annie looked intently at Edna, "Go back and put on that pretty brooch Billy bought for you when you went to Skegness."

"Why?" Said Edna.

"Because, Mrs. Dodds you are going to be on the photograph as well, Billy will want to have all his girls with him when he goes back to France."
Edna was about to protest but Annie looked set on the notion and to be close to Billy, if only through a picture in his jacket pocket, meant everything to Edna. She supposed it wouldn't make the picture too much more expensive. Edna had put in her purse just as much as she considered sensible and no more. If it was to cost more than that, then there would be no photograph. Buying some good food for Billy and his favourite smokes she would do over all else.

The tram was almost full, Hilda sat on Annie's knee, as they drew closer to town the pavements held more and more people. When they alighted the temperature outside the tram felt bitter after sitting in the warmth generated by the passengers. However, so much was happening all round them the chill was soon forgotten in their eagerness to see the sights.

The barrow boys were in Market Square, although noticeably older than usual, their cries of encouragement came over the air in deep gravelly tones, made so by years of smoking tobacco and breathing in fumes from grates backed up with 'slack'.

"Sweet oranges for the kiddies, figs for grandma, a nice juicy pear for mother and 'ow about some 'o them exotic nuts for the ol' man."
Their repertoire innocently saucy caused Annie to smile. Their mischief was

heightened by the approach of any young woman and sobered by the presence of women of senior years. As Edna walked by, one man called out, "Give us a kiss Edna!" She looked momentarily embarrassed, then in typical Edna fashion she went over to the barrow, squeezed an orange between her fingers and said, "It is Lady Edna to you, Lady Edna Dodds." She held out her hand to be kissed. The man obliged and laughed heartily. They waved to each other and as she, Annie and the children walked away Freddy said, "Who's that aunty Edna?"

"That's somebody I used to know a long time ago," replied Edna. Then under her breath she whispered to Annie, "I knew 'im when 'is nuts wer' fresh," she giggled, Annie just shook her head.

The Salvation Army band was playing carols in the Arcade and across the other side of Parliament Street, a man played the fiddle. The strains of 'Money is the root of all evil' followed the shoppers while another walked up and down in a sandwich board and front and back the message displayed upon it 'The meek shall inherit the earth'. Hilda clung on to Annie's hand tightly. Askews was at the corner of Castle Road, a small shop front with half a dozen framed photographs to advertise Lloyd Askew's craft. Uhm, no sign of Elsie's family group thought Annie with a rueful smile. Edna seemed nervous, Annie was perceptive enough to realise why.

She paused with her hand on the door handle and said, "This will be my present to you all for Christmas Edna, it will save me having to think of something else."

Edna kissed Annie's cheek, "I'll make it right," she said.

"You have already, more times than I could count," replied Annie.
The children were summoned to the doorway, Annie adjusted John's collar once more and said, "Now, bright eyes big smiles and no spring cleaning."
Edna gave Annie a puzzled look but by now the door was opened and the Eddowes and Dodds combined brigades stood before Mr.Askew, alert and ready for action.

The following few days passed quickly, the last day of school would be

Wednesday. Annie and Catherine were to have one last distribution before Christmas. Annie had left Hilda with Edna and made her way to The Ropewalk. The Appleyards lived halfway along, it was a pleasant looking house, reasonably large but quite simple and unassuming in design. The only outstanding features were a row of chimney pots all at varying heights, as though some were still growing, trying to catch up their taller fellows, and a plaque by the front door with the name 'Tamarisk'. Annie liked the sound of the word, she had been curious enough to ask Robert Appleyard what the meaning might be. It was apparently a tree or shrub more often found in mild areas. Today, as Annie walked around to the back door of the house, it felt far too cold for Tamarisk to thrive. She rang the old brass bell which hung from a bracket at the side, no one answered, she rang again, thinking it a little strange, it was their agreed day and time. Movement could now be heard inside, the door opened revealing Mr Appleyard.

"Come in Annie." His voice was faint, far removed from his usual stirring, deep bass delivery. "We are not at our best today, a telegram came this morning." Just for an instant Annie's breath deserted her, he looked so distressed. "Philip is missing, feared dead it says." He fought to keep his composure. Annie had read of the desperate situation at Gallipoli. Catherine had not spoken of it and Annie felt to do so was just too agonising.

"Would you prefer I go now Mr. Appleyard, I feel an intruder at such a time."

"Please stay Annie, Catherine hasn't been still since the telegram came, filling boxes, in and out of the pantry, emptying cupboards, it alarms me to see her like this and I don't know what I should do."

Annie knocked gently at the door of the sitting room, which Catherine had designated their 'store' in the absence of 'anyone to sit in it' as she had so pointedly put it. Norman seldom made the journey from Durham in the winter months and with Margaret residing at the Convent, only the possibility of Philip remained. Annie had ever believed Catherine to be ready to clear this room in a trice, then to immediately adorn it with every good and bright thing for Christmas if word came of Philip's leave. Somewhere behind the scenes, all that was needed for an instant transformation lay prepared for his homecoming, never spoken of but nonetheless completely in order and entirely splendid. Instead, eight boxes were positioned on the floor, their contents confirmed Annie's belief. Catherine looked up as Annie entered and thrusting a half bottle of brandy into one box which already appeared well filled she said.

"I have almost completed the packing, we shall need to make two journeys each, the donations have been excellent, more than could ever be dispensed in one. Never mind my dear Annie, whenever I said to Robert's mother 'I will do that to save your legs' she would reply with such indignation 'I do not want my legs saving, they are to be as my maker intended, well used and employed'. When she died she was ninety one years old and not once had she been transported mechanically."

Annie put her hand on Catherine's arm, "It is a day when walking might be beneficial but we shall walk together, whichever direction."

Catherine leant her head onto Annie's arm, for a few seconds she was silent then she raised her face to look at Annie. "What can I do for my dear Robert. He cannot push a pram of hope about the streets, what will keep him from defeat."

Annie had witnessed a father's pain when Harold died. Samuel suffered day after day, month into month and the years made it no less. Only his devotion to Sarah and his other children sustained him. "You will keep him from defeat Catherine, you and all those people whom he healed over the years, now it is the turn of others to restore Robert Appleyard."

Annie helped Catherine to her feet and the smile they exchanged, the understanding they shared would leave that room much less bereft when all eight boxes of hope and good things were taken from it.

Annie must collect the photographs from Askews, Billy and Frank were due home tomorrow. She could not think of words to adequately describe her joy at the prospect. If it was so intense for her , how much more it must be for

Edna and Ivy. Annie's thoughts raced ahead as she and Hilda approached the photographer's. Something made her look across Parliament Street, coming from a doorway she saw Samuel.

Annie began to wave. "Look, it's grandad Boucher."

Samuel crossed the Street and picked Hilda from the pavement, swinging her round like a top. The child laughed with delight. He put her down gently, kissed her curls and said, "My best girl." All Samuel's girls were his best, little Molly was seized upon in exactly the same way and only the size of his own grown up daughters combined with his advancing years, prevented him lifting them too into the air and whirling them round on that carousel of Samuel's glorious love. Then came Annie's big hug and today it was an Everton mint.

"Keep the chill out o' yer tubes lass." He pressed a threepenny bit into Hilda's hand, "yer mam will take yer to the sweet shop." He took a deep breath, " the old lungs protest some days Annie, likely full o' soot. We wanted to give our Frank somethin' to keep with 'im." He felt in his coat pocket and took from it a small packet. He carefully slid the paper bag from a jewellery box and lifted the lid. Annie looked at the ring, a simple gold band. She could see it was inscribed. Samuel replaced the lid and bag and returned it to his pocket. "It says 'always with you'." His voice trembled. "I shall be with my boy tomorrow Annie."

"We will see you all on Sunday at Davina's. I can imagine how busy Sarah is, baking and preparing for everyone, Davina tells her off every year for doing so much," said Annie. She was struggling to hold back tears and emotion almost crushed her chest as she turned to wave back to him. Annie would have liked nothing more than to have been at Davina's the following day waiting for that wonderful sight of Frank coming up the path. To be at Edna's when the sound of Billy's boots on the cobbles of the back yard sent his wife and daughters rushing to him. These first precious moments were intimate, they were for Ivy and Edna, no one else. Annie would wait until both men had recovered from being squeezed near breathless by their families, then she too would feel fit to hug them so tightly that their ears would pop.

The tram pulled up at Sherwood Road, Annie clutching the strong brown envelope containing the photographs, helped Hilda to the ground and they set off to Edna's, "We will only stay for a little while , I have lots to do when we get home." Annie was thinking aloud more than actually speaking to young Hilda.

Edna had just stoked the fire and the little house felt cosy and warm when Annie stepped inside. The girls had drawn pictures, bright Christmas scenes. Edna had pinned them to the cupboard doors. On each one was written, 'To dad' and displayed dozens of kisses all around the borders. A sprig of mistletoe was suspended above the scullery doorway. Fruit and nuts sat in a bowl on the sideboard, at the back some tobacco and cheroots.

"I'll put the kettle on," said Edna.

"Let's go to aunty Edna's privy before we take our coats off," said Annie to Hilda.

The sight which greeted Annie when she opened the privy door made her chuckle. The items which usually sat on the shelf, soda, spare paper and a tilly lamp had all been allocated space elsewhere and now, obviously in the privy to keep as cold as possible, twelve bottles of stout stood in a row.

Edna had tea ready poured when they returned to the scullery. The brown envelope lay on the table, Annie slipped off their coats and opened it. Edna could not contain her impatience and looked over Annie's shoulder.

"Are your fingers clean and dry?" Asked Annie.

Edna rubbed her hands thoroughly on the underside of her pinafore. Annie passed her the photograph.

"Just look at 'em Annie, when yer see 'em all done up like that, yer forget all the times the little buggers drove yer mad."

Annie thought it was a lovely picture. Edna had a sparkle in her eye and all three girls held a good mix of both their mam and dad in their features.

"Come on let's see yours then," said Edna.

Annie held up the group of faces, so mixed. William not really looking like Charles or Enid, yet Freddy so much like his mother, he had ever been of Enid's colouring and looks. George, her own dear George in fact looked very much like his uncle Frank, bearing smaller features than Harold but showing that same spontaneous warmth and good humour that his father had always displayed. Young John, timid looking, very gentle in his manner but steadfast in his love for all. Then Hilda, bright eyed, full of expectancy, ready to see the wonder in every new day. Annie herself had no other image than her memory of aunt Bella in which to find similarities. Aunt Bella was always old but surely she must have looked young and carefree at some point in her life, Annie found that difficult to imagine somehow.

"Charles ought to look at that an' count 'is blessin's," said Edna sternly.

Annie just smiled and looking up at the mistletoe said. "Do you honestly think you'll need that?"

"I've 'ung another sprig above the bed," said Edna, then gave a roguish laugh. "It won't last long, there'll be that much heat risin' up from below, them shiny white berries'll be all shrivelled up like soddin tapioca by the time I've done wi' Billy."

The two women enjoyed one another's company for half an hour or so but Hilda was ready to go home and Annie needed to bake.

"What time will you come tomorrow?" Asked Edna.

"I won't be here at all tomorrow, I shall leave you to yourselves until after the weekend," said Annie.

"God 'elp us Billy won't stand for that, if you don't come on Christmas eve at least, e'll be beside 'iself, yer know 'e will," Edna's outburst was sincere.

"Alright, I shall come for just ten minutes on Friday but that's all. Billy will be tired and wanting only his family."

Edna watched from the doorway as Annie walked away. "Wait a moment Hilda," said Annie. She stooped to pull the little girls collar up around her neck. "Put that hand inside your pocket and I will keep this one warm."

They hurried along, the air felt colder than when they left home earlier. Tonight there will be a frost, thought Annie, she would bring in plenty of wood.

Edna had found sleep unwilling to come, for hours she had lain awake, turning things over in her mind. Would Billy be bright or depressed, would he be exhausted, needing only peace and quiet or would he play with the girls. The news of the fighting and awful casualties had haunted Edna's dreams through all the months Billy had been away. She had decorated their home with greenery and gold ribbon, put good food in the cupboard, spent many nights knitting warm socks, kept their daughters safe and well, why then did she feel so nervous. Her hand travelled under the covers across the empty half of the bed. All this time she had wanted only to feel Billy there, afraid each day that this time, the telegram would be for her and not for some other poor woman. It was all confused and contrary. The longing, the fear, the jubilation at seeing him again but the dread of parting just ten days later.

Edna was glad to see the darkness fading, she would wash and dress. She put the girls' clothes to warm by the fire. Billy loved to see them in red, it was his favourite colour. They each had a red cardigan, today they would wear those. She pinned up her hair and just for a second looked at herself in the mirror, huffed in dismay at the bags under her eyes and quickly put on her coat. When she opened the back door, frostiness clung to the air, it was still far from light. In the meat safe was a piece of shin of beef, Edna was going to make a pie, Billy always enjoyed beef and ale pie, hot or cold. Shin needed to be cooked long and slow so she must get it on the range early. Edna had just got back inside and was putting the meat on the table when a noise in the yard made her turn. A figure stood silhouetted against the dawn sky. Looking out from the light into the dark made it difficult to see.

"Ello Edna, 'ave yer got that kettle on?"

He crossed the cobbles, that wonderful sound of Billy's boots, her man coming home from work. Edna stared into his face, thinner, eyes tired. As they stood, arms wrapped around each other, all the pent up emotion began to erupt in Edna. Tears fell as a tide, her shoulders shook, her breathing tightened.

"Eh' what's all the crying for," he lifted her chin, Billy's fingers shook too. Through her sobs Edna said, "I 'aven't put the shin on for your pie yet."

37

Billy kissed her again and again. "Love you Mrs.Dodds," he said. "Are they still asleep?"

"I'll make us some tea and put some porridge on. Billy sat to take off his boots. "I'll do that," her fingers worked at the laces, he looked down at the waves of her hair. He could not remember ever really noticing them before. Now every strand was vital, beautiful. He lay his coat and jacket over a chair.

"I'll only be a minute," he said.

Edna watched him disappear up the stairs and heard the boards creak as he stepped inside the girls' room. She made tea and put milk and oats over the heat. She quickly went to the shed for coal, washed her hands, stirred the porridge, poured two piping hot mugs of tea, then waited. Several minutes passed, the tea would be cold. Edna tiptoed up the stairs. Billy lay across the foot of the girls' bed, he was fast asleep. She fetched a blanket from the bedroom and covered him. Edna's very reason for living, all here in this little room.

Downstairs she prepared the shin of beef and while that simmered, she took her mug of tea , wrapped herself around in Billy's jacket and sat back in the chair. She would not have swapped this morning for anything, Edna Dodds was the happiest woman on earth, her Billy was home.

Christmas eve was a busy time for most women. The workshops would close at midday so Annie anticipated Charles to be home by two at the latest. The three older boys had gone off to kick a ball about with the other lads from the street. John and Hilda were in the living room making paper chains. Cheetham's had just delivered the meat, Annie took it outside to put it in the cool. She had closed the meat safe door when a voice behind her said.

"God Annie, all you and Edna think about is food."

Annie took Billy's hand and kissed his cheek, "You will never know just how untrue that is Billy Dodds but what on earth are you doing here?" Asked Annie. "Why aren't you at home?"

"I got back early yesterday, I wer' 'ome before proper daylight. I've told

Edna, a man needs a bit o' privacy to do 'is Christmas shoppin' else 'is family won't get any surprises. I wer' 'opin' you'd 'ave some idea o' what she'd really like."

"Come in out of the cold," said Annie.

"France is bleedin' cold, 'ere feels right bloody tropical compared to over there." Two little workers had heard a voice and abandoned their activity, paper chains forgotten they ran to Billy. He scooped them up one on each arm. "How about a kiss then young Hilda?"

"Look Uncle Billy," John led him outside, "we've got chickens……" before the boy could say the next word Billy launched into song

"In our back yard,
We feed 'em on Indian corn
Some lay eggs
An' some lay pegs
An' some lay nowt at all"

Annie stood in the doorway laughing, the children returned to their decorations and Billy sat by the kitchen table.

"I'm sure Edna would tell you that right now she has everything she could possibly want or need but I know you would like to buy her something, so I would suggest a nightgown. I believe she could do with a nightie." Annie knew Edna so well, if Billy gave her a nightgown she would wrap herself in its folds each night and sleep with her Billy. The coming months would demand a comforter, this interlude was precious but the parting in ten days time would be as much as Edna could bear.

"I can't tell 'er what it's like Annie, 'ow me an' Frank are still alive is a mystery, a bloody miracle. Lads are bein' shot to shivereens." His fingers clenched on the table top. "I got to know one chap really well, 'e wer' from Macclesfield, Jed, that wer' 'is name. 'E wer' alright, yer know, bearin' up like. We'd gone over again, it wer' like walkin' into the bowels o' Hell. Yer couldn't see, 'arf the time we didn't want to bloody see. Yer couldn't breathe an' me ears felt like they'd bin gouged out me 'ead, the bloody noise shook yer brain, like a terrier wi' a rat. I couldn't see Jed at first, I'd made it to the Boche trench, God knows 'ow. We'd been cut down to bugger all, then I seen 'im, comin' towards me, cryin' 'is eyes out. I can remember thinkin' that in all that soddin' bloody mess, 'e wer' still tryin' not to tread on the corpses, whether they was German or our own. 'I've lost 'em Billy, 'e kept sayin' it over an' over, I've lost 'em Billy'. When I finally got sense out of 'im, I knew why 'e cried. The wire had ripped 'is jacket, tore the pocket off. The picture of 'is wife an' kids wer' gone. 'E might 'ave bin still breathin' but that wer' when 'e really died Annie. They should 'ave sent 'im 'ome for a bit. 'E must 'ave been due leave anyroad but no, King an' Country Annie, not wife an' kids. 'E wer' in no fit state to go over again. Time after time they'd send a wave o' men over the top, in exactly the same soddin' place. Not a hope, not a bloody 'ope in Hell."

Annie held Billy to her chest, his tears soaked her frock. "I never seen Jed again." Billy wept bitterly.

Two little figures stood in the doorway, afraid to move closer. "Uncle Billy needs a cuddle," said Annie holding out her hand to John and Hilda.

All four clung together and not one of them, adult or child, truly understood this dreadful hurt.

CHAPTER FOUR

"For goodness sake Charles you have five children, it is Christmas, whether you like it or not is of little importance, today we are all expected at Davina's and that includes you." Annie spoke firmly, Charles' reluctance to mix with any company, other than at his work, was becoming wearing. Today he must forget his own distractions and give thought to the needs of others, especially his children.

The sharp exchange had led to a strained atmosphere between Annie and Charles, she had tried hard to move his mind along, to enter into the spirit of Christmas for the sake of the little ones but his manner was sullen.

"Come along Freddy." Annie called back to him. Several houses down the road he had spotted a cat sitting on a wall. The animal had purred its pleasure as the boy's hand smoothed the soft fur. Freddy displayed great affection for all animals and birds. Even the collection of snails he had put in a box by the back door one summer held his fascination. Annie had found him desperately trying to rescue one from the beak of a determined thrush intent on beating the poor creature to a pulp against the boot scraper. Of course each time Freddy drew closer, the astute thrush simply carried the snail a few feet away until, rendered to a most palatable delicacy it finally disappeared into the birds crop. Freddy had been dismayed and unbeknown to Annie, afterwards had taken the box, snails and all and hidden them in a wardrobe. Of the eight he was adamant had been inside the box, only seven were ever found.

His devotion to the chickens was equally fervent and when one became afflicted by the 'gapes' he had immediately gone to Bobbers Mill to seek the advice of Arthur Cropley at the farm.

' 'Tis that nasty little bugger the gape worm. The daft bird goes an' eats it but that worm 'as a barb on its head an' it fixes itself to the brainless bird's tonsils so it can't swallow the soddin' thing. All the daft bird can do is keep on gapin' like summat gone mad. What you 'ave to do is crush a strong smellin' cookin' onion, one that's goin' off a bit, add some salt an' mix it to a paste, force some down the birds throat wi' a pencil or stick an' wait.'

This gem of information from Mr.Cropley had inspired Freddy. Annie had helped him prepare the prescribed cure but Freddy himself had administered it. With the chicken positioned securely under one arm, Freddy had used a spill to thrust the magic potion down the poor creature's neck. He had shown no apprehension, entirely confident at the situation. When all the salt mixture had been transferred from the dish to the chicken, he carefully put bird down on the ground. For a few seconds it stood transfixed, a look of utter shock on its unusually wide eyes. Then it extended its neck to an incredible length, propelled itself around the yard like a Whirling Dervish, making the most dreadful, strangulated cries and flapping its wings in tandem with a piston like action of the neck, before finally coming to rest against the base of the clothes post like some inebriate. It shook its head, squatted, at the same time giving an almighty heave, passed an inordinate measure through the rear and immediately began to pick between the cobbles for any passing woodlice as though nothing at all out of the ordinary had ever taken place. It appeared perfectly normal and suffered no ill effects whatsoever. Annie felt Arthur Cropley must be an expert in all matters 'poultry', she would thank him when next they should meet.

"Can we have a cat Dad," asked Freddy, as they walked to Davina's door.

Charles made no reply, he had not heard the boy so tense was he at the prospect of this gathering. His senses were in turmoil, Annie was more than capable of running the business, he knew that, so too did the family. Frank must go back to the 'Front' in just a few days, Steve Wainwright's brothers were at the 'Front' now, what was Charles to say to them.

Ivy opened the door and greeted them all, including Charles, with genuine warmth. Her Frank was home, nothing else mattered, her happiness filled the hallway. "They are eagerly waiting for you."

She opened the door to the drawing room where a chorus of 'happy Christmas' exploded about them like a glorious umbrella of sparkles from a firework, raining down on their ears with all the splendour of a cascade. A sea of smiling faces, eyes welcoming.

Frank at once crossed the room, "Good to see you Charles," he said, shaking Charles hand. Then his arms wrapped around Annie. "It is so good to see you too Annie," still he held her tight, she could feel him shake with emotion. As he stepped back she observed in his eyes that same look Billy had given her. Frank would not have voiced his dread to Ivy or his mother and Davina, all his anxieties remained trapped within his own heart and mind.

"Give your uncle Frank a big cuddle Hilda," said Annie.

The little arms encircled his legs and John, as if sensing this moment called for his love too, pressed himself against Frank's side, clutching at the hem of Frank's pullover. It was William who then stepped forward, he held out his hand.

"We are all proud of you uncle Frank, dad will be going very soon, I shall look after the women, I promise you that." He shook Frank's hand so firmly, William's determination was quite obvious.

Annie dare not look at Charles, the moment felt desperate but salvation came in the guise of young Harold.

"I can play 'My Old Man Said Follow The Van'." He promptly put a harmonica to his lips and blew vigorously.

Jean grabbed the half empty log basket from the hearth and carrying it in front of her, proceeded to sing along with Harold's playing and dance about the room in music hall fashion, "and don't dilly dally on the way." The noise was dire, Davina and Sarah were in hysterics of laughter, the boys stood with hands over their ears, Samuel, Frank and Steve clapped encouragement and the rest groaned in pretend dismay, except Molly, who burst into tears and shrieked.

"I want to play the 'monica' it's my turn."

In all the commotion Charles and the war were forgotten. If any foe had attempted to infiltrate their midst, then it had surely been cut down by the ever resourceful Boucher Brigade.

"Come sit by me Annie," said Sarah, patting the seat of a chair. They numbered so many that to sit everyone around even Davina's large table was an impossibility. The youngsters sat with a plate on their knees, about the floor or wherever they could find a vacant space. The meal was of cold meats, cheese, pickles and relish. A large raised pork pie looked splendid alongside a bowl of spiced red cabbage and a plate piled high with crusty bread and butter.

"Ivy has prepared a wonderful trifle," declared Davina, "but the children must have only a small helping of the jelly as it is generously laced with sherry. I fear too much might adversely effect Harold's musical performance." Everyone laughed and the young boy, too innocent to recognise the friendly sarcasm, took it to mean that his playing had been much appreciated and he was to be called upon again.

"Nora will be 'ere about half past three," said Sarah. The Hymers are entertaining this lunchtime but are to be only themselves at supper so Nora has been given the evenin' off. Mavis is invited to Eddie's for tea. His mam an' dad send their best of course, Gertie an' Steve are goin' to Clara's to see all 'is family."

Annie had met Clara Wainwright at the wedding. Such a tiny woman, it seemed incomprehensible that so many children, boys so big and strong, could have been delivered into this world by someone of such diminutive frame. Steve's father George had tragically died of a seizure a few years ago. The older children had rallied round their mother and younger siblings, bringing them all so close. Annie could imagine Clara's fear for her two sons away at war.

44

The meal was wholesome and delicious but Charles ate very little and seemed remote from the general conversation, speaking only when someone addressed him directly. Annie had noticed Davina watching Charles intently, she sensed Davina's concern at his withdrawn manner, his distance from the rest of the group, not physically but in spirit.

Maggie and Mavis sat either side of him. Maggie looked down at her own dish of trifle, then across to Charles' dish. Seeing he had no silver dragees on his custard and observing the four on her own, she exclaimed entirely innocently, "Charles has no silver balls." She picked two from her dish and dropped them onto his. Annie knew Maggie had intended no malicious or snide remark, it had been done in the spirit of Christmas and nothing more.

Charles however, rose from the table and cast a gruff, "Very funny young Maggie, I need the lavatory," he left the room. For a moment an awkward silence prevailed.

"Let's all eat our pudding quickly then we can play bagatelle," announced Davina.

Jean, Maggie and Mavis helped Ivy clear away the dishes and the men set up the game. Gertie and Steve said their goodbyes and made an early exit.

Davina took Annie aside. "Chat to Sarah, she needs a diversion, Nora will be here soon but until then you must keep her from thinking of troublesome events. If Sarah could hide her Frank away so this evil war couldn't find him then she would, it occupies all her waking hours. I shall find Charles." Davina squeezed Annie's arm and smiled reassuringly.

The air was already growing colder as the afternoon advanced. Charles stood by the back door, scuffing his foot across an area of rough path. Davina pulled her coat around her shoulders and joined him.

"Do you know Charles, next year I shall be 64. Until a dozen years ago I felt I served little purpose, then I met Annie and this family." She sighed wistfully. "I lost Nathan, my husband, such a long time ago but I think of him still. Life holds many surprises, some wonderfully good, others brutally bad. I didn't ever give him a child you see, I failed to make him a father. If circumstances had been different I am convinced he would have been proud to have been a father and especially to have had a son. I am truly sorry that you suffered the loss of a wife, I understand Enid was very beautiful but you have such fine children Charles, you have Annie, together you create a wonderful family. Whatever happens you have achieved so much more than myself in 64 years has achieved. Take pride Charles, use it to drive your spirit. No one here judges you, too much love abides within this house for that to be so. It will be you Charles, you will ever judge yourself and that can prey heavily on a man's mind. Come back inside before you take a chill and I submit to pneumonia." Davina smiled into his eyes and at that instant she saw Nathan. It was not this hideous war alone which injured so cruelly and robbed fathers of their sons. She threaded her arm through his and led him back inside.

Nora had arrived a little late but bearing a large box of confectionary, a gift from the Hymers. They were aware of Frank's spell of leave and having no sons of service age themselves, their compassion towards Sarah and Samuel was sincere.

"It is time we all had a Christmas drink, I shall go to the kitchen for a tray, come along Annie you can help."
Annie was glad Davina had given her a chance to talk with her. She had not wanted to depress the afternoon by speaking of the Appleyard's loss in front of everyone. She had decided she must leave the children at Davina's for just a little while and walk the easy distance to 'Tamarisk'. Thinking of them alone whilst Annie had so much company was more than she could bear.

"I shall take Charles with me, it will present Robert Appleyard with an opportunity to encourage Charles on the subject of the 'Masons'. A number of times Catherine has suggested I persuade Charles of the many benefits being a member of the 'Lodge' might afford him, as I understand, both spiritually and practically. I cannot imagine Charles, despite such persuasions, ever turning from his usual activities. Robert Appleyard however, might be helped by the distraction of discussing with Charles this topic. Philip ever haunts his thoughts, even a single hour of relief must be helpful. Catherine is so good and kind, someone should sit with her at this time. It will achieve to remove Charles from here for a little while, he has made the day very difficult, I know everone will be glad to see the back of him."

Davina laughed with amusement. "My dear we shall take a glass of spirit for our fortitude, I think we deserve it. Then you must go to the Ropewalk and I shall enjoy every moment of playing with those dear children in your absence. Don't worry Annie, things have a way of working out although we may not feel confident at the time. We are all at the mercy of fate, the most humble and the most celebrated alike. Have you had your mint from Samuel yet?"

"No, not yet," replied Annie.

"Ah, then that explains everything, I shall make sure Samuel pops a mint into your mouth before you go." Davina paused, stood very erect, chest proud and in a bold assured voice, as though reciting a creed said.

"It'll do yer good, buggersham castle, it'll do us all good!"
Both women felt suddenly very much stronger, the brandy now seemed quite insignificant. They chuckled as they walked to the kitchen arm in arm.

Robert Appleyard and Charles were talking quite animatedly, one either side of the fireplace. Annie looked directly towards Robert from where she sat by the window with Catherine. He was a handsome man, even now in spite of age. His hair still very dark, grey had not yet dared challenge the attractive waves which framed a distinguished set of features. He used his hands very often to make his words more meaningful, like the conductor of an orchestra showing the light and shade, the power and the softness implied through the notes.

Annie felt quite sure Charles would do his best to appear interested, after all, an account of events at the 'Lodge' would to Charles, seem favourable to the games and activities at Davina's.

Catherine had shown such pleasure at seeing Annie and Charles at the door. There was little evidence of Christmas within the house. Some cards on the mantelpiece bearing pictures of holly and berries, of the characterful robin perched boldly on the snow capped post but those aside, the room held no cheer.

"Annie may I ask a big favour of you?" Catherine seemed troubled and unusually hesitant.

"Of course," replied Annie.

Catherine sighed deeply and cast a glance at the men before speaking.

"We have told Norman of the telegram, he wanted to come right away but we said no. This cold weather travel can be treacherous and unpleasant, there is nothing he can do. In the spring we would enjoy so much spending time with him, at Easter perhaps but now is not sensible or necessary. Robert feels we should inform Margaret." Annie could detect a change in her tone. Catherine continued. "Would you go with me to the Convent Annie, I would greatly appreciate your company?"

Annie smiled, "Let me know which day and at what time. I will take Hilda to Davina's and then come here to you. Billy and Frank must leave again on Friday, could it wait until after they have gone?" Said Annie.

Catherine looked relieved and took Annie's hand. "I feel no urgency to go there, even the Convent building repels me. It displays no welcoming features, merely a cold stony façade. I fear that without your encouragement I might fail Robert and turn back before even reaching the steps. It has to be me, he could not possibly enter you see, his own daughter so removed from him."

Annie recognised that resentment in her manner. Whatever lay behind it tormented Catherine deeply, Annie tried to sound calm.

"We shall see Margaret, it will be alright I'm sure. They are after all, only women like ourselves but choosing a different way of life."

"That is what I cannot grasp," said Catherine, "those words, 'of life'. How can they know anything of life shut away in that place." Catherine stood at the window and pointed to a man and child walking past. The little girl held tight her dad's hand and skipped alongside in blissful childlike fashion. Pretty blonde curls escaped from beneath a pink felt bonnet and bobbed up and down in a dance of celebration. "That is 'of life' Annie, joy, endeavour, hope, love from birth until death. Do you suppose we shall see such life inside the Convent or shall we rather shiver at the coldness?" Catherine watched the man and child disappear from view.

"I shall make us some tea my dear, join the men, Robert will not permit you to leave us without some account of your large family, their health and well being."

The interlude seemed to have mellowed Charles a little, as he and Annie made their way back to Davina's, his mood was gentle.

"He is a very intelligent and shrewd man Robert Appleyard," said Charles. "I asked him if he remembered mother. After she died, father was always reluctant to speak of her. I wanted so much to hear mother's name, Hilda. I would close my eyes and picture her, at all times tender and kind. She made me feel special. I suppose father was busy at the workshop and that is why mother and I spent a lot of time together, just the two of us. I could not feel that same closeness to father and I know it is true, although since he died it has made me ashamed, but if he and mother were talking, laughing together, I felt a terrible jealousy. If Enid had lived and William or Freddy had grown so close to her that I had become resented, then I would have despaired, yet that must have been so for father. I have regretted it since but more so after losing Enid.

Robert Appleyard told me that mother was serene when she died and that father stayed by her bed, holding her hand. I'm glad that he alone shared her last moments, I now realise that he deserved much more." Charles paused. "I don't believe that I have inherited his character Annie."
He looked vulnerable, his spirit too feeble to withstand the slightest trial.

"We will gather up the children and go home," said Annie. "The light is fading fast, time to get back to Hood Street and out of the cold." She put her arm through his. "We can only be ourselves Charles, do our best with each day but we are what life makes of us. Aunt Bella would tell me, 'always remember what you are'." Annie smiled fondly. "We are alive Charles, perhaps it is enough to simply remember that."

The days passed quickly with all the children at home, the hours were filled with their energetic enterprise. George and Freddy had begged some 'off cuts' of timber from James Handley's yard and from them were creating a sled. Snow had not yet fallen this Christmas but the boys, ever optimistic of waking to a white world, beavered away on their project.

William and Tommy Spooner had become good friends and spent much time either playing football at The Meadows or train spotting on Bobbers Mill bridge. Sometimes William's coat would smell so smokey from standing on the bridge as the trains chugged by below him, Annie would need to hang it over the clothes line for a while to freshen it.

She was expecting Billy, Edna and the girls. The sun shone making the air feel less chill so Edna, earlier in the day, had sent young Annie with a message, it read. Must be off me 'ead, told Billy I'd go fishin' wi' 'im if you could 'ave the girls for an hour. Can't expect them little mites to sit till their bums go numb. I'm only doin' it 'cause you said I 'ad to. If I catch me death then you'll 'ave to take all them empty stout bottles back to the shop for the deposit, it'll 'elp pay for me coffin.

Love Edna.

Annie had chuckled and sent back the reply. Your skin is too thick to let the cold through, see you all soon.

Annie xxxxxx

John and Hilda played in the living room by the fire. A new set of dominoes kept them amused, standing them up in a line, tumbling the first one so the last rattled against the fender. Annie had just banked up the grate and given them a barley sugar when voices in the yard announced Edna's arrival. The girls stood in the kitchen, each carried a small handbag, hand stitched and embroidered. The cloth Annie recognised as being from an old coat of Edna's. Both sides of each bag had been embroidered with coloured wool in bright cross-stitch and the handles were made from red curtain cord. Billy puffed on a cheroot, an old canvas dinner bag, containing his treasured fishing tackle over his shoulder. His rod he had placed very carefully by the coal shed door.

"We won't be long Annie," said Billy "I've promised my delicate little petal 'ere," he leant to one side and planted a kiss on Edna's cheek, "that we shan't stay by the river for more than one hour. When we get back I'll 'elp the lads smooth the bottom o' that sled."

Edna shuffled her feet and clung tightly to a bundle of old blanket. "I've filled it wi' boilin' water so I 'ope it don't crack when I'm sittin' wi' the damn thing between me legs. 'Ow would I explain that to doctor, frostbitten feet and a scalded fanny. Me mam allus says that if you keep your 'bits' warm then everythin' else feels warm an'all." Edna folded back the blanket to allow Annie a fleeting glimpse of the hot water bottle.

"Surely you're not going to carry that heavy stone bottle to the Trent Edna," said Annie in amazement.

"Yes I bloody well am," she replied, "an' when I get there it'll go straight on the spot."

Billy laughed and said, "Ave yer noticed Annie, 'ow she never worries about keeping' 'er tongue warm, that's out waggin' in all soddin' weathers."

Annie gave the children a variety of old buttons, pipe cleaners, bobbins and saved sweet wrappers to make into creatures of imagination. Some card and paste to create a dwelling for their menagerie to live in, suggesting they might first draw windows and doors on the card with crayons and cautioning them to let only Billy's Annie use the scissors. The activity would occupy the younger ones and keep them from annoying George and Freddy, whose carpentry and invention outside with their sled would doubtless be tested should these less crafted hands decide to help.

Annie had just plunged her fingers into a bowl of pastry when Frank's voice sounded in the yard.

"That's a masterpiece of woodwork lads, don't forget to make a hole for the rope to go through. If yer take it to Witford you'll be glad of somethin' to pull it up the slope."

He appeared in the doorway and laughed at Annie's obvious dilemma. Her hands covered in flour, she could not give him her usual greeting.

"Finish mixin' Annie, yer can give me a hug after." He sat at the table smiling. "I bumped into Billy an' Edna on the way 'ere, them two make me laugh, they're like a music hall turn. Billy went off shoutin' 'come on Mrs. Dodds, you've got to roll up me bread balls'. I won't tell yer what Edna's response was." Frank laughed wickedly and grabbed a knob of pastry from the bowl, squeezing it between his fingers to imply Edna's threat to Billy's afternoon!"

"Edna will be desolate when Billy goes, as will Ivy when you have to leave them on Friday," said Annie with a long deep sigh.

"I'm meetin' Billy for a pint in The Nelson tonight," said Frank. He paused briefly. "Tell Charles 'e's welcome to join us."

Annie wiped her hands and put the kettle on the range, "I will tell him but he may………."

"Frank interrupted. "I understand Annie, yer don't need to feel awkward. There are five kids in this home, 'e's best off 'ere."

"But in Billy's home there are three and in your home there are two more. Their plight is no less." Annie sat by him, taking away the piece of grey pastry which he had rolled nervously in the palm of his hand.

"I can't see me an' Billy comin' back from this Annie. We've been lucky, the war let him an' me come home for Christmas but it don't hand out many favours."

Annie wiped his hand clean with her apron, there was the ring, 'always with you'. "Me present from all of 'em." Frank turned it around on his finger. "If I don't get out alive Annie, will yer promise me somethin'?" She nodded but words would not come. "I know Ivy an' the kids will be alright, they 'ave Ivy's mother and Davina," he struggled for composure. "Mam an' dad, even with the girls to help 'em, I'm afraid for 'em Annie." His hands shook. "Dad 'as never really got over losin' Harold. I'm glad Harold went before all this. E'd 'ave been one o' the first out there, yer know what 'e wer' like. All them bright notions 'e 'ad o' the world. At least 'e died with 'em still intact. It's you now that keeps mam an' dad close to Harold, hold 'em tight for me Annie when the time comes, hold 'em good an' tight an' tell 'em that me an' Harold are doin' O.K."

The kettle boiled unnoticed 'til steam ran down the wall in rivulets, dropping to the flags where it lay in sad lifeless pools. Annie's and Frank's tears fell from their cheeks soaking the wood of the tabletop.

It was the shout of, "Come and look uncle Frank, it'll be the best sled ever," that raised his eyes.

Annie wiped their tears with a cool, damp cloth and said very quickly, "I promise." She made a pot of tea, mopped the water from the floor and cut some Christmas cake into slices.

"Freddy and George 'ave done a good job," said Frank, patting them heartily on the back. "That sled will fly down Witford Hill an' if Billy smoothes the bottom of it, I reckon it would keep on goin' til it reached Long Eaton." Frank chuckled and by now all the children had gathered for a piece of cake, especially the icing which was picked off and eaten separately, as if that sweet, make believe snow might magically produce the real thing.

"We're goin' to visit Ivy's mother tomorrow," said Frank. "Then Thursday I expect mam an' dad will come to Davina's."

Annie nodded her unspoken assurance and said. "At least since Mrs. Pilkington moved to Clifton, she and Ivy can see much more of each other."

They all waved as Frank reached the corner, he had turned and stood waving both arms. Even from a distance Annie could sense his pain, feel the hurt. Picking a brave dandelion from a chink in the cobbles Annie took it to Byron, telling the children the lone flower was too pretty to be trodden on. She placed it between those stones on the garden which held all her memories, there she sought strength before her own failed her.

Edna had made Annie promise to come on Thursday to say a proper goodbye to Billy. He would have to leave very early on Friday morning. Both he and Frank must catch the train to Dover, where they could board a troopship. Charles as agreed, had come home a little earlier. Annie had felt it best not to take the children. She had put Hilda and John to bed before leaving, the older boys could stay up until she returned, school didn't commence again until Monday, they could sleep on in the morning, it wouldn't matter.

Annie pulled the collar of her coat around her ears, strangely it was not as cold yet winter seemed more determined to make its mark. The sky above had hung still and heavy all day. As the postman had observed, 'it'll let summat down before mornin'. The streets were quiet, subdued after the Christmas weekend. Annie imagined there would be a number of homes now clinging to those last few hours before the men folk took that heartrending walk across the back yards, along the street and out of sight.

Edna had on her red dress and the brooch from Skegness. The girls wore their red cardigans and sat around Billy in the big chair, arms about his neck, the little fingers stroking his face with love in abundance. Three of them, all reluctant to leave his side, to be out of touch. Finally Edna peeled them from him and in that instant, Annie saw his heart laid bare
The goodnight kisses delivered a measure of soothing but Annie knew just how very much Billy ached.

"Will you be with Frank at the front?" Asked Annie.

"No, different battalion. I forgot to tell yer, blow me down when I wer' in town last Friday doin' me bit o' shoppin', I bumped into Alfie Cresswell's mam. E's wi' the Sherwood Rangers, cavalry would yer believe, somewhere in Egypt. Strange innit, me old mate sixfeet ridin' proud on t'other side o' world. If the poor bugger gets a guts ache now 'e'll 'ave to blame the bloody 'orse."

Annie leant forward and kissed Billy's forehead. "Never an hour goes by that I don't think of you and Frank and Edna lives for the day that brings you home."

Movement on the stairs confirmed that Edna had settled Annie, Susie and Liza. "They're tucked up for the night but they won't go to sleep unless you go up there Billy an' kiss 'em again. Let's 'ave a cuppa, I'll force feed you a mince pie Mrs. Eddowes, you'll 'ave to dunk it in yer tea, the soddin' things 'ave gone 'ard."

Annie grinned and followed Edna to the scullery. She spoke softly, "Don't forget to send the photo with Billy. I can imagine how easily lost it could be with all the men's movements, so fasten it to the inside of his jacket pocket with a nappy pin."

"I won't forget," Edna sniffed and pointed to a stack of thick woollen socks she had knitted. "I don't know 'ow else to keep 'im warm." Her voice trembled, before the tears fell Annie held her tightly.

"We'll get through this somehow Edna, I know we will. I won't stay for any tea, I have said my proper goodbye. Now Mr. and Mrs. Dodds must be left in peace to say their own goodbyes. Lock the door behind me Edna, keep the world away tonight. I shall come over tomorrow afternoon and dunk that mince pie with you then."

Charles sat quietly staring into the fire. Annie had been upstairs saying goodnight to the boys and to peep at John and Hilda. "Freddy and George are so looking forward to snow, to test their sled," she said.

"Mona Crabb has gone to Newark, her sister got a telegram last week.

Apparently Mona's sister has a nervous disorder, I cannot imagine Mona will be back at her machine for some time. You can tell Edna there is work for her, she can start as soon as she likes," said Charles. He took his watch from his waistcoat pocket. "I shall go up to bed very soon, what time must Billy and Frank leave tomorrow?"

"Very early, no later than five in the morning," replied Annie.

Charles rose to his feet. "I saw a rat in the yard, I've set a trap on the ledge in the coal shed, tell the boys not to go near."

Annie watched as he walked to the door. At times she wondered what went on in his mind, whom he thought about in his pensive moments. Enid with her tongue could cut a man down where he stood, then with her eyes, raise him again to stand and feel inches taller than before. Charles missed her still, Annie knew that. It caused her to feel no resentment. So many times she herself had longed for Harold, pictured his face and taken from it fresh heart. It was an unspoken understanding between them. Charles' and Annie's marriage did hold love and Annie would draw no comfort from Charles' signing up. It was Charles himself and William who struggled to pacify their emotions. It did not get easier, Charles' laboured tread on the stairs stressed every step of his climb. Annie felt pity for him.

It was still dark, the night hours had passed slowly. Annie had slept but briefly. She gathered her clothes from the chair and crept from the room, Charles was asleep. Downstairs, the fire had stayed in the range, she put a few pieces of stick and coal on the embers and dressed by its warmth. The kettle would boil soon. She took her coat from the hook behind the door and slipped her feet into her boots. The clock showed twenty past five. Very quietly she slid back the bolt on the back door and smiled at the sight of snow, about three inches was Annie's estimate on dipping the toe of her boot into the sparkly white carpet that covered the yard. The boys would be away to Witford this morning in a spirit of great excitement. Immediately about her the silence was tangible. So very still yet in the distance could be heard the dull drone of the trams as early morning movement awoke the city. Going down the length of the yard , a line of paw prints made by a cat, other than those the snow lay virgin white, untouched.

Annie could not hold back the tears as she thought of Edna and Ivy. The men would have already left, both women would now look out on a line of footprints, taking their most loved away from them. Footprints that would haunt their minds as their eyes followed that trail from the back door, out into the world, to the Western Front and beyond. Annie's family slept in their beds, safe, she felt heaven blessed, yet cruelly guilty for being so. She stepped back to close the door, at that moment a loud crack came from the coal shed. Death, even of a rat made Annie shake uncontrollably. A mug of hot tea tried its utmost to comfort but what she wished for more than anything was the feel of Harold's arms around her.

"God bless you Frank and Billy, God bless you always."
She spoke the words aloud, tomorrow would be New Year, it held both hope and dread. Annie drank the tea and swallowed hard.

CHAPTER   FIVE

The snow had lingered for several days before the temperature rose sufficiently to allow a thaw, to clear the pavements and make walking less perilous. The children were back at their classes and Edna had begun work, her girls were to go to Hood Street with Annie's boys where they would be happy until she collected them. It had been arranged that Annie would take Hilda to Davina's on Thursday morning, then proceed to Tamarisk from where she and Catherine Appleyard would set off for the Convent.

Annie felt just a little nervous, not so much at visiting a place which she held little knowledge of but more at being unsure of Catherine's manner when they arrived there.

Still a few small patches of snow lay at the foot of the laurel and box hedge in the garden at The Ropewalk. An optimistic blackbird perched on the bracket above the bell. It was Catherine's habit to cast any crumbs or other morsels out of the back door, his patience was rewarded, she opened the door holding a bread board, the crusts from the breakfast toast were deposited under the old Bay tree.

"I am quite sure it is the same bird each time Annie, his patience and resolve is to be admired. I was in Burton's store yesterday when a young woman of good breeding, nevertheless spoke so impatiently at the assistant, that I felt obliged to remind her of a 'home truth'. So I told her, 'do you know my dear, that your mother had to wait, with good grace, nine long months for you to arrive'."

Annie chuckled, Catherine could be very direct, nothing intimidated her. Annie could imagine aunt Bella and Catherine in one another's company, that would have made for a fearsome duo, she thought to herself.

Women generally were finding more voice, with so many men absent and the women taking on the male tasks, the change in society, albeit created by war, was very noticeable and in some ways fascinating.

Robert Appleyard smiled in greeting when Annie entered the room,

Catherine had gone upstairs to fetch her bag, he crossed the floor immediately to speak.

"Thank-you for accompanying Catherine today Annie," he sighed. "She has a big heart as you know, I hope that someday she might become reconciled to Margaret's chosen way of life. Our past very often dominates our future Annie. It is difficult to erase events from one's mind so they remain there, only to accumulate, like the drifting snow I suppose, making progress beyond laboured and wearisome."

Footsteps could be heard in the hallway, Catherine appeared, coat, hat, gloves and bag all in place, she kissed her husband.

"If we should be delayed, then in the kitchen you will find a pan of soup, don't wait, heat it up for yourself at the usual time."

"Give my love to Margaret." He spoke the words with such a depth of sadness. Annie felt concern for them both, losing Philip was heartbreaking but that aside, a deeper tragedy seemed to haunt them. Annie remembered Catherine's words from several years ago. 'I was an orphan at 15', she had not ever explained further but whatever befell Catherine's family had influenced her deeds and beliefs, of that Annie felt quite sure.

"We must resume our deliveries next week Annie, Burton's will have traded sufficiently by then following the Christmas closing to have gathered one or two items for our purpose. Shall we nominate Tuesday?"

Annie was not at all surprised by Catherine's determination to continue the activity. That robust exterior she displayed to the world kept Catherine safe. While ever she appeared so contained, no one was likely to offer sympathy and concern. Annie sensed that any sentiment of condolence would surely open the floodgate on tears.

"Yes, Tuesday will be alright, Edna has begun work, a machine became vacant at Winchester Street. Now Liza is at school Edna has the chance to earn. Her girls will come to me after classes until she collects them. I can leave Hilda with Ivy and Davina but I must be home by four," said Annie.

The Convent was a good walk away but Catherine had shown no

desire to ride and Annie was used to walking distances so they set off at a brisk pace. The closer they came to the Convent building, the more tense Catherine became, she fell silent her fingers gripped the handles of her bag so tightly the seams in the leather patterned her skin.

They stood at the base of the steps, Catherine took several deep breaths. "Come my dear, we will do what we must, then we can return all the sooner to Robert."

Catherine climbed the wide stone steps and without pause lifted the heavy brass ring and knocked fiercely. Annie stood at Catherine's side, wishing she had a mint humbug in her pocket. When Catherine lifted her hand as if about to knock again, Annie felt compelled to speak, the dark wood shook beneath the blows, the noise resonating through the corridors within.

"We have not been here anything close to nine months," said Annie, hoping to lighten Catherine's mood by the remark. The sound of the lock turning, very slowly, the creaking of the aged hinge, emphasised seclusion. Eventually the door was opened sufficiently to reveal a nun, who at first glance looked very unsure.

"Yes," she said, venturing to allow a little more opening of the door. The sight of two women had evidently eased her nervousness.

"We are here to see Margaret Appleyard on a matter which may be of some import to her."

Catherine was so matter of fact that Annie cringed. A smile was surely needed, Annie looked directly at the nun and smiled as warmly as she could.

"Please if you would wait here." The nun closed the door, locking it once more and left Annie and Catherine standing just inside. The floor was of the biggest flagstones Annie had ever seen, the walls were of stone, not sculpted or adorned but totally bare of any feature other than the natural graining and tiny speckles of lustre deep within the stone itself. Every sound echoed in the emptiness, the nun walked slowly, her tread was silent but halfway along the corridor she was obliged to stifle a sneeze which, amplified by her surroundings, made her appear far too small to have produced such volume. Annie tried to estimate the nun's age but with only the face showing and even that not fully exposed, to arrive at any conclusion was difficult. Only her eyes and fine lines about her lips suggested she might be of middle years. Annie had noticed the hands, they were not old in appearance, the skin looked soft and nourished. If they scrubbed the yard with soda or chopped kindlers, if they hung out the laundry in biting winds or cleared the grate of spent embers, then the painful chaps and sores must surely be healed by putting those hands together in prayer. It would ordinarily seem an unlikelihood, yet in this place the empty halls were filled with an unseen presence. The reality beyond that great door did not apply here. Catherine began to fidget.

"It is a long building, I don't imagine it is fully occupied, they may have to walk some way from where they abide to where we stand," said Annie.

"Then why were we not simply asked to follow her, it is a complete nonsense," said Catherine tetchily.

Several minutes passed before approaching footsteps could be heard. Two nuns drew near, the one now stood immediately in front of them, the other to one side, a pace behind.

"I understand you wish to speak with Sister Agnes, may I ask your name."

The nun was of ample figure, the beads around her neck lay across her chest but the crucifix they supported was suspended below her bosom and swayed gently with each movement. Her hand was extended to shake theirs, Annie was relieved when Catherine took the hand and replied, "I am Catherine Appleyard, Margaret's mother."

The younger nun was addressed as Sister Mary and instructed to bring Sister Agnes to the Reverend Mother's room. She hurried away leaving Annie and Catherine to walk slowly along the corridor with the senior nun.

Catherine was quiet, it was the Reverend Mother who spoke.

"We have received a number of callers over the past twelve months, almost every one asking to speak with a young Sister. These are times of great sorrow," she paused, fingered her beads then turned to look directly at Catherine. "Am I correct in my fears or might I feel relief for Sister Agnes?"

Catherine produced the telegram from her bag and passed it to the nun to read. Reverend Mother held it in front of her, Annie wondered if it was merely coincidental that the cross rested on the bottom edge of the paper, or if some intended blessing now passed from its sanctity to that tragic account of Philip. She handed the telegram back to Catherine.

"I am so very sorry," her eyes held tears, "Sister Agnes is loved deeply by us all, we shall pray together, perhaps you would like to join with us."

"No thank-you, I wish only to speak with my daughter for a few minutes, then I shall leave you to your prayers."

Catherine's reply was cold, Annie felt a terrible unease at being present. The situation was not hers to redeem and yet Annie longed to take the Reverend Mother's hand, squeeze it reassuringly and offer some comfort.

They were led through the passageway until they reached a doorway at which the nun opened the door, looked inside to check that Margaret was there and bid them enter, she then withdrew and closed the door behind her. Annie wondered if she would wait outside or if Margaret would walk with them when they were ready to leave.

Annie hesitated, staying at the back of the room. Margaret stepped forward and kissed her mother's cheek. She was not as tall as Catherine and even from several feet away Annie could see a strong likeness to Robert.

"This is my good friend Annie Eddowes," announced Catherine, "she is of course much closer in age to you Margaret than to myself but we nevertheless share our time and interests, Annie has no mother."

"I do have a very dear mother in law," said Annie, feeling slightly commandeered. She smiled openly at Margaret, to receive news of a brother's death and for that news to be imparted by a mother so unable to show emotion, must be especially wounding. 'Practical help is what's needed', that would have been aunt Bella's judgement on the situation but in such an environment, what practical help could one give. Annie would have preferred to be out in the corridor with the Reverend Mother or on her own as the case might be.

The room held evidence of a life of total devotion. So many hours of impassioned prayer had been offered up, that the mat at the foot of a personal altar beneath an image of perfect love, lay on the hard floor worn thin from Reverend Mother's innumerable hours of kneeling. A modest desk and chair, a shelf of scriptures and two candle holders, were the room's entire visible content but Annie sensed much more occupied this sanctum. Her own presence was an intrusion, she should leave.

When Catherine embraced her daughter and spoke her goodbye, Annie felt immense relief. In the event both Margaret and the Reverend Mother walked with Annie and Catherine to the front door. In some ways Annie fully understood Catherine's view on the solitude of this place. To have seen Liza, running towards them with her sheep on wheels in tow, or Freddy calling excitedly down the corridor to them, declaring the egg number for the day, would have brought the echoing space to life. Instead these cloistered walls kept the women within to themselves and their devotions. Perhaps such a concentration of faith would deliver mankind from evil, but it needed to make haste, for the war advanced daily. Annie had not the words to compose such profound prayer, she asked only that God bless Frank and Billy and that her own strength might hold. A greater communion with the Almighty she would entrust to these gentle women and be content at that.

At first Catherine spoke very little as they walked away from the Convent. Then as if she felt her manner demanded some justification or explanation at least, the story of Catherine's tormented past poured out.

"Mother and father were Irish, from County Cork, but they were unsuited in the most dreadful way you know Annie. Mother was a good Catholic girl and father was Protestant, although I remember how often he would declare proudly, 'I'm not ready to sip wine with the Saints yet, if they want me they'll have to come to the ale house and get me'. Their sin was to fall in love but sin had to be gone, it could not abide with either family. So they travelled away, first they landed in Wales but found no hospitality there. Virtually penniless they walked, begged rides, ate little and eventually found themselves just outside Worcester. They had skills, father was a farrier and mother could weave. At a farm place, kindly people gave them a meal and somewhere to sleep in return for labour. Mother would help in the house and work in the dairy, father, strong as an ox, would do whatever needed to be done, especially with the horses. They proved their worth and after a little while they moved into a small 'tied' cottage. They married, it was a civil wedding which never satisfied mother as it turned out. They continued to work hard, father laboured all hours putting away such money as he could, he was determined to do better for them, mother became pregnant. The chance to take over a forge at Bromyard was more than father could resist. They left the 'tied' cottage and lived like 'didikyes' in a shack alongside the forge. Perhaps they lived too meanly, the child was born, a boy, he lived but a month. I can imagine mother's despair, how her fingers would have travelled across those Rosary beads."

Catherine paused in her narrative and looked back to the Convent. All Annie could do was listen. The two women crossed the top of Parliament Street and Catherine resumed her story.

"The death of their son convinced them of a need to be better established before bringing another into the world. It challenged mother's serenity, a good Catholic woman did little to prevent conception, babies should come as a glorification of marriage even if that glory could not shine through the dense poverty. Father was the only farrier for some miles around, his skills were noted and many used his services. Mother made simple household rugs on a small loom. They managed to erect a more substantial dwelling and three years on, I was born.

I came to understand much later, that Joseph, the first born was never baptised or confirmed. Father imposed his belief that to belong to neither 'side' as he regarded it, would safeguard their children from the possibility of that condemnation he and mother had endured. For her, it meant Joseph's soul had no resting place, all the years I can remember of mother, she was never without her Rosary, fingering it constantly. Mother when she could, attended the Catholic Church in Worcester but father's will prevailed.

After me came Peter, Luke and Maria. The last birth brought complications, the baby was weakened and mother could not bear a child after that.

We grew up with father's neutral doctrine whenever he was present and with mother's desperate attempts to imbue us with, 'Our Holy Mother', when he was not. We were sent to school and all of us were blessed with bright minds except Maria, she was a little slow at learning. I suppose we were happy in our own way, like most children, we lived in a world of imagination much of the time.

The forge and our house sat back from the roadside down a narrow track, about fifty yards. Along the road, possibly a quarter mile as I recall, on a patch of rough ground lived a man, all alone in a makeshift abode. We had a natural curiosity, sometimes on our way home from school we would see him, chopping wood or digging the small area of earth where he grew a few vegetables. One day, Peter told mother we had spoken with the man, that he had given us some peas to pod and eat ourselves. I remember so well her reaction. It was as if Peter had told her we had communed with the Devil. It was not alarm she displayed but intense shame.

'You shall not go near that man, in the name of all that is Holy, you shall not go near that man and you a good Catholic girl Catherine'.

I corrected her, 'I am of neither side, father says so'. She slapped me, not once after that day did she ever kiss or embrace me." Catherine took a hanky from her pocket and blew her nose, sighed long and deep then continued.

"Travellers would call at the forge on their way to wherever, observe father at his work and talk as he shod their horses. Sometimes Peter would watch the scene, intrigued as much by the strangers as he was the anvil and furnace. The doctor held the opinion that Peter had taken the infection from one of these callers while standing by in the warm air of the forge. He became ill, mother tended him upstairs, sitting by his bed, counting her beads, praying over and over. She too became sick and father called me to him saying I must sit by her and Peter whilst he fetched the doctor. Their colour was unnatural, I held their hands in turn, sang to Peter, smoothed mother's brow but I shall never drive from my mind and memory the sounds they made. In my time of helping out at the hospital here in this city, I have heard the death rattle several times but this was so much worse. It was an agony as they stifled, it convulsed their chest and shoulders in a way most cruel.

The doctor had stood at the doorway downstairs and on hearing the sound, he had covered his nose and mouth. That alone frightened Luke and Maria half to death. His diagnosis was to frighten father more, Diphtheria! The two youngest became infected, father also, I was the last to succumb. All I could hear was slow death. No one came near, not from the village or from mother's Church, no one except the man. I saw him tend my family with love and gentleness. In the face of such hopelessness, he tried with all his heart and strength to defy that awful affliction.

Peter died first, then mother. No one would collect their bodies, 'not til the rest have gone', that is what he was told. Maria died next. I saw that man weep in despair over her tiny frame. Then Luke. Father began to rally, he recovered, as did I.

All through those days, the man ate only bread and milk, it was left by the roadside, no one would venture closer than that. He did not take the infection, unbelievable as that seemed he remained free of it. I later asked him, how could that be? He told me that before he entered the rooms where we lay, he packed his pipe with tobacco, lit it and filled all his airways with the smoke. Only then did he leave his pipe and go to us. And why did I live when my brothers and sister all died? 'You were barely alive', he said. 'So close were you to death that I did all I could think to do. I put my first two fingers together and thrust them down your throat 'til you retched and urged but breathed again'.

Annie shuddered as Catherine recounted that passage. She thought of Freddy's chicken, the spill forcing the potion down the birds throat. This was a terrifying account of a life. Catherine spoke again.

"Peter, Luke and Maria were buried in the cemetery by Joseph. Father had mother buried in a Catholic grave, away from her children. I remember his words. He cried as he said, 'I cannot do any other, she was a good Catholic girl'.

I honestly believe he did what he considered to be most decent but it preyed on his mind. We could not attend the burials, they had to be carried out quickly, father and I were deemed to be still infectious. We were confined to the house, quarantined from other folk for four weeks. When we visited the graves father wept bitterly for them all, as I stood by him at mother's graveside, I could think only of that day when she had cautioned me, 'in the name of all that is Holy, you shall not go near that man, you are a good Catholic girl'.

I knew then that I would never be that. Not one soul had come from mother's beloved Church, not one. All their married lives it had tried and tested their love, their peace, even in death it remained so. Within a month father had shot himself.

I was almost sixteen and would you believe it Annie a Priest called at the house. I was to live with the nuns at the Convent in Worcester where I would be cared for as my mother would have wished. Legally, I was not of age to live alone, although so close to reaching sixteen that it seemed irrelevant. I refused and sought the doctor's help. He was sympathetic and arranged for me to work as a maid in a house at Leominster. He knew the people and was aware of my ability to read and write quite well. I would live in, undertake general household duties but in addition spend a little time with the daughter, a few years older than myself and an invalid, bright of mind but feeble in body. I received good food and was treated kindly.

It took me more than twelve months to accumulate sufficient funds to pay the fare to Bromyard and purchase some tobacco for Thomas. I had come to know him well before leaving the forge. That man who had kept me alive, we chatted together and I promised I would return to see him just as soon as I could.

I was granted the whole day off to enable me to travel the distance by coach and spend time with this good man. My employers knew what had transpired, they sent food with me to give to Thomas.

He was just as I remembered, his environment completely at odds with the surroundings I had left at Leominster. He moved about within an area of no more than twelve feet square and that packed full with his lifetime's chattels. Nothing gleamed of silver or fell as silk, Thomas was surrounded by old books, papers, jars and bottles. Clothes stiffened by years of careless laundering draped the table and single hard chair. He took his ease in what could scarcely be described as an armchair, so battered and dilapidated it appeared, propped together at either side by rough wooden boxes. Through the slats I could tell the boxes too held more books and papers. The light was poor, candles stood on a ledge above a simple fireplace which sat amid such amounts of ash and debris its actual origin was difficult to determine. Only a heavily encrusted cookpot, emitting smell of onion offered any clue as to the fire's source. Yet I felt it wonderful, he was genuinely delighted to see me.

'Take a seat young Catherine, tell me you are well and happy' he said. He pulled one chair free of rags and clothes and dusted its seat with his sleeve. His smile recompensed any lack of domestic grace. It shone much brighter than the polished copper to which I devoted hours of time back at Leominster. We talked together as easily as the oldest of friends.

I had only two hours before I must take the coach home, that time passed so quickly. I promised I would come to see him again as soon as I could and I did, ten months later. I found him ill, I could tell he was very unwell. I could not leave him like that, not after all that had gone before. I ran to the doctor's house, it was a different doctor to the one who had arranged my place at Leominster. He was younger and very pleasant indeed. I explained about Thomas and he went with me at once. It was pleurisy. I had to return to my work but he told me not to worry, he would attend Thomas and do his very best. I gave him my address in Leominster but I could not describe to you Annie, just how wretched I felt as I travelled away from Bromyard that day.

Two weeks later, I received a letter from Dr. Robert Appleyard informing me with deep regret of Thomas' death.

I wept for my friend and I believe only then did I truly grieve for my mother, father and my brothers and sister. I felt utter desolation.

Robert Appleyard came to the house to tell me that Thomas had been buried in the small churchyard at Bromyard. Papers at his home had identified him and revealed a wife but she had died many years earlier. There was no record of offspring and no family could be traced. I asked who paid for his grave, little money had been found but a quantity of books had, text books mostly on the subject of physiology and medicine. They held no interest to any other so Robert had saved the volumes from being lost by acquiring them for himself and paying the costs of the burial.

The correspondence between Robert and myself, our brief meetings when circumstance would permit, began a friendship which was to grow into something much more. Three years later we were married. I was 22 and he ten years older than myself. His family were fine upstanding people but with no vanities. Our wedding took place at the small Church in Bromyard, Robert's family home was at Stoke Prior. We had a headstone placed at the grave in Bromyard, it read simply, 'In memory of Thomas James Else. A good man, a dear friend.'

Soon after that, Robert was offered a post at the hospital here in Nottingham. He specialised in conditions of the heart and lungs. Mining and textiles created problems in both areas of health. Nottingham needed his expertise.

We lived very happily but simply, in a tiny house close by the hospital and not until Norman was born did we move to a slightly larger property. In due course, along came Philip and Margaret, our contentment grew with each addition to our family. We remained there for many years, Norman had left home sometime before we moved again, this time to The Ropewalk.

By then Robert was a senior doctor and earning well but working so many hours, we scarcely saw each other. I started my voluntary work, the children were grown up, I had time on my hands, all my adult life I have tried to live by my deeds and let whoever sits at that final judgement, do as they will.

Mother was ever afraid, so afraid of sinning that she could not feel free to live. Removed from her children in life and in death. Father, a hard working man, skilled as a farrier and smithy but in most other matters, having little learning, he could not reconcile his doubts.

My greatest regret is that I could not be with Thomas when he died. There is not a single thing I can do that in my mind, will ever make up for that." Catherine stood still and looked towards the hospital.

"I was so pleased for Robert when Margaret decided she wanted to train as a nurse, she seemed so suited for the work. She qualified and worked at the hospital in Derby. Then things changed, she took leave and came home, spending hours at a time in her room. She returned to her work but in just a short while she declared her intention to give up nursing. When I asked her why, she answered. 'I have nursed and tended and sat with death, through it all, I felt I had made no difference. I feel a great need to pray for mankind, to heal his soul and let others take care of his body'.

She took orders at the Convent, a pledge of chastity, acceptance of a life of poverty, as though that were sacred. Well, I walk along these streets and I see people living in poverty, they cannot choose it for themselves, it is imposed upon them. I could name at least four spinsters here, at The Ropewalk and in The Park, who have never held anything to their loins warmer than flannelette or a hot water bottle but they do at least attempt to live."

Annie lowered her face so as not to show her amusement at this observation, Catherine voiced it with such intense opinion.

They had reached the gate at Tamarisk. Catherine's sigh was so long and deep, Annie could see the rise and fall of her chest through the effort.

Annie took Catherine's arm. "We shall continue with our distributions for as long as they are needed and we will call to see Margaret again. I shan't come in now, it is time I went to Hilda but I will be here on Tuesday."

Catherine spoke not a word but Annie felt the squeeze on her arm and knew at once they were in accord.

As she walked the short distance to Davina's , Annie knew in her heart that Catherine loved her daughter dearly, but missed her so very much. When Annie reached home she would go to Byron and add another memory to that place in the garden. Thomas James Else, could abide safe among the children and chicken at 14 Hood Street.

CHAPTER SIX

"He is still but a youth Annie, while William appears so grown up, his mind can be wholly content when playing football and British bulldog with the other boys, were it not for this war his thoughts would never stray from boyhood pastimes. We all hear day on day reports of the destruction, the desperation on all fronts. Even my generation, which has lived through other conflicts, struggles to comprehend the extent of this one." Bertha's hand trembled as she poured the tea.

The three older boys would visit Bertha on their way to or from The Meadows. Annie herself called on her when she could. It was easy to understand how Enid had found such a friend in Bertha. In her quiet way she instilled confidence, brought strength to a failing spirit.

"There has been no word from either Billy or Frank for some time, Edna and Ivy had a letter a few weeks after the men went back but nothing since." Annie sighed and her eyes appealed to Bertha for some reassurance.

"If things are as bad as we are led to believe, all men of age and fitness will be called up, I am afraid Charles will have no choice," said Bertha, then in an attempt to encourage, "I'm sure Edna and Ivy will get a letter soon."

Their obvious inability to stomach any of the 'seedy cake' which Bertha had placed invitingly on the table before them, confirmed an anxiety too intense to be calmed. Even Bertha could not find confidence in the situation surrounding them all.

Hilda had nodded off in the big chair, her effort in carrying safely, six lovely large eggs from Hood Street to give to Bertha had tired her.

"How will you manage if Charles goes?" asked Bertha, looking across the room to the little girl.

"Gertie is a godsend, more and more she has taken on responsibility at Basford, I sometimes think that Charles has purposefully encouraged her, ready for when the time comes. Even Charles must anticipate that brown envelope. He ignored Lord Derby's scheme so goodness knows to where he might be sent. Edna and May are constant in their loyalty and endeavour, since Alfred died May has lost herself in the work, Mabel is seldom home, she is doing well at her nursing and volunteers for additional hours, the hospital is so full of injured. Young Alfred wrote that he had met up with Frank, that was at the end of March so we know Frank was alright then. France is a land entrenched in death, a mire filled with corpses. Alfred's description was real, an account not softened to protect a wife from heartache. Still so young, he wrote to May as a boy would tell his mother of any distress, trusting her strength in all things. May sits at her machine and stitches her dread into every piece of cloth, those lines of thread hold together not only the garment but May's will too."

Hilda's eyes flickered open and she cast a smile to Annie and Bertha, while its warmth soothed their nervousness her innocent ignorance of the world's despair and suffering underlined their anguish.

"We had better be going, the others will be back from school soon." Said Annie.

At least the seasons held faith with life eternal. The trees so bare for all the weeks of winter, now proudly displayed branches adorned in blossom of every shade of pink, to white. Daffodils stood defiantly in bold, golden clumps between the pathways and gravestones at St. Andrew's Churchyard, as if proclaiming to all those passing by, that time of stillness below ground was merely a fleeting period of rest, a preparation for a new vibrant beginning, a glorious rebirth. The smoke from the city's chimneys, no longer hanging on the air, tickling the throat, stinging the eyes. In its stead, a faint but sure scent of spring flowers and freshly laundered curtains spread over clothes lines, that 'Clean Sweep' of springtime, almost a ritual, an accepted tradition. Annie felt this year it was done with a conscious intent to make everything as good and wholesome as it could be for 'the boys to come home to'. The women worked tirelessly, just like May Watkinson, it was the 'still' moments which weakened them, any chance to think, not the physical aches and pains of a day's labour.

As Annie and Hilda turned into the yard a healthy chorus of cackling suggested another good gathering of eggs awaited Freddy. The washing had dried well and Annie set about picking it in. She was debating in her mind whether George's socks would stand any more darning, when she heard someone knocking at the front door and calling her name, she went quickly to the front of the house, a young lad stood with an envelope in his hand.

"Are you Annie Eddowes?" He asked.

Annie felt unease, his shortness of breath evidence of a hurried passage through the streets.

He held out the envelope, "A lady in The Park told me to come straight 'ere an' give this to you."

Annie took it from him, she was about to ask if he needed something to drink before he went again but the lad turned on his heel and was gone.

"Thank-you." Annie called after him, Hilda had heard voices and now stood at Annie's side.

" Who was that Mam?" she asked.

"Let's go inside now," said Annie picking up the laundry basket. She sat Hilda at the table with some milk and a biscuit. The envelope seemed reluctant to yield to Annie's unsteady fingers, finally it surrendered a folded paper, a note written in Davina's hand, albeit less precise than usual.

Dear Annie.

Please come as soon as ever you can, we are distraught, it is Frank.

Water marks stained the lower edge of the paper, tears, Annie had seen such stains before, three times she had taken fresh paper and begun again when writing to Alice Hemsley following aunt Bella's death. The other children were due home from school in ten minutes or so, William and Freddy must take charge of the younger ones until Edna arrived. Annie hastily wrote a note for William to give to Edna.

Dear Edna.

Don't know how bad, only that Ivy has had word could you call back to the workshop on your way home and ask Charles to hurry, I can't know how long I shall be.

Annie

In the few minutes she had, Annie peeled potatoes and onions and took sausages from the meat safe, putting them in the scullery for Charles to see. She cut bread and laid it on the table with butter and jam. John was the first through the door, Hilda ran to him immediately.

"Mam's had a letter," she announced with authority, "I think it's from the war man."

Annie had no idea Hilda listened to so much conversation in the street. Charles and herself tried at all times not to discuss the war and all that surrounded it in front of the children.

"It's alright," said Annie to the group of young faces now gathered in the scullery looking intently at her for some explanation. "I need to go to Davina's for a little while but aunty Edna will tell your dad to come home early and William will be here with you. I may be back quite soon. Freddy will feed the chickens and you can all play together until aunty Edna gets here."

Annie took William to the coal shed under the pretence of needing fuel for the range.

"It's uncle Frank isn't it?" The boy was too close to manhood for Annie to deny him a truthful account.

"Ivy has received word but I don't know how bad it is, only that Davina needs me to go there as soon as I can. Keep the others here, no one is to go out on to the street, I may be back before your dad but he will come home as soon as possible and you know I will return the first moment circumstances permit. Don't say anything to your brothers and sister yet, I will tell you all there is to know as soon as I am sure of the facts, until then we must hope." She took William in her arms and held him tightly, repeating the words, "hope William, we must hope."

The boy looked directly into Annie's eyes. "Tommy Spooner told me that when his mam got the telegram she went real quiet, you know how she usually talks very loud on account of her deafness. Well she sent Tommy to fetch all the others and bring them home. When they were all in the room with her, she went up close to each one, as though she thought they might not hear her and slowly, one at a time she told them their dad was dead, that he

75

was a brave man and they could be proud to bear his name. When Mr. Dunn calls the register each morning in school and he shouts out George Boucher, 'here sir' says George, I wish he'd call out William Boucher, I'd be proud to raise my arm and answer, 'here sir'.

Annie, already so desperate to keep tears from erupting could hardly bear this trial. "Please William, don't weaken me now, look after the others for me whilst I'm with Ivy."

"I'll be strong for you Mam." William spoke the words with such feeling Annie knew she must go right away or those tears would engulf her.

The tram was busy and Annie willed the passenger sitting beside her not to chatter but the woman could not know of Annie's anxiety and the perpetual commentary reduced Annie's nerves to shreds. Every polite yes or no or even a simple Um, took a bit more effort. When she finally reached Market Square and alighted her legs near buckled beneath her. Before Annie could cross Parliament Street she needed to wait for a brewery waggon to pass by. The team of grey horses just as magnificent as ever, the polished brasses on their harness chimed rhythmically as they trotted close to Annie standing at the edge of the pavement. They seemed to sing to her.

'See you Sunday Annie Bundy, See you Sunday Annie Bundy'
Over and over 'til, too distant, only a memory remained. Harold, it was as if Harold had passed by with the horses, calling to her. Annie's legs felt stronger, her breathing had steadied. Whatever lay ahead she was not alone and neither was Frank, it would be alright.

Davina stood before her with eyes sore and swollen from crying, her fingers took Annie's and led her inside but words would not come. Davina clung to Annie as they walked across the hallway, at the foot of the stairs she paused, raised her head, drew a deep breath and began to climb.

"Would you like me to go alone, so that you might sit quietly for a little while," said Annie.

Davina nodded, her spirit entirely spent. Annie continued up the stairs, when she reached the landing, from the second door along, weary sobbing could be heard, an exhausting cry now rendered to those uncontrollable gulps of wretchedness. Annie opened the door slowly, worried for young Harold and dear little Molly. Ivy lay on the bed with Molly in the crook of her arm and her young son, who had been home from school just a short while, wiping his mam's face with the hem of her pinnafore. His expression would stay with Annie all her days, a little boy, only a year or so older than her own son John, comforting his mother with all the tenderness and concern of a parent.

"Don't cry Mam, I'm here now, don't cry."

Annie crossed the floor and sat on the edge of the bed, neither woman spoke but they joined hands. Could anything be worse than this, thought Annie, Harold's young voice the only sound beyond Ivy's sobs. Molly, mute from fear, huddled into her mother's side, clinging like a limpet to a rock. Annie could only try to imagine the torment assailing the poor child's mind, her head thrust ever more determinedly at the safety of Ivy's breast, nothing would prise her away from that sanctuary. For some fifteen minutes or so that is how they remained.

"Come downstairs with me Ivy," said Annie. "Harold, will you go down to aunt Davina and ask her to please put the kettle on the range." Annie's gentle request, delivered with a smile, achieved to persuade him.

"When Harold died George was just thirteen months old, I looked into his face, our son and whilst I wrestled with the question 'why', why did Harold have to leave us that way, I knew with all certainty that he would now trust me to keep George from all hurt, to shield him from any harm. He would expect me to strengthen our son's tread, day by day, not just as an infant but to manhood and beyond, just as he would have done. Frank would trust you Ivy, to protect Harold and Molly, your children. You must keep them from the hurt, for Frank, do this for Frank."

Slowly Ivy turned her eyes to Molly and with the gentlest of fingers, loosened the child's grip.

"Let's go to the kitchen and find you some milk, you must ask your brother what he did in school today, we always ask Harold that don't we?"

Ivy's words pulled at Annie's emotions, a sickliness came over her stomach, her pallor fell ashen. Davina entered the room, those few moments alone had enabled her to regain some composure.

"Come now, I have made us hot sweet tea, we all need to take some strength, Harold is downstairs waiting to show you his painting."

Molly led the way, her hair all tousled from nestling under her mam's arm. Ivy looked down upon it and declared. "We must brush out those tangles Molly and put on a dry frock."

The bodice of the little girls dress was completely soaked from tears, the small pink bow at the neck had become untied and fell forlornly across the damp cloth in two crumpled lengths of ribbon.

Harold stood in the hallway, he took his mother's hand. "I've got something for you Mam, Miss Wheatcroft said it looked that real she could almost smell it." On the table in the kitchen he had carefully spread out his painting, a bright red tulip with bold green leaves and written on the paper in his own hand,

'For Mam' XXX

Davina turned to the range and busied herself with the kettle and teapot, Annie knew why, to hold back tears was an impossibility, anything that would provide a screen to hide behind, Annie chose the coal bucket.

"I'll fetch some more." The half dozen nubs in the bottom of the pail she tipped into the fire and rushed out to the back yard, in the shed she shovelled the coal heap vainly from side to side, her hand shaking too much to control her endeavour, tears streamed down her face and fell among the black dust on the floor. A full ten minutes must have passed before she found sufficient calm to be steady enough to fill the bucket. When she returned to the others, Ivy was the first to speak.

"We shall be alright, you must drink some tea, then go home to Hilda, I shall need to ask one very big favour though Annie, would you tell Samuel and Sarah, I cannot face that, I just cannot." Davina's eyes also pleaded.

"I shall go to them in the morning, if no one else is aware as yet, then the news could not be given to them by another. Let them have this night."

Davina and Ivy nodded agreement, the unspoken love which passed between them all their only comfort, but it would hold them fast, it always had.

When Annie reached home she was surprised to find Edna there still.

"It wer' better for me to stay 'ere and put the meal on for yer than to rush off an' tell Charles to come 'ome."

Edna had potatoes boiling on the range and a pan of onions softened down between the sausages.

"I've shredded that cabbage you 'ad in the scullery, I can put that on now if yer want me to, the rest is all but ready."

Annie knew that Edna would be desperate to stay until she had learned the news of Frank, injured or dead, missing or accounted for. Edna needed to know, whichever it was could be her Billy at any time.

William appeared at the doorway. "Freddy has found seven eggs, one has a cracked shell so I've put it on a saucer in the scullery. Hilda and Liza are learning to do 'cat's cradle' with Annie and Susie, George, Freddy and John are pasting pictures from the old magazine Bertha sent, into the scrapbook." He delivered his report of events as though he were complying with regulations, satisfying some military command. "What news of uncle Frank, is it the worst?"

Annie sighed, "I need to explain to the others William, their younger minds are perhaps less able to cope than your own, I must first go to Mitchell Street. You shall leave me to talk with them, I will tell you now but please do not dwell on it, the telegram reads 'Killed in action'.
Your grandad and grandma Boucher have not yet been told. Until they are aware, the news must not be given to anyone outside this house."

Edna had sunk to a chair by the kitchen table. Annie gave William a look, which in spite of his youth and inexperience, he recognised as requesting him to leave Annie alone with Edna.

Annie put her arm about Edna's shoulders. "A day at a time, that is the most we can think of. Put that cabbage on Edna, we'll feed the children, they must be hungry."

"Yer don't need to be feeding my three, we'll be off now," said Edna with a snivel.

"Not until the girls have eaten, there is plenty. I don't imagine your appetite is any better than mine, even Charles will struggle to eat tonight, I shall plate up just a small helping for him. I cannot take Hilda with me to Mitchell Street in the morning, will you look after her for me. I shall tell Charles that you will be into work when you can tomorrow, it won't make your hours any less," said Annie.

"I'm not bothered about me soddin' hours, I'll bring the girls 'ere 'an they can walk to school wi' the lads but will you be alright goin' on yer own to Samuel's, I wouldn't want to do it."

Edna now intent on getting herself and her girls out of the way before Charles reached home, tipped the cabbage into the pan of boiling water.

"I shall be alright," Annie hesitated. "I promised Frank that if anything happened I would go to his mam and dad, he told me to 'hold em tight, hold 'em good an' tight Annie', he said." She swallowed hard and Edna looked at her quizzically.

"Did Billy say anythin' to yer?" she asked.

"Billy didn't have to, he knew how it would be if anything happened to him. When Harold died at the yard, you, Billy and I became so close we know one another's thoughts without questioning. You have not had word Edna, keep strong for your girls, don't let's despair, that is Ivy's right, not ours."

The children were assembled and fed and the washing up almost done when the back door opened to reveal Charles at the threshold looking concerned. He had heard Edna's voice as he passed by the window, his first thought had been Billy, Edna would not normally be at No. 14 at this time of day. When bad news came women sought solace in the company of other women, he knew it would be Annie whom Edna would seek if ever the dreaded envelope came.

Charles stumbled over his words awkwardly as he enquired of the circumstance.

"No Charles, we have heard nothing of Billy, Edna stayed here to be with the children, I had to go out for a while," said Annie.

"Annie, Susie, Liza, come on, we're goin' 'ome now." Edna called urgently across to the living room, where the youngsters played 'Jacks'.

William had heard his father's voice and came to the kitchen, before Annie could stop him he delivered the news to Charles, being cautious not to let the others hear. Aware that Edna's girls would not be far behind him he spoke so hastily and with such blunt expression, the words fell on Charles' ears like a threat. William did not wait for a response, turning away at once and going upstairs.

The harshness of the boy's action did not escape Edna. At that moment she could think of no words to say to Charles other than, "I shall see you tomorrow, a little later in the day." She would leave further explanation to Annie.

When Edna and the girls had gone, Charles asked Annie if the others knew.

"No, I shall tell them tomorrow, only William is aware and he knows not to tell anyone outside the house until I have been to Mitchell Street in the morning. I will explain to them all in the appropriate way. John and Hilda will need to be told with very carefully chosen words, Freddy and George are old enough to have more reasoning, if indeed any of us has of such a thing."

"Are they sure or is Frank declared missing?" Asked Charles.

"The telegram says he was killed in action at Verdun. Ivy and Davina are distraught, Harold and Molly have been told, the scene within that house cripples the senses, I could scarce' make hands or feet function to propel me home. Understandably, Ivy cannot face telling Samuel and Sarah, I shall go to them as soon as Edna arrives to sit with Hilda, she will be here early."

Charles was very quiet, it served no purpose for him to become morose. The children had yet to be settled to bed.

"I have a small helping of food keeping hot, I didn't think you would have an appetite for any great amount, you should eat something however and remain 'as normal' around the children. It is best to leave William be, he is shocked and upset, let him work it through in his own time."

Annie took a plate from the warming oven and set it down on the table. Charles appeared to be in a daze, his thoughts were not in that room with Annie and himself, she felt quite sure of that. She left him alone with whatever occupied his mind and closed the door quietly on his ponderings.

The sun was that brilliant, the sky so clear, Annie's feet were drawn to the arboretum. It was only a slight deviation, she would walk to Mitchell Street from there. Still early, the small park was quiet, only the birds showed signs of industry, the comings and goings in the laurel hedge, all made by male blackbirds and chaffinches, beaks filled with reinforcing materials for the ever filling nests, the sounds of encouragement given by the hen birds within, made Annie realise that these efforts were just the same as those of mankind. The birds suffered casualities too yet each year their determination was renewed. Annie sat on a bench listening, it was a 'constant', that undeniable evidence of perpetual hope.

A scuff on the path alerted her to the approach of an elderly man, he walked with a stick, his progress slow. Annie could not get up and walk away, it would appear as though she avoided him. He drew level with the bench and slowly, his old joints creaked their co-operation and he lowered himself to sit beside Annie. His slight fingers around the handle of his stick were deformed from arthritis, the skin yellowy brown with nicotine stain. He passed the stick to his other hand, as if to relieve some soreness, a row of knuckles now faced Annie, gnarled, weathered, his fist diminished by years of hard wear reminded her of a Jerusalem artichoke.

"Why are you sittin' 'ere on your own lass, 'ave yer 'ad bad news?"

Annie was taken aback by the directness of his question.

"We had word yesterday, my brother in law has been killed in France," replied Annie.

The old man sniffed and let out a long deep breath. "How old was he?"

Annie felt his concern was sincere, his manner, his deliberate enquiry held no suggestion of idle chatter. "Frank was thirty three," she said, "I'm on my way to tell his mother and father now."

The old man drew his stick across the path as if writing with it, in the dirt Annie could define an eight and a five.

"Is that your age, eighty five," she asked.

"I wer' born in 1831, I can't recall doin' anythin' worse than stealin' a chicken, yet I feel guilty for livin'. All them young men, some of 'em but lads, gone, dead an' I'm still 'ere, eighty five years an' I sit under the sun while they fade away under foreign soil. I grieve for 'em all lass." He bowed his head and his knee trembled.

Annie rose to her feet. "Frank wouldn't want you to feel this way, he would want you to enjoy the sun, to be proud of your span of years, to tell stories to the children, just for you to keep on going, otherwise none of this would make any sense."

Annie's words lifted his face to look up to where she stood. His eyes were watery. "Tell his mam an' dad that an'all, God help 'em."

His face lowered again and Annie, lost for words to comfort him, walked away along the path to the gate and the road outside, she could delay no longer, somehow she must direct her feet to Mitchell Street.

It was Friday, Annie had still to explain to the children, at least there was no school tomorrow, she could be with them and keep them distracted. She turned the corner and outside No. 69 she could see Samuel talking with a neighbour, as she approached he saw her and waved eagerly, his big smile tore at Annie's nerve, stay strong for Frank, you promised, she cautioned her spirit and raised her arm to wave back.

"Come on in lass we'll 'ave a cuppa before I go off with the barrow, you an' Sarah can catch up, she'll want to know all about them young 'ens, what they've been up to at school. Miss Pownall really fired up our Harold you know, now Sarah, bless 'er 'eart, thinks all her grandchildren will likely be explorers 'o the globe or invent a cure for every affliction, at the very least one o' them will make Sheriff o' Nottingham." He chuckled, Annie knew Samuel well, his light hearted chatter was delivered entirely for Annie's benefit, he could not know that today it made her heart so much heavier.

Annie spoke little, her mind attempting to organise the words to use when speak she must. They walked around to the back yard.

"Look at the poor old bugger, 'e's gone that deaf as 'e can't 'ear 'is dish rattle when Sarah puts it on the flags, she 'as to put it right under 'is nose, we're sure 'is sight's failin' an'all."

Eli, now growing old, padded slowly towards them, his once tan coloured ears showing age through their grey, mottled whiskering. Annie knelt to smooth his head, her fingers caressed his tired old back, she could feel so much more of his frame, like the old man in the arboretum, the cost to his strength caused by such a long span of years, visibly touching for the onlooker. Annie said nothing, lost at that moment in the memory of those early days with Harold and the young Eli.

"How am I goin' to tell 'er Annie, it'll do for my Sarah, it'll finish 'er ." Samuel's voice shook with an agony borne of love.

"How did you know?" Annie asked, standing now to console him. Eli, as if defiantly proving them wrong, sat with eyes intent and ears erect, what slight faculty he still had was surely concentrated on Samuel's grief.

"I could tell from your silence, the way your fingers searched our Eli for comfort."

Samuel's eyes were filled with tears, Annie took him in her arms. " We shall tell Sarah together, hold each other tight, good and tight."

Annie tried to give him strength but she felt her own diminishing. She must do this for Frank, she had promised. When they stepped inside the scullery Sarah cast a smile of greeting to Annie but her eyes had caught Samuel's. Married for so long, husband and wife dwelt within one another's heart and mind. Her shoulders swayed, she slumped to the floor, Annie heard the thud as Sarah's knees struck the flags, like the opening beat on the drum just before the company of musicians fills the air with sound. Her wails and cries rose in volume 'til Annie felt her ears would burst from the intensity. Samuel had enveloped his wife in his arms and the two clung to each other, down on the floor of the scullery, shaking with such pain Annie could hardly bear to be present. 'When the time comes Annie, hold 'em good an' tight'. Her arms could not reach around both Samuel and Sarah but she stretched as far as she could and even then, the hurt within her hold wrenched at her heart more than any other. Harold, Bella, the emotion at Enid and Saul's deaths, now wrapped around the loss of Frank creating a depth of despair more crushing than mortal flesh could endure.

Annie shed tears for them all, for these two parents, for Ivy and the children and for herself. They wept until there was no more to come, only their tight , uneven breathing remained. Eli had sought his old blanket by the dolly tub and lay in its folds, quivering.

Annie loosened her grip of Frank's mam and dad, stood up and crossed to the range, she put a kettle of water over the heat. Such a silence prevailed the house Annie took cups from the cupboard and put them down on the table, careful not to let one 'chink' against the other, so compelling was the stillness. They drank hot sweet tea, no one uttered a word, ears were too tired to receive and reasoning too fragile to process speech. Together they found calm.

"How is Ivy Annie? Those two young 'ens will need her to be strong." Samuel's concern now passed to Frank's immediate family. "I shall go to Davina's, Clara Collins will 'ave to put up wi' the crows in 'er stack for a bit longer. You should come too Sarah, they'll want you there."

Sarah looked so broken, Annie wondered if she would ever recover a sound mind or body but staying close to her Samuel was the very best thing she could do. Their own five daughters had yet to be told, the hurt was endless, Samuel would protect them as only he could, just as it had been when Harold died, this large, 'workhorse' of a man would keep their family safe within his love.

As Annie walked back towards Hood Street, a heaviness draped itself about her spirit, hope seemed futile, misguided almost, the inevitability of more sorrow leadened her steps. Billy's face came before her imagination, that rugged, honest, reliable set of features. Where was he, alive, dead, injured? Could he still be existing in some filthy trench, smoothing his fingers over that photograph fastened to his pocket by a nappy pin, longing for the warmth of his wife, the sight of his daughters' innocent loveliness.

Annie herself returned to a home intact, no one absent from the table, that is where she now felt the need to be, to see Hilda, to close their door on the world, just for a little while.

Edna looked up from her activity, "We've been very busy 'aven't we Hilda, making peg dolls. That one is you and this one is dad."

Edna held up a dressed doll, obviously meant to be Charles, she had crocheted a watch chain in single gold embroidery silk and sewn it to a tiny waistcoat. Hilda held aloft the other doll.

"This is you Mam, look at your hat, aunty Edna says you'll wear one just like this when I marry my sweetheart."

Annie smiled at the fashion of it, made from woven raffia, it sat upon the doll's head sporting a band of narrow braid, a downy feather retrieved from the edge of the hen coop and a tiny flower cut from red felt. The child was completely content.

"I think that aunty Edna and you have been very clever." Annie looked to Edna, "I shall ask her to make my real hat when we attend your wedding Hilda."

"Are you alright, you look bloody awful." Edna lowered her voice, not wanting to disturb the little girls concentration on the finishing touches to

Charles. The tiny fingers were intent on drawing the eyes, nose and mouth onto the pink cotton face of the male doll.

"I'm feeling a bit better now Edna, thank-you for everything, I shall make you something to eat," replied Annie.

"I'll just 'ave a quick cuppa wi' a piece o' bread an' butter, that'll do me now, then I can get off to the workshop to see what 'is nibs wants doin'.'"
Edna was knowing enough not to ask anything more. Any woman could have imagined the scene at Mitchell Street, it needed not to be confirmed in words, the senses already sore from the constant wounding each day seemed to inflict upon them, Edna's mind had embraced the creation of peg dolls, as much to distract herself as to amuse young Hilda.

"Don't walk back here this afternoon," said Annie, "after school we will go to the arboretum for half an hour, to feed the pigeons, then walk on to Winchester Street to bring the girls home to you."

"If you're sure," said Edna.

"Of course, it will give you chance to sort out their tea and have five minutes to yourself before we get there. I won't come in, I need to talk to the boys, it will be easier to do that before Charles gets home."

The understanding between the two women enabled Edna to grasp right away the fact that Annie's children needed to be told about Frank and Annie would not, for a moment, consider talking about such things in the presence of young Annie, Susie and Liza. William's reaction to the knowledge and his manner with his father had not escaped Edna's notice either, she did not envy Annie her task.

After Edna had left and the house fell still, Annie sat Hilda on her lap where she knew the child would very soon be asleep. Only the ticking of the clock on the mantelpiece and the occasional sound from the hens outside, intervened a few precious moments of quietude. The two dolls stood side by side on the top of the bookcase. Annie's own tiredness caused her thoughts to float at random, to lose the bounds of reality as they drifted into a drowsiness alongside Hilda's peaceful breathing. Her own doll carried an air of splendour, of gracious living and affluence. The male doll looked a perfect match, smartly dressed, successful in business, ambitious. It was not herself, that doll which looked across the room to Annie. It was Enid on the arm of Charles, radiant, beautiful, he displayed his gold chain, proud of his status, proud of his elegant wife. Annie Bundy could never be so celebrated, she had known only one truly glorious chapter in her life, when she walked proudly as Mrs. Harold Boucher, entirely sure in love and well being. So utterly perfect had it been, it could never be so again. Charles too could not find that ultimate union. The two dolls must abide together and 'be' the best they could be, that was life, even for a peg doll.

Hilda had stirred, Annie had put some stewing steak on to simmer and any minute now the others would be home from school. The sky was still clear and the air mild, a walk through the arboretum would do them all good. She put some stale bread in a bag and turned her mind to the children.

Edna was surprised to find Charles absent from the workshop, perhaps he had gone early to Basford with the wages.

"Is Annie alright?" Asked May timidly. Charles had told her only that Edna was looking after Hilda.

"Not really, but she will be as time moves on, yer know 'ow it is," said Edna, seating herself at the machine. Edna for that moment, had forgotten May was unaware of Frank's death and when she saw the puzzled expression on May's face, realized she must explain her remark.

The two women fell quiet, the idle chatter which often came from Edna could not be countenanced today, each worked in silence, the progress of the needle carrying with it their troubled thoughts.

Annie turned into Winchester Street with John, Hilda and Edna's three girls. The older boys had chosen to stay at home. Walking towards them from the opposite end of the street was Winnie Bacon, carrying a shopping bag.

"Cooo-ee," Winnie began to hasten her pace and by the time they reached each other she was quite breathless.

"You shouldn't rush like that especially with what appears to be a heavy bag." Winnie put her shopping down on the pavement beside her feet and patted her chest. "Ted's guts'll be the death 'o me, 'tis all very well the doctor sayin' 'ow Ted must 'ave fish to eat an' white meat! Like I said to 'im, doctor what do yer call white meat, even veal's pink. All I could think of wer' tripe an' Ted 'as never been keen. His mam used to force 'em to eat tripe but Ted hated the stuff that much 'e let 'is brothers 'ave 'is share an' 'e just 'et the onions. Well that explained a lot. When we was first married, 'is wind could near fire me out 'o the bed, it wer' never flatulence, not my Ted, oh no, it wer' pure gas. Mrs.Cannicot as lived next door to us then, asked me if it wer' safe to go out in the yard wi' 'er washin', 'I don't like the noise o' your dog', she said, 'it sounds vicious'. Well we never 'ad a bloody dog, it turns out that at night, she could 'ear Ted fartin' through the wall an' thought it wer' a big dog growlin', yer know one o' them as got floppy jowls an' big feet. An' fish, I thought a tin o' sardines 'ould do but no, white fish lightly steamed if yer please. That's where I've just been, Cheetham's for a fowl an' the fishmonger on Waverley Street for a fillet o' haddock."
Winnie at last paused to draw breath and Annie ventured to ask of Ted's condition.

"Doctor reckons 'e've got one o' them ulcer things, I allus thought they wer brought on by worry but Ted don't worry 'bout nothin', 'e takes 'isself off to the privy wi' 'is pipe an' paper an' if Haley's Comet wer' to fly past our chimney pot wi' the devil incarnate sittin' on its tail 'e wouldn't stir 'til 'e'd shed all as griped 'im, smoked half ounce o' cut plug an' read who'd been up before the beak last week. 'Tis me as does all the worryin'.'"

A cat appeared at the entry and walked stealthily in the direction of Winnie's shopping bag, obviously attracted by the smell of fish, it attempted a peep inside. Winnie caught sight of it from the corner of her eye, quick as a flash the toe of her shoe travelled the air and missed the cat's backside by a whisker.

"You can't turn your back for a minute without summat trying to torment yer, its not even our cat."

Young John had winced at the poor creature's narrow escape while the four girls had fixed their gaze the whole time on Winnie's hat, which in her haste to reach the shops, she had put on back to front. The brown ribbon which lined the rim now protruded from beneath and lay above her brow, flattening her hair to her forehead, it did indeed make her appearance most comical.

"Well I'm glad everythin' is well wi' you Annie dear, I can't stop, must get on an' do summat wi' this fowl. Cheetham said it'll need slow cookin', now yer know when a butcher tells yer that his meat needs to be cooked slow, it means it's survived more Christmases than enough!"

Winnie now sped away calling, "Ta Ta," as she went, the curious echoing farewell drifting back from the dark interior of the entry, to where Annie and the children now stood.

In fact dear Winnie had not once in the conversation asked how Annie was but circumstances stressed Winnie Bacon just as they did most everyone else. Annie knew Ted and Winnie had a grandson and a son in law serving in France, white meat and fish were not the cause of Winnie's preoccupation, Ted most surely worried himself to an ulcer over the young men and if the cat visited their back door later, it would doubtless be given a saucer of milk. Annie sighed and crossed the street to Edna's.

It was almost half past six, Charles should be home at any moment. Annie had sat the three older boys at the table and whilst John and Hilda played in the living room, she had explained the tragic loss of uncle Frank. William had obliged her and did not reveal the fact that he had been aware since the previous afternoon. Freddy and George both wanted to know if Frank had been shot by the Boche like Tommy's dad.

John and Hilda needed a delicate approach, their young ears

overheard remarks in the street which Annie would have preferred them not to hear, she could not be sure how they would react. John went outside to pick daises for Byron and Hilda asked for her crayons to draw a picture of a cat for aunty Ivy. Annie had done her best, their own young minds would deal with it accordingly, she had taught them to reason and if any one of them struggled, she would know by their demeanour and address their dilemma.

Charles had eaten his meal saying little and declining his serving of pudding. Suspecting something plagued his mind Annie had persuaded William, Freddy and George to go to bed a little earlier than usual, using the promise of a visit to the cattle market as an inducement. Charles sat in the chair by the hearth staring at the peg dolls, Annie expected him to comment on them, so intent was his gaze but instead his words completely surprised her.

"I went to Retford today, I shall need a sample of your signature for the bank. I am to go on a train to Manchester next Wednesday, to the headquarters of their Regiment on Burlington Street. They couldn't tell me where I will likely be sent so I will have to write to you from wherever it is when I can. I shall go to the bank on Monday and arrange for you to have authority to sign on the business account. It sits with adequate funds, there are only three bills of any consequence outstanding but they have always settled without the need of 'account rendered' in the past and I imagine they will do so this time. There are orders enough to keep Basford going for at least three months, Winchester Street will be in trouble before then if commissions for drapes and gowns don't pick up. Blackmore's school will likely place an order for the start of autumn term but midsummer will be bleak if you can't secure orders from some other source. These are hard times and the gentry are less inclined to hold receptions and refurbish while this war disrupts the city. Gertie is proficient in most aspects of the work but not in the books, that I'm afraid must fall to you, she does organise the women well however and keeps an accurate record of stock. May and Edna know the sewing itself better than any of the others but have never undertaken any element of management. They have shown a willingness to shoulder responsibility for you in the past, if called upon to do so again, then I'm sure they would oblige. I can do nothing to make it otherwise, I shall leave the ledgers up to date."

Annie looked into his eyes. "I am truly sorry Charles, please tell the children tomorrow to allow them time to prepare."

"To prepare for what exactly, my signing up, my departure or my likely demise." Charles' words were bitter. "I shall speak with them all before Monday, I can't imagine it will engage their thoughts too much other than William, who will declare the event with pride at the first school break and rush to Davina's to take care of the women."

Annie swallowed hard, he was so misunderstanding of his children's affections. "They all love you Charles, very much, you should never question that but you must remember they are children, they cannot comprehend the complexities of these times through which we live."

The night hours tormented Annie. She lay beside Charles offering warmth and comfort, nestling into his back she could feel his fear, his dread of the coming days but her attempts at sharing his burden were dismissed. It was the Sunday evening that Charles gathered his family around him and informed them that their dad was going to war. There were tears from the two youngest, an acceptance of dad's will by Freddy and George and a brooding silence from William.

Charles insisted he would attend the workshop as normal on the Tuesday. His train left early and he would need to be at the station no later than 6am on Wednesday morning. Annie sent word to Catherine Appleyard that she would be unable to help with next Tuesday's distribution but would call soon to explain.

Over the weekend, into a small holdall, Annie packed all of the items she thought would travel with Charles and bring him consolation. His uniform would be issued in Manchester so she could not secure the photograph, as Edna had done for Billy, inside the pocket of his uniform jacket but she wrote a note which she folded about the picture and pinned the two together.

Annie knew that to sign on the men went to Retford. It was the Sherwood Foresters or Rangers which many joined. At this stage of the war, whichever Regiment most needed reinforcement, then that one claimed the late recruits. For Charles it was to be the Manchester Regiment. Annie determined to stay close to home until he left, to be certain in her mind that she had given Charles every chance to seek what comfort and solace he needed before he must depart Hood Street, for only fate knew where.

It was too soon to tell Samuel and Sarah, or Davina and Ivy, their hearts ached enough, their thoughts could be for Frank only and that was as it should be. Charles had insisted the women should not be told until after he was gone. 'Makes it easier on us all, no need of false concern on their part or pretence at believing it on mine', had been Charles' cynical judgment of the situation. William had become more and more morose the closer it drew to Wednesday.

"We shall have tea early and spend time with your dad this evening, he will need to be given a confident smile from you William, to go away from us knowing you will be strong in his absence." Annie looked into his face, he now stood as tall as herself. "Support your brothers and sister, they will need you today especially and for many days to come."

Annie felt William was on the brink of tears but would not allow them to show. All these months he had so wanted 'his' father to be brave and do as the other men, to feel proud of his dad, the soldier. Now that had become the reality, William's emotions were in turmoil but Annie could do nothing to relieve him. It was all part of growing up, the realisation of principles and loyalties and how the two could conflict with such devastating hurt.

Annie baked Charles' favourite cake and packed it between thick socks. His shaving kit and brush and comb she had gathered onto the washstand, ready to put into the holdall at the very last. Pen, paper and envelopes, mints and chocolate all packed alongside the photograph.

That evening the love which ever surrounded Charles but which he seldom acknowledged, clung to his every move. Annie let the children stay up until their eyes would remain open no longer. William was the last to leave Charles' side. Father and son embraced so tightly, Annie knew that at last their doubts were banished, both were aware of just how much they loved each other.

That night Charles turned away from the wall to wrap his arm about Annie, to let himself know his wife's warmth, to carry with him the present, as well as the past. He stayed close, holding her to him until the hour arrived.

Annie dressed quickly and tiptoed downstairs to put porridge on the range and make tea.

Charles sat on the edge of the bed, he wished he could see his mother, spend just a few moments with her before this trial but those safe, carefree days were long gone. He donned his shirt and pulled on his trousers, looked around the room briefly before stepping out on to the landing. He paused by the door of the spare room. It was a curiosity that although he seldom went a day without thinking of Enid, he did not call to mind the events of that night in this room in spite of passing by the door at least twice each day. Now the memory of it was vivid, he needed to walk on, the children slept in their beds, he chose not to disturb them.

Downstairs he sat by the range to put on his shoes. Annie poured the tea and filled a bowl with warming porridge, the air was not cold but their spirits had need of soothing.

"It may be several hours before you eat again, I'll fetch the holdall while you drink your tea."

Annie checked the last items were packed and returned to Charles, he sat at the table, a sad figure. She stood by his side. "Write as soon as you can Charles, to let me know where you are. I shall keep everything going for you and we shall all wait here at home and hope you might return soon. Try to take that last mouthful, please." Annie coaxed him to finish the porridge, she helped him into his jacket, then put a cardigan around her own shoulders. There was already light in the sky, on the pavement outside the house she kissed him gently and handed him the holdall. She saw the wateriness in his eyes, before the tears fell he turned and walked briskly up the street. Annie felt instinctively that he would not turn to wave but she watched his progress until he reached the corner, with one long stride, Charles was gone.

She returned to the yard to find William in his pyjamas standing by the back door.

"I've sent him haven't I, it's me that's made him go to war." Tears rolled down his cheeks, Annie took him into her arms as he shook from sobbing.

"No William, it is not you who made him go, it is uncle Frank. When word came that Frank had been killed your father went straight away to the recruiting office at Retford. It is a thing of men William and thankfully, although you are very close to manhood, you are nevertheless still a boy and as yet entitled to enjoy the freedom of youth for a little longer but don't squander it William, for it never returns, not ever."

They stood quietly in the doorway until the boy's distress was eased. The victorious call of one hen declared she had performed her daily labour. Together Annie and William went inside.

On a tram, travelling towards the station with a handful of people up and about their daily task, sat Charles, clutching at his life contained within the holdall, watching from the window as all that was familiar, grew further away.

CHAPTER SEVEN

Annie hesitated, just for an instant but 'needs must' she told herself. Her fingers gripped the big brass ring and she brought it down against the door of the Convent with a purposeful thud. She turned to look back at the street behind her, it was busy, people moved about the city engaged in whatever provided their living but surely it held nothing and no one unknown to the Lord. She heard movement from within the Convent, the door opened to reveal that same nun whom Annie recognised from her previous visit with Catherine. The gentle face produced a nervous smile, she too remembered Catherine Appleyard's visit and the young woman who had accompanied her.

"Please may I speak with The Reverend Mother, I won't keep her long," said Annie.

"I will fetch her." The nun hurried along the corridor with what Annie felt sure was a more urgent pace. Only a very few minutes passed before she returned with the older nun.

"Good morning my dear, I do hope you do not bear more sad news for Sister Agnes."

Annie observed the gentle movement of the cross and rosary on her chest. Reverend Mother, while appearing serenely calm, never the less trembled within.

"Oh no, not at all," replied Annie quickly, "but what I am about to request may disturb you a little, I do hope not because that is not my intention."

The Reverend Mother turned to the Sister. "You may resume your duties, there is no need of concern.

It is Annie isn't it, I remember well the name, it being my own mother's name . How curious I should tell you that at only our second meeting when I don't believe I have ever spoken of my mother's name to the Sisters. She is dead now of course, were she alive mother would be 94. Well now Annie what is this request?"

"Once a week, usually on a Tuesday, Catherine Appleyard and myself distribute items of food, gathered from wherever possible, through the kindness of those able to donate. Catherine assembles these provisions at her home. We pack them into boxes and bags and take them to the families most in need. It has become impossible for me to continue helping Catherine. My husband went to war a month ago and I am needed at the workshops in his absence. It is crucial to the women who rely on their earnings that I maintain the orders and secure further commissions. I feel a compelling loyalty to them but for Catherine also, she is not a young woman, I worry for her. She has a determination to continue and I so admire her for it but I know the situation distresses her husband, he sees her tiredness.

Reverend Mother, I am quite sure that the stillness of the Convent allows the Lord to hear so clearly the prayers which you and the Sisters offer for us all but do you think he might understand if two of the younger Sisters were to help distribute to those families, give support to Catherine. It would be only once a week for an hour or two." Annie's sincerity weighted the appeal.

The Reverend Mother stood deep in thought, after a period of earnest contemplation she spoke.

"I imagine that you hope Sister Agnes might be one of these two young nuns?"

"It is not vital but I cannot deny that I hoped Catherine might see her daughter. I appreciate that you may feel it a little irregular," Annie hesitated, "Sister Agnes is devoted to her life here with you and all the Sisters, Catherine knows that and she does understand really but I believe she desperately needs to feel that, as a mother, she is still loved in some way."

The elderly nun smiled and nodded but her eyes did not meet Annie's, they seemed to gaze beyond Annie, to someone or something far distant. Annie continued.

"It is a busy activity and not always easy, sometimes a family is recently bereaved and food is not the only thing they need. Many of them would be afraid of your own total devotion, they don't regularly attend Church. We cannot fall on our knees to pray with them but we offer simple love as friends, in their own way, I do believe that they feel we have not come to them from Catherine Appleyard's house but have been directed to their despair by a God who cares, even for them, in spite of everything. Does this make any sense to you or is it simply my sentimental notion?"

Reverend Mother had lived long and for the earlier part of her life had shared the streets and ways of the world with the people of whom Annie spoke, she understood perfectly Annie's concern.

"So we deliver fortitude on the streets but deliver our prayers here at the Convent," she said.

"Yes, I suppose that is what I am asking," replied Annie.

Reverend Mother sighed, "I see no reason why we should not so engage ourselves but tell me, how are my young Sisters to carry these provisions, surely they must be heavy."

"Oh no," replied Annie, "we each have an old pram and we put the parcels in those, it creates no strain to our backs."

"So the Sisters each push a pram along the streets." The Reverend Mother's eyebrows rose in consternation but almost immediately a smile came to her face, she looked intently at Annie and both women burst into laughter, they laughed at the unlikeliness of it all.

"You know Annie I can almost hear my mother's voice saying, 'just get on with it Marjorie', that is the name my mother gave me, there I go again, how strange it is, that apart from my one brother who still lives and The Heavenly Father, how few people are aware, yet in the space of only ten minutes, I have told you these things Annie..........?" The nun was asking Annie's full name.

"Eddowes, Reverend Mother, I am Annie Eddowes," she replied.

"Well now Annie Eddowes, I trust you will prepare the way for Sister Agnes and Sister Mary, by talking with Catherine. I shall send them to her next Tuesday.

Annie leaned forward to kiss Reverend Mothers cheek. "Thank-you," Annie said softly.

As the heavy old door opened and the world outside passed before the elderly nun's eyes, she took Annie's hand.

"You are a mother too aren't you my dear," she said, "none of us feels so very differently you know, may God bless you Annie."

She stood at the top of the steps and waved until Annie turned the corner. The door now closed once more, Reverend Mother stood quite still, in her mind she could see two young women, each pushing a pram along the empty corridor ahead of her, she fingered her rosary, drew a deep breath and made her way slowly to that quiet room where only The Heavenly Father and now Annie Eddowes, knew so surely the fullness of her heart.

CHAPTER EIGHT

Annie thanked the driver for carrying in the bolts of cloth. A hasty inspection of the fabric had satisfied her of its quality, she checked his delivery note against the docket on the parcel and signed the receipt. She felt immense relief, the tender had been difficult, they were a comparatively small concern, too high and the order would have gone to another, too low and the business might fold. When word came that Eddowes' was commissioned to supply army regulation shirts to the Ministry for a period of ten months, with a review of costs at six months, Annie could have kissed the postman. This order would secure for the immediate, the jobs at Basford. Annie had pursued another to underpin the Winchester Street workshop. Christening gowns and wedding dresses had trickled in steadily and the ubiquitous work shirts, in spite of taking a knock due to the absence of so many young men, nevertheless sustained an existence through the pit workers and older men but Annie had needed to bolster the order books for the smaller workshop. Help had come in the form of shrouds, an item less obvious to many but required none the less. Basford had taken delivery of khaki cloth several days ago and the women had quickly familiarised themselves with the pattern. Gertie now ran the operation in her young enthusiastic way for 'King and Country'. It caused Annie to ponder the difference age could make. A younger mind, less hardened by life's contrariness and tribulation could approach the creation of military uniform with patriotic fervour yet many of the older women, veterans of domestic hardship, stitched their way to a wage only by overlooking the actual nature of the work. Their loyalties lay with family, their efforts concentrated on its preservation. The bolts of white linen which Annie had just taken delivery of were to be made into shrouds by Edna, May and herself.

It had been necessary to agree a rota, the children's well being was paramount so they had devised a plan to enable Edna to continue earning as before but her hours would involve the care of all the children for the later part of two afternoons. Each morning Edna would unlock the workshop for May, walk halfway to Annie's with her girls where she would meet with William, he would then take charge of young Annie, Susie and Liza bringing them back to Hood Street, then walking all the children to school. Annie would see them all safely off before setting out for Winchester Street with Hilda, the child would play in the back room whilst Annie worked. Two afternoons each week, Annie would need to go to Basford, at these times, Edna with Hilda would leave the workshop early to be at Hood Street when the older children returned from school. They would all eat together at Annie's each weeknight. Edna would lock the workshop on the three days that Annie left early for home, on the two days Annie went to Basford, May would lock up and push the keys through Edna's letterbox.

Annie decided that for everyone's sake, both workshops would close at midday on Saturday's, to allow all the women to organise their households and shop for food. Gertie held a key to the Basford premises and was diligent in securing what she considered to be her responsibility.

Billy's mam was to sit with her granddaughters on Saturday mornings, Samuel and Sarah were to take care of young John and Hilda for a little while so Annie could bring the books up to date at Basford and pay the wages. Annie did the banking each Thursday afternoon and paid Edna and May every Friday. The plan was not set in stone but for the most part it worked well with only slight adjustment to allow for the unforeseen, such as Edna's violent toothache one day and George and Freddy's bout of diarrhoea from eating 'scrumped' unripe apples.

Each Saturday Samuel and Sarah seized upon John and Hilda with obvious pleasure, the older boys often went to Mitchell Street after playing football or train spotting, so Annie was never surprised to find them all there on her return from Basford. Always Sarah would have baked and the children fed upon her 'goodies' readily. Annie redressed the balance by presenting Sarah with a small joint of meat, some eggs, a bag of mints for Samuel but the protests she met with never faded, repaying their generosity was ever to be a challenge.

Davina's house stood temporarily empty. Her cousin Isobel at one time used to visit with good intention yet wearing poor Davina to a state of 'Hardwick Syndrome' as she put it. The situation eased when Frank and Ivy married and set up home within Davina's house. 'Isobel is like a peevish child' Davina had declared 'she is jealous of two dear young people'. The resentment grew even more when in turn, Harold and Molly came along, with the result that Isobel's visits ceased, much to the delight of Davina. However a letter had arrived ten days ago informing Davina of her cousin's poorly state of health. Isobel had suffered quite a severe stroke. It was not in Davina's nature to ever ignore the plight of a relative or friend. She had determined herself to catch a train to Derby where she would stay for a little while and bring what comfort she could to Isobel.

Ivy had taken the children and gone to her mother's at Clifton. Since word of Frank's death, Ivy had rallied for the sake of Harold and Molly but some time spent with Mrs. Pilkington might enable her a measure of grief which Annie felt sure was still trapped within. On the occasions Annie had called to see Ivy, her quietness was too deep to be natural. The children coped well but their mother needed to mourn for her husband without that enforced jollity to inspire their son and daughter, an interlude at Clifton could only be beneficial all round.

Edna had brewed a pot of tea on the small primus stove in the back room. Hilda sat by May eating a slice of cheese and a teacake, her doll had been put to bed in an empty thread box, a picture of grandad Boucher's barrow lay half coloured on the floor.

"I think you aught to give that barro' some nice bright red wheels Hilda, cheer it up a bit an' make the brush handles yello'," said Edna trying to encourage the child.

"I had a letter from Alfred yesterday," said May, "it was only a short one this time, he sounds tired. They're reinforcing regiments at the Somme, he didn't say very much at all really, just sent his love to Mabel and told me to go down to The Meadows, pick some blackberries and make bramble jelly for when he comes home."

Edna sniffed and looked across at Annie. "Well at least you've 'eard from 'im, Billy 'avent written a soddin' word in weeks. The tea in her cup was flushed over the rim by the trembling of her hand, before the inevitable curses could assail Hilda's young ears, Annie said.

"Charles must be somewhere in Egypt by now, when he wrote from Staffordshire he had only two further weeks of basic training before embarkation." She hesitated, "I believe he could have come home for a day but he felt it best not to upset the children all over again."

Edna who had sat dabbing her lap with a remnant of flannelette, desperately trying to soak up the tea muttered a very pointed.

"Um that would never do."

May fidgeted on her seat. "Mabel earned her buckle last week, I didn't like to say anything, it seemed inappropriate somehow."

"Oh no, not at all May," said Annie, "we are so pleased and proud too aren't we Edna?"

"Course we are, you tell 'er I said she'll be Matron by the time I've finished sewing Mona Dallymore's weddin' dress, the soddin' pin tucks down the front are tryin' me patience, I can't concentrate on anythin' so fanciful," declared Edna.

"Well very soon there are some simpler items to stitch," said Annie, "the linen has arrived for the shrouds."

"Shrouds, bloody shrouds," shrieked Edna, "don't we 'ave enough misery wi' out sewin' shrouds."

"Hush Edna," said May casting her eyes to Hilda who now felt compelled to ask.

"What's a shroud?"

Both May and Edna suddenly fell silent leaving any explanation to Annie.

"Well, when someone dies the kind man whom we call the undertaker dresses them in a shroud, it is just something to be worn." Annie smiled reassuringly at Hilda.

"Is that what you will all wear when you die?" Asked the ever curious young mind.

"Well I won't," said Edna firmly. "When I pop me clogs I want yer to put me in me best red frock an' a pair o' them proper fine stockin's, not these thick things we wear. I want a dab o' rouge on me cheeks an' me hair done up in curls like Mary Pickford."

Hilda's eyes widened at Edna's detailed description and the whole thing struck the three women as amusing. May began to giggle, followed by Annie. Edna jumped up from her seat, grabbed a handful of braid, lay on the floor putting the tousled braid about her forehead and ears before crossing her arms over her chest and closing her eyes. Hilda laughed and tickled Edna's chin who in return winked roguishly.

"It looks as though Miss Pickford's wet herself," said Annie referring to the tea stain down the front of Edna's skirt.

"You are quite mad Edna," said May but the moment distracted the child from her enquiry and all three women resumed their work, able to feel a degree of light heartedness.

The arrangement with the Convent appeared to be working well. Sometimes on a Tuesday afternoon when Annie was on her way to Basford, she would see Catherine and the Sisters about their distribution. The first time Annie came upon the figure of a nun, parking a pram outside the door of Edith Spooner's, it did indeed seem incongruous, even Annie had to take a second look to confirm the reality. These were changing times, Annie often wondered what aunt Bella would have said about it all, her opinions and views always so correct, moulded as they were by the classics, the precision of mathematical equations and her innate command of an ordered mind. Aunt Bella would have truly struggled to adapt to this fast evolving society.

The look of surprise which Annie had been given the first time she had called at the bank amused her somewhat. Working class women were never seen standing before the teller and the more gracious and wealthily endowed ladies had trusted clerks to undertake matters of finance for them. So it was with some relief Annie had found herself standing before Edwin Garbett. It had brought back to mind the day he had stepped in to help her steer Charles away from trouble at The Standard. Annie felt sympathy for Edwin, as with Charles,unkind tongues had questioned his presence still, when men from the streets around him had left their homes to fight. They were unaware, as indeed Annie had been, of his fits which from a boy had interfered with his activities. The sudden death of his father, Edwin had found him dead on the privy, had made his condition even more severe and when he fitted at the bank, traumatically and in view of colleagues and clients, the terrible nature of epilepsy became known to a very many people, the tongues which had once derided him now spread an account of his alarming seizure. Annie imagined that for Edwin neither circumstance offered peace of mind, he must surely feel inadequate in any case. Only the acute shortage of young men and the fact that Edwin was competent and entirely honest, persuaded the bank not to let him go. He had told Annie this was his sincere belief one day when he walked with her to the tram stop. It was a sad and misguided avoidance which now, most people chose to apply to Edwin Garbett.

Davina's visit to cousin Isobel had been extended due to her deteriorating condition and while Ivy was at liberty to come back to The Park at any time, Davina had insisted Ivy take a key, she and the children nevertheless remained at Clifton. Annie became just a little anxious that it might not now be Ivy's intention to return. Mrs. Pilkington was a woman younger that Davina, in truth there was little work for Ivy to do at The Park over and above tending her own family. Her mother was doubtless a ready child minder and painful memories would be less present at Clifton. These thoughts troubled Annie, Davina would be so desperately lonely without Ivy, Harold and Molly. They were all very fond of Davina, Annie had no doubt of that but Ivy was now with her own mother and to be so, must surely bring comfort. The longer this situation continued the less likely would be their return to The Park, the blessings were mixed, as with all things it seemed ever necessary to rob Peter in order to pay Paul.

Annie would try to bring Sarah and Davina into one another's company more, she could think of no other course, matched in age and nature, it offered a sensible solution. Samuel too would find easement if he knew his beloved Sarah was safely ensconced by Davina's hearth whilst he dealt with those blocked chimneys and lost himself amongst the crops at the allotment. Once everyone had established a settled routine Annie felt sure Ivy would bring Harold and Molly to visit their grandparents and dear aunt Davina as they had ever called her.

It was Wednesday afternoon, in just a short while Annie would need to put away her work and go home to be there for the children's return from school. Edna and May were engaged in putting the final touches to the wedding gown. Mona Dallymore was a tall well built young woman and as Edna had so eloquently put it, 'ad the girth of a cab horse', the fine detailed embroidery to complete the hemline, both women had worked on in order to meet the deadline. Annie continued to add to the number of shrouds, at least they were uncomplicated and presented no challenge to concentration. Hilda had mastered simple knitting and sat in the office chair where her careful manipulation of the needles produced an acceptable garter stitch which grew in length day on day. Her ability for a child of three was impressive, Annie believed it came from the productive environment of the workshop. When the women were occupied at their machines Hilda must amuse herself and the little girl wanted to create something by her own hand. The scarf was to be a present for Annie, to keep her warm next winter as she travelled to Basford.

A knock came at the door, May was closest and about to secure the last stitch on her length of hem. The knock came once more, now ready May crossed the room to open the door to the caller. A lad stood there, his cap and jacket identified him even before he extended his hand to pass an envelope.

"Mrs. Dodds?" He said, "are you Mrs. William Dodds."

May could not answer, she stood completely overcome. Edna and Annie had both heard the lad's words but only Annie stood and joined May at the door.

"Yes," said Annie, "Mrs. Dodds is here."

She stepped to one side enabling him to see Edna, still seated, the hem of the wedding dress across her knees, her fingers paralysed yet so accustomed she held the needle upright, away from the satin lest she prick her finger and fetch blood.

Annie signed for the telegram and the lad was gone. Hilda slid down from the chair, crossed the room and stood by Edna, taking the needle from her fingers. It pained Annie to witness an act so mature from one so young. Even childhood was not permitted to go untouched by this war, responsibility, awareness of trouble, imposed themselves upon the young long before they should. Annie put the needle in a pin cushion and gently gathered up the dress from Edna's lap.

"You open it, I can't," said Edna, "please, you do it Annie."

May's chest pounded beneath her blouse, still she had not uttered a single word. Annie took the paper from within the envelope and her eyes travelled along each line.

"Edna, it's alright, Billy is alive, wounded but alive. It says he is being shipped back to England and will be taken to hospital. You must await further word, I don't imagine they could know to which hospital he will be sent. As soon as he reaches whichever one it is they will let you know. That is how it was when Harry Payne was injured." Annie's relieved expression did little to sooth Edna.

" 'E lost 'is leg for God's sake," cried Edna, "God Almighty Annie, what'll it do to Billy?"

"Listen to me," said Annie. "You have no way of knowing what Billy's injuries are and until you do, tell yourself this, Billy is alive and out of the fighting, he's safe Edna, Billy is safe."

May burst into floods of tears, now Annie directed her voice at May. "Make a pot of tea, do it right away, I have to take Hilda now and go to Hood Street. After you have drunk the tea, finish the hem of that dress and hang it on the rail. None of us will be able to think about work again until tomorrow, pack away and cover the machines. Edna, you lock up as always and come to the girls. It is going to be alright, I know it is."

Annie's gentle authority restored calm but the tension deep inside all three women would find small relief until the identity of the hospital and the extent of Billy's injuries became known to them.

Everyone had eaten, the children, now aware of the telegram and its content had gone outside to play. Optimism came more easily to the young, for Annie, Susie and Liza, dad had suddenly become closer, they had heard the words 'coming back to England', that was enough.

Since May 21st when the Government had introduced British summertime, the darker mornings had seemed nothing but a nuisance, farmers might well call for later daylight hours to gather crops into the evening but getting children ready for school, preparing dinner bags for the men in that gloomy light betwixt night's end and day's beginning, brought yet another torment to the already harassed women. Now at almost midsummer, the evenings seemed without end, daylight held for so long. Calling the children in from play was a summons repeated several times before finally, exasperated mothers threatened the certainty of a sore backside if their calls were not heeded.

Eight breathless, weary children made their way to the backdoor of No.14. Annie had allowed John and Hilda to stay up late, Edna's girls needed to settle their young minds on the day's news. Play with all Annie's brood enabled them to find a safe feeling, dad was injured but alive, surely everything must be alright if they were permitted to play so freely. Bad news invariably sent them straight to bed so grown-ups could talk and weep unseen.

"Come on, you'll be like Nellie Draper's stuffed owl in the mornin'," said Edna. "That thing gives me the creeps, it perches under that glass dome in 'er livin' room an' its eyes follo' yer all round the place. When I 'ad to sit wi' 'er that day she 'ad the vertigo, I turned the bloody thing round to face the wall. Billy says it reminds 'im of 'is old schoolmaster, Ebenezer Arkwight, as if a name like that weren't bad enough the poor bugger 'ad 'orrible poxy skin an'all an' wore thick, tinted spectacles that made 'is eyes look like piss 'oles in snow."

Annie marvelled at Edna's graphic description as she ushered her own children into the house.

"I'll see you tomorrow," she cast a bright smile at Edna.

Annie was determined they should remain optimistic, when Edna received further word it would be all important that she travelled to the hospital right away. It would be a journey of such mixed emotions, Annie imagined either Edna's or Billy's mother would accompany her.

It was a strange coincidence that on the same day Edna got her letter from the hospital, Annie too received a letter from Charles. He was in Cairo, it imparted little information other than to tell her that because of his background, his management experience as such, he had been assigned to the Supply Corps. He wrote of a man whom he had travelled with, Clem, he didn't reveal a surname. Clem was from Long Eaton, until being called up he had worked as a bailiff, such men were usually possessed of a hard disposition. Traditionally, the pit owners held much of the housing also. When a man died below ground, his family above were shown scant compassion. With barely enough time to bundle their modest chattels together, women weakened from grief and lack of sleep were obliged to pack their lives and vacate the tenancy. Clutching makeshift holdalls and shepherding frightened children, they fled the domineering bailiff and wandered from mother to mother in law, aunt to cousin, wherever the love of extended family might keep them safe for a little while. Almost without exception, the bailiff's power over his fellow mortals seemed to drive a cruel streak in his nature. Perhaps this Clem was that one exception, Annie hoped it might be so and that Charles' new found friend did not take pleasure from the sight of despair, that he had not in the past, closed his eyes and felt satisfaction at the memory of a thoroughly callous eviction. Now the miners' families were not alone in this tide of humanity. So many widows, so many mercenary landlords, the divide which separated the haves from the have nots grew ever wider.

Edna had been told that Billy's injuries, while serious, were not life threatening, she would catch an early train to St. Albans, then a bus to Hemel Hempstead. Billy's mam would go with her, it would be necessary for them to find overnight accommodation closeby the hospital. Annie was to sleep the girls at Hood Street on Wednesday and Thursday night. Edna would collect them sometime on Friday evening.

May was on edge, the reality of war had invaded the workshop. Edna's nervousness and apprehension clawed at poor May's composure. She could not force down as much as a biscuit and over and over she would mutter the words 'oh dear' and sigh so deeply.

"For God's sake will yer stop that bloody moanin'," Edna cried out tetchily. "Me nerves are in tatters as 'tis wi' out you makin' 'em worse."

Annie had already gone home, school ended for the summer break in nine days time, yet another rota had to be worked out.

"Sorry," said May feebly. "Every day I go home I'm afraid to open the door, I have to make myself look down at the mat. There was a brown envelope there yesterday, it lay face down for more than an hour before I turned it over. It was for Mabel, nothing to do with Alfred at all."

May burst into tears and Edna feeling bad for having shouted, took May in her arms and comforted her as best she could but it was a curious contagion, the touch of a hand, an arm about the shoulders, any embrace intended to restore would instead pass the heartache and intensify the crying before some inner strength eased both parties of their affliction.

"Give my love to Billy tomorrow Edna," said May, what time do you leave?"

"Billy's mam is comin' to stop at our place tonight, we've to be at the station by twenty to seven," replied Edna.

It was a strange feeling, sitting alone to eat a bite of supper, no sound of Annie, Susie or Liza. Edna forced herself to eat the egg and bacon, her spirit already fickle, she knew that tomorrow would call for a stiff upper lip. Billy wouldn't want her snivelling over him whatever the sight might be and Billy's mam was not a young woman, someone must bolster her spirits too. She should come very soon, 'by half past eight' she had said. Footsteps outside in the yard announced Phyllis Dodds' arrival, it was almost 9 o'clock.

"I'd 'ave been 'ere long ago if it weren't for Doris Sugden an' 'er damn dog, she never goes anywhere wi'out the scruffy cur. Just as I wer' about to put me coat on the soddin' thing wer' sick all over me scullery floor. Doris said she'd clean it up but I weren't about to leave 'er in me 'ouse so I 'ad to see to that before I come. I told 'er 'tis Sid's bloomin' pigeons, that dog goes over every inch o' their yard lickin' up all the droppin's. I asked 'er do yer ever feed the thing, tis no wonder it spilt its guts on me flags. Them pigeons are nowt but a damn nuisance, one got me best counterpane last week, right down the middle."

"What did Doris want anyway?" Asked Edna.

"She came across wi' a pat o' Colwick cheese for Billy, she knows 'e's allus liked the strong one, 'er Sid won't eat it 'til the maggots are in it. This one's fresh, we'll take it to the hospital, I've put a couple o' Lovatts cobs in me bag for Billy to eat it with."

The soft cheese from Colwick Weir appeared on most tables in the summer, combined with watercress and crusty bread it created a meal of delectable flavour. The average mortal chose the pat with the blue lettering on the wrapper but those of stern spirit and cast iron palate would take the pat labelled red. An intensely sharp bite even when fresh but when at a matured stage of development it could 'blow yer socks off'.

Edna sighed, "No use takin' 'im any smokes, it won't be allowed in hospital."

"Billy could sit outside an' smoke," suggested Phyllis.

"No, I'll take a couple o' bottles o' stout, don't see any reason why 'e couldn't 'ave them."

Edna put away her supper dishes and took down the laundry from the airer. As she folded the girls' dresses, it occurred to her that Billy would likely need some clothes when he was discharged to travel home, surely he would wear 'civvies' now. Only then did she realise how little she actually knew. Would he recover and be sent straight back to the front, would he be given leave first or was the war over for Billy, would he be coming home for good.

"What should I do mam?" Said Edna.

"Well if I wer' you I'd put in a shirt, trousers an' jacket, just in case, 'ow they think you can organise yerself when they don't tell yer 'owt is beyond me." Phyllis muttered her frustration as she unpinned her hat.

Edna lay awake for a long time before tiredness eventually brought sleep. She called Phyllis with a cup of tea then found her fingers unwilling to be steady as she combed her hair. Too nervous herself to eat, she prepared bread and jam, which Phyllis had declared to be, 'a bit 'o comfort for me innards'. The two women were out of the house and on their way to the station soon after six.

Edna had not been on a train since going to Skegness with Billy. The station was a draughty, noisy place. Back then her excitement at travelling to the coast had been immense, now however, her emotions were confused and the sight of the huge locomotive pulling in alongside the platform amid whistles, smoke and steam hissing from beneath like some mighty weapon of war filled her tired head with panic. Travelling away from her girls, from No.24,

Edna was no longer that worldly young woman from Sherwood. The last ten years had been spent making their family, Billy and Edna Dodds and their three daughters, she had sought nothing more. As her free hand guided Billy's mam on to the foot plate it was the thought of seeing her husband which calmed the fear and delivered Edna to her seat. The heavy doors slammed shut along the length of the carriages, another high pitched whistle and deep shudders of movement as the great lumbering engine opened its mouth to the coal and with a belly full of fire, now carried Edna, Phyllis and all the other passengers out of Victoria Station, past the factory chimneys and the pit heads beyond. The grand dimensions of The Castle became smaller with each violent thrust from a piston, yet the uncertainty grew so much larger with every billow of smoke the powerful engine sent from its stack. They shared the compartment with a young woman, probably no more than twenty one or two years of age, two older men and one very large older woman. At first no one spoke, then conversation between the two men broke the silence. Their debate did nothing to lighten the mood, The loss of The Hampshire and the drowning of Lord Kitchener at Jutland, their very differing opinion of Churchill, the disaster at Verdun, the push at the Somme. It seemed these men could find no other topic than war. Edna noticed the strained look on the young woman's face, the nervous contortions of her fingers.

"Are you goin' far," asked Edna.

"To the hospital," she replied.

"We're goin' to Hemel Hempstead, my husband Billy's been injured, 'e's in hospital. Don't know 'til we see 'im 'ow bad 'is injuries are but the letter said not life threatenin'."

Tears began to fall down the young woman's face. "It's my Tom, I'm going to see my Tom, they sent word I should come right away. He was improving but last Tuesday he haemorrhaged, lost a lot of blood."

Her words became faint, all Edna could hear was a wrangle between the men over the virtues of Lloyd George as opposed to Asquith.

"For Almighty's sake, will you talk about summat else, bloody politicians, admirals an' generals, they can all crow like a cockerel on a dung heap but when it comes to it, 'tis our men 'do' while the big wigs 'spout'."

Taken aback by Edna's outburst they chuntered some displeasure and buried themselves behind their newspapers. The plump, older woman who sat beside Phyllis cleared her throat and said.

"My Les 'asn't got a leg left, twenty pairs o' socks I knitted for 'im an' 'e 'asn't got a single leg left."

In any other situation Edna would have found the woman's remark amusing but today it grated on her senses. She leaned across to the young woman. "You can travel all the way with us, it'll be alright."

"I have to change at London, Tom is in hospital at Worthing but thank you anyway," she withdrew to some place behind her closed eyelids.

Phyllis began to fan herself with her hat. As the morning had progressed so the temperature had increased, the compartment was warm and stuffy. Edna rose to her feet.

"Let's walk along the corridor for a bit Mam, we can get some air out there."

The train had very few empty seats, it occurred to Edna that many of the passengers were women, most of whom sat with that look of trepidation, their reason for journeying most likely to be similar, if not the same, as her own.

The day had turned out to be the hottest of the summer so far. The brief period at St. Albans had presented little opportunity to view their surroundings and to cool down. Anxious not to miss the bus which would take them to the hospital, both Edna and Phyllis had gripped their bags of precious items for Billy and concentrated solely on furthering their journey to its ultimate destination.

"Here we are ladies," said the conductor who had been slightly amused by Edna's request. 'Don't you let us miss the stop, we've been travellin' since 6 o/clock this mornin', the train wer' full an' 'ot as Hades, me poor backside's stickin' to the seat o' your bus wi' the heat an' Billy's mam's got a Colwick cheese in 'er bag, if that turns, them at the hospital will want to fumigate the both of us afore they let us in'. Had been Edna's desperate plea from where she sat at the back of the bus, close to the conductor and his all important bell.

Standing at the front of the hospital both women drew a deep breath and cautioned each other to be strong. Inside, a woman espied them through the open door of her office.

"Can I help, you appear a little lost," she said with a friendly smile.

"We have come to see Billy Dodds, Private William Dodds, of The Sherwood Foresters. This is his mam and I'm his wife," said Edna with a concerted effort at correctness. "I have the letter with me." She reached inside her bag and produced the paper. So many times had Edna read it, the creasing and fingering were very evident.

"If you would like to come with me I will take you to the ward," said the almoner, as she had introduced herself.

Edna and Phyllis walked slightly behind as seemed to befit her officialdom, whilst her manner was pleasant, at this moment Edna felt very humble.

The corridors revealed wards spilling over with sick and injured, many lay beneath bandages and coverings so extensive, only a familiar voice and a stretched heart string would give a relative any clue to kin, a lover that spasm of hope. The smells were a cocktail which refused to blend, the heavier elements settling underneath the lighter but releasing their potency whenever the mix was stirred. The sounds caused a torment to the ears, ranging in tone from cheerful, encouraging chatter to suffering moans of despair. Edna gripped her bag more tightly and took deeper breaths, a growing nausea seemed intent on turning her stomach to gall. Finally the almoner led them to a side room where a nurse sat at a desk amid considerable paperwork.

"This is Private Dodds' wife and mother Sister, very anxious to see him, they have travelled from Nottingham."

"Thank-you Mrs. Beale, I shall take them to Private Dodds in just a few minutes." Sister smiled a welcome and an expression of mischief passed to

Edna as she said, "My dear, I hope you will not be too eager to take him home, he needs to remain with us for a little while yet but I confess my ward would be a poorer place without him. I envy you Mrs. Dodds, you have a diamond, an absolute gem."

"What's 'e been up to, I've been married to 'im for ten years and only the landlord at The Nelson 'ave ever told me they'd be poorer wi' out 'im." Edna had abandoned her attempts at correctness with the Sister's declaration of Billy's brilliance.

The nurse chuckled, then her manner became serious. "Billy sustained injuries to one side of his head as a result of shellfire but he is healing well, there will however be some measure of loss to the sight in his left eye and the hearing in his left ear. I'm afraid his left arm was severely damaged and could not be saved. He is lucky Mrs. Dodds, while you probably feel otherwise right now, I have to tell you that for others, my words in this very room have been as much a tragedy for me as they were for them. Billy exudes life, each of us in this place has thanked God for that, some days we are all tested, even we nurses." She took Edna and Phyllis's hand in turn and squeezing them tightly said. "Chin up, ready?" Her question was answered by their nervous smiles. "I shall take you to him."

She led a numbed Edna and Phyllis to the end of a bed where Billy lay with the unbandaged eye closed, a thick wad of dressing and bandaging just below his left shoulder. Sister gave Edna a wink, patted her arm and left them to themselves.

Phyllis stood motionless with tears rolling down her cheeks but Edna moved to the side of the bed. Billy heard the movement and without opening his eye said.

"Where's that pint o' stout you promised me nurse, you wait 'til my Edna comes, I'll tell 'er, I only let you near me bits 'cause you bribed me."

"Do you want another bandage Billy Dodds, 'cause if you aren't careful I'll get 'em to bind your 'bit' an' put it in traction like Paddy Malone's leg when 'e fell off back o' brewery waggon. 'Is missus reckoned it wer' never the same after that, she allus swore they stretched it too much. His inside leg changed from 26 to 28 on that side. For years, 'til 'e wore out all 'is trousers, 'e went around wi' a turnup on one leg and none on th'other. I offered to stitch 'em so both legs 'ould match but she said 'no', at least 'e got one proper turnup. Poor bugger, when their Elsie got married she put 'er 'andbag on the ground an' made 'im stand wi' 'is odd leg behind that for every photograph."

Billy slowly opened his eye and a big grin straddled his face.

"My Edna, God it's been quiet wi'out you, they told me I'd likely be deaf in one ear, I began to think I'd lost hearin' in both but your soothin' tones 'ave restored me my love."

"Shut up Billy an' give us a kiss," said Edna with a joy in her heart that near consumed her. She fell against his chest with no thought for his soreness and if he felt any, then it was disregarded as husband and wife found each other again. Phyllis sank to the end of the bed, clinging to the rail, age and weariness suddenly took the upper hand.

"It's alright Mam, I'll be 'ome afore you know it an' you'll be less likely to clip me round the ear now I've only got one of 'em."

Poor Phyllis sniffed and said all she could think to say. "I've brought you a strong Colwick cheese from Doris an' a wedge o' fruit cake, the one you like wi' dates an' spice."

"Now that's more like it Mam." Billy reached for her hand. Edna produced two bottles of stout from the bag along with a tray of treacle toffee. They chatted about the girls, the neighbours and of Charles' departure, eventually Billy asked if there was news of Frank. "It's been that bloody bad, when you're out there, it's daft really, but you hope, every day you hope that you'll see a mate."

Billy lowered his face to the bed, as if afraid to look on Edna's response. She took his fingers and closed her own around them.

"Frank was killed at Verdun." Neither spoke for a minute or more, then Billy raised his face again and said. "Tell our girls their dad is comin' 'ome soon, tell 'em that 'e's never goin' away again." His voice faltered for an instant. "We're bloody lucky Edna, I don't know why us but we're the lucky ones an' we never forget the others, never." He wiped a tear from his cheek.

"How is Annie managin'?"

His enquiry led to an up-to-date account of the workshops. He asked about their journey on the train, where they would spend the night and find a meal.

"There are places close to the hospital, we'll take a room at one o' them an' come to see you again for a little while in the mornin'. We 'ave to be at St. Albans to catch the train by ten past midday, said Edna.

His clothes were deposited in the small cabinet by the bed, when Edna pulled out the drawer, there it lay, the photograph and in one corner, the nappy pin secured it to her letters. It gave Edna a curious feeling, all those miles, all those months, this image of home had endured with Billy. Edna smoothed her fingers across the faces, recalling that Saturday at Askew's. It seemed hardly possible to be able to touch the picture again knowing all that had happened since.

Billy had pronounced all his goodies, 'enough to make a man too big for 'is boots'. A brief exchange of kind regards with Sister and an assurance on her part that Private Dodds would soon be back in Nottingham, enabled Edna and Phyllis to make their way to a café for a 'cuppa' and something to eat before finding a place to rest the head if not to sleep, until the morning brought a few more precious moments to spend with Billy.

The journey home would be much less daunting. Men can bloody well talk about whatever they like on that train tomorrow, thought Edna, my man's comin' 'ome. Churchill and Kaiser Bill can take their right flanks and their left flanks and shove 'em right up their rear guard! Edna Dodds was invincible.

Back at the hospital Billy ate Doris's strong cheese, his mam's cake, drank his stout from Edna and wept for Frank. He was compelled by emotion to do all these things.

"Nurse, nurse." He called out in his confusion and distress.

"What is it Billy?" Sister held him in her arms as he cried floods of tears.

"I've wet the bed Sister, I've been an' wet the soddin' bed."

She cradled him until all his torment was released.

Billy Dodds, everyone else's brightness, needed, for just a little while someone to shine about him.

CHAPTER NINE

Annie stood back to view the room, each week she had opened the window, given the furniture a quick dust over but with so many other activities demanding her time, the room had not seen a good bottoming in years. Despite the sadness to which these four walls could testify, Annie had not once felt any sinister influence when moving about the bed where Enid had lain or the chest from which Annie had taken the pretty mauve scarf. She had made a comfortable new cushion for the chair in which Dr.Baragruy had sat in anticipation of the worst. Still the images of that day were vivid but Enid through whatever means had not sent sign of unrest, in fact Annie was content to believe that Enid was at peace.

Davina had stayed on in Derby following cousin Isobel's death, to attend the funeral and spend a couple of days with Lawrence, Isobel's son, whom Davina had not seen for some time. On returning to Nottingham she had learned from Ivy that an opportunity had presented itself for her to work as a housekeeper at Rylands Boarding House. It would be a 'live out' position so Ivy would be staying with her mother at Clifton and Harold would attend school there, as indeed would young Molly very soon. They had all visited Davina and whilst the reunion had been tearful, it had to be acknowledged that the arrangement did offer a greater prospect for the future. Davina's house saw few callers and those invariably of senior years. Ivy was still a young woman, a very sad widow at present but time healed and Davina would not wish for Ivy to be all her days without that special love and warmth of a husband. Davina knew better than most, just how empty a bed could feel when reaching out in the darkness only the crisp cotton of the sheet, cool and lifeless, ever met those searching fingers.

Sarah and Samuel had been given the firm promise of regular visits. If Ivy's hours of work at busy periods prevented her being away from Rylands, then Mrs.Pilkington would take Harold and Molly on the bus to call on both Davina and Sarah, their close bond would ever remain.

So it had been fortuitous that at the time Annie was despairing of how to cope with the children's summer break and the demands of the business, Davina had pleaded with Annie to be allowed to move into No.14, just for the period of August so that she might be there constantly to mind the children and relieve Annie of such worries.

'I have barely unpacked my bags since returning from Derby, I shall simply transport them to your house Annie dear', had been Davina's logical approach to it all. Annie recognised the good it could serve in easing Davina's feeling of loneliness and solving the very real problem of her own need to be at the workshop. 'I must go home when school resumes, I cannot leave the house unattended for too long', Davina had declared, anxious not to give any impression of imposing herself.

The spare room at No.14 was now ready to welcome its new occupant. Annie had placed her pretty embroidered duchesse set on the dressing table. On her way back from Basford the day before, she had picked wild honey suckle from the hedgerow by the canal, this now sat in a pale pink jug on the window ledge.

The arrangement could not have been agreed without certain conditions being attached. The children would help with the chores and not receive liberal amounts of spoiling in the form of sweets. Annie herself, would continue to do all the laundry, shopping and preparing of meals, unless of the latter Davina wished to create one of her own favourites, but other than that, she must accept her age and natural limitations. Most crucial of all was the appointment of young Sylvia Robinson, a very pleasant and able girl, who had left school at the end of term. Instructed well by her mother, she would live in at The Park and become, just as Ivy became, a maid of sorts but mainly a companion, a young friend for Davina. Sylvia would commence her work at the start of September.

A carriage drew up outside, Annie could hear cheerful chatter, Davina was obviously instructing the driver to bring her bags to the door, regaling him with an account of her purpose over the coming month as he dutifully obliged. Davina's voice rose in pitch as she became more excited, Annie felt she should rescue the poor man.

"Annie dear, I have kept my baggage to a minimum, this warm weather I shall have need of only light attire," said Davina as the affable driver carried the fourth bag to the front door. "Thank you kindly young man, I hope it might be you who comes for me when I require return transport."

Davina pressed money into his hand, the delighted smile which came to his face confirmed Davina's usual generosity.

Annie lifted one of the bags from the floor to carry up the stairs.

"Oh no dear, they are far too heavy, we must remove some items first. "Davina stooped to open the catch of a leather 'Gladstone', her fingers defied the protests of age as she pulled wide apart the sides of the bag. "I have no further use of these, some are quite old you know. If the children take care of them I can imagine that in time they could prove valuable. There could be no better opportunity to rid my cupboards and drawers of surplus items."

The open bag revealed gentlemen's hair and clothes brushes with rich ebony handles in a leather case which glowed like a polished chestnut. An elegant wallet still with a label from new. A hip flask with a decorative silver cap, cuff links of gold. A cravat pin, the very best of clothes hangers, sleek, varnished and bearing the names of 'well to do' outfitters. A second bag held a beautiful embroidered silk bedcover and two perfume atomizers, the pumps covered by gold thread crocheted in intricate design. By the time Davina had unpacked all the so called surplus, her clothes and personal things needed for her month's stay could easily be contained in just one bag.

"I cannot possibly allow you to give away all these things to us. Surely you must have some family member to whom you could gift them." Annie was genuinely alarmed at the sight of so many valuable objects arrayed about her hall floor.

Davina caught hold the stair post and lowered herself to the second tread, she patted the one above, signalling Annie to sit there. "I have just returned from Isobel's house in Derby, Lawrence is now in the process of sorting all his mother's things. He offered me many of Isobel's little treasures, jewellery, embroidery and tapestry, figurines and so on. I accepted only a photograph of happier times, taken at Redmonds when Isobel attended a Christmas assembly. The photographer captured a perfect image of Isobel, elegant, confident and so obviously proud." Davina sighed deeply. "I said to dear Lawrence you must remember I am no longer a young woman, my own house is filled with a lifetime's accumulation. We feel compelled to keep those pieces of our hearts, the ones which cause us to smile as well as those which make us sad. Birthday cards, letters of love, dried posies. I'm afraid it is now Lawrence's unfortunate duty to discard many of Isobel's keepsakes, hurtful to him though it is, if he does not then the distress is merely stored until it afflicts his own dear children. I have no offspring Annie as you know. Your family is dearer to me than any other in the whole world, believe me when I tell you that I would much prefer to be allowed the happiness of giving your children these few things whilst I am still alive. She paused briefly, "Nathan too, would be pleased to know that your fine young men will one day make use of them. Hilda, when she marries, might lay the bedcover over her bed and remember aunt Davina, that curious old lady who begged to be adopted."

Sitting behind Davina on the stairs, Annie could not see her face, had she been able to do so, Annie would have looked on a longing so intense, so deep felt it would surely have haunted her mind for evermore. As it was Annie rose to her feet, squeezed past the plump figure of Davina, held out her hands as a hoist and pulled her dear friend from the lower tread saying.

"They will never forget you and that would be so regardless of these wonderful gifts. Now, come along, we must install you in your summer residence."

Annie gathered up the bag containing Davina's clothes and led her to the bedroom. The gifts were safely put away, to be distributed at the appropriate times and the household at Hood Street settled comfortably around Davina Wright's presence.

The children were in bed, Annie had hung out a line of washing, bed sheets and pillowslips, to bleach under the moon.

"It's time you sat down Annie, you've not stopped since you got up this morning." Davina sat in the kitchen patching the seat of George's trousers. She had set about all the little odd jobs which, not being imperative, Annie had put aside for the dark evenings of winter. The brassware sat highly polished on the mantel and in the hearth. The three older boys had been despatched to The Meadows with basins, to gather blackberries. Twelve jars of bramble jelly, richly purple, topped with covers cut from the good areas of a worn out white shirt which Davina had boiled in an old pan on the range to sterilise, now stood in a row on the pantry shelf, looking for all the world like an assembly of Bishops at a prodigious Mass.

A goodly number of fresh eggs had been preserved in isinglass for when colder days of midwinter rendered the hens less productive. It was the mending basket however that Annie declared as displaying a miraculous conversion. From a pile that would bring a sigh to the most nimble of fingers, it had been reduced to just a pair of pants needing new elastic and a petticoat coming undone at the hem. Davina was proud of her handiwork, at home little challenge presented itself, now reassured of her capabilities she had announced to Annie her intention, on returning to The Park, of joining 'The Women's League of Friends' from Church. Taking turns to host their gatherings, the product of their endeavours was used to raise funds for good causes and as Davina had so rightly pointed out, never before had there been so many good causes.

"Now what are you doing?" Asked Davina in an exasperated tone of voice.

Annie laughed, "I am putting a summer pudding to stand for tomorrow, I'm sorry Davina but my fingers will not be still, just like Edna's. We are both so looking forward to Billy's homecoming. The girls can hardly wait and Edna has floated through the workshop door every morning this week. Even dear May has been singing at her machine, daring to feel positive in spite of everything."

Davina let out a long satisfied sigh, "It is good to have one of the men back with us, though it won't be easy for Billy. I know him only slightly, mostly from your descriptions Annie but his wounding is severe enough. His strong character will doubtless see him through but I worry for his frustrations. Billy is a 'working' man, not used to sitting at a desk, spending his hours with letters and figures. He is far too young to be idle, somewhere there is employment to suit Billy ideally, the real task is in finding it."

Annie lay in bed with a diversity of thoughts. There had been no further word from Charles, William had written a splendid letter to his father, full of news from home and bearing detailed descriptions of the family's activities. Annie had enclosed a simple note from herself, wanting William's words to impress Charles and prompt him to write to his son just as soon as he could.

'Cairo is a very long way from England', she had reminded William, 'it is inevitable that the mail will take considerably longer to reach us than if your dad was in France'.

Edna would stay at home tomorrow, not being sure what train Billy would catch, Annie had insisted there be no absence from No.24. 'You stay at home until at least Monday Edna'. Annie had persuaded her to forget the workshop until then. It was impossible to predict quite how the days would be. Edna, naturally was feeling very protective of Billy.

'I'll carry on workin' an' 'e can stay 'ome wi' the girls, I'll not 'ave 'im rushin' off to find 'isself a job for a one armed, 'arf blind, 'arf deaf, daft silly sod,' she had vowed on receiving the letter which informed her of Billy's discharge from hospital on Friday.

Now that day was almost upon them, tomorrow Edna would wake up to the reality. It had been agreed that on Sunday, they would all eat a meal together at Hood Street. Annie felt no concern over her own children's reaction to Billy's appearance, he was simply uncle Billy, now bearing scars of war but that same glorious human being who made them laugh and told them stories taller than the factory chimney! Annie considered it advisable however, for their first reunion to be in the familiar surroundings of No.14. aunt Bella had always said 'close your door when everyone is safe within, keep the world at bay'. It seemed Bella was wise beyond her lifetime, those words infinitely appropriate at the present, 'keep the world at bay', Annie fell asleep repeating Bella's wisdom over and over to herself.

Billy checked the small cabinet by the bed to make sure he had not left anything inside. Last Christmas seemed a lifetime ago, now at last, a bit worse for wear but still on his feet, Billy Dodds was going home.

"Are you leaving us then, after all we have been through together we can't persuade you to stay?" Said Sister jokingly.

Billy grinned, "Wild 'orses couldn't keep me from Edna and our girls but if you want to ask me again in a couple o' months time Sister, dependin' on 'ow much Edna's tongue 'as wagged, I might come back 'ere for me 'olidays."

"You're a fraud Billy." Sister kissed his cheek and laughed when he puckered his lips. "Only the most seriously wounded get kissed on the lips Billy Dodds, you've nought but a graze. Now you have been to see Mrs. Beale haven't you?" She asked.

"Yes Sister, I know 'ow bloody useless I am, mustn't get frustrated, accept me disabilities an' all that. Me pension'll provide, so long as we don't eat too much." Said Billy with a note of cynicism.

"Mrs.Beale is trying to help, you'll be surprised how much you can do but not yet, give yourself some time, enjoy your family, make up for all those months you've missed."

Billy sighed, "I know Sister, I know. Albert wants to see me 'afore I go. I promised I'd take a parcel back to 'is missus. Their place isn't far from ours, I could walk it in 'arf an hour, strange really, we didn't know each other 'til we met in 'ere. Is 'e goin' to be alright Sister, poor bugger 'as 'ad some rotten days."

"Albert's wound was so badly infected but you Midlanders are a tough breed, tell him you'll be waiting for him, we shall do our very best, I've every confidence in Albert," said Sister.

Albert lay back on his pillows staring at the ceiling.

"I'm doin' a bunk now Albert, got to get clear o' the gate 'afore they spot me."

Albert moved awkwardly across the pillow and winced as he reached out to his cabinet.

"Hold on there Albert, just tell me what you want, I can get it out o' the cabinet." Said Billy, feeling the pain in Albert's every move.

"I've got a bit o' somethin' for me kids, will you take it to Florrie for me, she can't get 'ere very well, tis awkward," he paused, "wi' the young en's, you know 'ow it is. Tell 'er I'm doin' alright, I'll be 'ome as soon as I can. Do you mind doin' that Billy?"

"Yer daft sod Albert, would you mind doin' it for me if it wer' t'other way about? I'll take it round to Florrie next week, no worries."

"Mind 'ow you go Billy, give 'er my love, she's a good lass you know, my Florrie."

His voice weakened and his face contorted with pain as he lay back on the pillow. Billy took Albert's hand, squeezed the fingers and turned away quickly before emotion spilled over. Packing the parcel for Albert's children into his holdall, Billy looked around the ward and called out.

"Cheerio lads, I'm off to join the circus, they're lookin' for a juggler."

Then with a last thank you to the nurses Billy, virtually blind in one eye, deaf in one ear, carrying his bag with his one arm, thanked God he was alive and went out into the world, humbled yet defiant, weakened yet strong and intent on just one thing, his family.

It was a curious journey and Billy had come to the conclusion that his appearance, while it caused some to unwittingly gaze and subconsciously scan the bus or tram floor for his missing ear, it could nevertheless produce a surprise blessing, 'no charge lad', had been the conductor's response when on the bus Billy held out the fare. He had approached the ticket seller at the railway station with a suitably open mind, no concession there however. Then a warm smile and a tanner pressed into his palm immediately after the transaction, with the words, 'God bless yer lad, 'ave a pint on me'. At times he had felt like a sideshow at the fair, then generous praise from a well meaning but little knowing individual had made his nerves jumpy. Worst of all had been that tortured look in the eyes of some, that remote, glazed, averted stare which held grief, that hurt from loss as they glimpsed a survivor when their own loved one had not.

"It's your dad." Called out Edna to the three girls, sitting at the scullery table in the midst of their tea. Edna had been back and forth, to and fro' the living room window all afternoon. Now the sight of Billy walking down from the corner took her emotions to new heights of frenzy. She prodded at her hair and pinched at the skin of each cheek. Annie, Susie and Liza had abandoned the table like a sinking ship and now stood with Edna, noses pressed to the glass, their legs limbering up in readiness for the sprint.

"Come on Mam," Annie pulled at Edna's arm, "make haste." The child could wait no longer, rushing through the scullery door and out the back. Her feet flew over the cobbles, only just behind, Susie, her long straight hair shedding the pink satin ribbon as she ran to catch up. Liza protesting at being held by the hand crossed the street with Edna 'til all reached Billy. A knot had formed in his stomach, a dread of falling apart before his girls. Instead the sheer warmth of their love melted over him, securing all those raw nerve ends, like sealing wax over twine. Edna took the bag from his hand, but before she could grasp his fingers with her own, Liza had seized her dad's hand and was not about to surrender it to anyone. Her sisters gripped his sleeve and Edna steered their group swiftly across to No.24. Neighbours could wait, for now she wanted to tuck up her family safely inside and lock the door. Like Annie, for a little while Edna must keep the world at bay.

When the children had finally been persuaded to go to bed, 'your dad'll still be 'ere in the mornin', Edna had assured them, she set about emptying Billy's bag.

"What's this? She held up the small parcel wrapped in brown paper.

"I promised to do a favour for a mate. We didn't meet until the hospital, Albert, Albert Haynes. His missus is called Florrie, do you know 'er? They live down the bottom o' Forest Road, where it joins up wi' Glover Street," said Billy.

Edna thought for a moment or two, "No, can't say as I've heard the name," she replied.

"They got seven lads, she 'asn't been to see Albert, 'e says 'ow 'tis difficult for 'er to get away. P'raps she's nervous at travellin', anyroad, Albert went right off 'is smokes, for days 'e wer' burnin' wi' temperature, infection in 'is stump. He sold two packets o' Woodbines to Jimmy Green. Jimmy wer' discharged from hospital last week. Albert asked one o' the nurses to buy some sweets wi' the money while she wer' off duty an' bring 'em in for 'im when she came back to the ward. They're for the kids, 'e asked me to take 'em round there an' tell 'is missus that 'e'll be 'ome as soon as 'e can."

"Will 'e get better?" Asked Edna anxiously.

"I bloody well hope so, Sister seemed to think 'e'd make it." Billy took a deep breath. "Make us a cuppa, they do their best in hospital but the brew there never tastes the same as at 'ome."

Edna chatted as she put the kettle to boil. " Annie wants us all to go to Hood Street on Sunday to 'ave dinner wi' them. Davina Wright is stayin' there 'til the end o' the month. Ivy's not comin' back from Clifton, except to visit. She's got a job at a boardin' house close to 'er mam's . Mrs.Wright said it made only sense for 'er to stay at Hood Street until school starts again, make things easer for Annie, what wi' the workshops an'all. When she goes 'ome to The Park, Sylvia Robinson is goin' to live in like Ivy used to."

"Ah well, get it all over an' done with," said Billy.

"Yer' don't need to worry about Annie's lot even that Davina's got no side to 'er, she's alright I reckon." Edna carried two mugs of tea to the sitting room and sat beside her beloved Billy.

"Liza asked me if she could put some zinc an' caster on the side o' your 'ead, she thinks it looks sore."

Billy laughed and swigged his tea. "Make haste Mrs.Dodds," he winked at her, " tis' not me bloody 'ead that aches for want o' soothin'!"

Annie pushed the carving fork between the crackling, it felt tender, a large joint of pork shoulder filled the room with mouth watering smells of dinner. Davina had laid the table and an extra side table, carried through from the sitting room. Her Apple Charlotte she had declared a triumph.

"I'm not sure that I shall need help at home, my cooking, albeit only the odd pudding, seems quite acceptable and I could keep the house clean if I did a bit each day," said Davina.

Annie shook the roasting tray, coating the potatoes in hot dripping. "Davina you would lose all appetite and find no need of cooking at all if you lived entirely alone. What about the winter months when the fires need to be tended, besides, Sylvia is looking forward to her work and her mother will have spent great effort ensuring that her daughter is proficient in all domestic tasks. It would be unfortunate if they learned that you no longer required her," said Annie.

Having the worry of the business and concern for the children's well being was enough, to think of Davina in that large house, growing older and lonelier would prey on Annie's mind endlessly. At least Sarah had Samuel and Catherine had Robert.

The boys and Hilda played outside, William was beginning to think himself far too grown up to be included in their usual fun and games. Annie had found him peering into the mirror at close range, desperately seeking any sign of facial hair or a stray whisker on the chin. Freddy had roguishly identified Rosie Potts as William's sweetheart, only to be strenuously denied by a very red faced William who in a fit of pique, had stormed off and hidden Freddy's scrapbook. The dispute had run on until Annie could stand it no more and cautioned both to behave or be in bed by six o'clock each night for a week. The scrapbook had magically reappeared and Freddy had declared Rosie Potts to be sweet on Tommy Spooner as well, in his innocence believing this offer of mitigation might placate his elder brother. It achieved simply to drive his ill humour and William persisted in a mood of irritable adolescence. Each day Annie willed the postman to bring a letter from Charles but still the boy waited.

Voices of greeting outside confirmed Edna and Billy's arrival, excited, lively voices, happy at seeing one another. Annie stood in the doorway observing the scene. Hilda had a troubled expression, still so young, she could not hide her shock at seeing Billy's disfigurement. He too had noticed the child's anxious face, he knelt in front of her.

"What are you thinking Hilda?" He asked giving her a big grin.

Her lower lip trembled.

"Does it hurt Uncle Billy, ask the doctor to make it better."

"It don't hurt a bit Hilda, honest it don't. Liza put some ointment on it, that done the trick, an' just to make sure, aunty Edna kissed it better."

The little face leaned forward, her eyes closed, her mouth puckered to the size of a shirt button, she planted a kiss on Billy's lips, opened her eyes and whispered, "Love you lots."

Davina, who had been standing beside Annie in the doorway, quietly turned and went upstairs, dabbing her eyes with a teacloth which just happened to be in her hand. She sought her bedroom, suddenly Davina felt an intruder at this reunion. All the men folk in her life had gone. Her own dear father very many years ago, Nathan too, Harold and Frank. The only vestige of family she had dwelt within this house and ironically, they not aware. Charles must never know, all the years he had recognised Saul as his father, the truth would sour not sweeten.

"We are going to eat in a minute Davina." Annie called up from the hallway.

"Coming dear, just needed to put on a dab of gardenia for Billy." She made her words sound cheerful and mischievous. She must do her best to eat dinner, normally that was no problem for Davina, food, especially tasty roast pork to be shared with a large family around the table held immense delight but right now she felt the much greater need of a mint.

The meal was enjoyed by everyone, the dish of crackling had been passed around until only one piece remained.

"Go on Billy, clear it up," said Annie, "we've all had plenty, besides, Davina's pudding looks delicious so we must save room for that."

Billy crunched on the crispy pork, a trickle of juice ran down his chin. George had been deep in thought, finally having settled to his notion he said.

"Do you know Uncle Billy, I reckon you should never again have to pay for a pint at The Nelson."

A puzzled silence fell on the gathering.

"Ow do yer' make that out then George." Asked Billy, giving Annie a wink to imply that she need not worry, he would not be upset by any innocently patronising remark made by a child.

"Well," said George, "if mam and aunty Edna made you one of those three cornered hats, you could sit at the bar like the Admiral himself. One arm, one eye," he paused briefly, looked across at Annie and said, "was Lord Nelson deaf as well mam?"

Davina laughed 'til she was in imminent danger of wetting herself, gales of heartfelt, joyful laughter, everyone joined in 'til their sides ached. Edna was the first to speak.

"Annie I swear, if you dare make 'im one o' them 'ats, I shall never come to this 'ouse again."

William, his own troubles forgotten said. "The proper name is tricorn, it's a tricorn hat, tri means three."

"I don't care if it's a soddin' tencorned 'at, Billy can't 'ave one, 'e'd never be out o' the bloody Nelson," said Edna.

"You can't have more than a fourcorn hat, there are only four corners on a square," observed Freddy.

The happy nonsense accompanied Davina's Apple Charlotte and by the time the children were excused from the table and sent outside to play, a wonderful feeling of contentment prevailed the adults.

"I'm told, no that's not quite right, I am ordered," said Billy, "to rest up an' do nothin' more strenuous than mind our girls while my missus goes out to work."

Annie smiled at the tone of perplexity in Billy's voice. "Just for a short while, until school starts. You've been away from them a long time, the girls are sure to clutch at your company until they feel things are back to normal," said Annie encouragingly.

"Anyway," said Edna, "you can take yourself to The Nelson for an hour on Wednesday if you want, me mam's collectin' them at 11o'clock to take em' to our Ada's. It's 'er youngest one's birthday, they're all goin' to the swimmin' baths an' on to the chip shop after for some dinner."

"Then I'll go to Albert's 'ouse while they're with their grandma. I'm in no hurry to go to the pub, I'm not sure I could stand the noise in there, not yet anyroad," said Billy.

He crossed to the back door and stood watching the antics of the children. Edna quietly explained the nature of Billy's errand to Annie and Davina. The dishes were cleared away under a more pensive mood. This cruel war was never far from their minds, however hard they tried to hold it at bay. As Annie stacked the plates back in the cupboard she felt a rush of sadness at Charles' absence from this day's joyous togetherness. Perhaps he and Clem had found a valuable friendship, in the past Charles had seemed unable to form any deep alliances with other men from the neighbourhood, always walking to The Standard on his own and leaving without company to walk back alone. The cards, the drink, they were the attraction, not the camaraderie, the easy banter with like minded men. Perhaps tomorrow would bring a letter from Egypt. It would be good to hear news of him, to know that he was safe.

"Hello chap," said Billy to a dog which had stopped by his feet to have a good scratch. "That's right you scrub at the little buggers, there'll be a few fellas about the place wi' a lot more sympathy for your kind now, lousy bunch o' sods we was."

The mongrel, having temporarily eased the irritation, stood with his tongue out to the air.

"I know chap, we was thirsty an'all, 'tis already gettin' hot I reckon the kids'll be glad to jump in that water today. Yer best get yerself 'ome, find a drink."

As if comprehending Billy's words of advice the animal trotted off, Billy watched for a few seconds, drawing level with a lamp-post, it cocked its leg, piddled and the process of eliminating one or two fleas began again. Billy smiled but moved along swiftly at the onset of a sympathetic itch. Being able to look at a clear summer sky, to walk on ground that was English induced that same sensation, deep within a lad which was felt when the best looking girl in school smiled across the playground at him. Billy held tight to the parcel, Forest Road stretched out before him, a long row of houses, probably built to the same plan originally, now differing according to fortune. The front of a dwelling revealed a surprising amount, bright curtains, a door that displayed evidence of being nurtured by the application of linseed oil, and a container of flowers, cried out to the passer-by, 'we're doing alright'. A home where the nets, washed each spring, now barely held together from wear, a door opening up its grain to the weather having lost the priority bid, bread must ever succeed over oil and the only flower, a simple dandelion arranged by The Almighty in a chink by the base of the wall, these features cried out to the passer-by, 'we are struggling'. Billy was looking for No.67, right down the bottom end Albert had said. Just before it merged with Glover Street, there it was, a plain house in a row of mixed fortunes.

Billy knocked at the door with the back of his hand, his fingers clutching the parcel. A woman with a gentle face, naturally so, not enhanced by powder and lotion but made of soft eyes, a cautious smile, stood back from the open door.

"Yes," she said.

"Don't worry Mrs.Haynes, 'tis not bad news, nothin' like that. I'm Billy, Billy Dodds from Winchester Street, I asked my Edna if she knew you, now my Edna knows most everybody but blow me, you must be the only one she 'asn't tracked down. I've been in hospital wi' your Albert, I wer' discharged last Friday."

Before Billy could continue, she spoke. "Come in, I'll make some tea."

Billy stood in the small front room, neat and clean, it held little regular ornamentation, a wedding photograph, obviously Albert and Florrie, some smaller photos of various children, one glass vase in which rested an Empire Day Flag and a child's paper windmill, but a curious array of objects, made from card, wool, buttons, any piece of discarded 'scrap' available to their creator. They sat on every ledge, by the window, the mantel, a small corner shelf and occupied the entire of a glass fronted cabinet with the exception of one porcelain figurine which bore the look of a family heirloom. Florrie called across the passage way. "Don't stay in there on your own, come through to the scullery."

At one end of a 'scrubbed top' table, Florrie poured tea, sitting at the far end was a young lad, intent on his activity. A cup of flour and water paste, an old paint brush, an assortment of bits and bobs, all held his attention.

"Sit down Mr.Dodds," she said.

"Call me Billy Mrs.Haynes, it don't seem right you callin' me mister when I've shared a ward wi' your Albert for weeks. He's asked me to bring this parcel round to you, somethin' for the kids." Then Billy looked across at the lad, "Why aren't you out playin' in this lovely sunshine wi' your brothers instead o' bein' stuck in 'ere under your mam's feet."

The boy looked up from his activity, the pale, retreating face, unsure, nervous, released no sound from the mouth but nevertheless told Billy why Albert's wife had found it difficult to travel to the hospital. Billy left his tea and walked around the table, pointing at a shiny green button among the boy's bits and pieces he said.

"I reckon that 'ould look good if you stuck it there, on that piece o' gold card, it 'ould shine like the eye of a fish, a nice carp as swims in the Trent."

The young face opened to a tentative smile, Billy grinned back, now the smile spread, it travelled around every feature so fast, his eyes, cheeks and mouth became illuminated, as though someone inside his head had lit a powerful lamp.

"His brothers are down The Meadows with the other kids," said Florrie.

"Why don't 'e go?" Asked a puzzled Billy, " 'tis lovely out there today, a lad got to kick a ball about an' grubby 'is boots a bit, 'tis what makes a man."

Florrie lowered herself onto a chair and took a sip of tea. "He used to go but I had to stop it, they were tormentin' him. He can't understand, they think it's fun but he don't know enough to give as good as 'e gets. He's safe in here with me. I always wanted a girl, I was close to me mam but she died young. When me and Albert got married, I thought to meself, I'll 'ave a daughter one day, I was always goin' to call her Victoria after the old Queen. A grand name for a girl, give her a good start. Well, Raymond came first, then Eric, Brian after him, William and George came with a bare eleven months between, next it was Jack. Albert said if it isn't a girl next time Florrie lass, then it wer' never meant to be an' that's that. Well it was another boy," she looked across to the lad with his paint brush and paste. "I didn't notice anything different, not then, he was just another baby, like all the others. After a week he got awful chesty, it was difficult to feed him, so much phlegm, he kept on bein' sick, we called the doctor, I shall never forget the way he spoke, it weren't like he was really bothered.

'You do realise he's Mongoloid Mrs.Haynes, he'll never learn very much, neither will he be a long-liver'.

He said it like I was foolish to be worryin' me head over him, Albert does his best but it have never sat right with him, I suppose bein' a man he found it embarrassin'. 'No more lass', he said, 'no more'. Eventually it got a bit easier. I knew then I'd never have a daughter. I looked in the crib, a mother senses things, I was sure that all his life, for how ever long it might be he'd have to struggle, every day would be a battle for him. I couldn't give a daughter a good start with that grand name so I gave him a head start instead, I willed him to win you see, I called him Victor, that was eight years ago."

Billy couldn't bear it, "Mrs.Haynes, Victor can't spend all 'is days cooped up in 'ere, it isn't right. Me an' him'll go fishin' together, 'tis quiet down by the river, nobody to bother 'im there."

Florrie smiled, "You're a kind man Billy Dodds but you don't understand. People stare, gawp at him, gawp at me an'all. It's hard, you don't want to be puttin' up with that."

"Bloody Hell Mrs.Haynes, 'ave yer not looked at me, one soddin' ear missin', me eye is buggered, the side o' me head looks like a baboon's backside an' I've only got one bloody arm. Me an' Victor was made for each other. When we walk down the street together I won't know if the miserable buggers are starin' at me or 'im, an' Victor won't know if they're gawpin' at 'im or me."

"They would likely be starin' at the both of you," said Florrie slightly amused.

"Ah but that don't matter, it feels different altogether when you know you're not the only one. I'll call for Victor on Saturday, just after dinner. My girls 'ould rather go shoppin' wi' their mam than be bored to death on the banks o' The Trent watchin' a fishin' float."

Florrie looked worried, her hands fidgeted with the hem of her apron.

"I might only 'ave one arm Mrs.Haynes but I wouldn't let any harm come to my girls an' I'll look after Victor just as if 'e wer' me own. The kid is safe wi' me I can promise yer that. Besides, I could do wi' Victor, a one armed man 'ould struggle to set 'isself up for fishin', but wi' a set o' young fingers to help, well that 'ould be bloody magic for me." Billy rubbed his hand over the lad's hair, "We'll be best mates won't we Victor, when your dad comes 'ome we'll 'ave some tales to tell 'im."

Victor beamed his pleasure and his finger, covered in paste, pointed to the piece of gold card. There it was, the shiny green button affixed to the spot Billy had suggested. Billy chuckled.

"I'll show yer a real Carp, beautiful they are, they glisten like posh women's jewellery, you'll see."

So it was agreed, somewhat reluctantly on Florrie's part, that at around 2 o'clock next Saturday, Billy Dodds and Victor Haynes would go down Trentside fishing.

Billy related the days events to Edna when she came in from work.

"The girls aren't back yet, your mam'll be worn out tonight, all your Ada's lot an' ours an'all, she'll be too tired to walk 'ome."

Edna laughed, "Mam won't be long now, she'll stay at Ada's 'til ten minutes afore Morley's due 'ome then she'll be off. It's not so much that she don't like 'im, 'arf the time she don't know what to say to 'im. 'E don't seem the same as other blokes 'is age. Mam reckons 'e got a funny mix of 'ormones, funny peculiar that is. Mam says if 'e 'ad a few less o' the one sort an' more o' the other 'e could 'ave been a Mary instead of a Morley!" Edna giggled roguishly. "Still, it 'aven't stopped 'im firin' 'is gun, bless 'is 'eart."

In truth, Edna for all her outspoken observations, embraced the whole of mankind, she had shown genuine concern when Billy had explained Victor's plight. Fishing was Billy's way of relaxing, Edna worried about his handicap, the awkwardness and possible perils of being as Billy now was, but she had come to realise over the past few days that Billy needed normality, when he actually pulled on his jacket one evening and said, 'I'm off to the pub for a jar', secretly she would be pleased. If this Victor helped her Billy recover his familiar ways and Billy helped the lad find a life then it was a sensible arrangement all round, it had Edna's blessing.

Billy had carefully sorted his bag of tackle, the bread bin had offered up three stale crusts and his rod was still threaded with line from his hour by the river last Christmas. With a small bag of toffees in his pocket, he had kissed Edna and the girls, telling Susie to ask Mr.Waterford for a bucket of 'yellow whitewash' winking at Annie as he spoke. To young Liza he said.

"When yer go into Cheetham's tell 'im that yer dad is back from France an' because 'e hasn't 'ad any for so long 'e's fancyin' a nice piece o' pig's squeak. Can yer remember that?"

"Yes," said Liza repeating the request, mentally storing it for the appropriate time. "A nice piece of pig's squeak."

Edna shook her head, resigned to her husband's mischief.

"Be careful down by that river, if yer fell in now you'd go round an' round in circles when yer tried to swim, God help us why can't yer play bloody draughts or summat an' give me poor soddin' nerves a rest."

Billy walked up to the corner whistling, his old dinner bag across his shoulders. It was good to be carrying his fishing rod again, all the months he had gripped a rifle, the feel of his old familiar fishing rod lifted his spirits. He had managed to dodge Winnie Bacon, the first time she had spotted him, one evening earlier in the week, he had been obliged to tell her a white lie. After ten minutes of non-stop chatter his one good ear throbbed under the strain. 'Tis good talkin' with yer Winnie but Edna's indoors waitin' to do me dressin', he had lowered his voice to imply a confidence, 'delicate little place, if it don't heal it might 'ave to come off'.

Winnie's pupils had dilated at the sheer effort of keeping them trained on Billy's face, he had quickly turned to cross the street, adopting a slightly awkward gait and called back, 'I can allus tell when it needs doin'. Winnie had disappeared into the entry with her own dire illusion. Today however, she had not made an appearance so Billy's progress was unhindered.

He reached the door of No.67, leaning the rod carefully against the wall Billy knocked at the weathered wood. Florrie greeted him politely.

"He's ready, you will watch out for him won't you, what time will you bring him back?"

"Give us a chance Mrs.Haynes, we 'aven't even gone yet. I reckon we should be back 'ere by 'arf past four," said Billy.

"Victor," the boy's mother called through to the scullery. He stood to the side of her looking a little unsure of events.

"Look what I've got in me pocket," said Billy, he lifted the bag of toffees for Victor to see, the little face widened at the prospect and his tongue made a quick swipe of his lip. "We'll 'ave one when we get to the river, come on then, while the sun's out."

Victor encouraged by Florrie, crossed the threshold and stood looking up at Billy who winked, picked up the rod and said.

"You hold on to the strap o' me bag lad, that way Billy can't get lost can 'e?

Victor giggled and repeated the word's, "Can't get lost." He let out a long breath which bubbled about his mouth as it combined with some spittle. "Can't get lost." He giggled again and gripped tight the canvas strap.

They made a rare sight indeed, Billy showing the scars of war, young Victor, yet engaged in his battles but no one caused them any real bother.

"Smell the water lad, all yer can smell in the streets is man an' 'is muddle. 'Ere yer can smell the grass, elderflowers, even the fish, I swear I can smell when a plump bellied carp swims by."

Billy stood taking deep breaths, scenting the air, Victor, still clutching the strap, did the same. Billy found a good level spot, lay the rod against a clump of bog grass and pulled the strap over his head.

"Pull on that sleeve lad, go on, give it a good tug."

Victors fingers gripped the cloth as Billy wriggled his shoulder from the jacket, shaking it free of his right arm where it fell to the ground.

"Now first things first." Billy felt into his pocket for the toffees, he held out the bag for Victor to take one. The eager hand delved in and pulled out a chunk of treacle toffee.

Billy laughed, "Well done lad."

Both rolled their cheeks as the sweet toffee began to soften on their tongues. "Now I've got a job for you young Victor." Billy took the crusts from the bag and very quickly, dipped them in and out of the water. "You just watch this." Billy pinched small pieces from the damp bread and rolled a couple between his fingers to make bait. "Can you do that?"

Victor took the bread and carefully did as Billy had shown him, looking up for approval.

"Just the ticket, now this is the tricky bit, it 'ould be easy if Billy boy 'ad 'is other hand but 'e left it behind in Hemel Hempstead so 'e 'asn't an' that's that, nowt I can do about it." Billy released the end of the line from where it had been wound around the first eye on the rod. Now a tiny hook had to be tied on. He managed to open the small 'baccy' tin which held the hooks, lifting one between his fingers he spoke softly to Victor. "You see the little hole at the top, well I need you to take that line and thread it through the hole. Nothin' to worry about, take yer time."

The concentration on the child's face was so intense that for a moment Billy dare not utter a word. Victor's fingers, amazingly steady, directed the end of the fishing line to the eye of the hook with such precision, it slipped through effortlessly.

"Magic lad, soddin' magic." Now Billy placed the hook between his teeth to tie the knot. He lay it on the lid of the tin and with his penknife cut away the unwanted length of line. All the time Victor's eyes watched intently. "We've got to hope young Victor, that Mr.Fish 'asn't 'ad 'is dinner yet." Billy put a tiny ball of bread paste onto the hook. "I 'ave to cast now so you need to stand over there, by that tree out o' the way o' the hook."

The bright orange float now bobbed in the water. Billy sat on a large tuft of grasses and called Victor back to his side.

"You sit on me jacket, we 'ave to watch that float, when the fish swims along, if we're lucky, 'e'll see that bit o' bread an' put it in 'is mouth, like we did wi' the toffee."

Billy looked over on his newly found friend, quiet, comfortable, entirely trusting of Billy's company. Poor Albert, perhaps it's different when you've already got six lads thought Billy but after what he had seen and done at the Front, this simple individual, devoid of all malice, Billy found very easy to love and impossible to reject. For about fifteen minutes they sat, listening to the ripples of the water, Billy holding the rod between his knees, gently reeling in the line when the float drifted away. Then suddenly the orange tip near' disappeared below the surface.

"We've got the little bugger, look lad." Billy reeled steadily, lifting the rod to reveal a pretty gold carp, wriggling on the end of the line. Billy swung the fish onto the bank and rested the rod once more against the bog grass. "Have a look Victor, isn't that bloody beautiful?"

The child stroked the side of the fish. "Beautiful," he said, "bloody beautiful."

Billy chuckled, "You'll get me into bother wi' your mam." Billy removed the hook from the lip of the fish and threw it back into the water. "It don't hurt 'em, 'tis a bit like you 'avin' your nails cut, that gristly bit at the front o' their mouths is right tough."

Victor frowned, deep furrows crossed his brow, Billy laughed. Their activity continued and after taking the fourth carp from the hook Billy said.

" 'Ere, you throw it back this time, don't suppose you've ever 'eld a fish afore."

The small hands, nervously at first, took the fish from Billy's fingers. It wriggled but Victor seemed determined. With the carp firmly ensconced between his palms, the boy began to walk away. Billy was just about to call out when something stopped him, a curiosity, a sense of expectation maybe, he observed quietly. When Victor had walked, still holding the fish, a good four yards downstream, he squatted on his haunches by the water's edge and gently lowered the carp into the river.

"Bugger me," said Billy, " 'e's carried it downstream so we can't catch it again."

Billy recalled the doctors words, 'he'll never learn much' that's what the doctor had told Florrie. Billy looked up at the sky.

"Were you watchin' Frank, did yer see that Jed? 'Ow many times did that bloody whistle blow, 'ow many times at that same soddin' spot did they send us over the top, shot to shivereens, blasted to buggery. We couldn't see 'owt for dust an' smoke, our 'eads rattled wi' the bombardment but Captain said, 'send 'em over', at that same bloody spot wi' not a hope, not a soddin' hope." Billy sniffed and dragged the back of his hand across his face, he spoke again to Frank and Jed. "This lad 'as gone downstream to send the fish back, to give it a chance, 'e's got more sense than the whole bloody lot of 'em." Billy laughed and cried at the same time.

The youngster walked slowly back to where Billy stood, looking up into Billy's eyes he said. "Can we go home now?"

Billy clicked his heels together and raised his hand to his forehead.

"Yes, Sergeant Victor."

He held the salute for a good thirty seconds or more. The child smiled at Billy and repeated the words. "Yes, Sergeant." Putting his chubby little hand to his brow. Victor liked this game it made him laugh. Billy packed away the bag and with the knack he had developed over the past week he put on his jacket.

"I reckon it's time for another toffee Victor, then we'll get you 'ome to your mam so she can see you're alright." More than alright, thought Billy to himself. With the rod in Billy's hand and Victor once more holding fast to the canvas strap, they made their way. "You know lad, you an' me'll go to the cattle market next Saturday, Annie ,Susie an' Liza are likely to go wi' us there. Pigs an' chickens, loads of 'em, you'd like that wouldn't yer?"

Victor grinned, "Pigs and chickens," he gave that long breath which bubbled the spittle in his mouth, "Pigs and chickens." The face widened as he turned to look at Billy, a broad smile straddled his cheeks.

Frank and Jed had gone, he had lost Harold all those years ago. Most people would have looked on Billy's newly found friend and considered him a poor substitute but Billy knew different and if Frank, Jed and Harold stood with Billy and Victor in the street now, they would know different an'all. Billy began to whistle as they walked along.

Florrie opened the door with a look of relief.

"Told yer we'd be alright didn't I. Next Saturday we're goin' to see the pigs an' chickens down the cattle market, isn't that right Victor?" The lad's happy expression answered the question.

When Billy turned the corner into Winchester Street he could see Winnie Bacon outside her house talking to Nellie Draper. He quickly adopted that slightly awkward gait and crossed to the other side of the street, he called out.

"Good evenin' ladies."

As he walked round to his own back door he smiled at the notion. All the women the length of Winchester Street by Monday morning would be scrubbing the shirt collars with sunlight soap and pondering a dire illusion.

He laughed out loud, " God bless yer Winnie," he said, as the smell of onions frying and the sound of his wife singing while she worked, reminded Billy that his dressing needed doin'.

CHAPTER TEN

"Oh botheration." Davina said sharply as a knock came at the front door, the moment was crucial.

"Hilda dear, do you think you could see who is at the door, if I stop stirring at this point the custard will turn to scrambled egg."

Davina felt harassed, the stewed plums sat in a bowl on the table, the vapours of steam rising from their juicy goodness filled the kitchen. Hilda, not yet tall enough to reach the front door knob easily, stretched up on tiptoe and with all the might her young grasp could muster, eventually achieved to release the catch. She opened the door to find herself looking up at a tall man, unknown to her but smiling back at her, genuinely charmed by the pretty face.

"Is your mother at home?"

"If aunt Davina stops stirring it will turn to scrambled egg and mam is at the workshop with aunty Edna so we're cooking the pudding. Do you like plums?" The child's confidence amused him.

"I like plums very much, in fact I think they are probably my favourite fruit."

Davina appeared bustling across the hall from the kitchen, the sight of a young man whom she had not seen before made her anxious, then she noticed he held a package, not an envelope, her quick reasoning told her this was not a telegram. The few minutes spent with the custard had left her a little agitated.

"Can I help you young man?"

Her breathing was quite short and a small dash of custard lay just above a button on her bodice where it had fallen, when unable to resist a quick taste of the confection, Davina had licked the spoon. He smiled and spoke politely.

"I called at an address in The Park several days ago but found no one at home. My leave ends tomorrow so before I must return to France I again went along to the house, although I could find no one there, a lady from the property next door saw me and called me to her gate. She kindly directed me here, it is Mrs.Boucher, Mrs.Frank Boucher whom I seek."

"Do come in, you must forgive me, I got rather carried away by the importance of a smooth custard, now I regard that to be of little consequence, you have come to tell us about Frank I imagine," said Davina.

"I'm afraid I did not know Frank, I have made a number of visits over the past few days, all of them of the same nature, only two of them were from my Company." He handed the package to Davina, very carefully, almost tenderly.

"It is with the greatest respect and deepest regret I deliver Frank's personal things to you." His eyes crossed the room to where Hilda sat with paper and crayons. "Does Frank have other children?"

"I should explain," Davina paused, "my dear, I have not yet asked your name."

"Sands, Andrew Sands."

"Well Mr.Sands, I am Davina Wright," they shook hands, "before those explanations I shall make us some tea."

Davina smiled warmly, the Lieutenant was in no hurry to leave the pleasant atmosphere of No14, he answered.

"That would be very kind, thank-you."

Davina again bustled across the hallway to make the tea and check her endeavours with the custard the minute her back was turned, had not been contrary enough to develop those dreaded lumps.

"What are you drawing?" He stood to view the child's work. "Ah, a chicken and a very fine looking chicken it is too," he said.

"We've got chickens, Freddy looks after them, William used to help him but he says he's too grown up for that now, William loves Rosie Potts but Freddy says Rosie Potts has pimples."

Hilda's innocent chatter fell on his ears like a therapy.

"So you have two brothers, that must be fun," said Andrew.

"Four," Hilda cried out proudly. "William, Freddy, George and John. John is little like me we aren't allowed to go to Bobbers Mill bridge train spotting. Mam says it's bad enough having three smoked scallywags to deal with, the weight of their jackets snapped the clothes line. Mam told them to hang them over the line to sweeten but Freddy had found some nubs of coal on the street that had fallen off the waggon, he put them in his pocket to bring them home and forgot to take them out. William called Freddy a 'dough bake' and he went upstairs and broke William's birds eggs. George says Rosie Potts loves Tommy Spooner best. Mam told grandad how naughty they'd been so he took them to the allotment to dig potatoes, they got that hot and thirsty, grandad let them have a drink of cider but it was very strong, William and Freddy were drunk and George got sick all over grandma's rhubarb." Hilda looked intently at Andrew's face and asked, "Have you got chickens?"

Davina returned with a tray of tea.

"I hope Hilda has kept you entertained, she has a bright mind."

"I have the very best of company," he said smiling down at his young friend. He did indeed feel her to be a friend but five children, now without a father, he wished that he had known Frank.

Davina poured the tea and with great satisfaction, offered shortbread, her own making. "Now, the circumstances require considerable explanation." Davina sipped her tea and began.

Lieutenant Sands listened politely, Davina, rather like Hilda, could not simply relate bare facts, always additional information brought depth and colour to the narrative. By the point at which Davina thought she had imparted all the necessary enlightenment, the young officer felt he did after all know Frank, along with all his extended family, but something about this home, Davina and Hilda, the open friendliness made him genuinely sad at leaving.

"Annie will be sorry to have missed meeting you, she works so hard and although she says little on the subject, I am sure she hopes every day to hear from Charles, to know that all is well," said Davina.

They stood at the front door.

"Are you quite sure you wouldn't like me to take the package to Clifton. If Annie is busy, it only presents her with yet another task," said Andrew Sands.

"You have already spent much of your precious leave on these unfortunate duties, we are indebted to you," said Davina, offering her hand.

He held it briefly as he kissed her cheek, "Goodbye," he said, with haste he turned and walked away.

Davina raised her hand to wave, tears welling in her eyes.

"Do take care," she said softly.

Another young man returning to The Front, travelling with small measure of comfort for his thoughts, at least in his pocket was a unique gesture of love, Hilda had written two kisses at the bottom of the paper, carefully folded her picture and presenting it to Lieutenant Sands she had said. 'If you see my dad will you please give him this and if you don't see him then you can keep it'.

Hilda's brightness, as yet not sufficient to enable her a grasp of geography, she could not comprehend the distance between France and Egypt. Davina sensed that simple drawing of a chicken, along with kisses, would accompany Andrew Sands over many miles, she closed the door with a sigh, the world was beset by tribulation, Davina's custard was smooth as syrup, yet the latter had suddenly become remote from her mind.

It had been agreed that on leaving Basford the following Saturday Annie would go straight to Clifton with the package for Ivy. She sat on the bus, a strange presence of Frank came to her from that brown paper, resting in her lap. She had not eaten since breakfast, an empty, sinking feeling crept through her stomach, she felt inside her pocket, a paper bag with some sherbet for Harold and Molly was tucked safely away, at the bottom she was lucky, her fingers found a barley sugar, goodness knows how long that's been there, she thought. It comforted, in just a few minutes they should reach Clifton Green. Mrs.Pilkington's house was only a short walk from the bus stop.

As Annie had travelled, her mind had taken her from Ivy to Samuel, this would bring back all the intense hurt but how could Ivy not tell Samuel and Sarah about the return of Frank's things. As Annie stepped down from the bus a child's voice called out. Molly had been watching as the bus drew in, a number of children were playing together on the green, Harold was in a makeshift goal. Not the tallest for his age but having strong, muscular thighs, he was always the likely choice for goalkeeper, he had bruises to prove it. Mrs.Pilkington sat on a bench, one eye on the children, the other trained down on her crochet. The cast she had in one eye had become even more pronounced with the years. It was a curious fact as Sarah had once remarked, that in spite of Mrs.Pilkington's wayward vision, she did not require spectacles for fine work yet both she and Davina could not properly see to knit or sew without them. Annie, aware that the sight of a package would intrigue Molly and Harold and anticipating their disappointment when it was put away until they were in bed, as it would surely be, she had in her pockets, two bags of yellow sherbet and two liquorice sticks. Annie sat by Mrs.Pilkington on the bench, waving to Harold in goal and assuring Molly that she would watch as she skipped and count how many times. The child could be heard chanting the popular skipping ditty, 'Salt, Vinegar, Mustard, Pepper,' over and over, 'til finally tired from the heat, she ran back to the bench.

"How many did I do aunty Annie?"

Having no accurate answer, talking as she had been with Molly's grandma, Annie thought it wise to respond with a generous number.

"Twenty eight, you did twenty eight skips," said Annie and immediately regretted the wisdom when Molly turned to the girl behind her, handing the skipping rope over and declaring with childlike boasting.

"You only did twelve." They were shooed off to play.

"Little children should be seen and not heard." Mrs.Pilkington cautioned them.

Annie would give the sherbet presently but she needed to spend a few more minutes with their grandma.

"Ivy will be at work until at least eight o'clock, the boarding house is busy at the moment. She is happy enough there, the pay is as you would expect, as I'm here for these two she can work extra hours. There are one or two perks, a couple of weeks ago a well cut gentleman gave her a florin, told her she excelled as a maid, that his room had been kept delightfully clean. The other day a lady insisted Ivy accept the remainder of a box of peppermint creams. They were so rich in flavour that I could still taste mint when I ate a trotter twenty four hours later."

Annie explained about the package, she would have preferred to hand it to Ivy herself but she could not wait until so late, on the way home there was still the shopping to be done. Mrs.Pilkington lay the package on the bench, sniffed and said.

"Not much to show for a life is it?"

Annie felt defensive, whether the remark had intended any slight she could not be sure but it had been delivered with no attempt at softening the words.

"Such a shortened span cannot be considered a life but two very fine children are nevertheless a great deal to show in Frank's name," said Annie.

"I tried to persuade her to go back to The Park, such a grand house and that Davina so fond of them. What family has she, none as I understand other than distant cousins."

The cold nature of Mrs.Pilkington's remarks alarmed Annie, she must find an opportunity to talk with Ivy. No longer was Annie inclined to believe that the future for Ivy and the children would be best served here. Her mother, while watching over Molly and Harold seemed far more concerned about the loss of a possible inheritance than the tragedy of Frank's death.

The treats handed to the children with a big hug for each, Annie caught the return bus and hurried through the shopping list, her mind barely able to concentrate so badly did she want to be at home. When finally she turned the corner into Hood Street to be spotted by George, his legs propelled him towards her with such speed.

"Let's have a couple of those bags Mam," he said, relieving Annie of weight. "William has had a letter from Egypt, he read it out to us all, dad sounds to be doing alright. His friend Clem has taught him lots of new things. What's for tea?"

His eyes were suddenly diverted to the bags and on seeing some iced buns from Lovatt's he began to whistle. Annie smiled to herself, home, untidy, hardly ever still, always demanding of her efforts, but home, how good it felt.

Davina would be returning to The Park and the children to school in one week. Concern for Ivy had occupied much of Annie's mind throughout the weekend but Charles' letter continued to draw her thoughts. Anyone reading it without prior knowledge of the situation could quite easily have imagined Charles to be sending an account of his progress at his recently acquired position at a department of Fortnum&Mason. Indeed Annie wondered if Charles was engaged in the same war that Billy and Frank had fought. Clem featured strongly. It was difficult to picture Charles and his newly found friend stoically feeding beleaguered troops with life preserving supplies. Perhaps for William's sake he had purposefully written an enhanced description of his duties and actions so as not to worry the boy. Annie had told herself this many times since reading the letter yet that one passage seemed very sharp, not cushioned to be sympathetic in any way,

'I wish I had met Clem long ago, even on the train as we travelled to Manchester he said he could teach me a thing or two, well I've learned a lot from Clem, I begin to see ways of the world I hadn't glimpsed before. When I get home son, things will be different, better, you'll see'.

Annie pondered the words as she stitched a pocket onto another Blackmore's School blazer. A knock came at the workshop door, Edna called out.

"I'll get it."

Sylvia's mother stood at the doorway looking flustered and nervous. Annie put down her work and went to her.

"Come inside Mrs.Robinson, we are working on Oliver Blackmore's order at present, there is always a period of panic as term time draws closer, we do have a few days grace, the boys go back to Blackmore's four days later than our children return to school, thank goodness," said Annie cheerfully.

She tried to put Gladys Robinson at ease. They went through to the back office, Gladys sat preparing herself to speak, turning her wedding ring around and around on her finger.

"I couldn't pacify her Mrs.Eddowes, all last evenin' she cried her eyes out, 'tis not the work she's afraid of, our Sylvia's a good girl, she'll work with a will at any task an' she's allus been quick to learn, 'tis sleepin' in a strange place, not comin' home at night. I told her Mrs.Wright is a lovely lady and that she'd be alright there but no, for hours she cried an' cried. Gladys paused to blow her nose, then with a sniff and a greater intake of breath she continued." 'Tis only a few months that her dad was killed, Sylvia took it bad, I know I should be firm with her but I can't bear to see her so upset again."

The tears began to flow, she searched her pocket for a hanky, Annie knelt in front of her.

"Tell Sylvia to come here to the workshop, she needs to be occupied and to begin with, May will show her how to stitch buttons and labels."

"She knows how to sew on buttons and she can invisibly hem a skirt," said Gladys proudly.

"Then all the better," said Annie, "don't worry I shall speak with Mrs.Wright, she is always understanding, send Sylvia here in the morning at eight o'clock, tell her to sleep well tonight so she will be bright and eager to learn more when she joins us here tomorrow."

Edna had overheard some of the conversation, enough to put two and two together.

"Now what will Davina do, I know 'ow she says she'd manage but me an' you know different, she might be alright for a week or so then she'd be miserable as sin an' you'd be forever runnin' over there sick wi' worry," said Edna with her usual degree of tact.

Annie knew it was an accurate prediction, not wrapped in tissue as some might have presented it. Dear Edna, nothing less than a reliable truth ever passed to Annie from Edna.

"I think I have a solution, at least I hope I have, I must speak to Ivy very soon." Annie let out a deep, deep sigh.

"Blimey," said Edna, "if it needs that much hope then God help yer." She went back to her machine 'tutting' as she walked. May glanced at Annie, offering a reassuring smile, inured as May was to the need of travelling in hope.

The next day, Tuesday, Sylvia had been at the gates of the workshop when Edna arrived to unlock the door and May had come determined to encourage the timid girl. May of all people could sympathise with a timid disposition. The morning had progressed well, Edna had even managed to tempt Sylvia to smile, relaxing the girl as they chatted over a cup of tea. If this was Annie's plan then so be it, Edna's loyalty was sound as a bell, she may have concerns of her own but whatever Annie chose to do, Edna would try her utmost to help, it had ever been so.

It was time for Annie to leave for Basford. It had been a testing few days for Gertie, two machines had been idle while women visited their men folk in different hospitals. The numbers of wounded grew at an alarming rate, the City Hospital was desperate for bed linen. The women had worked their dinner break and some until later in the evening to meet an order for sheets and pillowcases.

As yet, Annie had not mentioned Sylvia's crisis to Davina, she must talk to Ivy, it was the physical difficulty of finding time but it could not be delayed any longer, tomorrow she would go to Clifton, ask at Rylands if she might be permitted to speak briefly with Ivy on a matter of some urgency, then return to the workshop and pack Blackmore's order. Davina could tend the children with a simple meal.

As she walked to the tram stop Annie could see, several yards along the street, Catherine Appleyard pushing the pram, her pace very hurried, even for Catherine! It had been sometime since they last met, Annie ran to catch up.

"Slow down just a bit Catherine," Annie called out as she came within a few feet of her friend.

"Why my dear Annie we have not bumped into one another for ages, we are all so busy, at times I think too busy for our own good but war demands such effort of us all."

Annie recognised that old sparkle in Catherine, her words almost defiant. The loss of Philip had perhaps been soothed by those frequent glimpses of her daughter. At least she sounded very positive, Annie knew her friend well, Catherine needed to be positive, to be driven by a cause, that was when she functioned best.

"I don't suppose you can think of a young woman who might be available for a few hours work each week," said Catherine, "it wouldn't be worth a fortune I'm afraid but to top up an existing income it could prove ideal."

Annie thought the question heaven sent. "Perhaps you could tell me more about the position, it would help me think of a suitable candidate if I knew what was required of them," said Annie.

Catherine leaned forward to stabilize a precarious box of provisions intent on falling from the pram.

"I still call at the hospital, a little voluntary work keeps my mind employed. They are so stretched, bed space is at a premium. We live in a large house, most of it serving no purpose than to gather dust. I could think of no other way to really help, we are accommodating three servicemen at Tamarisk. They no longer require full nursing care but for a further period, good food, rest, a short time to gather strength," she sighed. "Sadly at this stage they will return to their Regiments. These young men give everything for us Annie, it is a small gesture in return. However, I find myself with hardly any time to spend with Robert and that cannot be right, not at our time of life. A young woman to help me with the laundry and cleaning would make such a difference. I do intend this to be an ongoing arrangement for as long as might be required, the hospital must free up beds, the numbers of wounded are incomprehensible."

Catherine was indeed positive and at this moment Annie felt a rush of inspiration. The Ropewalk and The Park were a comfortable distance from each other, easily covered on foot, if Ivy returned to Davina's the additional hours of work would enable Ivy to feel much more fulfilled. Davina's abilities had become evident over the past month, looking after Harold and Molly if their mother needed to be at Catherine's would come readily to Davina now she had found her confidence. Ivy would feel less confined and meet more people, it made a great deal of sense.

Mrs.Pilkington could think whatever she liked, Davina was an individual of tremendous qualities, she would do as Davina saw fit, Mrs.Pilkington could like it or lump it. Annie promised to let Catherine know by the weekend. Their conversation empowered the feet of both women, Catherine to the next house of distribution and Annie to Basford.

The ride to Clifton was not without event, at Lenton an elderly man had boarded the bus, at first he had made his way to a seat in silence, the only clue to his likely dementia being a roguish wink at a lady of similar age and his enquiry of her, 'Are you comin' 'ome to meet me mam, she's baked us a cake, your favourite'. Given that he must have been in his eighties and the elderly lady near' convulsed with fright Annie had felt compelled to coax him to another seat. He had smiled at Annie, told her that she had always been a good daughter and launched into song, 'It was only a bird in a gilded cage'. The conductor a kindly soul accepted Annie's belief that the old man posed no actual threat but must be returned to Lenton for his own safety, so with a slight delay, at the next stop the conductor escorted him across the road and placed him in the care of a group of people waiting for a bus to Lenton. As the driver pulled away Annie looked back, it was amusing yet sad, he appeared to be dancing with an imaginary partner. The colour had returned to the face of the elderly lady who now sat dabbing her forehead with her hanky. The conductor smiled at Annie, 'there but for the grace of God', he said and quite unintentionally took up the strains of the old man's song. Annie wondered how long it would be before the old man found himself in a 'gilded cage' like the bird, having lost his freedom.

Annie found the rear door to Ryland's Boarding house a much less impressive image than the auspicious, pillared façade to the front. The door was ajar so Annie knocked and called out.

"Hello, is anyone there, Hello."

A voice replied from somewhere within.

" 'Old yer 'orses, I'm comin' this place'll be the death o' me".

An elderly man appeared, a course Hessian pinafore, saturated with water hung from his shoulders, his hands were reddened by hours of pot washing, one dripped a greasy residue on to the floor.

"Well, what do yer want?"

He said with not so much a lack of courtesy as an absence of any activity which might enable him a feeling of self respect was how Annie perceived his demeanour.

"I wonder if I might speak with Mrs.Ivy Boucher. I know that she is employed here, it is a matter of importance but I will not detain her for more than a minute or two." Annie smiled to encourage a favourable response.

"You'd better wait there, it's been a right ding dong of a day so far, they found one old bloke dead in 'is bed this mornin', doctor come an' said it wer' 'is 'eart 'e reckoned, but they've took the body for one o' them post mortems. Isaacs 'ave been like a bear wi' a sore 'ead all day, 'ad to buy a new mattress see, never mind the poor old bloke as died, Isaacs don't like partin' wi' a shillin', since 'e been manager 'ere we've all 'ad to give 'im 'is pound o' flesh. Dillys Hocknall says old man Isaacs 'ad a string o' pawn shops but when 'e died, his missus sold 'em all an' bought a big house in Mapperley, she give their two sons Manny's bicycle an' fifty pounds each, told em they could do as they liked but she wer' goin' to make up for all the miserable years she'd been livin' mean as cat shit over one o' them shops. Dillys says Mrs.Isaacs married again, some fella a lot younger than 'er. Now I don't know if 'tis true or just rumour but I've 'eard as 'ow they had a pawnbrokers sign engraved on Manny's 'eadstone wi' the words, 'Guide me o thou great redeemer'."

On that, the man turned and disappeared, Annie waited just outside the door, the greasy little puddle which had dripped from the man's hand was now being slowly consumed by a thirsty crack in the flagstone, the dust and dirt which had been sent within by a passing broom became animated, brought to life by the offer of a drink. Two bins stood to one side of Annie, escaping from their battered lids a smell of rancid fat and rotting greens. The yard had been recently swept but in the middle, missed by the broom, a large rat dropping lay, dark black, sinister. Annie's imagination likened it to the chrysalis of a rare creature, any moment it would split from end to end, freed of its sheath it would burrow through the shabby bins and gorge on grease and cabbage stump, then hide behind the besom 'til dark when it would take to the sky to seek its purpose!

The shuffle of feet drawing closer brought Annie back to reality, this was a creepy place, she would be glad to remove Ivy from it. The man reappeared.

"You'll 'ave to wait she's finishin' the room, Isaacs 'as already let it, could 'ardly wait for 'em to shift the corpse. I bet the poor sod that's sleepin' in there tonight'll 'ave a few shivers."

He laughed, it seemed to bring on a bout of coughing, the knot which tied the strings of his apron across his belly rose and fell with each spasm 'til finally the cough subsided. He wiped his brow with one corner of the Hessian.

"Bloody pit."

He walked away mumbling curses. Annie looked up to the sky, it displayed more goodness than the inhospitable yard. Eventually, an out of breath Ivy arrived looking worried, she was surprised to find Annie.

"Is something wrong, are the children alright, why are you here Annie?" Asked an anxious Ivy. Annie took her arm and led her away from the doorway.

"Ivy I need you to answer me entirely honestly, after talking with your mother the other day, I think I now understand why you chose not to return to Davina's. Are you really happier here, or as content here, as you were at The Park?" Annie looked intently, poor Ivy burst into tears. "You have given me answer enough. Tell these people you will work the week out, they will replace you in that time I've no doubt. I must not keep you now to explain further but you are needed at both Davina's and Catherine Appleyard's. Tell your mother how you feel, encourage her to fill her own life with more activity, then she might not dwell on matters which you and I find awkward and ungracious."

Ivy's tears eased and she nodded accord.

"Did you tell Davina what mother had said?" Ivy's expression was tortured.

"No of course not, don't fret Ivy, when your mother calls as I'm sure she will, Davina's happy nature will rub off on Mrs.Pilkington, she will begin to see things in a better light."

"Ivy Boucher, a tray of tea is required in room 5, now." A determined voice bellowed from within.

"You go, we will see you in just a few days."

Annie sped from the yard, what a soulless place, then a smile came to Annie's face, how she would love to place Edna in Mr.Isaacs boarding house, hide behind a drape and simply listen. The smile advanced to laughter at this glorious thought.

"I wouldn't call the King me uncle." Said Annie to a mystified child playing on the green.

Aboard the bus Annie sat back and closed her eyes, she felt tired, the motion gently swayed her, the air was warm, the chatter of passengers became muffled by her drowsiness. She still had to pack Blackmore's order, it was already late afternoon but somehow everything felt better, very much better.

Davina's reaction when Annie related the recent events was a joy to behold and when on the following day, Annie had gone from Basford to The Ropewalk to inform Catherine of Ivy's availability to help at Tamarisk, the relief and delight which immediately poured from both Catherine and Robert made the extended bus journeys and late sessions at the workshop very worthwhile indeed.

Sylvia, under the guidance of May, was settling well to her work, even at a machine she displayed confidence and her hand stitching was already quite accomplished. May's placid temperament and sincere pleasure in teaching her own skill to another, ever resulted in success. Edna's deep pleasure at having her man back home filled every nook and cranny of the workshop with a sense of peace. Only one thing tormented Annie's mind,

'I begin to see ways of the world I hadn't glimpsed before, when I get home, things will be different'.

Annie could not convince herself of Clem's worthy influence or of Charles' undeviating conviction to good. His letter would seem to suggest Cairo held less threat to the immediate but of the future, Annie was even more unsure.

Davina had arranged a carriage to transport her to The Park on Saturday afternoon. No.14 would miss her presence greatly. Annie and the children had assembled to wave goodbye, even the older boys were saddened but Hilda and John could not fight back the tears. Davina, overcome by emotion, could scarcely speak to the driver. When the carriage had turned the corner out of sight, Hilda begged Annie to take them to The Meadows, to gather wild flowers for Byron. The late summer sunshine was a great inducement.

"Very well, just for an hour," said Annie.

The walk was pleasant, the usual activity with balls and cricket bats covered the area with young people, observed by a much smaller number of parents and grandparents. William, Freddy and George were soon in the midst of the noisy, exuberant throng. John had spotted a boy from his class at school, the two now set off to explore the hedgerows for vacated birds nests. Hilda's dexterous fingers made daisy chains and Annie gathered the late summer flowers for Byron. A familiar voice said.

"Hello Mrs.Eddowes, I'm surprised you are not in search of blackberries."

Annie turned to see Edwin Garbett, holding a basin with one hand and waving the very purple stained fingers of the other. So involved had Annie been with her own thoughts, she had walked past without noticing Edwin.

"Mother sends me here each year, a sort of tradition. When I was younger I thought it a subterfuge, a cunning plan to place me where I might be espied by a young lady. Now older and wiser, I believe it has been nothing more than mother's taste for jam, especially spread on milk loaf." He laughed as convincingly as he could but Annie recognised the regret, a loneliness.

"September will be gone all too quickly, then the days will be less inclined to activities such as these," said Annie, adding a foxglove and a stem of pink campion to the bunch of flowers.

"Have you heard from Charles?" He asked.

"Yes, a letter came a week ago, he is well. I imagine there could be only limited detail Charles could write to William of the situation, the letter was for William you see." Edwin looked surprised, Annie felt obliged to explain. "I purposefully wrote the briefest note to include with William's letter to his father, it is important for the boy to feel close to him, a letter of reply addressed to William meant so much. He read it out to us all so we have been comforted to learn that all is well," said Annie.

She found herself chatting easily to Edwin as they walked, telling him of Ivy's return, Catherine's generous undertaking, of Sylvia's aptitude for her new job. Edwin had found Annie's account of her visit to Rylands amusing, so few people ventured to converse with him, this comfortable exchange of simple opinions and happenings was a rarity for Edwin.

"Well I must gather up my brood, that alone will take several minutes, always there are desperate cries, 'just a bit longer Mam'."

Annie and Edwin said goodbye to each other, he to take home his mother's blackberries, she to finally prise her children from the ongoing games.

"Who was that you were talking to ?" Asked William, between gasping for breath, his brow ran with sweat. Freddy and George had succumbed to the heat a while back and abandoned the game to lay on the ground, drawing grasses through their front teeth. The small dry seeds which adhered to their sticky cheeks and foreheads now began to irritate. The two boys intent on ridding themselves of this itch rubbed with their palms resulting in the most grubby looking faces imaginable. Annie sighed.

"That was Mr.Garbett from the bank," she replied to William's enquiry.

"You don't often see blokes picking berries," observed William.

"Well your grandad picks berries at the allotment to take home to grandma," said Annie.

"That's different, I think it's strange," William persisted.

"His mother is elderly, you gathered blackberries for aunt Davina because she was unable to walk here. Anyway, all that aside there is no debarment to a man gathering berries, here at The Meadows or any other place for that matter. Now come along, you will all need a bath tonight," said Annie. Loud moans of dismay fell about her ears. Annie looked down at the flowers she held in her hand. "We must hurry, these need water or they will be wilted before we give them to Byron."

It achieved to propel their feet a little faster. They would be hungry after all the exertion, if they must suffer a bath then she would at least give them their favourite tea, eggs, sausage and chips with soft white bread and butter. Annie's mind wandered as she shepherded the children across Forest Road. Poor Mr.Garbett, life could be so cruel. William's questioning of a circumstance which most people would not have given a moments thought to reminded her of Enid, that same trait, unwilling or unable, whichever of the two, to accept anything which did not coincide with her own order of things. Annie would mention Edwin Garbett's loneliness to Billy, perhaps he could join Billy and Victor on one of their outings. The thought amused her, three musketeers, not exactly swashbuckling but highly dependable and curiously attractive.

"What are you chuckling at Mam?" Asked George.

"All of us, the way we are, the nonsense of things," said Annie.

Not really understanding her reply but nevertheless too weary to pursue the matter, they proceeded in silence, tired legs, empty bellies and a dream of chips confined their attentions, all they wanted now was home.

Ivy had returned to Davina's and commenced her work at Tamarisk. With the exception of Hilda, all the children were at school, including Molly who had taken to lessons like a duck to water. Davina, rather than being overcome by latent tiredness as Annie had anticipated following the rigours of August, instead set about her every day with impressive zeal. It had taken Annie considerable amounts of persuasion to convince her that a gathering for George's birthday would demand just too much of everyone. The loss of Frank was still devastating, Charles was away and after all, George was to mark his twelfth birthday, no longer a little boy but growing strong and tall, he would understand full well the need of allowing the family's nerves to settle around their soreness.

Ivy at the first opportunity, took Harold and Molly to see Samuel and Sarah. It had been a couple of months since they had seen each other, to have the company of their grandchildren once more filled these two wonderful people with love.

Whilst Eli held the children's attention, Ivy opened her bag and took from it a small jewellery box.

"I kept the box at home, in the drawer with Frank's belt and tie. When I opened the package, the ring was there, inside an envelope written with Frank's number and Regiment." Ivy took a deep breath. "I know you told Frank that the ring was from all of us but you bought it Samuel, I thought that it should be returned to you."

She handed the jewellery box to him, Samuel's hand shook so much he could barely grip it. Slowly, he removed the lid, the ring nestled into the soft lining, the rough, work hardened skin on his fingers clung to the fibres of the cloth, then as those words became visible, 'always with you', a pain inside Samuel took his breath, for an instant it was as if that vital beat of his heart, that life giving surge of the lungs had been stopped, a hurt so strong it took Samuel to the edge of death.

"Samuel," Ivy took his hand, "Samuel," she said again. Sarah wept into her apron, Ivy was frightened. Eventually he raised his head and spoke.

"One day your Harold will be a man, when you give 'im this ring, tell 'im that for all 'is days 'is dad will be with 'im, all 'is days." Samuel rose from the chair, crossed the room to his wife and took her hand.

"Come now lass, your grandchildren are out in the yard, Ivy will put the kettle on the range an' you must open that bun tin. I'm goin' down the allotment to fetch a few bits for Ivy to carry back to Davina, I won't be long."

Samuel rubbed his hands over Harold and Molly's hair.

"Our Eli is an old man now, you must remember that an' not be too upset when 'e breathes 'is last. I reckon some days 'e feels like givin' up. 'e's sore an' tired, that's all, nothin' really wrong with 'im 'cept soreness an' tiredness," said Samuel. He walked to the gate, Eli's eyes followed him but the dog's weary frame stayed where it was, on an old blanket in the yard.

Ivy had told Annie of her concern for Samuel, she had meant no hurt in taking the ring to Mitchell Street but now it worried her greatly, Samuel had been so distraught.

Two weeks had passed, this Saturday afternoon Annie would go to Samuel, sit with him a while and try to release his spirit. Since seeing the ring he had withdrawn to a place where not even Sarah had been able to reach him.

The machines at Basford were once more fully employed but Annie found Gertie in distress, struggling to cope with the morning's work.

"What is it Gertie?" Asked Annie, the red swollen eyes the tell tale of troubles.

"Steve's brother Henry, the telegram came yesterday, his mam is so upset."

"Oh Gertie, you should not be here at all, why didn't you send me word, I would have come early this morning had I known. You must go right away, I shall see to things here."

Gertie took her jacket from the peg, "Are you sure?" She said, Annie took her arm and guided her to the door.

"Do tell Clara that I am so sorry and give my love to Steve. I shall be at Mitchell Street for a little while this afternoon but I won't say anything, it is best you tell Samuel and Sarah when you see fit. We shall all be at home tomorrow if there is anything I can do."

The morning at last came to an end, Annie was relieved to see the women off and lock the workshop door. They had all been subdued, as she had given them their wages, each had borne that look of compassion. Not one had escaped the sadness, husband, brother, son, all knew Gertie's struggle.

When Annie arrived at Sarah's all the children were there feeding on apple pie. She looked about the table, as she did so Hilda's tongue appeared and did a circuit of her mouth, gathering every stray trace of sweetness, she smacked her lips and declared.

"That was delicious."

"I hope you haven't eaten all of grandma's pie," said Annie. Sarah stood at the range, quietly stirring the contents of a pan. Annie kissed her cheek, lifted five slices of belly pork from her bag along with a packet of rice.

"Where is Samuel?" She asked.

"Down the allotment, stringing onions, I cant get 'im to eat 'ardly anythin', I told 'im what's the use in growin' stuff if 'e won't eat it. 'E said there'll allus be somebody whose hungry." Sarah looked up from the pan, "I reckon 'e's like that daft dog," her gaze transferred to Eli, lying by the dolly tub in the scullery. "I put food down for 'im yesterday an' the silly begger let a cat come in an' eat it. Used to be if a cat come near 'e'd eat the cat given 'arf a chance."

"I'll walk the children to the allotment to see their grandad, let's do these dishes then we'll go."

"I can do a few dishes, what else am I supposed to do with meself an' I've told you afore, you don't need to be bringin' stuff 'ere for us."

Annie could tell Sarah was close to tears, she called the children.

"Come on, we're going to see grandad."

A light plume of smoke could be seen rising from the allotment, a pungent smell of yielding garden trimmings as the fire overtook them rendering them to a rich potash. As they drew closer to where Samuel worked, the additional aroma of onion cooking assailed their noses.

"One or two rotten ones, just as well burn them first as last," said Samuel. Already three long strings of onions hung from the stronger boughs of the old apple tree. "This will be the last lot then I'll hang them all from the beam of the shed to dry."

"What can we do to help Grandad ?" Asked George.

"You young 'ens can pull up the shallots, save my back, I'll show you what to do," he led them to a patch of ground at the other end of the allotment. "Now, they come up like this," he pulled a clump from the earth, shook off the loose soil and pulled them apart. "They have to be separated, all the loose skins need to be gently rubbed off, then Hilda can put them in that box." He pointed to a shallow wooden tray by the path. "I'll take them home to grandma an' when you come next time she'll 'ave some nice jars of pickles for you," said Samuel.

He left them to their task and returned to Annie, sitting on the seat by the apple tree. He prodded the fire with the fork, it crackled a response, sending more smoke to the sky above. He lowered himself to the bench beside Annie, picked up a shiny, golden onion from the ground at his feet and threaded the twine around its neck. He let out a long weary breath.

"When you come to us that mornin', to tell us Frank had been killed, I weren't surprised. When 'e went back after Christmas I couldn't make meself believe that I'd see 'im again. I'd lie awake at night, tryin' to picture 'im. 'Tis strange, 'e went away that New Year's Eve lookin' older than 'e was, yet I allus pictured 'im as a young lad. It wer' the same when we lost Harold, it wer' 'is young boyish face I could see when I closed me eyes. Sometimes I thought I could feel their 'and in mine, like it was when I took 'em down the street, just lads trustin' their dad for everythin'. I felt one comfort when you told me Frank wer' gone. Wherever 'e lay under that foreign soil, I lay with 'im, holdin' 'is 'and, 'e weren't on 'is own 'cause is dad wer' there an'all." Samuel's effort to speak became tormented by the tightness of his breath. "They took it off 'is finger, they didn't understand, I never wanted the ring back." He swayed back and forth in grief.

Annie leant her head on his shoulder, took his tired old hands between her own. Neither spoke, for a good ten minutes that was how they remained. Annie knew no words could make the hurt better. She felt his breathing, he could feel hers, an unspoken understanding existed between them, it eventually brought calm.

"All done Grandad, it's all done." Satisfied cries came from the far end of the allotment. Samuel tied the last onion, raked the skins onto the fire then called out to William.

"Put all the loose shallot skins in the pail and bring them 'ere for burnin'." Samuel carried the strung onions into the shed for storing and announced it was time to go home. William was given a bag of beetroot to carry, Freddy a bunch of carrots, George must bring the leeks, John was awarded the care of a lovely speckled marrow and young Hilda held a savoy cabbage which Samuel had left attached to its stalk to enable her to hold it like a posy. Samuel himself carried the box of shallots and Annie was given three large parsnips.

The children walked ahead chattering away to one another, Annie and Samuel shared a quietness but the silence held no awkwardness, their understanding deep and full. Annie hoped that before she must turn away from him to take the children to Hood Street, before she raised her hand to wave, Samuel's fingers might delve into his pocket and deliver that strength giving mint, then she would know that he was alright.

Annie and her family walked to the back door of home, this was truly a desperate day. They were laden with vegetables, enough to last the week and beyond but Annie would have gladly traded them all, good, wholesome as they were, she would swap them for just a single mint. It had not been offered, Samuel's sons were gone and his heart with them.

CHAPTER ELEVEN

It seemed premature, William was fourteen, all boys left school at fourteen except those at Oliver Blackmore's but in Annie's eyes he was still too young. He had shown no inclination to find work and whilst William's presence at Hood Street made life easer for Annie, he was at least there for his brothers especially young John until Annie reached home, she knew that for William's own good he must be usefully and sensibly employed.

Billy had told Annie that a couple of places were available at Player's, when she informed William he had scarcely acknowledged her words so in spite of the boys moodiness Annie had taken him to the factory, escorted him to the office door and waited outside. After several minutes he had come out of the office accompanied by the manager, one Reg Yeats. A man of average build and height but with a striking port wine birthmark over one side of his face, that however was not the feature which caught Annie's eye the most, she found it very difficult to turn her attention from his braces, they seemed intent on hoisting up his trousers to such a degree, the waist band sat at his chest. Annie felt they must have had a previous owner, much taller and longer in body yet the trouser legs ended neatly just on his shoe, skilfully turned up by Mrs. Yeats no doubt. Perhaps he had lost a brother in the war, dead men's clothes were circulating families and communities in the desperate struggle to stretch the budget and ease the heartache. The spread of this natural resource did little for the latter.

He cleared his throat and with no unnecessary stipulations, often used by bosses to inflate their own importance, he looked directly at Annie and spoke.

"I'll give 'im a months trial missus, some turn out to be worth their salt, an' others don't."

"Thank you Mr. Yeats," said Annie. She turned her face to William, her look of expectancy prompted him to offer his hand to his new boss. The agreement made, Annie hurried William away before any opportunity to change minds could present itself.

At the end of the trial period Annie felt apprehensive, her attempts at coaxing some response from William when she ventured to ask about his work, produced only very modest results. She had taken a deep breath and called at the office of Reg Yeats, at least she would then have a truthful account of the circumstances.

"Sit down Mrs. Eddowes." He lifted a stack of papers and a carelessly abandoned coat from the chair. "We don't get many mothers in the office askin' about their sons, is 'e your one an' only?"

Annie recognised his hint of sarcasm, this over protective mare too possessive to allow her young colt to look over the hedge. Annie smiled, his manner caused her no offence.

"I have four sons Mr. Yeats and one daughter, I am responsible for feeding and clothing them in my husband's absence. I am also liable if their manners or actions should fall short, that too could be no one's responsibility but my own after all. William has missed his father through this war, I don't offer that as an excuse for what at times can be his difficult temperament but neither can I simply send him into the world of men without once casting my eyes over his progress and that Mr. Yeats is as much for your sake as for his."

"Well that put me in me place didn't it." A big grin straddled his cheeks. "Your lad 'as a bit of attitude, seen it scores o' times but this place'll knock it out of 'im." He noticed Annie's sudden look of concern. "It won't be me as sorts 'im out it'll be the men 'e works with, don't look so worried, it's all part of a lad's development, turns 'im into a man. Wally Dale come 'ere six years back, just like your William, thought a few 'airs sproutin' 'ere an' there made 'im God's gift. When Wally's month wer' up 'e come back to this office an' said to me, 'Mr.Yeats, I can pack a fag and a punch now, before I come 'ere I could do neither'. He turned out to be a good 'en, now 'e's in France." Reg Yeats sighed and momentarily seemed regretful. "I'm glad 'e wer' 'ere first, this place an' them men," he pointed towards the door of his office, to the factory floor beyond. "They made 'im a man an' if 'e 'adn't learned that afore 'e went to the Front 'e wouldn't 'ave stood a bloody chance, if you'll pardon me for swearin' missus." He spoke with such conviction Annie felt an immediate regard for Reg Yeats, she would trust his judgement.

So William had begun full time at Player's, working a 48 hour week finishing at noon on Saturdays.

The difference in the two brothers was marked. Freddy had already lined up his job on leaving school, he had come home one day from visiting Arthur Cropley at the farm in a state of great excitement, 'Arthur says I can start the week after my birthday, the geese and turkeys will need to be fattened up for Christmas and the hoggets finished for market. He'll teach me how to work the horses and pay me a fair rate'.

Annie had smiled at his enthusiasm but stressed the fact that in the mean time another year of school demanded his best effort, even farmers, especially farmers, must adapt to changing times and knowledge was the key to every success.

William it could be said, gave the impression of enduring his days while Freddy clutched at every moment, finding delight in learning and achieving. Annie could imagine William packing the cigarettes, not considering his last box of the day to be a job well done but merely a means to a pay packet. Not dreaming of promotion and eventual management but knocking off at 12 o'clock on Saturday to drift through the weekend aimlessly.

When Annie pictured Freddy, he was always planning his next project busily occupying each minute of his day and yet despite their differing characters, she believed both would make good men. Annie loved them dearly, be it William in a mood or Freddy on a mission she was proud of her two young stepsons.

"You're a 'rum en' Charlie boy, we're out 'ere in the middle of a soddin' sandpit wi' nowt but flies an' hairy arsed blokes but you don't go lookin'." Clem rested his back against a stack of crates and lit his cigarette. "Are yer goin' to 'ave one today or are yer in denial of a smoke an'all."

Clem held out the packet for Charles to take one. Not often but when the mood took him, Charles would smoke a cigarette, something he had never done back home.

"There's summat different about these women, they smell different for a start, ours slap a dab o' rosewater behind their knees, if you're lucky, I've 'ad some as smelled like the bloody dog on a wet day but these, it's spicy, aromatic, hot, yer can feel the heat afore yer even get started." Clem laughed, "Who'd o' thought it eh, Clement Clegg, now there's a name to conjure with, under the Arabian stars wi' a sultry beauty. Our Dennis, now 'e wer' one for the women. When 'e wer' born, our 'ouse wer' that poverty stricken they 'ad to wrap 'im in newspaper to keep 'im warm. His father wer' down the pub, 'e wer' never any place else. I reckon that sealed fate for Dennis. When 'e wer' thirteen 'e got a job at factory, done alright, settled to it, we all giv' our wages to mam, never 'ad nothin' for ourselves. I couldn't abide that man, 'e must 'ave wooed me mam just to get 'isself a skivvy, once 'e got the ring on 'er finger 'e might as well 'ave put a bloody shackle about 'er neck an'all. When me own father died we all cried, 'e wer' no age, God bless 'im. Summat 'et at 'im inside, 'e went to skin and bone, faded away like." Clem drew on his cigarette and blew a swirl of smoke into the air. "Dennis began to feel 'is feet, like a young fella does, 'e'd been at factory four years, 'e wanted money, a lass expected summat if only a bag o' chips. 'E started a fiddle, just 'arf a dozen at a time, 'e weren't greedy. 'E'd put 'em down the sides of 'is boots, 'e 'ad welts all round 'is ankles where the nails an' screws dug into 'is flesh. 'Is mate Arnie 'ad a stall down the market, Arnie sold 'em on for 'im, it wer' only coppers all of it. Dennis got away wi' it for a couple o' years but a snitch at the factory must 'ave spotted summat. Old man Clayton 'ad Dennis in the office just as 'e wer' off 'ome, end o' the shift, made 'im take off 'is boots. Well there they were, a few bloody screws an' nails but Clayton brought a case of it.

Poor Dennis wer' giv' five years, he owned up to the lot, from when 'e first started to fiddle yer see. Well 'e served 'is time an' when they let 'im out o' clink, first thing 'e went to look for wer' a woman. Prudence she wer' called, only our Dennis could pick a soddin' Prudence, she worked behind the bar at Wheatsheaf, she giv' 'im the glad eye, told 'im to meet 'er later, after work, lived on Battersby Road. Poor bugger, got 'is end away alright, that Prudence wer' like a combustion engine, Dennis said 'er thighs thrust like pistons under a full 'ead o' steam, 'e told me all about it, five years 'e'd been banged up, 'e couldn't contain 'isself now. Prudence 'ad a bloke, she weren't married to 'im, but they was shacked up together, 'e worked at scrapyard, mean bastard they said. Three days later, about seven in the mornin', a young paper lad wer' cutting' through by the canal, 'e got to Drummond Street quicker that way. 'E come upon a body, a bloke wi' 'is 'ead stove in. The lad 'ad watched 'is grandma die the week afore, seen 'ow 'is mam pulled the bedcover up over 'is grandma's face. 'E took a newspaper from 'is bag an' spread it over our Dennis's head, thought 'e wer' doin' the right thing, respectful like, yer know. Dennis wer' born to a sheet o' newspaper an' died wi' it. 'E didn't deserve that, none of it, a few soddin' nails an' screws an' the need of a woman. We couldn't prove nothin', no point in tryin' but I've allus believed it wer' that mean bastard as lived wi' Prudence. When we buried 'im I swore I'd do summat for Dennis, so 'e'd know I cared, summat that 'ould make 'im laugh up there on 'is cloud wi' the angels."

Clem stubbed out his smoke with the sole of his boot, coughed and spat into the dust.

"I got meself a job at the factory, old man Clayton didn't know I wer' related to Dennis, different surname see. I kept me nose clean for the first six months then I started. A man could put 'is 'and up to 'is face to 'ave a scratch an' nobody 'ould think owt about it. Just afore knockin' off time I'd scratch me nose, me chin, whatever I decided to give an itch to. I'd slip a few nails an' screws into me mouth, hold em under me tongue, keep 'em there 'til I wer' well clear o' the factory gates, then cough 'em out. I could taste the metal in me spittle, it wer' like that taste o' blood when a tooth come out. Iron, that's

172

what it were, Iron. I did it for that long traces of iron residue must 'ave got into me gut, constipated! God Almighty was I constipated but I cheated Clayton, took the stuff right out under 'is bloody nose an' 'e never knew it. Soon after that Dennis's father snuffed it, 'is liver wer' pickled in alcohol, 'e wer' yella as a guinea, looked more 'chinky' than the chinaman as worked in hospital laundry. I giv' all the money from sellin' the nails to me mam, told 'er to buy 'erself summat, I'd 'ad enough by then, couldn't shit to save me life, 'ad to take Senna in the end, talk about the world fallin' out o' yer bottom. I reckon all five soddin' continents come out together, I could tell which one wer' Asia, it wer' 'ot enough to scald me arse, I wer' walkin' round like a neutered Tom for days. Jacked in me job at factory an' got work as a bailiff. Best thing I ever done, found meself a nice little earner, you'd never believe what folks'll sell when they're desperate. If you've got an eye for an antique there's a killin' to be made. When we get 'ome Charlie boy you an' me'll show them buggers a thing or two."

Clem laughed loudly, slapped Charles on the back and said.

"Afore we leave this place dammit, I will get a bronze beauty to wrap 'er legs around your 'old fella', got to live each day as though it might be yer last. When we go up the line we might be shot to oblivion an' when we walk these narrow streets after dark we could end up wi' our throats cut. Live Charlie, live while yer bloody well can."

Clem was different to other men Charles had mixed with, their lives prior to meeting on the train to Manchester that day they both left for training, were in every way dissimilar, yet Charles felt drawn to Clem, he was a friend, a good mate. Clem's endless chatter made Charles feel safe, Clem was bold, brash, loud, all the characteristics which Charles would normally shy away from. A measure of Charles longed to be like Clem but the other part of him, that dominant part lived still in the memory of his gentle mother and the beautiful, fiery Enid. Annie he thought of as a bystander to his life's events, someone who witnessed, who knew his trials, someone who from kindness, stayed his strength, he needed Annie but Clem would not understand these sentiments. With Clem it was black or white, good or bad, less defined fancies were not worth Clem's time in pondering. The two men rose to their feet, Clem stretched his back and sighed.

"Come on my son, put them muscles to work, the bloody sinews seize up too quick these days Charlie boy, not enough of the old 'pull an' push'." He laughed. "Another batch went out last night, poor devils, I reckon the barracks are lookin' a bit too lean and empty. The bloody cavalry took a real poundin' at Gaza. They'll 'ave to do like the Aussies an' put 'em on camels. I 'eard one bloke say there were nothin' closer to the sulphury smell o' gunfire than a good fart an' nothin' nearer the smell of a fart, than the stench of a soddin' camel's breath. 'Tis one way o' seein' the world Charlie, we'll be up the line soon I reckon, older blokes are gettin' dragged in now, they'll be in 'ere keepin' shop," he began to whistle.

Charles took a heavy crate from the stack, reconciled the stores sheet and pulled the trolley to the loading bay, as he hauled it up the tailgate of the truck, he brushed his face against the canvas flaps, they smelled of sulphur, he shivered. Unlike Clem who sought every scrap of information, Charles did not ask, his simple belief being that what he didn't know couldn't hurt him.

Annie had sent him a new photograph with her Christmas card, the children had grown so much in the past twelve months, they had all written something and William a long letter. The boy was in his fifteenth year, working now, he would be a man when Charles got home, if he got home.

"What you cogitatin' now?" Clem stood on the ground in front of Charles, quick as a flash he put a length of pole under his arm, "Get yourself down 'ere Eddowes, you miserable, celibate cretin before I 'ave yer balls gouged out an' welded onto the Major's ceremonial scabbard."

The two men chuckled, as they loaded the truck. Clem would sometimes write on the side of a box, draw a picture, 'got to send the boys a laugh' he'd say. Today it was an image of two ample breasts.

"Wish I could make the nipples look real, yer know, like them artists can make an apple look round on the canvas, not just flat."

Underneath his drawing he wrote the words,

'Lots of love from Nefertitty' XXX

"You silly bugger," said Charles as he carefully positioned the box, picture side out, at the back of the truck!

Annie found Edna and Sylvia alone, Edna's eyes conveyed her concern, she had not voiced it to the young girl but for May to be absent with no word was unusual and ominous.

"I shall go to find May if she has not arrived by ten, just to make sure she is alright." Annie tried to sound confident for Sylvia's sake. "Perhaps she is unwell this morning, she did eat a piece of pork pie for her dinner yesterday, I know she buys the bigger one to save money, the smaller ones are poor value but it lasts her so much longer and none of us feels able to waste food."

Sylvia smiled, Edna gave a look of resigned compliance and Annie stitched shrouds with an ache in the pit of her stomach, willing the door to open and for May to walk in, all of a fluster but with a benign reason for her delay. It was not so, the hands on the clock had ticked around torturously slowly and just after ten o'clock, Annie put down her work, took her jacket from the peg and looked to Edna saying,

"I might be a while, don't worry if I am not back before Billy brings Hilda, she'll be happy drawing pictures in the office."

It was fortunate that Billy had taken Hilda with him to call for Victor, the three of them were going to feed the pigeons in the arboretum.

"Once Billy gets out wi' Victor they're gone for hours, what those two get up to God knows so you'll likely be back 'ere before 'e is. I've told Billy workin' a night shift means you're supposed to sleep by day, 'me an' Victor do sleep' he said, silly bugger caught a train to Derby last Friday, 'ad an hour on the station lookin' at the engines an' stuff, then caught a train back 'ome. Billy told the guard to wake 'em up when the train pulled in at Nottingham. Our girls think Victor's lovely, we've found out that 'e likes music. The band wer' playin' in the arboretum Easter weekend an' Victor wer' dancin' an' singin', set our Susie off, now she wants a trumpet, God 'elp us."

Annie knew Edna's chatter came from her anxiety. May had been an almost constant companion to Annie and Edna for many years, they both now harboured a dread of the worst.

Annie hurried towards Melton Road, she was thinking of Billy, his spirits had been lifted tremendously since he had begun night shifts at the telephone exchange. It was a job his disability could cope with, Billy's determination and limitless energy, his entirely likeable nature had very soon endeared him to his colleagues, one of whom was also an ex-serviceman, an amputee like Billy, he had lost a leg.

Albert Haynes had survived, eventually being discharged from hospital but with the very sad reality that he could not be fitted with an artificial limb. The infection in the wound had resulted in further surgery, not sufficient stump remained to support a prosthesis. His general health was poor and Florrie struggled endlessly. Annie sensed, though Billy had a great attachment to Victor and genuinely enjoyed their outings, it was a loyalty to Albert also which made Billy so resolute. The bond between men who had shared the horrors of battle and survived painful periods of recovery in hospital was so great they now lived as brethren, it was a kinship stronger than bloodline.

Annie reached May's house, she peered through the window, all was quiet, no sign of May in the living room. She knocked at the door once again. In order to reach the back door Annie must go to the end of the road, turn into a narrow 'cut' and follow the row of houses in reverse until she reached the gate to May's back garden. The door was unlocked, Annie called out, a sound from upstairs led her to a bedroom, May sat on the end of the bed, she was dressed the way she had been the day before, her hair was pinned, her face was grey, her hands white and cold. She rocked gently to and fro' clutching to her chest a framed photograph. Annie sat beside her.

"May, you must warm yourself."

Annie tried to persuade the fingers to release their hold, so many hours had they been locked around Alfred's picture they had become set. Annie wrapped her own hands over May's, this warmth eventually enabled May's hands to open, she did not speak as Annie tenderly took the picture and lay it on the bed.

"When is Mabel due home?" Asked Annie. May slowly turned her head to look into Annie's face.

"Mother is looking after Mabel, you know mother always looks after Mabel, it's liver for tea, Alfred likes liver, he'll get kindling on his way home from school, I'll make the fire up then. Are you cold?" May's eyes demanded a reply.

"Yes, I do feel chilly shall we go down to the kitchen, it will be warmer there," said Annie.

When May rose to her feet it became apparent she had wet herself, unable to move from the spot, she had urinated where she sat, the bed too was wet. Outside the air was mild, it was almost the end of April but inside, especially in the north facing bedroom at the front, it felt chill. Annie needed to take May downstairs, to strip off her wet clothes, wash her and put on dry but the fire in the range had gone out. Annie sat May on a kitchen chair.

"I will only be a minute, you stay here." She picked up an enamel jug and ran to the next door neighbour. "Please could I ask you for a jug of hot water?"

Annie briefly explained, not revealing details but simply saying there was a problem with the range. May's neighbour seemed not to be nosey and handed the jug back to Annie with a smile.

"That was no trouble at all dear, if you need any more just knock," the kindly woman said.

Annie felt thankful for this small mercy at least, but the tension in her chest had turned to heartburn.

She washed May and dressed her in clean clothes, encouraged her to drink a cup of milk and to eat a slice of bread and butter. It was like tempting a small child, indifferent to its meal.

Somehow Annie must get word to Mabel at the hospital, she could not leave May unattended. The telegram lay open on the kitchen table, Alfred had been killed in action at Nivelle whilst displaying great bravery, Annie read the words, each one intensified the discomfort in her chest. She must confide in the neighbour, there was no other solution. Annie stood at the open back door, taking deep breaths, trying to quell the heartburn. A familiar voice in the garden of the house at the other side was heaven sent. Winnie Bacon, it was definitely Winnie, there could be no mistaking that voice. Annie called through the fencing.

"Bless my soul, 'tis young Annie, now whatever is the matter dear. I was just 'ere 'avin' a cup o' tea with Elsie afore I go 'ome. I 'ad to fetch some laxative from Hastilow's for Ted, I've told 'im 'til I'm sick o' tellin' 'im, that damn nougat allus bungs 'im up, 'e will buy it for 'isself off market stall, 'tis full o' nuts, 'e's spent more time in privy since Saturday than 'e 'as indoors."

"Winnie I need to ask a big favour, I don't know what else to do, someone must go to the hospital and bring Mabel home, she hurriedly told Winnie and Elsie of May's plight."

"I'll go right away," said Elsie, don't fret you stay with May, mam will go to the workshop to tell Edna what's 'appened before she goes in to dad."

The exchange of dialogue had miraculously cured Annie's heartburn. What a coincidence that Winnie's daughter should live alongside May. Elsie knew May as a neighbour of course but May had no reason to be acquainted with Winnie, they would likely have caught a glimpse of one another over the years but nothing more. Annie held no awareness of Elsie's address, either way it was a Godsend. Both women had left immediately, Winnie calling back to Annie as she hurried away.

"Elsie's door is open take May in there and make yourselves a cuppa."

Annie turned into Winchester Street wondering if the day could possibly bear anymore misery. Mabel had been told that her brother was dead and found her mother in such a state of shock the woman's mind was addled. The poor girl was exhausted from nursing long hours and already a witness to pain and bereavement through the course of her work in spite of not yet reaching the age of twenty years herself. It had grieved Annie to leave Mabel but she could stay no longer, it was nearly three o'clock. She would stop briefly to speak with Edna and Sylvia then she must go home with Hilda to be there for the others. Now Edna's eldest was turned ten years, she was entrusted with the care of Susie and Liza, they walked together from school to No.24. If for some reason Billy was not there, then they simply ran to the workshop and stayed with Edna until she finished her work.

Sylvia's expression as Annie entered was a mix of fear and hope, that combination which seemed to defy the features of an older, established face. Still youthful, Sylvia's eyes cast the fear while her mouth opened and rounded to receive the hope, some offer of sweetness to take on the tongue as comfort.

Annie could not see Hilda at first, she had curled herself, like a kitten in a basket, on the big chair at Annie's desk, fast asleep.

"Billy's tired 'er out poor mite," said Edna, "Winnie called so you don't need to go over it all now, you get yourself an' Hilda 'ome, we're alright 'ere aren't we Sylvia?"

The girl nodded, Annie squeezed Edna's arm, smiled warmly at Sylvia, gathered the sleepy Hilda and made her way.

"You have to walk now my love, my arms are aching so," she lowered Hilda to the pavement and caught hold her hand. Hilda's other chubby little fist rubbed the sleep from her eyes, their steps were laboured.

John came rushing towards them, he had been waiting by the gate to see his mam and sister turn the corner. His eyes were brimming with tears and he could scarcely speak for sobbing. Between his cries Annie heard the cause of his distress, they had bumped into aunty Jean on their way home, Eli was dead. John grabbed at his mother's hand for consolation, Annie walked, her two youngest at either side of her not knowing if she held them from falling or if it was they, innocent children who kept her from collapse.

Annie seemed quiet, her mind elsewhere.

"Are you well Mrs.Eddowes?" Asked Edwin Garbett, looking up from his counting.

"I am so concerned for May Watkinson, her son Alfred has been killed in France, the news has disturbed her mind, I can only hope her confusion will be temporary. I wish I could do more to help Mabel but with the workshops and the children, the days are full. I'm on my way to Basford now. May is a dear friend, to see her empty chair and the silent machine is dreadful for us all. Edna isn't saying very much but I know she is grieving with May, she has Billy home you see, safe from the fighting, injured but safe. That is wonderful but now Edna feels she has been blessed and not poor May, it torments her."

Edwin felt a great respect for Annie Eddowes, he was saddened to see her so upset.

"I am very sorry , you must tell me if there is anything I might do to help."

Suddenly Annie realised she had delivered distressing news, to have given such a tragic account to Edwin of all people, he should not be subjected to stress.

"I didn't mean to trouble you Mr.Garbett, it was quite wrong of me," said Annie.

He smiled, "Most people imagine that if they should venture to tell me bread has gone up a penny a loaf or that the 56 bus was late then I might instantly fall to the ground, salivating like a rabid dog and so they choose to tell me nothing. You however, have always spoken to me as though Edwin Garbett had no such tendency. I have been grateful for that. Please believe me to be concerned for this family but not to be troubled."

Annie thanked Edwin, enquired after his mother and left the bank.

The Basford works were two machines down, the absence of women at hospitals, of women holding children close in the aftermath of bad news, resulted in a continuing upheaval. Annie tried desperately to keep positions open but not knowing when or if these harassed women would return, placed production under severe pressure.

Another threat to family life was the cold and calculating attitude of some landlords. The women already juggled the care of children, housekeeping and employment through virtually a twenty four hour period, Annie knew what that was like, she had sewn shirts in the cold of Aunt Bella's front room, when other than men on night shifts at the pit, folks slept in their beds, tending George and Bella by day to keep them from the poor house. An increase even small on rent, could drive the budget to collapse and spirits with it. The men, having greater physical strength to resist and defy were fighting, only God knew where, so landlords bullied the vulnerable women. These men engaged in a campaign entirely engineered by their own ruthlessness and greed. Mostly older in years and exempt from the call of duty, they had free rein. For a woman to find that her job was gone when she rallied her strength was sentencing her to almost certain eviction.

"Dad is getting worse Annie," said Gertie, he sits at the allotment on that old bench for hours. He was supposed to sweep all the chimneys on the vicarage but in the end, the Vicar had to get somebody else to do it. Mam kept reminding him but he doesn't seem to hear, it's as if he's miles away. His appetite is poor, Maggie bought him a Thornton's egg at Easter, more than half of it is still in the box. Mam says he lies awake at night, she can tell his eyes are open, staring up into the gloom. He buried Eli where grandad buried his whippet but he won't burn Eli's blanket, he's put that on his old chair in the shed."

"I'll take all the children on Sunday and persuade him to go with us to the embankment, he needs to be distracted from dwelling on all the sadness,

Harold, Frank, even Eli was a friend to Samuel, he is missing them so much. The boys will keep his mind on happier things and Hilda always creeps inside his heart," said Annie with a sigh.

"Watch out," Clem called urgently. "Bloody thing, it's gone between them two crates, I'll poke the little bugger's arse 'til it wishes it 'ad stayed on the Turks' side, I'd step on the ugly critter if I thought it wouldn't pierce me sole wi' that soddin' sting. I don't know what yours are like Charlie but my boots are that thin on the bottom I can tell when I tread on me spit."

As if to illustrate, he spat on the ground in front of him, picked up a length of pole and walked over to the crates, intent on evicting the unwelcome scorpion from its hiding place.

"Damn it, I can't see the sod, it'll be when I put me 'and on a box or summat that I spot the bastard again."

Charles said, "Give me the pole," he began to beat on the side of a crate, louder and louder, "watch for it coming out, call to me when you see it." At first nothing happened but Charles persisted.

"There 'e is , give 'im a bloody 'eadache Charlie boy." Clem cried out excitedly and to his immense satisfaction Charles brought the pole down on the confused scorpion with such force it separated the body from the tail which now lay in the dirt of the floor, writhing on a nerve. Clem leapt about with glee. "Done for the little bastard you 'ave Charlie, 'e'll never fuck again."

"What should we do with the sting?" Said Charles.

"Wait 'til the bugger stops twitchin', then wrap it up an' send it to 'Kemal' wi' a note, 'stick this where the sun don't shine'," replied Clem, slapping the side of a crate with his palm and whooping with delight.

Charles brushed the remains of the scorpion onto a shovel and carried them outside. When he returned, Clem had set about finding himself a pair of boots.

"Sod the bloody lot, I can't kick Mustafa's arse wi' out a good pair o' boots."

The summer heat had forced Annie to open the workshop door, she must now trust the older boys to behave in her absence. John and Hilda had gone to stay with Davina and Ivy.

'It will be much easer for us if they come here for a week or two, children amuse themselves well if there are sufficient of them. John is ideal company for Harold and Hilda for Molly, Ivy knows that when she is busy at Catherine's I am perfectly capable of watching the children and we are not beyond going for the odd excursion. A ride to Papplewick or to Strelley is always a delight in the summer'. Davina had declared with the caution, 'No use arguing, my mind is made up'.

The children themselves had raised no objection and Annie, too weary to oppose the plan had accepted gratefully.

Freddy had acquired a fine looking cockerel in the spring, he had called on Arthur Cropley at the farm, the boy's eagerness had inspired Arthur and having numerous male birds to be killed for the table, he had picked one out as being a decent example and told Freddy to, 'put 'im in wi' your 'ens an' watch, if 'e skulks in a corner, cut 'is 'ead off an' eat the soddin' thing but if the bugger chases 'is women 'til feathers fly an' 'e gives 'em all a portion then feed 'im on the best an' nature'll do the rest'.

Freddy had devoted his holidays to three broody hens which in succession had sat on six eggs each, with the consequence that the garden at No.14 was now wired around almost completely and within this enclosure, twelve chicks at varying stages of development, picked and scrabbled under the watchful eyes of their mothers and the cockerel positioned himself atop the hen house, issuing threats and bird type abuse at every magpie, rook and jackdaw that was bold enough to fly anywhere near. Annie had explained to Freddy that this increase in bird numbers could not be accommodated through the winter months, some of the older birds must go for the 'pot' and a few of the pullets he would need to sell, long before the colder weather drove the rats' hunger. She imagined the forbearance of neighbours was due in the main to Freddy's carefully worded, but enthusiastic prediction of a steady supply of the freshest eggs at a reasonable price.

A large ginger cat which had appeared, lazing on top of the dividing wall had been deterred by George's determined endeavours with a water pistol. It had finally given up on its predatory stalking and taken itself off to somewhere less wet.

George's even temperament and brightness equipped him with an ability to pour oil on any rough waters, friction which arose between William and Freddy, if not calmed quickly, could soon intensify. In fairness, troubles were usually of William's making, his moods, even now at almost fifteen could be very difficult to understand, George's patient, diplomatic tactics thankfully achieved a result more often than not.

May had improved a little, still not yet herself by any means but the few words she did utter seemed sensible enough. Mabel had been living on money she had saved from her work but close to running out of funds she had returned to her duties at the hospital, nominating night shifts as most appropriate, given her mother's health. At least May would be safe in bed whilst Mabel was out of the house. The management at the hospital had been considerate and accommodated Mabel in her request. The arrangement seemed to be working and Mabel had told Annie that at last she felt a degree of normality in the days. Annie had called on May a number of times, finding her quiet, some would have said peaceful but Annie was far from convinced that May's mind had found a healthy calm.

News from the front had put everyone in sombre spirits, the death toll grew to hideous numbers, that stubborn streak of patriotism which forced smiles and laughter in the face of adversity was shallow, the heart beneath instantly felt a sickness, a nauseous guilt at allowing mirth in any measure when men suffered day on day, dying, dead, lost in fields of carnage. Women walked the streets, about their work but searching for solace when home no longer held comfort. The names, Ypres and Passchendaele, kept people from their food and from their sleep, some most tragically of all, from their senses.

Annie was just finishing a letter to Alice Hemsley, she had determined herself to keep in touch with Alice after aunt Bella died. No more than three times a year they exchanged letters, always at Christmas, very often at Easter and again around late summer. The boys were asleep, the following afternoon they were all going with Billy and Victor to a football match at Mapperley, it was the penultimate match in a youth tournament, designed initially to take the young minds away from all the troubles, to concentrate teenage boys' thinking on regular activities rather than fighting and belligerent talk. A knock came at the front door, it was almost 11o'clock, no one called at this hour. Annie put down her pen, the knock came again, she lit the lamp in the hallway and opened the door a crack.

"Who is it?" She asked anxiously.

"It's Edwin Garbett, I think I have May Watkinson with me." Annie found the answer confusing but recognised the voice and opened wide the door. "I was on my way home from a meeting, I found this lady wandering along Gafney Street, it was apparent she was in distress, I asked her name and she answered, 'May, I'm looking for my Alfred, he's not come home, it's time he was home'. I didn't know where to take her Annie, I remembered your friend, the lady you told me about so I've come here, if this isn't your May, then perhaps you might help me get this lady to hospital," said Edwin.

"Oh May, you are in your nightclothes, whatever were you thinking, bring her in Edwin, she must be so cold." Annie took May's hand and led her through to the kitchen, there was fire in the range, Annie lay more coal on the embers. "Edwin, would you put a kettle of water over the heat, I must go upstairs and fetch a wrap for May."

Annie walked as quietly as she could along the landing to her bedroom but William's face appeared at his door.

"Who is it, I can hear a man's voice, what do they want?"

"It's alright William," said Annie, "it is nothing to do with your dad, all is well, it is May, she has been walking and become very confused, it's fortunate that Mr.Garbett found her and brought her here, try to go back to sleep."

Annie hurried back to the kitchen, she covered May in a blanket and rubbed her hands to bring back circulation. The fire began to crackle and the kettle to gently hum activity. Edwin had already found cups and the teapot.

"Milk is in a bucket of cold water in the scullery," said Annie. "We will warm her through then I'll put her in my bed for the night but I must get word to Mabel, she's working night shift at the City Hospital."

They sat with May coaxing her to drink the warming tea. Edwin's patient gentleness Annie found remarkable, she could not imagine Charles looking on this situation with such compassion, out of his depth, lacking patience and fearing any show of tenderness he would have very likely gone immediately to bed leaving Annie and May to their own devices.

"Come along Mrs.Watkinson, drink some more then you can tell me all about Alfred and you have a daughter too, tell me about Mabel." Edwin's prompting induced a smile.

"Mother says Mabel will break all the boys' hearts when she grows up. Alfred got all his sums right, Mr.Dunn says the boy listens, that's why he learns so well," said May proudly.

Unbeknown to them, another boy listened from the stairs, satisfied it was as Annie had told him, William returned to bed. That foible of William's, that doubting trait to his nature would not allow him a ready acceptance.

"I will go to the hospital now Annie, find Mabel and tell her," said Edwin, "will you be alright?"

"Yes, I shall be quite alright, tell Mabel that her mother is safe tonight but perhaps she could come straight here when her shift ends in the morning."

When Mabel, tearful and stressed, arrived at No.14, Annie had already dressed May in one of her own frocks, pinned her hair and persuaded her to eat a small bowl of porridge.

"It must have been the newspaper," said Mabel, "I don't buy any because of mother but yesterday the lad must have pushed one through our door by mistake, mother had been reading it when I got up. What must I do Annie, I have to work, we have no money aside from my wages."

"I think you have no other choice than to speak with the doctor, your mam is very ill Mabel, it is more than we are qualified to understand. Take May home and stay with her, I will call on the doctor and ask him to attend your mam this morning, try not to worry, I'm sure doctor will help and advise but you have to tell him what has happened, that your mother was walking the street in just her nightgown."

Annie felt such pity for the young woman, it was an impossible situation, for May's own safety she must be watched night and day.

The boys had not stirred early. The crisis had been removed from No.14 before they got up. William's time spent sitting on a tread of the stairs had filled his head with more knowledge of May's tragic illness than Annie realised but in the event, he mentioned none of it to his brothers.

"I told you they'd be callin' on you an' me Charlie boy, when things get really bloody tough they send in the cream, the elite, 'no one else to drive the truck', my eye, we're shit 'ot we are Charlie, the dog's bollocks, they know a good set up when they see it, 'tis our fourth run, gettin' used to it now, know the way. I feel like the charabanc driver on 'is way to Skeggy' 'cept I don't 'ave to peer into the distance for the first sight o' sand, the soddin' stuff's everywhere, God knows 'ow it gets to where it does, we're sittin' in a bloody great truck nearly three foot off the ground, I've got me trouser legs stuck inside me socks an' me flies done up to me chin yet I can still feel sand chafin' the crack o' me arse an' me old fella'll start whistlin' soon, I can feel 'im gettin' ready to blow," said Clem.

Charles chuckled, "You're a daft bugger Clem," he said, "it's my boys birthday today, he'll be fifteen, William's a good lad, reckon if I get home, him and me will be spending a lot more time together."

"What do yer mean, if you get 'ome Charlie boy, we've got plans don't forget, can't let me down now, you an' me'll be walkin' into The Wheatsheaf an' folks'll take off their caps an' whisper to each other, 'that's Clegg an' Eddowes', we'll be as famous as Wrenshaw's 'osses. A bloody empire that's what we'll create Charlie, a soddin' bloody empire."

Clem began to sing and Charles scanned the landscape for any unwelcome company. The butt of a rifle rested in his lap, the barrel on the ledge of the window. He had found a friendship in Clem, unexpected, unlikely, yet stronger than any Charles had found before. He picked up the strains of the song and joined in, both men spurred on by the presence of the other, sang loud and hearty.

Bang! A crack of gunfire shook Charles from his thoughts and turned his head towards Clem, slumped forward, still. The truck veered perilously close to soft ground, Charles grabbed at the wheel, tears welled in his eyes, a trickle of blood had begun to fall from Clem's ear. Fear, driven fear told Charles he must not stop the truck. He let the rifle down into the footwell and with one hand on the wheel he heaved Clem's body over towards the door, both men were slight of build but it was dead weight, Clem was dead. Charles wept bitterly, pushing, heaving with all the strength his right arm could muster, veins rose across his forehead under the pressure, holding the wheel with his left hand, he slid himself over the seat 'til he held Clem with his side and shoulder against the door. Warm blood transferred to Charles' face, he dare not look at Clem, he was dead, his only friend was dead and he could not look at him. The weight of the body near numbed Charles' right arm but the truck moved on. He put his foot down harder, then another 'crack' rent the air, Clem's body shook violently from the impact.

"Dear God, Oh dear God help me," Charles cried out through his tears as more hot blood poured over his shoulder, spattering his face with each jolt of the truck when he put his foot down as far as it would go.

Annie Shuddered, her entire body shook as the sod struck the coffin, that final sound, that thud which took this earth to the next with such absolute surety. Her wonderful friend Samuel, that tower of love and strength, her constant since Harold's death, now lay in the ground, she could not bring herself to look on Sarah, her own grief was as much as she could stand, if her eyes fell on Sarah, Annie knew she would crumble to nought.

"Dear God help us all," Annie whispered to herself. Samuel's death had reduced his family to faintness. The girls were so broken hearted they could not bear their mother's grief too, only Nora had stifled her own outpouring in order to stay Sarah.

Jean had returned home from her work at Burton's to find her mam fussing over Samuel's lateness. 'He spends far too many hours on that allotment, the time he gives to that patch o' ground, you'd think 'e wer' farmin' acres. Uncle Moses 'ad 22 cows an' 50 acres at Ruddington but 'e still come in to see me aunty Pearl every once in a while. I could run off wi' the coal man an' your dad wouldn't notice I'd gone', had been Sarah's pitiful lamentation. Jean had gone to the allotment to hurry him home. Nowhere to be seen she had opened the shed door. Samuel sat on the old chair, Eli's blanket across his lap. At first she had smiled at the sight, thinking this retreat to be Samuel's refuge from her mam's tongue, his special place of peace. He was not sleeping, Samuel had passed away quietly among his tools and onion strings, his hands resting on Eli's bed. Jean had taken it badly, to be alone when she found her beloved dad, having to leave him there to tell her mam had tormented the young woman so much, she had scarcely uttered a word since and at the funeral, without Annie there to steer her through she would have stood transfixed in the cemetery until day passed to night and back to day again.

When they reached Mitchell Street Annie sat with Jean. The memory of May's trauma alarmed Annie she must talk with Jean, to be sure that her mind was sound.

"It's alright Annie, I just miss him so much, dad was always there if we had a problem, he always had the answer too. Quietly, in his own way he led this family through thick and thin. I want to hear his laugh, feel that big hand on my shoulder, see those glorious eyes and know I'm safe." Jean looked into Annie's face. "It will never be the same will it?"

Annie took a deep breath, "No, it will never be the same Jean, but for him it was never the same after Harold, then even harder after Frank. Samuel carried us while all that time mourning his sons. We must look after Sarah for him, just as he would trust us to do." Jean nodded and smiled. Annie struggled with emotion but her instinct told her Jean would be alright.

Davina had kept the four youngest grandchildren at The Park, William, Freddy and George had stood like men, only their swollen eyes and restless fingers, evidence of their misery. Gertie, Mavis and Maggie were comforted by Steve and Eddie, who supported Samuel's youngest daughter through the funeral as best they could but poor Maggie wept so bitterly.

Ivy looked up at the sky the entire time, so desperate was she to avert her eyes from the grave she almost tumbled over a grassy mound into the Vicar's arms. She had rushed home to Davina's and not one of the gathering had felt it kind to dissuade her.

The mints had gone many months ago, now Samuel too. Jean was right, things could never be the same again.

"Well done Eddowes," the Captain looked up from his papers on the table before him, "got yourself out of a sticky hole."

The words attacked Charles as mightily as any advancing army. The first time an officer had used the expression 'a sticky hole', Clem had muttered under his breath, 'that's what I could do with right now, a warm, sticky hole'. As for 'well done', it didn't feel at all well done. Clem had stopped two bullets which more likely than not, would have killed Charles if they hadn't buried themselves in Clem's flesh first.

"There are the usual casualties to transport back, including Private Clegg. I have ordered some days of leave for you Eddowes, I understand you have not taken any in months. Unfortunately it will not enable you to see your family, we cannot simply cross the channel from here but a man can find some relief when away from his post, if only briefly."

Charles made to salute, the Captain raised his hand a few inches above the desk and dismissed the formality in a gesture of common regard.

"Just take the dead to more respectful ground and do your best to stay alive Eddowes, a salute would help neither."

It was a puzzlement to Charles, driving the truck back alone as he was, his load, seven cadavers, among them Clem, rather than weaken him it seemed to fire his resolve. If it was to be, then like Clem one moment he would be alive the next dead, with nothing between. It was quick, no pain, no time for regret, just oblivion. Whether his silent travelling companions some how kept him from harm Charles could not know but he reached the barracks and not so much as a lizard had bothered him.

A private Duffy worked with Charles to lift the dead from the truck, they would be buried immediately, some had already started to swell. The heat of this place was at times oppressive yet the nights fell to a chill that forced a man, when not asleep, to move his limbs, shake his nerves too or miserable cold drove his want of home and played tricks with his mind.

So, leave it is then, I shall take my leave, said Charles to himself. He would go into the Souk, buy gifts for the children, silks for Annie but first he must do something for his friend. In her last parcel Annie had put some cologne and a bar of coal tar soap. Charles shaved, he washed and put on clean underwear, cut his nails and combed his hair. He took the cologne and patted his cheeks and forehead with the cooling lotion. Charles gazed into his shaving mirror and spoke out loud.

"This is for you Clem, it is all for you."

He sighed wearily, put money in his pocket and went out from the barracks into the narrow streets. Charles could not allow his mind to stray from its course, he knew where to go, he felt his feet were directed onto the very same ground that Clem's steps had taken, 'this is for you Clem, all for you'.

Charles paused, aware that he was being observed, two women stood at the top of a flight of stone steps, looking down into the alleyway. The younger one smiled, not in a way that said nice day, good to see you, not a spontaneous greeting, a courtesy. No, this smile developed in slow motion from deep within, from a sensual place, mysterious, beguiling. It began at the fullest part of the lips, creeping ever so slowly to the corners of her mouth, a slight opening in the middle, just enough to permit a flash of pearly white from her teeth. Her eyes seemed to narrow, as if concentrating on the image before her, to shut out inconsequential background. Dark tresses fell across her bare shoulder, her bosom sparkled above the material of her dress, the skin glistened with aromatic oils. Gold bands decorated her upper arm and fell loose about her ankle which she slid through the opening of her skirt where it wrapped around at the front. She flexed her toes and her smile performed a seductive dance as it spread and withdrew, over and over, beckoning Charles from the street below to her place of charms, her court of abundance.

Charles slowly climbed the steps, he did not feel good, not good at all. The older woman stood to one side, the younger one took Charles' hand and led him into a room, dark, cool, then along a narrow passageway to another area, dim, draped in the middle.

"Come," she said, her voice soft, deliberate. She lay on a rug surrounded by cushions of every rich shade, purple, burgundy, midnight blue, all braided in gold, "Come," she said again, her hands stroking the air, not once taking her eyes from Charles' face.

His fingers trembled as he took off his jacket, awkwardly he undid the fastener at the waist of his trousers. Her hands signalled him to come to her, her flesh smelled of cloves and cardamom, so soft so warm. Charles' breath was tight in his chest, when he closed his eyes he saw Enid, vividly, if he opened them he could see Annie. Open, close, open, close with each thrust of his body, tears stung his cheeks. He felt bad, wrong, but this was not for himself, this was for Clem. The act was done, Charles rolled away to her side, putting his palm over his eyes whilst his breathing steadied. Finally calm, he dressed and paid her. She sat upright her back against the wall, her legs spread-eagled but covered randomly by her skirt. She spoke, her words delivered very slowly.

"English man and Arab man are like horse and camel. One is shod the other is not, one feels the ground move beneath it , the other feels only steel."

Charles swallowed hard, turned on his heel and left.

The Souk could wait until tomorrow, Charles wanted sanctuary, he wanted his bunk, Charles longed for his family and home. He hurried along the streets, mumbling words to Clem.

"Now you can sit on your cloud with the angels and laugh Clem Clegg, you can have a good laugh at Charlie boy but I did it all for you, bloody hell I miss you Clem."

He sniffed and walked into the barracks, when he reached his bed, he sank on to its familiar feel and lay thinking but thinking was painful, he didn't want to hurt anymore, it was done and that was that.

He took pen and paper, rolled over onto his stomach and with the paper rested on the bed, he wrote.

Dear all,

I am lying on my bed with nothing to do for five days, you would think a period of leave after months of duty would be a relief, it is strange but it does not feel that way. The work brings a sameness, a routine, in the stores with Clem we'd have a laugh, jolly each other along, the hours passed quickly.

The last few days have been long and challenging so this time of leave is to relax and enjoy the Souks. I shall go there tomorrow, they sell everything, I shall surely find something pretty for you Hilda and some interesting items for you boys.

You should see the chickens in Egypt Freddy, they are smaller than our own, darker in colour, some are actually black. They run about everywhere like the pigeons in slab square, they seem to eat anything they can find and lay eggs wherever they like. Your friend Mr.Cropley at Bobbers Mill would consider them poor specimens.

I have driven one of the big trucks, we were taught to drive at the beginning, it was difficult at first but when the necessity arises we just have to get on with it, everyone is in the same boat as it were.

Clem is somewhere else now, I don't imagine we shall meet again but I remember well all that he told me. Everything that happens here we shall remember always I think, it is so different to home.

I hope to get a parcel off to you within a couple of days so it should reach you in time for Christmas.

Give my regards to everyone. I can picture you all at Davina's for a get-together. Hope you, William, have enjoyed your birthday and that Freddy will have a good time too in a few days. Samuel will no doubt have some boyish activity planned as a surprise. He would find this place most un-Boucher like, someone told me today that English men feel only steel, I don't believe that is true but word from home definitely finds our softer side so please all write soon.

I think I shall sleep for a while, I have come over very tired. Could you send more soap, I have enough cologne.

With love to you all,

Charles

CHAPTER TWELVE

Mid Summer 1918.

Catherine held up a runner bean, "Your Freddy is very enterprising Annie, I swear the beans this season are at least two inches longer than usual, those bags of chicken manure must have made all the difference, just how he managed to explain the smell to the tram driver I can't imagine, they only sat in the shed for three days before Robert used them but it took a week with the window open to disperse the odour. Half a crown well spent, that's what I say."

Annie chuckled, "It was to be a florin but Freddy decided he needed to cover his tram fare as well so I'm afraid you were charged an increased rate."

Annie sliced the last bean into the colander and Catherine scraped the strings from the table and put them in a bowl.

"My dear, Freddy has every angle covered," said Catherine, "these trimmings I must save in the cool of the meat safe and he'll collect them together with any other green stuff I manage to gather up, such as the outside leaves of cabbage and lettuce, you know how they mount up when there are several men to cook for. Freddy assures me the hens will eat all these waste scraps and in so doing, add to the goodness of the eggs. As Robert says, he has a remarkable grasp of true economics, if there is any justice in the world the lad will become Chancellor at the very least." Catherine sat back in the chair and let out a satisfied sigh. "We have come a long way Annie, it feels like an eternity, this war and all that goes with it, yet since the first time Margaret came to Tamarisk to help with the distributions the months have passed by so quickly. I shall ever be grateful to you for sending me such a salvation, after Philip was lost I allowed myself to become selfishly preoccupied but to be in Margaret's company, I really should say Sister Agnes I suppose," Catherine laughed. "Well, it gave me the 'boot up the behind' which I desperately needed. Although I miss seeing her I cannot deny that I am truly delighted that Margaret is nursing again, albeit as a 'Sister of Mercy'."

Catherine again laughed, loudly but with no suggestion of resentment. "She will be too busy for very much prayer so fair's fair, I shall pray most diligently whilst Margaret works at the hospital." She paused, "you are giving me an unconvinced look Annie Eddowes but I can promise you that I shall indeed commune with the Almighty. I have never been one to renege on an agreement."

She gave Annie a wink, which for someone of Catherine's stature and years seemed altogether out of place. Annie felt amused, so the Lord above had apparently agreed a deal regarding Sister Agnes, her tireless efforts nursing the sick and injured at the main hospital in Southampton, working alongside the overstretched nurses already there was acknowledged and an ongoing dialogue between Catherine and her maker was to be a sincere gesture of thanks for his part in all this.

"Margaret must surely be witness to so much hurt and suffering I feel nothing but great respect for her," said Annie.

Both women sat quietly for a moment then Catherine asked, "What news of Charles, how is he?"

"I believe Charles has changed, he writes a very mellow letter these days. I noticed the difference just before last Christmas, although he hasn't actually written as much, I think his friend Clem was killed some time ago. It is very true when they say one can read a great deal between the lines, his last two letters have made me feel concerned, I am sure he is missing home badly. William however is my main worry, Freddy and George are always content but William seems to be ever searching for something. His years of adolescence have been spent without his father, I have tried to guide him through them, to answer his questions and dispel the boy's confusion and doubt but a youth needs a father most when he approaches manhood. It sounds silly now but I can honestly remember as plainly as if it were only yesterday, the wonderful feeling when his little hand held mine as we peered into Freddy's Moses basket. My own dear George has kept me strong since his dad died and of course John and Hilda I carried as a mother does, William and Freddy were ready made." Annie smiled fondly. "I have genuinely loved them Catherine, now they are far too deeply ensconced within my heart for it to be otherwise."

"We give our children life Annie," said Catherine, "we give it free of encumbrance, we don't merely advance a lease, if we are fortunate then we shall always be a part of that life but it is their's nonetheless, we cannot demand it back to suit ourselves, I realise that now."

Annie kissed Catherine's cheek, "I should be on my way, I told Davina I would be there by 4 o'clock. She has been desperate to have a get-together, last year was just too emotional but Ivy and I conceded to a birthday tea for Molly this Sunday. Everyone will be present, Sarah and the girls will be already there. I am so behind with housework that I begged to be excused until now so I could catch up at home. Which reminds me, Mabel is concerned that you might want her to vacate the house on Melton Road. It seems unlikely that May's mind will be restored. I visited her last week, she sits in virtual silence, she causes no trouble. Since she was moved to Mapperley, Mabel has felt guilty at occupying a house alone when a small family might abide there."

"Tell Mabel that the owners are kindly, sympathetic people, let the situation remain for now, if it persists beyond the end of this year and Mabel, in the meantime has not found anyone to share the accommodation then perhaps it would be sensible to make changes. Now, you should run along to Molly's birthday tea, pop your head around the sitting room door before you go to say goodbye to Robert and the young men, he does so enjoy their company." Catherine paused, a twinkle of mischief came to her eyes. "I do believe Reggie is sweet on dear Ivy, he is a lovely young man Annie, those blonde curls alone could make a girl swoon, the way he whirls her round when Robert puts on the Gramophone. I was so pleased when Robert acquired this amazing music machine, we push the furniture to one side and dance. It is great fun and God knows we need to give these young servicemen some fun before they go off again. I wouldn't be surprised if Ivy hadn't developed a fondness for Reggie too, would that be such a terrible thing Annie?"

"No, not at all," replied Annie, "but the children must be included in any attachment."

"Oh, Reggie has met Harold and Molly a number of times, they join in the dancing. It was amusing to see Donald waltzing with Molly, he is so very lame still and the difference in their height produced a comical and yet quite touching spectacle. Eric has particular need of encouragement, he witnessed the most dreadful scenes at the Somme, his stomach wound almost killed him, he eats small amounts often but would retreat very quickly to a world of his own if we didn't persuade him of his colleagues' need for his comfort and support." Catherine stifled tears, "I pray that none of them need return to the fighting."

Annie felt real concern for Ivy, it would be wonderful for her to find happiness again but if this Reggie were to rejoin his Regiment, Annie shuddered at the thought.

News had encouraged everyone to hope that an end might at last be in sight. 'The big push' is how The War Office described the current state of military activity. No one was in any doubt over the cost, those whose men had survived and continued to fight on, dared not look forward with optimism, as Annie had heard one woman observe, 'Tis like sayin' none o' the men in our family 'as ever gone bald, tempts fate, afore twelve months is up there'll be one walkin' round wi' a scalp like marble'.

Robert and his young company were playing cribbage, a small stack of pennies beside each man.

"I bid you goodbye gentlemen," said Annie with a big smile. They all made to stand but she quickly dismissed the courtesy.

"You must come along to one of our dance afternoons Annie," said Robert, "bring Billy and young Victor, I understand the boy has a great liking for music, in fact bring everyone, all yours and Edna with her girls as well, we shall have a splendid time."

"I'm not altogether sure these young gentlemen are ready for such a challenge Robert," said Annie, only half in jest.

But they all laughed and Annie promised she would bring everyone to join in the fun one afternoon provided it was a Saturday or Sunday.

Davina's garden looked colourful, the roses and orange blossom greeted Annie with their scent. Since Samuel had pruned the shrubs and fed the beds with soot, the blooms had been prolific. It was a tribute to his skill and effort, Sarah would no doubt leave with a fine bunch of flowers to put in the windows at Mitchell Street. Everyone felt Samuel to be very close still, Annie sometimes imagined she could hear his voice talking to Eli in the back yard.

Annie recalled the day she had decided to enjoy a few extra minutes of summer sunshine so had walked through the arboretum on her way home from Basford. Sitting on a bench, quietly reading The Gazette, was Edwin. They had exchanged greetings then Annie had said she must not delay, home and many chores beckoned.

'I'll walk with you'.

He got to his feet, put the paper in his pocket and began to chat, their conversation flowed freely as they walked. He told Annie that sometimes he thought his father was calling to him, then he would remember that could not be. 'Our minds play tricks on us, I believe it must be the same for most people, memories taunt our subconscious, don't you think Annie'?

Edwin had gathered a small posy of daisies from the edge of the lawn, 'for you', he passed them to Annie, she laughed it was an innocent act of kindness, almost like that of a child.

'Thank you', she had carefully put the stems through a buttonhole on her jacket.

Edwin sighed, 'It should really be a gardenia or an elegant lily but daisies are all I am entitled to give'. He had nodded quickly and walked away from the arboretum gates, leaving Annie with a feeling of sadness. His gentleness reminded her of Harold, in another place at another time she could have found a special corner of her heart for Edwin. Charles had never held Annie in his love, only possessed her as a belonging, showing her no malice or neglect but displaying no passion either. There was only this place and the present. Annie had looked on the daisies. 'Just you remember what you are my girl'. Memories, Edwin was right about the memories. Annie too, had sighed and hurried home.

Annie opened Davina's back door and called out, a chorus of voices welcomed her and seven eager young faces looked on her as they ran from the sitting room to where she stood.

"Look Mam," said George, "aunty Maggie has given one to each of us." He held up a tin whistle.

"We're learning to play 'Danny Boy'," said Freddy. He put the whistle to his lips, followed by the others. Annie sang along with Maggie and Jean.

"O Danny Boy, the pipes, the pipes are calling............" That's as far as we've got, what do you think?" Asked George.

"I think that is excellent," said Annie, "you must practice at home until you can play it all the way through, your dad will be impressed."

"Come along Annie dear, tea is ready, Ivy has made a wonderful cake, I told Freddy it must be those lovely big eggs, the sponge has never risen like that before," said Davina with obvious delight.

They gathered round Davina's big table, laden as it was with all good things. Sarah's baking too was very evident and Jean had bought ribbon from Burton's to put around the cake. They sang to a delighted Molly the old music hall song *'She's as beautiful as a butterfly'*. Freddy and George sat at either side of Annie.

"Did you know Mam, that hens lay better when they listen to music?" Said Freddy knowledgeably. "I shall play to the hens at home, I reckon they'll like 'Danny Boy', Arthur Cropley says he had the best day of eggs ever when Colliery Band marched past Bobbers Mill on Jubilee day."

Annie smiled to herself, this was her place, her time, anything else was needless and nonsensical.

As they walked home to Hood Street they all sang 'Danny Boy' and with each note, Annie counted her very many blessings.

CHAPTER THIRTEEN

Every once in a while fate appeared to get things right. News from the front now allowed the stout hearted to believe victory was in sight. On the strength of this optimism, Mavis and Eddie had quietly married.

"Annie we couldn't wait any longer, you know what it's like. Eddie said if we didn't get wed he'd explode." Mavis giggled and looked sheepish. "He said it was like havin' water on the brain only it didn't stop him thinkin', he just had to sneeze into his long johns most nights!"

"Whatever would Sarah say Mavis?" Annie tried to look stern but couldn't hold her expression and they both laughed as they took another biscuit from the tin and dipped it in their tea.

"I only wet it up to the fourth row of knobs, any higher and it falls into the cup," said Mavis, carefully transferring the Lincoln biscuit to her mouth, first sucking the softened half before munching happily on the remainder. "Weren't we fortunate to get this place, it was alright livin' at Eddie's mam's but when Mabel decided to move out to live in nurses quarters and your friend Mrs. Appleyard arranged for us to rent the house we couldn't believe our luck. I do think about May very often, won't she ever get better?"

"May at times seems remote from us all," said Annie, "I do feel so sorry for Mabel, I think there could be no worse illness, her mother is alive yet gone from her, seldom does May know her when she visits, to have to watch helplessly such a rapid deterioration must be painful beyond our comprehension." With a heavy sigh Annie rose to her feet. "I should get along now, John and Hilda are at Davina's until tomorrow, William will likely be at the embankment with a young lady. Freddy has whispered in my ear the name Celia Tozer, poor Rosie Potts would appear to have faded from the scene. George will be at the allotment and it wouldn't surprise me if Freddy joined him there when he finishes at the farm. He was so eager to tell me all about his task, I was getting their tea ready yesterday when Freddy arrived home and he couldn't wait to give me a detailed account of how he castrated four young boars. He has all the confidence in the world." Annie began to chuckle. "Water on the brain indeed, give my love to Eddie, tell him Freddy has aquired numerous skills and is now surgically qualified." Both women laughed and Mavis stood in the doorway waving vigorously until Annie went from view.

The strains of 'Danny Boy' drifted from the back garden to the street as Annie approached No.14. Freddy had persisted long after all the others had abandoned their musical efforts, his conviction that music inspired the hens to greater production seemed justified, every day eggs sat in a bowl on the scullery table, large, firm shelled and inviting through their attractive buff colour. Freddy had a marketing ploy, a downy feather alongside the eggs when he sold them. 'Proof of freshness Mam' he'd say, with a wink of satisfaction.

"Where are George and William?" Asked Annie, handing Freddy a chocolate bar. He grinned.

"I stayed with George and helped him pick down the last of the apples, we put them on the shelves in the shed and it must have been about 2 o'clock when I came back here and he went down The Meadows. William has taken Celia to the pictures. It don't get dark 'til half past six, he can't wait that long so they're kissin' their way through a Douglas Fairbanks cowboy film. I bet if you asked him he wouldn't be able to tell you whether the horse was black or white. Waste of money I call it, they might as well have sat in the under stairs cupboard for an hour."

Annie put her shopping bag on the table, carefully lifted from it the parcel of 'books' from Basford which had travelled with a piece of brisket, a rabbit and some belly pork. The meat was quickly transferred from Mr.Cheetham's greaseproof paper to plates and put in the meat safe. Annie crossed the hallway to deposit the 'books' in the living room until she could attend to them later, a letter lay on the mat, just inside the front door, it was from Egypt. Charles had written frequently over the past months, last year his letters had been very few, Annie sat on the bottom tread of the stairs and opened the well travelled envelope, the letter was dated October 2nd, almost three weeks ago.

Dear all,

Thank-you for the parcel, it is surprising how accustomed we have become to food, which before arriving here we would not have considered fit. All of us at times have had bad stomachs, I believe the flies are mainly to blame, they persist with such intent we have surrendered to their occupation. At home, if a bluebottle comes indoors we attack it with so much violence, its spattered remains can completely obliterate the significant line of an obituary notice on the folds of a newspaper. I remember when Elliot Dewhurst's cortege went past The Standard, one man said to me, 'I thought as you'd be out there wi' yer black suit following' on wi' all the rest o' the hand shake brigade'.

I didn't even know he'd died. When I got home I found the paper on the scullery shelf and looked through the deaths. I could barely make out the name but sure enough, there it was, just legible beneath the deceased bluebottle, 'Elliot Dewhurst, died suddenly at his home aged 49 years'. Here nobody bothers about flies anymore, they just are, like everything else which rules our days but when the parkin and biscuits arrived I got that mad when a fly came close I swatted it with the stores list, now four crates of salt tablets and kaolin and morphine have been covered in bluebottle innards. The parkin is especially good, it softened as it travelled.

Morale has improved since we took Damascus, they seem to think Beirut will follow soon. We try not to look at the burial ground and God knows how many were shovelled into the wilderness before the heat drove their smell. Whichever side takes the territory, they'll win a land filled with death and never lose the stench, that will always be just under the surface, every time they stir the rot will seep.

Lieutenant Olds reckons by Christmas we shall be packing up, it's what we leave behind that torments, when the time comes men will cry, for their mates and at the whole bloody insanity.

Tell Billy I spoke with an old friend of his, he's been injured but not critically. He won't be able to ride a horse for a while though, Alfie Cresswell can't sit down. They shot his mount from under him and the poor devil fell on a jagged shell case, caught him right where east meets west. I had to distract him while they cleaned him up so we chatted and it turns out that he went to school with Billy. It was his third horse, one more would have been enough to pull a brewery waggon, Alfie reckons four cavalry mounts would be the equivalent of two of Wrenshaw's greys.

Hope George had a good birthday, Samuel would be pleased that the boys have taken on the allotment. Sorry May is no better but it sounds as though the new girl is working well with Edna and Sylvia. One of the men was knitting in the barracks last month, his wife sent him the needles and wool, seems he always knits the socks in their house. His mother taught him how so he could occupy himself when he had rheumatic fever at the age of ten. He says no one can turn a heel better than he can!

Will end now and try to sleep. Last night I lay awake picturing the workshop gates at Winchester Street, I couldn't remember which side the latch lifted, left gate or right, it's bothering me so write soon and let me know,

Love to everyone,

Charles.

It was an unusual letter, it obviously reflected Charles' mood at the time of writing but normally Annie gave the letters to the boys to read for themselves and Hilda would listen when Annie read aloud the appropriate passages to her. Yet William, Freddy and George were all now working, should she deny them this account of war or would that be a slight on their intelligence. Such letters were enlightening after all and when their father came home it might help them to understand what he had endured.

Suddenly a loud, triumphant chorus of cackling erupted outside and the tin whistle played 'God save The King'. Freddy had learned this piece too and delivered the notes in fast, flamboyant succession, it made the serious and respectful national anthem sound like an Irish jig. Annie smiled to herself, Charles would learn so many new things about his children. Even John and

Hilda had developed strong characters and William for all his complexities had turned out to be a fine young man. Annie put the letter back in the envelope and lay it on the sideboard.

They were all invited to Tamarisk the following afternoon. For weeks Robert had been asking Annie to bring the family to one of his dances, Reggie had rejoined his regiment at the beginning of September, Ivy was anxious but had heard from him twice since then and so far was well and in good spirits. He seemed to be almost relieved and proud to be part of the final push, his regiment was in France.

Annie had a lot of work to do before joining the others at The Ropewalk, this afternoon she must attend to the books for the Basford operation. Housework, baking, cooking all put her under pressure to be caught up in time but inwardly she looked forward to the event, everyone needed a little cheering up, winter loomed ahead. The long Summer days had brought endless hours of toil, it seemed almost sinful to sit down and rest while any daylight remained so weariness had crept into most peoples homes. Yet the prospect of dense fog and damp cold, or hard frosts and lingering snow caused mixed feelings. Regardless of whatever an individual chose, season followed season with no allowance for the preference of humankind. As Catherine had quite sensibly pointed out, 'If we leave our get together very much later we might be plagued by too many chaps and chilblains to wholly enjoy holding hands and propelling toes through an hour of non-stop nonsense to music', as she referred to Robert's gramophone afternoons.

Annie cleared away the meal, William had returned home in surprisingly good spirits, eating his food heartily and making enquiry of

George and Freddy as to progress at the allotment. Even a roguish remark from Freddy failed to ruffle William's feathers beyond a taunt in return. 'Wonder what Celia thought of the cowboy film, perhaps she was that frightened of the 'injuns' she had to hide underneath William's pullover 'til Douglas Fairbanks shot big chief Cock n' Bull'.

'You're just like Ernie Searle at work, he can't get himself a girl because his breath stinks, you smell like Arthur Cropley's gaiters Freddy Eddowes, jealous, that's what you are'.

George had quietly waited his moment to declare, 'Rosie Potts has a bigger bosom that Celia Tozer'.

In exasperation Annie had sent the three of them to the living room to read their dad's letter. It would take her an hour or two to bring up to date the books from Basford, two accounts needed to be sent off on Monday and there would be little time to spend on paperwork tomorrow. Annie had been quite firm when telling Catherine they would not stay for tea. The younger ones had school the next day and Billy would have to take Victor home to Florrie before she got worried. Poor Florrie, Billy watched over the boy like a hawk but his mam still became fretful if they were out over long. Edna would prefer to have a bite of tea at Hood Street anyway, 'me an' Billy an' our girls aren't used to anythin' posh, if we was to sit around a grand table sure as God made apples, one of us 'ould spill summat all over the bloody damask', had been Edna's prediction.

The morning had been hectic, Annie had filled the cake tins and baked two big apple pies. A Colwick cheese and some jellied veal sat on the slab with a nice wedge of cheddar, she had made an egg custard and a jelly. It became apparent when Annie had cleared away the dinner dishes and despatched Freddy and George to the scullery to wash, that William was dragging his heels.

"But why don't you want to come with us William, it will be fun, it is only for a couple of hours at most. Everyone will be disappointed, especially

Harold and Molly, they look up to you. Besides, you should learn to dance, Celia will expect you to take her dancing from time to time, it is more enjoyable when you feel confident." Annie tried to persuade him but he remained adamant.

"I shall stay here and mind the chickens, I might even play them a tune."

Annie was too weary to argue merits. "Very well but if you insist on staying here I want you to weed Byron's spot for me, it hasn't been done for weeks."

"Alright I will," said William. He was too passive, Annie began to suspect William had plans of his own and they would doubtless involve Celia Tozer.

When George and Freddy had passed inspection, no tidemarks about the neck and fingernails scrubbed Annie sent them on ahead.

"I'll catch you up, walk slowly, I just want to nip upstairs and put on a dab of lavender. Her real intention being to have a quick word with William.

He stood before her with a blank expression. "A young woman likes to feel special, she is thrilled when a nice young man shows her attention but she also needs to feel respected and admired. We shall not be late, I intend to be back not a minute after five. Billy, Edna and the girls will have a quick bite of tea and Victor of course. If Celia is to come here in our absence," William made to protest but Annie continued, "she is very welcome to stay for tea and meet your brothers and sister. I trust you to behave well, Celia is a very pretty young lady I am told. We were all young once but even in youth we must be responsible. You do understand William?"

"Yes." He looked directly into her face. "You'd best put the lavender on, must cheer up the servicemen after all they've been through. I shall probably write to dad later, the latch lifts on the right hand side of the gate at the workshop."

Annie turned away before her desire to give him a stiff telling off simply added to his contrariness. Why did William so often bring tension to the days. Perhaps when Charles returned to them the boy would change yet he was all but a man, surely the mould was set.

"Come on Mam," George's eager voice called out from the corner, Annie hurried but her heart was heavy, until a few moments ago the afternoon had been something to look forward to, now she could only ponder William's strange mood. Perhaps she should not have allowed him to read the letter. Freddy and George were as always and they had read it too. As they walked the boys began to chant a rhyme.

'Poor Ernie Searle, can't sleep a wink,

The girls don't love him 'cause his kisses stink'.

"Don't be cruel," Annie called out to them and shook her head in dismay, at least their minds were set on simple boyish mischief.

"Race you to the bus stop George."

Freddy's legs strong from his labours on the farm, sped down the street, George in hot pursuit. It was almost impossible to believe that George was now working at Raleigh. He'd impressed the manager at his interview three weeks ago, his quick mind had enabled him an easy grasp of his task and now he set off to work each day with eagerness. Annie had tried always to instruct them well in money matters. Some men displayed a poor grasp of the subject, it inevitably led to domestic crisis. Each weekend, she accepted their pay packets, together they counted the content and one third of the amount she gave back to them, all three were treated in exactly the same way.

'You must save all you can, you will need money as you get older, you are earning now but there is never a guarantee of employment, fortunes can change. Put your money safely away in your tins and when you are old enough you can open a bank account'. Two days after Annie had returned to him that third of his first pay packet, George had come home from work with a small parcel.

'For you Mam', he said and handed her a brown bag. Two bars of scented soap from Hastilow's were inside. Just like his father before him

George delighted in giving. Annie had shown her great happiness in receiving George's lovely gift but insisted he limit such gestures to Christmas and her birthday. 'Save hard George, save for your future'.

Now two happy lads stood at the tram stop waving to her. William would not spoil this afternoon, she wouldn't let him. Annie began to sing 'Danny Boy' and pictured Victor dancing with the girls and Billy, graciously leading Catherine around the room with his one arm whilst dear Edna prayed he would not tell Mrs. Appleyard any jokes! If only Annie's eldest boy could accept their ordinary lives and not question so much. Annie sighed, William missed chances to be content and his difficult moods affected everyone. He would be sixteen in just four days, the gathering of family and friends at Tamarisk could have been an early birthday treat. If Lieutenant Olds was right then the war would be over and families reunited at last, Annie truly hoped so. Two and a half years had passed since Charles had left, it was too long, everyone wanted him back, especially William. In the meantime perhaps Celia could bring a little happiness, Annie would invite her to tea on Thursday and instruct Freddy and George to behave impeccably.

"Come in Annie bring those young men through to the sitting room, we are looking forward to the arrival of Edna and family, we are severely outnumbered by the male contingent, four more females will considerably redress the balance. Davina has declined to come, apparently a troublesome corn the size of Castle Rock has convinced her that a quiet afternoon with a book will afford her a better chance of a pain free evening. Where is William?" Catherine had suddenly realized that only two boys had followed their mother.

"I'm sorry Catherine, I did try to persuade him, he is at that awkward, self-conscious stage. I think he imagines his lack of dancing experience would cause all eyes to focus on him and William's mind will not countenance his learning to be so publicly witnessed," said Annie.

Catherine laughed, "It is such a pity, what an ideal situation in which to practice, we are none of us even slightly accomplished, as Eric observed in a rare moment of light heartedness, 'we move about the floor like fleas under the threat of DDT powder'. Robert does tend to wind the gramophone a little over enthusiastically, striking the correct tempo proves challenging. The dances Robert and I attended in the past were very gracious affairs, requiring elegance, as you well know. The accompaniment was always a group of seasoned musicians, more likely to keel over dead from being stifled by their stiffened collars, than to play a wrong note," Catherine chuckled, "I think we might well devise a new dance, we could call it a celebratory polka to mark the end of hostilities."

Freddy and George were introduced to Donald, Eric and Benjamin, the latter being Reggie's replacement, a young officer of very pleasant manner and good pedigree. Ivy had brought her own two youngsters plus John and Hilda.

"When you get home Annie, take the parcel out of the overnight bag," said Ivy, "it is William's birthday present from us all, keep it hidden until Thursday."

The bell clanged at the back door, Catherine rushed off to answer it, the medley of voices proclaimed the arrival of Edna and entourage, within minutes the gathering was completely animated. Victor looked somewhat overcome until Billy introduced him to the servicemen.

"Now lads, I want you to say 'ello to me sergeant 'ere, 'e's the best a tommy could 'ave." Billy stood to face the boy, clicked his heels and raised a salute. "All present and correct sergeant Victor."

Almost in unison Donald, Eric and Benjamin did likewise, happy to participate in Billy's fun, as they deemed it to be. For Billy, each time he saluted Victor a large measure of respect occupied his mind, it kept him close to his mates, especially Frank and Jed. It acknowledged Albert Haynes' sacrifice of health and ability but for Victor it was encouragement and his wonderful smile in response was Robert's signal to start the music and ask everyone to take their partners for the first dance. Much to Annie's amusement, Lieutenant Benjamin Carlyon made a beeline for Edna who looked especially attractive today in a floral dress which Annie had not seen before. Billy too, had noticed the young officer's intent and gave Annie a knowing wink.

"Will you dance with me Edna?" Asked Benjamin.

She looked him up and down, "I've seen more muscle on a spare rib but go on then why not." He circled her waist with his arm, "You're the first Benjamin I've ever met, knew a Ben once but that wer' short for Bendigo, 'e wer' a visitor at the Mission, black as the ace o' spades 'e wer'. Esme Tutin lodged 'im at 'er 'ouse for a month, she 'ad to go out an' buy two more lamps for 'er livin' room, she said after dark it wer' like sittin' down wi' a set o' teeth, she couldn't make out the rest of 'im but sing, 'e could sing like a linnet," said Edna and she began to hum to the music.

"My mother had a fancy for Disraeli when she was a young woman, much to father's puzzlement, although father is a die hard Tory he has always considered Disraeli an odd looking little man. I suppose we all see differently, 'a toad is a diamond in a ducks eye' and all that. When I was born, the first boy, in fact the only boy as it turned out, mother was torn between two names, thankfully she chose to name me after Benjamin Disraeli. Her other great fascination was Wolfgang Mozart, can you imagine, I would have been forced to adopt a pseudonym, no Englishman could fight the Boche with a name like Wolfgang. You have a pretty name Edna," he said with a charm that clung to his every perfectly enunciated word. He was well educated, mannerly and although of very different upbringing to Edna , his conversation was warm and entirely genuine. Edna could be no other than herself.

"I was named for me aunty Edna on me mam's side o' the family. She 'ad eleven kids, eight o' them wi' a wooden leg, a waggon run over 'er in yard. She wer' bloody tough, aunty Edna could cover the ground nearly as fast as anybody else. Like me mam said, it wer' a pity she couldn't shift fast enough to get out of uncle Walter's sight, mind you 'e only 'ad to take off 'is breeches an' 'ang 'em over the bedpost an' poor aunty Edna 'ould be in family way again. All them little 'ens, she 'ad to take in washin' to 'elp keep 'em all in food an' boots, uncle Walter worked at the Coopers, 'e wer' proud of 'is bungs, reckoned they fitted as tight as a gin but it paid bugger all. Aunty Edna wer' allus in water, the scullery floor, the cobbled yard, it used to worry 'er so every month she'd treat 'er peg leg wi' linseed oil, keep it from rottin' she thought. Uncle Walter 'ad some strange foibles, 'e allus giv' us kids a farthin' each when we went there at Christmas, 'e wer' generous like that but their fire wer' dire. One log, three nubs o' coal, 'e wouldn't put more 'an that on, it used to feel bloody freezin' in their 'ouse. Mam reckoned it wer' because 'e wer' afraid o' the sparks settin' Edna's leg afire. 'Tis a wonder she didn't die o' pneumonia years afore, she lived to be 72, it wer' some sort o' palsy took 'er in the end. Mam said nobody in the family could understand what 'e did after funeral, as soon as Edna wer' buried, uncle Walter went 'ome an put the soddin' wooden leg on the fire. Well, 'e never give a thought to all that linseed oil, it must 'ave been near saturated in the bloody stuff, blaze, God Almighty, mam says it wer' the only decent fire that grate 'ad ever seen, it took an hour for it to die down enough for the women to put the kettle on it." Edna chuckled, "Uncle Walter reckoned she come back to haunt 'im, 'e said as 'e could 'ear 'er stompin' about on the flags in the dead o' night."

"Gosh," said Benjamin, "what happened to him?"

"Oh, 'e wer' alright, lived five or six years after that but went deaf as a post, couldn't hear a bloody thing. Chimney stack crumbled on next doors 'ouse, fell through uncle Walters roof into spare bedroom, 'e never 'eard a sound, it weren't until a soddin' crow flew into 'is room an' tried to pull 'is moustache off that 'e woke up. We reckon aunt Edna must 'ave give up hauntin' 'im, 'e couldn't 'ear owt so it 'ould be a bloody waste o' time any road. I've 'eard o' that Mozart bloke, was 'e German then?" Asked Edna.

"Austrian," said Benjamin, "almost the same thing really."

"I'm more your Harry Lauder an' Marie Lloyd type meself, summat yer can sing along to," said Edna, once again humming and quietly singing to the record which just happened to be The Merry Widow Waltz, given Ivy's presence it was a most unfortunate composition but no one seemed to notice the irony.

Benjamin happily led Edna about the room until the record stopped. "Thank-you Edna, promise me another dance before Robert declares the event over."

"On one condition, you ask Annie for the next dance, me an' Annie are best friends, 'er Charles is in Egypt, where's your regiment?"

"Italy, I shall rejoin them very soon, been with them from the start, don't want to miss the last of it. Took a shot in the leg, I was lucky, it went straight through, healed well so I shall be off again soon. Too many mates over there, some living some dead. Your Billy's been through a tough time by the look of things."

"Takes a lot to get my Billy down, 'e'll manage wi' just one arm." Edna sighed, Benjamin smiled, nodded his understanding and sought Annie as the music began again.

Robert had wound the handle a little too much but the young ones whooped with delight.

"Look at Susie and Victor," said Billy, who had made sure his wife was returned to him for this dance. "What's 'e like then our Lieutenant Carlyon?" Asked Billy.

Edna grinned. "E's alright, 'e joins 'is regiment again any day, in Italy." Billy looked across the room at George and their own Annie dancing together. "Penny for 'em," said Edna.

Billy kissed Edna's cheek, held her even tighter with his one arm and whispered, "Shall we try for a boy?"

Ivy danced with Eric.

"Reggie will be alright, everyone seems to think it will soon be over, the papers are all predicting peace by Christmas. Reggie's a strong character and a clever bloke, before he joined up he worked in his dad's business, with glass, mostly stained glass like church windows and so on. Reggie told me that when he finished making a stained glass window it looked dull as ditchwater until he held it up for God to see, then every fine detail would be instantly illuminated and made perfect. Reggie said it was he who put the glass together but it was God who made all the final touches. A look of remoteness came to Eric's eyes, Ivy could feel the quivering of his fingers. Too many dark images stalked Eric's mind, God, Heaven, Death and Hell fought a constant battle behind his brow, the effort of finding some peace within drove Eric to extremes of weakness. Ivy squeezed his hand and spoke softly.

"Come with me to the kitchen, Catherine has laid out sweet biscuits and we must pour sherry for the adults and lemonade for the children, I need someone to carry the second tray."

Donald danced with Catherine, his lameness now much less severe. "I shall miss you Mrs. A., when the Captain starts his shouting I shall hear you calling us for dinner instead. When I sink my teeth into the bully beef I shall taste cracklin' and sweet soft pork. When the whistle blows I shall hear Robert put the record on and whatever obstacle they put before me I shall dance around with you in my arms."

The music stopped, he lifted her hand and kissed it. Catherine swallowed the painful lump in her throat, it would lay heavily inside her for many weeks to come but at least she could now speak.

"Surely they won't send you back, you've played your part, it can't be right," said Catherine close to tears. "What will happen to Eric, he needs to go home to his family, it could be his only hope of restoration." Catherine's thoughts were vexed. All three men were to report to their regimental headquarters in three days time.

"The army Doc. will sign Eric out Mrs. A., his innards couldn't take any more, they'll know that for sure. As for me, no show without punch, got to be there for the grand finale. Don't you fret, I'll be back to see you and Robert before too long."

Ivy and Eric appeared with a tray each, Catherine clapped her hands.

"Now help yourselves, it's just a small intake of sweetness to keep up our energy levels," declared Catherine.

The children's eyes scanned the tray, there were shortbreads, brandy snaps, coconut rings, Grantham gingerbreads and macaroons. Victor had delved in eagerly to locate his favourite, a coconut ring. George roguishly demonstrated his ability to roll his tongue and push its tip through the middle of a coconut ring where it became affixed and moved from side to side of

George's mouth as he waved it like an eye on a stalk. Victor at once copied the mischief, his determination to get the biscuit to stay on the end of his tongue caused the most comical contortions but his persistence paid off and he waved the coconut ring from side to side so fast that it flew off and landed in the middle of a Maidenhair Fern on top of a jardinière beside the wall. Just for that instant Victor was afraid he had done a bad thing and his lower lip began to quiver but everyone burst into laughter which intensified when Edna bit into a macaroon and a flaked almond fell into the bodice of her frock. Edna quickly turned away, retrieved the wayward piece of nut and with a big grin popped it into Billy's mouth. It brought a welcome smile back to Eric's face and Victor carefully removed his biscuit from the plant then sucked on it with simple contentment. The sherry warmed everyone's spirit, a fire crackled in the hearth, the room had become very warm, the normally pale cheeks glowed a healthy pink and Annie found herself dancing with Billy when Robert again cranked the gramophone.

"I had a letter from Charles yesterday," said Annie. "he wrote that I should tell you he had met Alfie Cresswell, Alfie was injured but not too seriously." She went on to relate the events as described by Charles.

Billy laughed. "Poor ol' six feet, 'e's allus 'ad trouble wi' 'is arse, 'e's managed to keep 'isself alive thank God. I look forward to seein' 'im when 'e gets 'ome. I'll ask Edna to make a special cushion for 'im, just to show there's no 'ard feelin's, so to speak."

Freddy now danced with Susie. The girl had blossomed since her dad had come home and stood almost as tall as her elder sister Annie. Her fair hair still determined to grow completely waveless nevertheless framed her face perfectly, the lack of curl caused no slight to her prettiness and her childlike naivety, although lost on the youthful Freddy, would have charmed any older man into utter submission.

"Why are posh girls different to ordinary girls Freddy?" Asked Susie, confident that her all time friend, now a working man would have the answer to her quandary.

"How do you mean, different?" Replied Freddy.

"Well Joe Spooner says that girls who live at The Park and The Ropewalk have a china and us Sherwood girls have a fanny."

For a few seconds Freddy was baffled, then realized why Susie was confused. "No, you've got the wrong word, posh girls have a vagina. It's all the same thing really, like at the farm, Arthur Cropley's mare is at the top rank of importance, he couldn't manage without her. Now she'd have a vagina and the cows and sows have fannies."

"So, Mrs. Appleyard has a vagina then," said Susie.

A little nonplussed, Freddy said, "Yes," and quickly changed the subject.

The five youngsters had danced themselves to exhaustion, refusing to be still even when the music stopped. Now tiredness found Liza, Molly, Hilda, Harold and John slowing down before the record finished. Robert announced the last waltz of the afternoon. Edna was obliged to honour her promise to dance once more with Benjamin. Annie found herself with Eric but Freddy was quite innocently seized upon by Catherine.

"I must claim this waltz with the handsome young Freddy Eddowes," she declared and took his hand. Freddy could feel the heat advancing up his neck to his cheeks where it burned ruddy red. To find himself partnering who he deemed to be the highest ranking female in the room seemed suddenly to have become an acute mortification. His arms were not long enough to lead this tall lady about the room with a formal distance between her and himself. His nether regions developed a will of their own and Freddy Eddowes felt his very first flush of manhood as his mind clung in desperation to a 'china'. If anyone noticed his blushes then they made no comment and when all the goodbyes had been said and they walked away from The Ropewalk, Freddy felt an overwhelming need for familiar things, he'd clean out the chicken house, gather the eggs and play Danny Boy as he'd never played before.

Annie had finally persuaded Edna to leave the last of the dishes and take the girls home. Billy had already gone with Victor. It had been a busy day, William was alone when they returned and Annie had not asked about Celia in front of the others but Annie's few minutes spent with Byron had confirmed Celia's presence earlier in the afternoon. The weeds were all gone, everything was neat and tidy, across the small gravels which spelled Byron, two sprigs of Cotoneaster, covered in bright red berries, had been lovingly laid. William would not have thought to do that without Annie's suggestion. Celia Tozer obviously had a sensitive side to her nature, the notion pleased Annie.

A letter addressed to Charles was propped against the mantel clock. "I've not sealed the envelope so you can write tonight and put your letter in with mine. I'll post it on my way to work in the morning." William looked expectantly at Annie, he anticipated a quizzing.

"I have two accounts to finalise for the Basford workshop, you can post those too," was all she said.

William had missed a good time at Tamarisk, telling him what they had done there would mean little to him, Annie knew that, she was tired, too weary to examine his hospitality toward Celia. If he had written to his dad and tended Byron's grave then he had done as she asked and more. Running the business in Charles' absence had been hard enough but overseeing William's transition to manhood was a duty she would not be sorry to hand back to Charles, she dared to believe it might soon be possible.

Somewhat reluctantly, William had agreed to ask Celia for tea but only on the condition that George refrained from singing his usual rude ditty and that Freddy would not rush his food and burp at the table.

Annie left Winchester Street early to allow herself time to go to Basford and do the banking yet be home to prepare a nice spread for the boy's sixteenth. William had pretended to be not the slightest bit interested in his birthday, he was past all that silly excitement. Annie however, had caught him looking in the sideboard where he knew she put any presents for safekeeping. A parcel from Davina and Ivy, one from Edna and family, another from Sarah and the girls, her own from them all, tormented his curiosity where they lingered on the shelf above the best crockery.

Today the wind carried a bite, Annie pulled her collar around her ears, she had been too busy to shop for herself, her shoes were worn thin and the cold pavement transferred its chill to her toes. It was always warm in the bank at least, those few minutes should allow her nose to shed its tinge of blue and her feet to regain some sense of feel. As she approached the bank, two men left the premises urgently, muttering as they hurried past. Annie heard one say.

"Shouldn't be allowed in a public place, enough to frighten a woman to death, 'twas once that folk were locked up for less."

Annie opened the door on a commotion, several people stood transfixed whilst something took place before them.

"Edwin?" Annie saw a man on the floor, his entire body shook with spasm, no one appeared to be making any attempt to help him, Annie knelt beside Edwin, his tongue seemed to flail within his cheeks, his eyes rolled to the tops of their sockets showing alarming dominance of white. She grabbed his arms as he writhed, his head swung violently from side to side, his back arched like a fatally injured animal trying desperately to defy death. His strength seemed to increase beyond the capacity of his being, it was as much as Annie could do to hold him down, to prevent him from physically damaging himself. A fine line of blood escaped from one corner of his mouth, his lips tight closed. "It's alright Edwin, you will be alright." Annie tried to calm him, to reassure him, a wet patch crept across the front of his trousers. "Could we clear the bank for just a few minutes, please Mr. Birkett?"

Annie's authority over the situation was welcomed by the inert manager who at once ushered the assembly of shocked clients to the door and on to the street. Finally, Edwin's seizure subsided, his tortured body became still.

Annie loosened her grip on his arms and gently smoothed his brow. His expression for several seconds was blank, only very slowly did awareness of people and place return to his mind. Edwin opened his eyes and made a vain attempt at speaking but no words would form. His teeth had punctured his tongue in one place, Annie sat him up and wiped the blood from his lips with her hanky.

Embarrassment and dismay consumed him, Annie felt compassion for Edwin but intolerance towards the bank officials who stood by without even a meagre gesture of help.

"You are intelligent gentlemen, could your ability and discretion not extend to your colleague?" Annie's tone revealed her condemnation.

"Perhaps you could escort your friend home now that he is partially recovered Mrs. Eddowes, you do seem most aptly disposed to the task," said Gerald Birkett.

"With respect sir, I have no knowledge of Mr. Garbett's address, therefore escorting him home would prove extremely difficult, further more I must be at Hood Street in time for my children's return from school. You however hold the details of Mr. Garbett's address, Edwin being in your employ."

The manager, suitably contrite, expressed his gratitude for Annie's assistance through the distressing incident and authorised a clerk to call a cab to take Edwin home.

"Mr.Carter will accompany his colleague, you can be sure that we shall see he reaches home safely." He walked Annie to the door. "Tell me my dear, how is Mr. Eddowes, might we hope Charles will be returning to us all before too long." Gerald Birkett annoyed Annie, he was so patently shallow.

"Charles thankfully writes that he is well, those of us whom have kept loved ones through this war and are ourselves of sound health must be truly grateful to the fate which so favoured us, don't you agree Mr. Birkett?" Said Annie. He nodded, offering a contrived smile. Annie turned to look at Edwin, now sitting silently on a chair.

"Goodbye," she called back, "it is William's birthday today, he is sixteen."

As Annie walked into the wind's bite once again she pondered her last words. Why had she mentioned William's birthday, what relevance did it have to the situation. Edwin would have thought it strange and as for Gerald Birkett, he must have considered it entirely removed from the nature of such a circumstance. Annie sighed and quickened her pace.

She laid a table of good wholesome fare and placed the various packages for William by his plate, envelopes too. Annie's natural curiosity had made her count their number, eight cards. Hilda and John played with a puzzle in the living room. George was first back from work, followed soon after by Freddy, William as yet, had not made an appearance. Annie while she had a chance took George and Freddy aside and spoke firmly.

"One day you will feel as William does now, it is all part of growing up. Celia is joining us for tea you will behave sensibly and kindly, not just to her but to your older brother too. It is good to have fun sometimes, it is important that we learn to laugh at ourselves but today we shall cause no embarrassment, do you promise that you will not provoke him?"

Freddy still carried the memory of his dance with Catherine Appleyard and readily agreed his compliance. George grinned but recognising his mother's genuine concern, gave his word.

The chickens were fed and shut up for the night, Celia had arrived more than half an hour ago, everyone was hungry but still no William. Not knowing what else to do Annie bid them all sit to the table and eat. If William was not there within the hour, then she would go in search of him. Perhaps some of the men at Player's had come to learn of his birthday and delayed his walk home. Poor Celia had clutched a small package and an envelope since arriving, now she placed them with the others on the table, she made a pathetic spectacle as she nibbled on a piece of bread and butter, gazing down at a slice of gammon ham on the table before her as though if she focused her eyes sufficiently it might be transformed and William would then appear, sitting cross legged in the middle of her plate, encircled by the pattern of green ivy leaves and gold rim. At last, just on the hour, the back door opened and the errant celebrity made his entrance. Annie resisted to demand an explanation, it was Celia's feelings she wished to spare, instead she said,

"We were so hungry William we just had to start but you will soon catch up, come and sit down, we are eager to discover the contents of all your parcels."

His demeanour was gruff, he pulled up a chair, noisily. "So what would you have me do first, eat to catch up or satisfy your nosiness?" He looked intently at Annie, he made her feel uncomfortable, she took a deep breath.

"On top of the pile is Celia's gift and card, I really think you should apologise to her for being so late and ask if she still wishes for you to open them."

William turned to Celia. "Well, is that what you want?"

His abruptness startled her, she simply nodded and this time took a generous bite of bread. He opened his presents and cards, uttered a subdued thank-you then took up his knife and fork. Hilda had been so looking forward to William discovering his parcel, she had made him a case, all by herself for his new pen knife, that was a gift from the boys. Annie had given him a fob watch. Davina and Ivy had sent him a very smart blue waistcoat. Edna and family had very carefully wrapped a model locomotive, a replica of a G.W.R. engine. Sarah and the girls had brought him handkerchiefs, a tie, socks, braces and garters. Celia's package had contained a bottle of cologne. His dismissive approach to these items, given with such love, now brought tears to Hilda's eyes, Annie smiled at her youngest and diverted the child's thoughts with a promise of three chapters from Gulliver's Travels in Lilliput when she was washed and ready for bed.

"Come on now, you too John there is school tomorrow. You older ones can chat together, say goodnight."

Two timid voices responded with a sad, weary goodnight, directed almost entirely at Celia, even at their tender age they felt sorry for the pleasant young woman.

Annie purposefully prolonged their preparations for bed and read four chapters of their book. It was favourable to being downstairs in the atmosphere created by William's surly mood. When she eventually returned to the kitchen she found Celia clearing away the dishes with George and Freddy. William sat alone in the living room, his cards stood along the mantelpiece, his presents lay forlornly on the sideboard.

"I'm going to walk Celia home now," he said.

"What has happened William?" Asked Annie. "You seemed happy enough this morning."

"Why did you have to step in at the bank today, what had it got to do with you. People are saying that you were on your knees attending Edwin Garbett when he threw some sort of fit."

"Would you have preferred me to leave him without help?" Replied Annie sharply. "Is that really what you would have chosen for me to do?"

"Well no one else poked their nose in from what I hear. Will you tell dad about it in your next letter or will you overlook that bit of news?"

He stood and walked from the room, as Annie watched him cross the hallway she felt that in spite of the passed sixteen years, the heartache, all the love and life they had shared, she really didn't know this young man at all.

CHAPTER FOURTEEN

Annie could smell tobacco smoke, it drifted around the corner of the house to meet her, John and Hilda had smelled it too and looked up at their mother curiously. William stood outside the back door, he drew on a cigarette and as they reached him he sent a plume of smoke into the air. Hilda was wide eyed, this was something new and different, William had never smoked before.

"May as well, they're all I see for hours on end every day. Don't worry, it's only a 'Weight', nothing hardly in the bugger, now someday when I show this City what William Eddowes is really made of I shall be smoking the big ones. Reg Yeats calls them, 'the better kind'. You don't see many of them on the streets or in the pubs, they lay in silver cases, tucked inside the pockets of fine cut suits. They don't get lit with a sulphur, oh no, at one side of the waistcoat there's the watch and chain and at the other, fitting neatly into the pocket there's a lighter, initialled by an engraver." William drew again on the cigarette and as the smoke was momentarily confused by a gust of wind, he said, "You need to know which way you want to head, W.C.E., that's what shall be inscribed on mine and an elegant scrolled pattern, something classy. Aim high John, isn't that right Mam?"

William rubbed his hand over young John's hair and smiled at Annie. He had shown little ambition in the past so if William had at last raised his sights it could only be a good thing, yet Annie felt unease.

"If we are fortunate, then endeavour and effort are rewarded with success and those enviable comforts which make life less harsh, but these must be earned, that is why seldom is such 'manna' the property of the young, years of application are first needed to achieve it."

Annie returned William's smile, Hilda, fascinated by her elder brother's most recent behaviour, stood beneath the smoke, intent on his every move until her nose, irritated by the tobacco fumes produced a hefty sneeze.

"Does it taste as good as aniseed William, you can have one of my aniseed balls if you like," said Hilda, reaching into her pocket for the small paper bag.

William stubbed out the butt, laughed and produced a threepenny bit, handing it to Hilda he said. "You can buy some more of those when you go to the shop, I'll wait 'til I can have some of 'the better kind'." He lifted the bag of shopping from Annie's arm and carried it inside.

Since armistice Nottingham's folk had revelled, wept, argued and celebrated through a diversity of emotions. A few weary, battle scarred men had returned, many more were still abroad or in transit. Families waited anxiously and those in high office promised every good thing would welcome the City's sons. William listened to these prophesies, he recalled his father's prediction in the letter, 'Things will be different when I come home, better, you'll see son'.

Celia had forgiven William's lack of courtesy that evening of his birthday. His arm about her waist and his searching kisses which explored her neck, her ears, for stray doubts before planting his own lips over hers, sealing any way of escape, tracing the lining of her mouth with his tongue, satisfied William that not a single breath of uncertainty had found release and convinced Celia of his devotion, she was captivated, entirely at his bidding.

Her father was a shoemaker, late in life marrying he had been too old to go to war and had fathered only one other child, a boy, two years younger than Celia and still attending Blackmore's school. Jessie Tozer was a respectable man, quietly successful and of pleasant nature. His wife Gwendolyn was a cousin of Robert Cheetham. Twelve years his wife's senior he had done with strutting and posing, that male characteristic which through the process of parading brilliance and charm could often lead to physical scraps in order to claim the territory. He was master of his craft and at peace with his lot. Gwendolyn, while not a raving beauty, nevertheless cut an elegant figure about town but her need of knowing everything about everybody, limited her circle of friends to those of a similar ilk. Celia displayed softer features than her mother and the gentler disposition of her father.

"There's a bit of a 'do' at The Institute tonight, I told Tommy Spooner to come but I don't suppose he will. When he isn't working at Handley's he's either washing up glasses at The Standard or bagging up coal in Jenkin's yard, poor bugger never stops," said William, peering into the bag. "Good, you've bought some tunny fish, I like that better than pilchards, doesn't make the bread soggy, you'd be surprised how soft the sandwiches can be by dinner time. Ernie Searle's mam put ripe Colwick cheese and pickled cabbage in his the other day, the bread had soaked up that much juice, by knocking off time he had to suck them off the paper. Reg Yeat's said, 'Are yer tryin' to plait watta' lad, you'll not manage that, 'tis only Yorkshire folk as can do the like'. One bloke heard him, Percy Fosdyke, he comes from Harrogate and he called out to Reg, 'Us Yorkshire men learned th'ard way, 'ad to plait watta' afore us could walk on watta', a true Yorkshire man'll not let a little thing like watta' get in 'is way'." William chuckled. "Steve Wainwright's brother is home, got back this morning."

With that William went up to his bedroom leaving Annie with the good news. Gertie had obviously not been aware when she had spoken with Annie at Basford earlier in the day. It would be a great source of happiness for Gertie to go home to and Clara would be overjoyed.

Although it seemed unlikely that Charles would return to them before the end of the year at the earliest, William had taken on a much improved demeanour. Annie at times, felt the boy set off to his work each day half expecting his dad to be waiting for him at the factory gates, seeking his first born to greet and hold before spreading his love more thinly between the rest of the family. William carried within himself a guilt, a torment, which despite Annie's assurances he could not drive from his mind, the belief that he, William, had sent his dad to war. He wanted nothing as much as Charles' safe return. What he would have done had Charles been killed he could hardly bear to contemplate. At times he searched for someone else to blame, to take this burden of guilt from his shoulders, to rid himself of the doubts and know that his dad loved him first and foremost. Now Charles' homecoming was spoken of with confidence, William had allowed himself to be less perplexed, not so preoccupied with insecurities. Since his tantrum on his birthday there had been no evidence of displeasure or outbursts of ill temper, he had chosen instead to say nothing at all when Annie told him that the bank had dismissed Edwin from his post.

When on her second visit to the bank following the incident there was still no sign of Edwin Annie had inquired of the teller as to Edwin's health. The man had gone through to a back room and returned with Gerald Birkett.

'Would you care to come to my office for a moment Mrs. Eddowes', he had led Annie to a rather grand room, heavily panelled in oak, his chair almost throne like, his desk furnished with a splendid paper knife with an onyx handle, an ink pot and pen to match, the blotting pad bound at the corners in rich dark leather. A photograph of a lady, presumably Mrs. Birkett, a choker of pearls about her neck at least two inches deep or more, but to redeem him somewhat, evidence of his simpler side, a small dish of caramels, a newspaper opened at the sports fixtures. He cleared his throat and held the small chair for Annie to sit.

'It was with regret that I informed Edwin of my decision. You will doubtless consider my action to be harsh and unworthy but I must safeguard my staff and clients from such distressing scenes. I assure you Mrs. Eddowes I took no personal satisfaction from the outcome, I do in fact have regard for Edwin Garbett, he is honest, capable and affable, unfortunately, through no fault of his own, he is not reliable. For that reason only I could do no other. I have written an excellent character reference for him, I cannot commend his health, no more can he, his integrity will not permit him to offer his services without mention of his epilepsy I feel sure. We can only hope that a position, which does not require the applicant to be directly involved with the public might present itself'.

Gerald Birkett had smiled at Annie and tendered his plea of mitigation. While she felt intense disappointment for Edwin, he had worked at the bank for many years, inwardly she could not deny the severe shock a fit might give to an onlooker, especially one unused to and unaware of the condition. Annie had acknowledged Gerald Birkett's courtesy, thanking him for his time in explaining.

When Annie had related these events to William, he had for the entire five minutes or so, sat at the table, his fingers fidgeting with his penknife, opening the blade and closing it over and over. When she fell silent , he had put the knife back in the case which Hilda had made and said. 'Do you think dad will join The Lodge when he gets home, Celia's dad goes there, Reg Yeats scoffs at it, he says the Masons is only like Boys Brigade except the Brigade is 'Sure and Steadfast' while the Masons is ever open to friendly persuasion'.

To read the course of William's thinking proved too difficult and time consuming so Annie had replied as best she could, suggesting Charles' immediate concern would be his children, everything else would evolve as life intended.

Now William's voice called down to her from the landing. "Do you think my new waistcoat is too smart for The Institute?"

Annie stood at the foot of the stairs. "What is the occasion?" She asked.

"One of the men is leaving Players, he's going to Huttoft to work on his uncle's farm, Reg says we'll have a sing song to wish him well and a few drinks to give him a good send off," replied William.

"You aren't supposed to be drinking alcohol at your age, surely Mr.

Yeats knows that," said Annie anxiously.

"It's alright," said William, wrapping his hands around the knob on top of the newel post as though he moulded it to shape as he spoke, "Reg says all the beer is watered down now anyway so we young ones can have two halves of mild and it would still be less than a glass of communion wine."

Annie sighed, "Wear your blue waistcoat you will feel good in that."

William stepped inside The Institute and was knocked back by the smoke, blimey, he thought, he had stood on Bobbers Mill bridge when The Jolly Fisherman, No.80080, passed underneath and it had been several minutes before he could see Tommy a few yards along but even that didn't compare with this dense cloud of tobacco fumes. The voices of men becoming gradually imbued by Wrenshaw's cocktail of malt and hops filtered through the haze and loud, raucous laughter erupted randomly across the room as the punch line of a joke drove their abandon further and tales of past exploits, vividly embellished, were bandied from group to group.

"Come on lad, I'll buy yer a drink." Reg Yeat's strong hand came down on William's shoulder and he steered him through the throng to a small bar at the far end. "Give the lad half 'o mild Jack," he turned to look at William with a smile on his face. "Don't want your ma' comin' after me with a complaint, she's not yer everyday sort o' lady is she?" Said Reg.

"William felt embarrassed, "She's not my real mam, just my step mother, my own mother died when I was eighteen months old."

Reg looked intently at William. "Well lad, I reckon you can think yourself lucky, my mam kicked me arse out the door the very day I were thirteen. I got a job barrowin' on a building site, from then I 'ad to be responsible for meself. Oh yes, I went home of an evenin', got fed an' watered an' bedded down for the night but mam's attentions 'ad to pass down the line to the next eldest. Sometimes I felt like I could 'ave vanished from the face o' the earth an' nobody 'ould 'ave noticed. I wer' bright enough an' a cussed little sod, made me way an' done alright, but 'this'," Reg's voice shook with emotion, "'this' lad," his finger pointed at the birthmark, "how many different names do you suppose there could be for men to call 'this'. ' Little Reggie face afire', 'freak cheek', 'cats lights', I've 'eard the lot an' what I would 'ave giv' for me mam to 'ave come to that place just to see if I wer' 'appy in a man's world. Mrs. Eddowes isn't the woman as birthed yer, so what, as a mother she's a bloody good 'en, so drink up lad an' count yer blessin's." Reggie raised his glass. "To mothers past an' mothers present."

William watched as the Adam's apple rose and fell with each swallow, not until every drop was gone did Reg lower the glass to the bar, a swipe of his lips with the back of his hand and a deep breath of satisfaction seemed to be for William's benefit.

"Welcome to a man's world William Eddowes, get that down yer neck, we've all got to sing, *'To Be a Farmer's Boy'*, to Alf. With that he slapped William on the back and moved away across the room.

William was pensive, his first intake of alcohol had freed his imagination. Wonder if there are any more red marks on Reg's body, perhaps his face is just one of several, he thought to himself, Reg might even be piebald like the gipsy ponies at the fairground. William stared into his empty glass as though it were a crystal ball.

"BOO!" He near' jumped out of his skin. "You wer' miles away, bet it wer' that Celia you was thinkin' about, you'll go 'boz-eyed', that's what me mam allus says when she thinks I'm lettin' me imagination run away wi' me, I can't help it, my Rosie 'as got the sort o' bosom makes yer want to bury yer 'ead in. I sometimes think I could 'appily die o' suffocation, a sort o' sacrificial stiflin' in the name o' Spoonerism." Tommy's big grin beamed at William.

"A Spoonerism is an accidental transposition of sounds in adjacent words, don't you remember Mr. Dunn teaching us that?" Said William.

"No I bloody well don't, you soddin' clever dick Eddowes, what was yer thinkin' about anyroad?"

"Ponies, piebald ponies," replied William. "Come on, I'll buy you half of mild, then we've got to sing to Alf so he'll have something to remember when he's planting mangolds and shovelling dung at Huttoft."

The two young friends eventually tired of the noisy dialogue which seemed to move up a decibel each time the barman opened his till. Outside in the air, the familiar streets and arched entries where childhood games had been played seemed altogether more sociable than the 'social' which they had just left. They stopped to have a cigarette, neither of them had lit up in The Institute. Under the soft light of the street lamp they leaned against the wall, quietly enjoying the comfortable silence, after a few minutes, Tommy cast his eyes over William's waistcoat.

"That's a bit 'o new innit?"

"Birthday present from Davina Wright and Ivy," said William.

"Ah, very nice too, a real Celia pleaser I reckon that is," said Tommy.

"What do you mean by that?" Asked William.

"Well, she's the sort as wouldn't feel spoiled sittin' wi' a bag o' chips an' a pickled egg on killin' 'ouse wall, now I'm not sayin' there's 'owt wrong wi' 'er, she's very nice, but my Rosie thinks fourpenneth wi' salt an' vinegar an' a cuddle behind Walter Ingram's Angel is just what the doctor ordered of a Saturday night." Said Tommy.

"You don't mean to say that you take Rosie into the Churchyard, that's creepy," William was genuinely shocked.

"No it isn't, me poor dad God rest is soul, wherever it is, used to say, 'if they didn't bother yer in life then they aren't goin' to bother yer in death'. Well Walter Ingram never bothered me nor Rosie, she reckons she's only done what her sister done but the other way round. Rosie would 'ave 'ad another older sister but the baby only lived three days, 'er mam told Rosie, 'she's gone wi' an Angel'. My Rosie says she's come wi' an Angel." Tommy laughed wickedly.

"Bloody Hell Tommy, you didn't really do it did you?" Asked an incredulous William.

"Only the once, we didn't mean to. It wer' one evenin' last summer, Rosie 'ave been regular since so she's alright. We sat on the grass, just around from Walter Ingram where if you look between the headstones yer can see the top o' Castle in the distance. Rosie wer' pickin' daisies an' threadin' 'em, you know, like girls do, well, all of a sudden she starts shoutin', 'there's summat crawlin' in me knickers', she wer' frantic. By the time she called out, 'it's crawlin' 'ere an' creepin' there an' named the spot it 'ad got to afore she dropped 'er drawers in desperation to shake the little bugger out I 'ad an 'ard on like Nobby Green's donkey!" 'I can't walk 'ome wi' you lookin' like that' she said, 'you'll 'ave to do summat', so we did. It wer' bloody earwig's fault, it 'ould never 'ave 'appened else."

"You were lucky to get away with it," said William, still feeling stunned.

"That's what Rosie said, so she's limited me activities, anythin' below the bosom's out o' bounds, she reckons I cant do much 'arm in the bosom area," Tommy grinned, "I tell yer what Will, it's a bloody good compromise. 'Ave yer 'eard when your ol' man's likely to be back yet?"

"No, you'd think they'd send him home soon wouldn't you, he's been gone for years, do you think he'll look different?" Asked William.

Tommy sniffed and thought for a few seconds. "Bit older, out there in all that 'eat he'll probably look a bit brown an'all. Do yer remember when Archie Clark come back from Cleethorpes the summer afore last, 'e wer' colour o' Virol. I reckon anybody as didn't know 'is mam would 'ave giv' 'er a few funny looks until it wore off. Anyroad, I best be on me way, we got two coffins to put together in the mornin', one of 'em a great big bugger, six foot tall 'e wer' an' built like a brick shithouse. Real nice bloke though, giv' me a penny more 'an once for 'eavin' im on to footplate o' tram." Tommy stubbed out his cigarette end. "See-yer Will," he walked away down Sherwood Road, hands in his pockets, whistling, 'To Be a Farmer's Boy'.

William watched his friend growing smaller as his figure became more distant. A cat strolled from an entry and rubbed itself about William's trouser leg before crossing the road and disappearing into the darkness. Something glinted on the pavement a few yards along, he walked over to it, a tanner, I don't know how Tommy missed that, William thought to himself. Then he remembered the evening Tommy and the others had come to the house carol singing, Charles had put down his newspaper, felt in his pocket and given them each a sixpenny piece. William could do nothing to stop the tears which rolled down his cheeks.

"Come home dad, come home soon," he spoke to the coin as if it were the very same one Charles had put in Tommy's hand all those many months ago, wiping his tears with one hand he held tightly in the palm of the other the shiny sixpence, his fingers lovingly secured its passage all the way to Hood Street.

CHAPTER FIFTEEN

"Let me have your coats, you can play by the fire, your brothers will be home soon." Annie hung up their coats and went quickly to the living room, she had laid papers and sticks in the grate before leaving, she had only to light it.

To find Ivy so happy had pleased Annie greatly, Davina's generous nature enabled her to sincerely rejoice with Ivy and the children but Annie knew the loneliness which must follow could not be far from Davina's mind. Reggie was back from the war and eager to resume work with his father. He had written to say he would visit and yesterday, amid tears, laughter, remembrance and hope, Reggie had asked Ivy to be his wife.

'If this war has taught me anything then it is the realization that every day is precious and not one can be guaranteed'. He had kissed Molly and shaken Harold's hand. Ivy had accepted with a flood of tearful emotion but they were happy and no one would express anything other than genuine pleasure at their engagement. There was much to plan and arrange, somewhere for them to live, close to Reggie's work, school for the children but for the present, both would be content in the knowledge of their love. Molly and Harold would be closely observed for any sign of apprehension, as yet they had displayed only excitement. The children liked Reggie and trusted him, Annie believed they would accept it all quite readily. She had experienced that sense of uncertainty, the self doubt which plagued the already vulnerable mind at such a time. For Ivy however, Annie felt confident that Reggie's obvious devotion might make the passage to this new life a little easier than her own had been, she did hope so.

George and Freddy had gone to visit Bertha with eggs and apples. William was with Celia at the embankment, or at least that had been his intention on leaving the house just after dinner. The fire soon crackled life and leaving John and Hilda to their snakes n' ladders, Annie put the kettle and flat iron on the range then set about the pile of shirts and linen.

Charles had written that with any luck he could be home before Christmas, now at the middle of December it began to feel a very real probability. Men were returning, they would arrive on the streets and be immediately soaked up by their families, so thirsty were they for that first taste of life giving nourishment the men disappeared like water into a sponge, seemingly for days before wives and children finally quenched, would sit back satisfied and a few at a time, men, often bewildered and strangely timid, trickled free.

Annie folded William's shirt and lay it on a chair, a knock came at the back door, carefully placing the iron back on the heat she crossed the scullery to answer the knock. Edwin Garbett stood in the yard, a nervous smile came to his face.

"Hello Annie," he said. "I have wrestled for weeks over what to do."

"Come inside out of the cold." Annie noticed how pale he looked and thinner in the face.

"You're busy I can see, I won't hinder you," said Edwin.

"The kettle has just boiled, I am about to make some tea so please, sit down for a few minutes at least, you need to warm yourself. I felt the temperature dropping as we walked from the tram stop. We called on Davina Wright at The Park this afternoon, I feel guilty at neglecting her of late but always I fight the clock, especially through the week. It will be easier when Charles gets back."

"Is he well, surely it cannot be too long now, Charles seems to have been absent for ages, the children have certainly grown, he will see such a difference, especially in the older boys." Said Edwin.

"Things are still quite confused in Egypt, some men will need to remain there well into next year. Because Charles has five children which he has not seen for two and a half years they hope he will be aboard a troopship in time to land on our shores by Christmas, in fact if it is to be so, then he will almost certainly be at sea as we speak."

Edwin watched as Annie took cups from the dresser and reached up for the tea caddy on the shelf. He felt embarrassed to think of this woman, so slight of build, holding him down, keeping him from harm.

"I wanted to call that same week, to thank you for what they told me you had done. I'm afraid my own recollection is pathetically vague but how could I present myself, I was quite convinced that you would not welcome any contact whatsoever following such a debacle. These weeks have passed to months and despite my very real misgivings, I could not let the year end without saying thank you Annie, thank you so much." His fingers shook and the cup rattled in the saucer as he took it from Annie's extended hand. "Thank you," he said again.

Annie laughed, "You have no need of so many thanks Edwin, simply one for the tea is sufficient," she sat at the end of the table, the old ironing blanket and shirts lay at the other. Edwin sipped the warming cup, he had a fragility about him. "I am sorry to hear about your job, have you found another position?" Annie asked

"I am on trial at Jacobson's. If I can go a month without growing fangs and sprouting fur then Mr.Jacobson might remove my leash and even pay me a wage. I do at least have a reasonable grasp of figures and accounts. There I am able to work in a room out of sight and hopefully, out of mind, I imagine the name Edwin Garbett strikes terror at the slightest mention but tucked away behind the scenes as I am there, in time this traumatized population may achieve to forget."

He raised his eyes from the table where he had fixed his gaze on a strangely formed knot in the pine, its dark features and extended contours seemed to stare back at him like the one eyed Cyclops.

"If I fail this test then I shall travel the roads to wherever fate may take me, as dear Mr. Macawber would say, 'Something will turn up'." He grinned.

"And what of your mother if you should adopt this nomadic lifestyle?" Annie looked at Edwin quizzically.

"Don't you think she might welcome the chance to be free of her son's madness?" He replied.

"What I honestly think Edwin, is that you have no understanding of mothers, absolutely none at all." Annie rose to her feet to take the iron off the heat.

"No, please don't delay your ironing, I must go now. I am truly delighted to hear that Charles is very close to home at last."

Annie stood at the doorway, Edwin turned, raised his hand to wave and called out, "Goodbye, have a very happy Christmas."

Annie stepped out into the yard to wave back, "Good luck at Jacobson's."

She shivered, the kitchen was warm, just those few seconds outside had made her feel chill. She spread George's shirt across the old blanket and welcomed that sense of warmth as the iron travelled over the cloth. Annie was pleased to learn that Edwin had found work, Isaac Jacobson, an accountant, had the reputation of being a stickler for correctness and for being not the most philanthropic of souls. Annie sighed, Edwin had once been a colleague of Charles' at the bank after all, they should go out for a drink together every once in a while. If Clem was, as Annie feared, no longer alive, then Charles could do a lot worse than make a friend of Edwin.

William had walked Celia safely back to her door but declined her invitation to go in, suggesting it would be less than polite to appear now, so close to Sunday tea time. Celia had accepted his decision with good grace and they had parted company with a kiss at the front gate.

Gwendolyn Tozer had an insatiable curiosity and on the previous Sunday, earlier in the afternoon, she had interrogated William as though she were some kind of official responsible for national security. He had left feeling unsure as to whether Mrs. Tozer's questioning was to satisfy her concerns as to the Eddowes' pedigree or if she was indeed the appointed inquisitor to King George.

William liked Jessie Tozer, a very mild mannered man, he had shown him the workshop where he created all manner of footwear. The smells of leather and Dubbin, the rows of tools, neatly stored to be instantly available when he needed them. Boxes of nails and tacks all fascinated William but most intriguing of all was the array of circular needles, all of varying thickness and strength. Jessie's apron was so shiny from the polish which had impregnated the cloth, it hung on the hook catching the light from the window. William ran his fingers up and down a pair of sleek riding boots, they took his thoughts to grand places, well heeled individuals pursuing a lifestyle which reflected success and wealth, he tried to estimate in his mind, the boots' worth to Jessie Tozer, considerable no doubt. If he had made sensible enquiry of Jessie, then William's overly rich imagination might have been tempered by the answer. Work boots made up the majority of the items and provided the shoemaker with his daily bread, a reliance on riding boots for gentlemen and elegant dance shoes for the ladies would have provided a much less secure future.

William was still day dreaming as he walked home, ever searching for something as yet out of reach. When he turned the corner into Hood Street, walking towards him was Edwin Garbett, they drew closer and met.

"Have you been to our house?" Asked William tersely.

"Yes, I have," replied Edwin, I needed to thank your mother for her kindness when I was unwell at the bank. I should have come before, it is very remiss on my part not to have done so but today I decided it could be delayed no longer." He smiled warmly but William's expression offered no pleasantness in return.

"Father will be home at any time, it could even be this evening, we are all eager to see him."

"So I understand, you have waited a long time William, I am genuinely pleased that this Christmas will be a very special one for you all." Edwin sensed that there would be no attempt at further conversation by William, he nodded and wished the young man well, walking on towards Sherwood Road.

William turned his head to observe Edwin's progress. He had no reason to resent this man, Edwin Garbett, the man who throws fits, yet William did resent him, Edwin had no business here at Hood Street, or at The Meadows picking blackberries or in the arboretum feeding the pigeons. If William held such power as to banish the likes of Edwin Garbett then he would, he would drive him from the city with no hope of return. It made no sense, not to William, this feeble man should have perished years ago from one of his dire seizures, why did he still live when William's own mother had died of that most natural of events, from bearing a child. William kicked a piece of crumpled paper along the pavement until he reached No.14. 'Things will be different, better, you'll see son'. He leaned against the wall and lit a cigarette, his mood was only prevented from sinking further into anguish by the approach of Freddy and George.

"Got something for you William, it's a surprise from Bertha." George's glee at finding William immediately present bubbled over as he stepped in front of his older brother, he had anticipated having to wait for William's return from Celia's to see the reaction to Bertha's gift. George had been standing with his hands behind his back, now quick as a flash, he produced a bowler hat.

"It was Mr. Duffin's, Bertha says now you're walking out with a young lady and working alongside men you are entitled to dress accordingly. Put it on Will, go on, let's see what it looks like," the eager George pleaded with the moody William, almost dancing with excitement.

William looked at it, brushed his hand over the nap on the rim and placed it, slightly askew, on his head. He drew on his cigarette and blew smoke over the top of his brothers.

George, full of mischief said in a theatrical voice, "Shine your shoes for thruppence Squire, give us a tanner an' you'll see your chin whiskers in 'em!" He made to doff his cap and gave a bow. Freddy laughed and joined in the banter.

"Need a cab guv' only a bob to The Ropewalk, finest 'orse this side o'

Newark, 'e'd be pullin' Royal carriage if I 'adn't o' nabbed 'im first."

William had uttered not a single word, he straightened the bowler hat, felt for the fob watch in his pocket to check the time, threw the remainder of the cigarette to the paving and ground his shoe over it as if he needed to destroy every last trace of its existence. Slowly he swaggered along the side of the house to the back yard, casting over his shoulder to George and Freddy his response to their fun.

"One of these days lads, one of these days."

CHAPTER SIXTEEN

Charles had forgotten just how reassuring were the dependable chimes of St. Andrew's church clock. The air was clear and cold, nothing hampered the progression of sound across the sleeping city. The bandstand seemed smaller somehow, the view across the grass bank to the railings beyond in the fickle light of dawn, closed in on him. Charles had travelled landscapes of sand and shimmering heat, journeyed across the ocean wave where no visual boundary confined him, now the arboretum felt like a tiny enclave, surely beyond those railings, behind the bandstand, hostility awaited his appearance, the chimes called out 'home' but the shadows which drifted along the laurels making him aware of their presence but concealing his adversaries caused him to shiver from an irrational dread. Had he become like Enid, frightened at the prospect of pain, crying before any actual hurt assailed him. He rubbed at his tears with fingers numbed from cold, he hadn't felt his toes since stepping off the train, surely a man should want nothing more than to rush home to his wife and children, to drive from his mind all the misery of the past two years but ghosts haunted Charles, they stalked his thoughts and bound his expression of love. Soon the streets would awake, Charles picked up his bag and made his way. He had not eaten for many hours, he was not hungry yet an emptiness cried out to be satisfied.

As he passed the end of Winchester Street his eyes automatically turned towards the workshop, the half light cast a strange animation over the old gates, Charles quickened his pace, feeling exposed and vulnerable to the demands of daylight he sought No.14. Why he felt the need to walk silently to the back door he could not explain but as morning broke and without so much as a whistle to announce his approach he opened the door to find Annie filling dinner bags for the boys. Startled, she dropped the bread knife, it clattered as it struck the flags, he crossed the room and gathered it from the floor.

"You shouldn't pick it up yourself, sharp luck," he said, placing it on the table.

He smiled nervously, his empty stomach weakened him. Annie took Charles in her arms, his face felt so cold, his cheeks chilled from the early morning air.

"I can't move my arms," he said, "need a mug of tea to bring Charles Eddowes back to life."

Annie kissed him, rubbed his hands between her own to drive away the white deadness from his fingertips. "Sit by the range," Annie led him to a chair, recognising his weariness she untied his laces and took off his boots, she rubbed his feet to bring back warmth. His presence again after all this time, the events which had dominated both their lives since that morning he had walked away from Hood Street, now sapped even Annie's strength. The tears stung her face, her fingers trembled, it was only the sound of footsteps on the stairs which saved her. William stood in the doorway, his trousers so hurriedly pulled on that one twisted strap of his braces hung between his legs, his feet bare, his youthful whiskers adorning his chin in a determined show of potential manhood.

"You're not as brown as Archie Clark was, Tommy said you'd be real brown, like an Abdul."

William's words grew fainter as he began to weep. Charles stood, crossed the room and threw his arms about his son. Annie poured boiling water over the tea and fought the knot in her stomach which would have her be sick with relief.

They were four days away from Christmas, Charles had presented his children with the finest gift of all.

"Let your dad have a hot drink William whilst you go back upstairs to dress properly and rouse Freddy and George, they will want to talk with him before work, you all will. John and Hilda can miss school today." It was Friday, the last day of lessons before the Christmas break. "Drink this Charles." Annie passed him the mug, she had taken a half bottle of brandy from the cupboard and put a measure of its strengthening goodness into the tea. "You must eat something or it will go to your head."

She took bacon from the slab, within minutes it sizzled over the range, releasing that appetising smell. An urgent procession of feet covered each tread of the stairs so fast that all three young men stood before Charles their breathing short from exertion and excitement, eyes and arms so animated that he virtually disappeared beneath their welcome. Freddy found no need for words, he clung to Charles not making a single utterance and when he raised his face from his dad's shoulder Annie saw a smile which had surely been ever close by, just patiently awaiting this moment. For Charles it was more sustaining than any brandy. George walked across to his mother the tell-tale glint of a tear in his eye, whilst his two stepbrothers almost consumed Charles with their eagerness.

George whispered, "It's all over, the war and everything, isn't it Mam? You'll be alright now, he's safe."

Annie could no longer hold back her emotion but it was her son, her own dear George who held her in his arms and comforted her with his deep understanding.

"For 'eaven's sake, get yerself 'ome, we'll be alright," said Edna. Annie had left Charles with his two youngest whilst she hurried to Winchester Street to tell Edna of his return. "We'll finish these curtains today, I shall be glad to see the back o' the damn things. Why folk 'ave to live in 'ouses wi' windows ten foot high is beyond me. They reckon there's a peepin' tom goin' round Radford, 'e wer' chased away at one place an' they said 'e wer' no taller than the back leg of a pit pony, 'e ran off carryin' two 'ouse bricks as 'e used for standin' on. Billy says if the short arsed bugger comes round our way, them two bricks'll be mighty useful." Edna began to chuckle. "They'll be the only soddin' nuts to get cracked this Christmas, the bloody war 'as even done for them." Edna sighed and gathered the heavy folds of fabric to her knees.

Annie smiled at Edna's frustration. "The world will eventually find some normality I'm sure, perhaps by next Christmas imports and exports will be as before. Anyway, Nobby Green has cob nuts," said Annie.

"Well 'whoopee-doo' for Mrs. Green," said Edna roguishly and waved

243

one hand at Annie. "Go on, clear off, get 'ome to 'is nibs, if you're lucky Charles might even 'ave brought some back from Egypt for yer." Edna gave Annie a very suggestive look then immediately began to treadle her machine and sing a ditty.

> The dapper little fella who stood under me umbrella
> Wer' only keepin' shower off 'is worsted.
> No reason for me mother to send me little brother
> To fetch me 'ome afore we got all flustered!

Annie waved to Sylvia and Bessie Clark before hastily making her way home. Truthfully, she did not know what Charles wanted. He had eaten some breakfast, shown love to his children, sitting cuddled up to John and Hilda, staring over their heads to the shelf at the two peg dolls but giving slight response when Annie had told him she would be straight back. She must unpack his bag, remove that reminder of his absence and coax his spirit. After such a time it was strange for them all and his family had so little knowledge of the life which had held Charles in its grip since he entered the war. As Annie walked she pondered the coming days, the weekend would enable William, Freddy and George to begin the process of adapting to their father's presence in the house again, it should allow Charles a respite from outside pressures and Annie herself, the chance to lay his anxieties to rest. Billy had come home from the war with severe physical wounds yet his deep contentment at nestling down amidst the restoring properties of his family had banished all his hurt. No terror stalked Billy's mind, instead he looked to the future, confident that old sores were completely healed. Billy Dodds was alive and blessed, his gratitude at being so, charged him with the duty to live for all those who had not come home.

Charles was a complex character, where others smiled readily, without aforethought, Charles analysed and judged. It undermined the opportunity for friendship and any chance of simple pleasure.

Annie could hear not a sound from within when she opened the back door. In the living room Charles rested in the big armchair, fast asleep. John and Hilda sat beside him on the floor, the fire was low in the grate. Annie cautioned them to be quiet, she lifted the coals, one at a time with her fingers to render the task silent, beckoned the children to follow her, pulled to the living room door and tiptoed to the kitchen.

"Your dad will sleep for a while, he needs to sleep, we'll make something nice for him, some shortbreads and an apple pie."

Annie took the bag and carried it upstairs out of sight, she would empty it later. Placing it by the window of their bedroom her thoughts at that instant travelled back in time to the day, with George and Byron, she had moved into No. 14. That day had felt so final, leaving behind aunt Bella's home, Winnie Bacon that friendly face Annie had taken comfort from so many times, those familiar features of Winchester Street, dear Edna and Billy dwelling as they were in the place where Annie had known her greatest happiness. She had stood at the window then, insecure, lonely even. Two more children and eleven years on, why did she feel a part of herself was abiding elsewhere and that this house, while causing her no actual grief, as yet had not wholly embraced her. Only when she knelt at Byron's spot did a sense of peace soothe Annie's mind. Her past lay quietly there, not demanding anything of her, just a reassuring memory.

Hilda had just lifted the last finger of shortbread from the baking tray when the door opened and Charles hurried across the room.

"Need the privy," he said. Without a further word he went to the yard where John was collecting eggs. Annie heard the boy's excited cry on seeing his dad was awake

Charles sat inside the privy, listening to the contented sounds the hens made as they pecked on a cauliflower stump. He had forgotten that smell of age which hung about the lime washed walls, the echo of his own breath as a sigh or a sniff travelled first to the roof before finding escape through the gap

245

at the bottom of the door. That hollow in the cobbles where the suds lingered after Annie had used the water from the dolly tub to wash the privy floor and the latch on the door, worn smooth by so many years of use it now fell into the catch with room to spare and rattled its reminder of 'time gone by' with the slightest movement of air. He shivered, it was cold, as he pulled up his trousers something fell to the cobbles, a button, Charles had sewn several buttons onto his clothing over the past two and a half years. The first time he had taken the needle and thread his thoughts had immediately turned to Annie and the workshop. Clem had laughed at Charles' precision, 'six times through each hole then wrap the thread twice around the base of the button before securing at the back by passing the needle through the last loop'. Charles had explained the practice to Clem, declaring all Eddowes' buttons were sewn on firmly. Clem had listened with a big grin on his face.

'What you need Charlie boy is a woman to rip your buttons off, first real woman I went with sent me 'ome wi' just one button on me flies, mam giv' me an old fashioned look an' asked, 'what 'appened to you then'? Got caught up on the gates o' paradise mam I said, she never bat' an eyelid, just took down 'er sewin' basket from the shelf, stitched the buggers back on, 'anded me the trousers an' said, 'you want to be careful if you go there again, them gates must be rough'. Charles fought a pang of grief as he picked up the button and put it in his pocket.

John had already gone indoors with the eggs, the cockerel stood by the wire of the enclosure, his head to one side, his beady eye observing Charles, someone different. The bird made a low sound of acknowledgement then strutted around his hens as if warning Charles to respect his authority, as though reminding him that such a long absence required Charles to win his place and not presume it.

In the kitchen Hilda had taken delight in laying the table, setting a place for her dad beside her own. Annie poured soup into bowls, Charles sat where his eager daughter bid him.

"I have presents in my bag, when we have eaten we shall open them." Charles achieved to excite the children even more with this remark and John, remembering his present from Egypt the previous Christmas, wondered if it might be something similar, a bird carved out of wood, like no bird John had ever seen, painted in rich gold and red and with features so sharp it sat on the ledge in his bedroom like a rare predator awaiting the chance to swoop down from its perch, outstretch concealed talons and carry off an unwary victim. Hilda's gift last Christmas had been a bangle in the form of a snake, as yet too large for her wrist it adorned the neck of a jar of bath crystals which Hilda insisted were far too pretty and sparkly to be dissolved in water so they remained on the washstand, unused since aunty Jean gave them to her.

Charles looked across the table at Annie, "I tried to find some softer coloured silk but it is all so vivid over there that I chose something entirely different, I hope you will like it."

Annie smiled warmly, "We have the very best present Charles, the last two Christmases have been an effort to enjoy but this year will be easy for us all."

"What time do the boys get home from work," he asked.

"George will be home first, he's always here first isn't he Mam, then William, except for when he bumps into Tommy Spooner, mam says she can't think what they find to talk about that takes so long but Freddy says they discuss the birds and bees, I don't like bees, Molly got stung by one in the summer and aunty Ivy had to pull out the sting with a pair of tweezers. Freddy will be the last home, he's always last, he has to help Mr. Cropley shut up the poultry and the Guinea fowls will go anywhere but in the shed. Last week they had to give up on one and it roosted in the big elm tree outside the house, as soon as light broke it began to shriek like Guinea fowls do. Freddy says Mrs. Cropley couldn't sleep a wink after five o'clock in the morning and she told Mr. Cropley that if he expected her to churn the butter then she needed her night's sleep and she wasn't going to stand for being woken up at the first crack of sparrow's fart by a stupid Guinea fowl."

Hilda finally paused for breath and Charles, astounded at the dialogue flowing so freely from his little girl began to realise how much all his children had developed since he left that day for Manchester.

Annie chuckled at Charles' obvious surprise, "Your older sons chatter and your bright daughter listens intently, her education will doubtless be very much wider than was ours at that age, growing up as we were without siblings."

Charles too could not resist to laugh and in response to Hilda's informative delivery said, "Then I shall look forward to seeing George home first, followed by William and lastly Freddy and you Hilda can help me unpack my bag."

"What about John can he help too?" Said Hilda.

"Yes, John can help as well." Charles had found some measure of ease, his stomach ached less and warmth had reached his fingers and toes, he felt safe.

The soup was good, it tasted entirely English, an important consideration for Charles. Even the salt beef and army biscuits, despite their British origin, when eaten amidst the sights and sounds of Egypt, that foreign place where life could appear and disappear at the whim of a mirage, lost their identity and became just another part of the timeless war. Now every spoonful delivered a concentrated flavour of home and the shortbread, which Hilda declared to be especially good because she had made the pattern on the top, might have been despatched in a luxurious hamper for the festive season, alongside mature Stilton cheese and Vintage Port, so fine did it look and taste. Only when Charles passed his empty plate to Annie as she cleared away did it occur to him how tired his wife looked.

"Where is my bag?" Asked Charles, his eyes scanned the kitchen.

"I took it up to the bedroom," said Annie.

"Why, was it in your way, am I in your way?" Charles' tone was hurtful. Annie looked quickly at Hilda and John, they were anxious.

"I simply carried it upstairs to remove from our sights the reminder of your absence, we don't want to think about that now, we need to look forward, we are all together at last." Annie's reply caused him to feel regret at his outburst.

"Come on, lets fetch the bag down, it's warm in here, the bedroom is too cold to enjoy unwrapping presents there." Charles left the kitchen and Hilda ran after him, John hesitated, his eyes searched for reassurance from his mother. "You go too John, everything is alright, I'll finish these dishes quickly and then when your dad comes back with the bag we can see what he has brought from Egypt." Her smile settled the boys doubts and he followed his sister. It was almost three o'clock, Charles had slept by the fire in the living room for several hours. George was usually home by half past five and William soon after. Freddy had no actual clocking off time. When the day's work was done, it was time to go home but he and Arthur Cropley had an understanding, animals were not the same as people, they lived by the seasons, not by the clock. Arthur paid Freddy well and took pains to explain and instruct the young man in the ways of animal husbandry. Freddy in return showed eagerness and loyalty, he seemed totally satisfied at the arrangement. However, Annie suspected all three boys would do their utmost to get back to their dad and when made aware of Charles' arrival at No.14, their respective employers would allow them to finish in good time.

The sound of chatter and feet descending the stairs made Annie rush to wipe her hands and appear happy and at ease when Charles and the children returned to the kitchen.

"I have taken out what belongs upstairs," said Charles, putting the bag down on the table. Hilda's legs fidgeted from anticipation, John waited quietly observing his father's every move. Charles took an oblong parcel from within the bag, teasing Hilda he held it for several seconds as though concentrating hard, then, "I remember now, this one is for William." His hand delved inside the bag again and withdrew a knobbly shaped package, he looked at it with a puzzled expression, rubbing his chin with his fingers. "Now let me think, who is this one for, ah yes, Freddy, this one's for Freddy." Hilda danced a jig on the spot as Charles once again reached into the bag, this time he pulled out a parcel, looked at Hilda then back at the parcel before saying. "Yes, I feel quite sure, this one is yours." He handed it to the delighted child who right away cast her eyes at Annie, seeking permission to open it.

"Wait until John has his then open them together," said Annie, hoping her response suited Charles' purpose. The two youngsters now pulled feverishly at the wrapping, John held up a small leather pouch.

"Look inside then," said Charles. John's gift was a magnifying glass with a most unusual handle. "That is made from the tooth of a crocodile." Charles gently smoothed his finger along the handle. "That was once in the mighty jaws of a great crocodile swimming in the river Nile."

John's eyes were wide with wonderment, he held the lens to look through at Hilda. "Your nose looks huge," he cried and set off to examine all the everyday items within the room under the magical power of his present.

Hilda had taken the paper from around her own gift to reveal a pair of dainty slippers, they were of rich plum colour decorated with braid of gold and a glass bead. She called out her pleasure at their prettiness and sat on the rug to take off her boots and try on these exciting new shoes.

Charles laughed out loud, he placed three parcels on the dresser. "They are for the boys, this one is for you." He handed a long narrow packet to Annie, his fingers were nervous, awkward and he at once looked away. "I shall make some tea, we all agreed that tea tasted very different in Egypt, perhaps it was the water or the milk, very often we had to use condensed milk, anyway it just wasn't the same at all."

Annie lifted the lid on a long box lined with deep amber coloured silk, laying the length of the box a necklace of gold chain, very fine indeed. At the front three droplets of ruby red, one slightly larger at the centre, each set in a delicate gold mount, Annie's silence made Charles all the more nervous, he put the lid on the teapot clumsily and the noise it made seemed to bring her from a state of shock.

"It is so beautiful Charles, so very beautiful." No more words would come, suddenly her throat felt dry.

Hilda had whirled around the table in her dainty slippers like a doll on a musical box, humming *The Merry Widow Waltz*, a favourite piece of music from her memory of Robert Appleyard's dance afternoon. John had discovered a spider in the corner underneath the coat rack and cried out.

"It's got whiskers, did you know Mam that spiders have whiskers?"

At that instant Charles and Annie found each other's gaze, he held her briefly, kissing her forehead, for those few seconds he had no thought for the past.

It was drawing dusk, Annie had made a stew with some knuckle, it simmered gently over the heat, the apple pie sat on the slab awaiting its time to be accompanied by a jug of rich yellow custard for pudding. There was a noise outside in the yard, Annie heard the sound of the chicken house door falling into place, William appeared muttering annoyance.

"Those mindless birds have lived in the same place all this time yet still they lead me a song and dance when I shut them up, anyway I've closed the latch on the coop, Freddy will probably check, he won't trust me with his precious hens, he can please himself but the stupid things are all in, where's dad?"

Annie could remember William's initial excitement at the arrival of the very first chickens, now they were simply a nuisance in his view. How very different to Freddy who still studied their every feather as keenly as he had done on that first day. Freddy saw them as perfect examples of production, just as technically gifted as the men working at Raleigh producing bicycles, if not more so given that they created without the need of any other material than food and water.

"Your dad is in the living room, you are in good time, it is kind of Mr. Yeats to let you go so early."

"Oh Reg said I could knock off at dinner time so I went to see Celia's father to ask him if he would take dad to the Lodge one night. That's what dad needs now, he's done his bit for the country, he should think about himself from now on, push the business forward, make a comfortable living, expand, let others do the donkey work. It happens you know, it's who you mix with that makes the difference, like attracts like."

Before Annie had chance to speak William was across the room and into the hallway, all she could do was despair at his immaturity. Even now, after all this time of separation, it was not Charles whom William truly hankered for. His dad was home safe, uninjured, William's troubled conscience had found relief, now he pursued an ideal, a notion of status. Freddy bore Enid's looks but William held that element of his mother's nature which prevented her ever being satisfied. Yet a vulnerability seemed to lie just below the surface of William's world, Annie shuddered at the memory of Enid's last hours.

A happy whistling could be heard outside drawing closer. George stepped in through the back door carrying a parcel, his face broke into a wide grin, he gave Annie a wink, put the parcel in the scullery, dipped one finger into the jug of custard and licked it hungrily.

"It feels good doesn't it Mam, all day I've been thinking we're lucky, the family is intact despite everything." He stood at the range and smelled the stew, planted a kiss on Annie's cheek. "Do you know Mam , I wouldn't call the King me Uncle."

The meal had produced a comfortable atmosphere around the table. Freddy had arrived home bearing a bottle of sloe gin, a gesture of goodwill to Charles from Arthur Cropley. 'Tell your father me and Mrs.Cropley send our best regards and next Monday we shall send a fine goose an'all, a bit o' Christmas for all of yer'.

The boys had opened their presents from Egypt. William had discovered a marquetry box made of light and dark woods, their differing grain arranged in random pattern yet as a whole, perfectly united. Inside the pieces of a chess set, the one side of dark, mysterious ebony, the other of delicate, exotic ivory. Freddy unwrapped his knobbly shaped package to reveal a large egg timer. Charles had explained its significance.

'It is a half hour timer and the sand is from the Sinai Desert. Over there they say if a man dips his hand into the Nile at Cairo in July, by the time all the sand has run down, then the water that he touched will be in Rosetta'.

George had very carefully unfolded the brown paper from his gift, it was

252

a circular plaque of copper, a design of olive leaves hammered into its surface. He had sat gazing at it for a minute or more, holding it at various angles to the lamp.

'That's clever, that really is clever', he'd declared, 'I shall hang it on the bedroom wall so that it catches the beam from the street lamp outside, then I can lie in bed and watch the patterns change with the light'.

Annie felt relieved at the relaxed mood which now calmed the gathering, the boys had all come home early, Charles had eaten well, it was William's question, albeit asked in complete innocence, which changed sharply the sense of wellbeing.

"What happened to your friend Clem?"

Annie could see Charles' expression change instantly, tension narrowed his cheeks as he took a deep breath.

"He was killed, shot dead by the Turks."

A desperate silence prevailed the family until George rose from his place at the table, crossed to the scullery and returned with the parcel he had placed there earlier. Handing it to Charles he said.

"From all of us, what's passed is past, this is for what's to come."

Charles struggled for composure but his youngest child came to his aid, Hilda called out excitedly.

"Open it Dad, do open it, I don't know what it is, no one has told me."

George grinned and winked at his brothers. Charles' fingers pulled at the string, his breathing was tight, it hampered his efforts. At last the twine yielded, the paper fell away at the top.

"What is it?" Asked Hilda, looking slightly disappointed at the rather drab box.

"It's a camera," said George, "it's not brand new, second hand but the man assured me that it works perfectly. He said you can take fine pictures with that of all the family. He showed me what to do, stand over there by the dresser, go on all of you, stand close together. You can take one Dad, of mam wearing her new necklace."

After one or two seconds of hesitancy Charles obliged his eager family and stood by his wife and children. William and Freddy, now almost as tall as their father, flanked them at either side with John and Hilda in front.

"You'll have to nudge up a bit, I can't fit you all in," said George, "smile, say cheese." The camera clicked to register the process done and George then handed it to Charles who looked bewildered. "All you have to do is look through that little window, when mam is in the middle, like a picture in a frame, press that little lever. Put your necklace on Mam." George was not going to let the moment pass.

"It won't look right with this frock, it's a beautiful piece of jewellery to be worn with an elegant low cut bodice," said Annie, trying to relieve Charles of this task about which he seemed uneasy.

"Go upstairs and put on something low cut then," said George.

Annie smiled, "I haven't anything low cut other than underwear," she moved to begin clearing the table.

"That's alright," replied the ever determined George, "dad knows now how to work the camera, I shall put it in your bedroom so he can take the photograph when you get ready for bed. Mr. Askew will develop the pictures, he did some for Norman Fowler, Norman works with me on pedals and chains, he used to work with Les, his son, 'til he joined up. He brought the pictures with him one day last week, showed them to me at dinner time, I didn't know what to say, they all looked the same, photos of Les standing in their back yard, still in uniform, just back from France, he had a smile on his face and tears in his eyes on every one. Anyway, I didn't really need to speak, Norman said, 'what's passed is past, now all that matters is what's to come', I thought that said it all." George picked up the camera from the dresser where his father had placed it and walked purposefully up the stairs.

Annie watched Charles, he sat by the range staring at the black cast canopy. He seemed not to hear the happy chatter of his young ones or to notice the way in which William observed him from the doorway. The canopy was dark and blank, on that Charles could create whatever image he chose .

Annie set about the dishes, she would need to go to Basford in the morning and check with Edna that all was well at Winchester Street, the curtains now completed, must be delivered to The Ropewalk in time for Christmas. Her thoughts occupied her mind and the washing up engaged her efforts so she did not notice William until he stood right beside her.

"Did you know about the camera? George might have said, I'm sure dad guessed it was all George's idea." William rattled the coal bucket with his boot, his resentment very apparent. "Dad will think I didn't bother."

"I am quite sure William that your dad has no thought for the camera or for who's idea it may have been. One day he will be less preoccupied but for now he dwells on the loss of his friend Clem. We must help him to move on, to find purpose." Annie paused, she let the pan which had engaged her effort in scouring slip back under the water and turned to face William. "When George's dad died, Billy's grief almost overwhelmed him, we truly feared for him so distraught was he, so mindless of himself. You see they were real friends, not just casual pals, one day you will come to understand exactly what that means. Billy missed Harold so much the hurt was unbearable. Don't create expectations William, you must allow your dad to find some peace, in the meantime enjoy his company, be happy with Celia, simply be content."

William gave a deep sigh before going outside to the yard, he closed the back door to keep in the warmth. Faintly, Annie could smell tobacco smoke and as she once more took up the scourer she imagined the young man's look of intense frustration.

"I thought you'd be in bed by now, why are you sitting there in the cold?" Annie had banked up the fire and put laundry to soak before following the others.

"I slept this morning didn't I, besides, I'm waiting to take your photograph, George will give me no peace until I have, he won't be satisfied until I show him the picture. We shall have to use up the film over Christmas, then I can take it to Askew's."

Annie chuckled, "I can't begin to think what the result will be, such a lovely necklace and me in my petticoat but you are right, George is sure to ask in the morning. It will have to be quick or I shall be immortalised in print covered in goose bumps from the cold."

Annie took off her frock and sat in front of the mirror. She held up the gold chain, the red droplets caught the soft light. Carefully she put it around her neck and secured the fastener.

"There, how does it look?"

She turned to Charles for approval. Her hair, naturally thick and wavy, still pinned up as she always wore it, suited her face. Without the collar of the frock her neck was long and slender, just a wisp of hair which had escaped the order fell in a soft curl by one ear. Charles gave no answer, he held up the camera but his hands shook, finally the shutter clicked.

"It will probably be blurred when Askew develops it," he said, "it isn't easy keeping completely steady."

In the darkness Charles had no need of closing his eyes to picture Clem, his friend stood before him, laughing, as Clem did.

'You're a rum 'en Charlie boy, out 'ere in the middle of a soddin' sandpit wi' nowt but flies an' hairy arsed blokes but you don't go lookin'.

Charles could feel Annie's warmth beside him. 'English men feel only steel'. That was not true. Charles now climbed the stone steps, he lay down among the braided cushions and felt the all consuming want of his wife, here, now. There was no vision of Enid, no image of Egypt and the war, just Annie. Shedding tears for something he could not define, Charles made love, the world was excluded, all pain, every memory, banished from the moment, from this one perfect act.

Sleep came to them both, the camera sat on the chest of drawers, keeping silent witness, only ever to reveal a blurred reminder of this night and along with the rest of the household, await what was to come.

CHAPTER SEVENTEEN

" Well would you believe that."

Billy bent down to retrieve a very soil encrusted object from the spit of ground which together, he and Victor had just turned. Billy had no lack of physical strength but some tasks were made frustratingly awkward when tackled with only one arm.

The end of hostilities, the sense of utter belief in England's green and pleasant land had led men to the spring of 1919 with a jubilant defiance. The mood was buoyant, rickety gates and weathered doors, flaking walls and blocked gutters, all had been remedied through this fervour of patriotism.

Billy thrust the spade into the ground and with one forceful stomp of his boot, made ready for turning an impressive spit of soil. Victor, with both hands and sheer determination, lifted the spade and turned over the surrendering sod of earth, each time awarding himself the cry of satisfaction taught him by Billy.

"*Ubergeben*".

It was not the triumphant euphoria which drove Billy's endeavour, he stopped short of strident cries of victory. More than one young German had died at his feet, 'them or us', lost its potency when eyes fixed in their very last expression set their gaze and lips passed final words to whoever still stood to witness.

"*Meinen kinder, mein leibling*".

The young German spoke these words to Billy as life left him, it was not until some days later that Billy learned they were not the last defiant words of an aggressor but a declaration of greatest love for his family.

"Time for a breather lad." Billy sat on a makeshift bench, rubbing at an old pipe. "This must 'ave been buried up for years, made o' clay, look Victor."

Billy's roughened thumb had taken the soil from the bowl of the clay pipe, Victor carefully lifted it from Billy's fingers and studied this strange item.

"Dirty, needs washin'," said a puzzled young Victor, trying to understand why Billy was so taken with it.

"When we get back 'ome we'll soak it in a bucket o' water, dry it out on the range. I reckon a bit o' baccy in that 'ould do me nicely," said Billy with a chuckle as he imagined Edna's response to this notion. He produced a bag of toffees from his pocket and they both leaned back against the fence of the allotment.

Early in the new year Albert Haynes had suffered a stroke, Florrie had sent for the doctor but within a few hours a further stroke occurred. Albert died in his wife's arms, quietly, without uttering a single word. The four eldest boys were earning wages and somehow Florrie kept them all in food and boots but her struggle touched Billy. When the rent of an allotment came up, he saw it as his chance to help supplement Florrie's larder and provide for his own, with Victor's help it would work.

The day was pleasantly warm, a bumble bee made its way from flower to flower of the pear blossom and birds pulled at every scrap of nesting material, disappearing into the dense ivy which traced through the gaps in the hawthorn like darning wool through the rubbed heel of a sock.

Billy looked at Victor sitting beside him, happily chewing on his sweet, his feet swinging below the bench, those familiar sounds of bubbly lip smacking and simple sighs of contentment.

"I've got a secret to tell you Victor," said Billy with a big grin on his face.

"A secret," replied Victor, his tongue sweeping his mouth to gather any escaping sweetness from the toffee and a sniff to prepare himself for his usual repetition. "A secret." He gave Billy a pleading look and held out his tongue to confirm the toffee all gone. Billy laughed.

"Go on then, you've worked hard." He handed Victor another. The hours they spent together provided Billy with a companionship few men would understand. The boy would always be just that, a boy, all the demands and responsibilities of manhood, never to rob Victor of his innocence.

"I'm goin' to be a dad again, Edna's goin' to 'ave a baby, what do yer think o' that?" Said Billy.

Victor smiled, pulled Billy to his feet and handed him the spade. It was as if he understood the need to work even harder if there was to be another mouth to feed. Perhaps not just a boy, thought Billy, Victor's simplicity was a joy but underlying was a rare perception, it made Victor an enigma, a wonderful mystery to beguile a 'black or white' world.

Edna stared into the bucket by the back step, something lay in a few inches of murky water. She gently tipped the bucket from side to side. "God only knows what Billy's brought back from the river this time but it's dead whatever it is," she muttered.

On one occasion Billy had returned from the Trent with a water vole which Victor had found, frightened and injured. 'Probably escaped from the claws of a cat' had been Billy's theory on the creature's condition. Victor had sat with the vole on his lap as if willing it to revive, miraculously it had but by then it was too near Billy's time of work at the exchange for him to return it to the riverbank, so it had been contained in a bucket of shallow water with a stone from the wall to afford the vole some dry land, there to remain until the following day.

Edna opened the back door and called out, very often Annie and Susie would be in the scullery making a start on the potatoes for tea or folding down the washing. If Billy was upstairs in bed Liza would creep in beside him, it was not unusual to find them both fast asleep. Today however, the house appeared empty, then Edna spotted a note on the dresser.

'We've all gone to me mam's to fetch dad's old wheelbarro'.

Edna shook her head in dismay, filled the kettle for a much needed cuppa and turned her attention to their meal. Each day this week she had wanted to nip off early and go to Hood Street, to tell Annie about the baby but Charles had been absent from the workshop every afternoon. The Basford works were demanding more of his time. Gertie's first child was due in less than a month, she had finally given in to Steve's concerns and now stayed at home, gathering her strength for the impending birth.

Annie had been in and out of the workshop very briefly but Edna had not wanted to announce her news in front of the others, not just yet but Annie, she did need to tell Annie. After all they had been through Edna considered Annie to be her closest confidante.

Charles' demeanour had become more relaxed of late, the business kept a steady pace, not showing any rapid growth despite the predictions of great things for all who grasped the nettle. In fact the promise of homes for heroes now seemed a little rash. Men were queuing for jobs and whilst the mood of optimism held good as they awaited a chance to sign on and take their first steps on this road to prosperity, it was ever the case that the unlucky at one queue simply extended the length and added to the disappointments at another.

Billy and the girls turned the corner into Winchester Street, young Annie held one handle of the barrow and Billy the other whilst Susie and Liza took turns to ride.

"That's enough now, you two must walk, my shoulders are aching," said Annie.

It was only at moments such as this that Billy resented his disability. To need the help of a child, especially for such a simple task, grated at his humour and yet when he was with Victor it felt perfectly natural. They each had need of the other, entirely reciprocal. They had walked Victor home to Florrie before going to Billy's mam's to fetch the wheelbarrow. The girls always enjoyed a visit to their grandma. Phyllis Dodds' household was an engaging mix of clutter and items of import. It was not at all unusual to see the stays of a corset removed for laundering, randomly placed in a Royal Worcester vase, or her ample bloomers airing over the gilt framed picture of grandad Dodds. Today they had found her unpicking an outgrown jumper, the wool being wound around the back of a chair, until it comprised a 'hank' which, after careful washing to remove the kinks, would be sufficient to knit up again into some bed socks and a tea cosy. A bowl of bread dough sat rising under a tea cloth in the hearth and laying across the table was a dead rabbit.

'Your uncle Wilfred dropped that in but I told 'im it'll 'ave to wait 'til I've got me 'ands out o' the dough afore I skin that', she'd declared with not the slightest hint of urgency as her fingers pulled undone another row of stitches from the ever shrinking jumper.

'Wilfred said there wer' a right old rumpus outside The Nelson yesterday, it started wi' just two men arguin', then they all pitched in. It wer' Doreen Piper as put a stop to it. 'Er 'ouse is next door to the pub, the noise wer' drivin 'er mad. She wer' tryin' to give Isaac Jacobson's grandson 'is piano lesson but the shoutin' an' cussin' goin' on outside wer' no fit accompaniment to 'is tasteful rendition of, 'O for the wings of a dove'. Doreen went out there wi' a 'Flit' pump as she keeps for when 'er Angus comes 'ome from the dogs an' doused the lot of 'em. That stuff don't 'arf sting if yer get it in yer eyes, well they got it everywhere. Accordin' to Wilfred this one fella said to the other, 'I 'ear you compromised my missus'. Well nothin' 'appened to begin with but another bloke shouted out, 'Yes, an' 'e did it wi' Esther Glasson an'all'. Then first chap realised what compromised meant an' all Hell broke loose. I've heard as the Jacobson lad can play 'O for the wings of a dove' note perfect an' 'e's only eight. What made anybody want to write a song about a soddin' pigeon is what I cant get over, them birds o' Sid's across the street are nowt but a damn nuisance'.

At that juncture Billy had declared it time they were off home and after the girls had kissed their grandma goodbye, the barrow was hastily gathered from the shed whilst Phyllis lifted the well risen dough from the hearth to the table and with the rabbit alongside awaiting the firm hands of Phyllis to rip its skin from end to end, those same capable hands kneaded the dough to the strains of, *'O for the wings of a dove'*, as she sang, full voiced over the bowl, the flour she used to coat her hands drifted across the table giving a fine dusting of white to a pair of reading glasses and a coal bill which leaned against a bottle of syrup of figs.

"Just how do you suppose you're goin' to manage that barro' Billy Dodds," said an anxious Edna from where she stood by the sink, a potato in one hand, knife in the other, "you'll wear yourself out, what wi' the allotment by day and the exchange by night, God 'elp me Billy I cant stand the worry."

Billy stood before his wife, kissed her forehead, patted her stomach and whispered in her ear, "I wer' christened William and where there's a Will there's a way."

Trying to appear less than placated, Edna drew the knife down the side of the potato and issued the warning. "If that dead vermin, whatever it might be, isn't removed from my bucket and got rid of afore I tip the peelin's, I'll take that bloody barro' wi' the bucket in it and tip the soddin' lot in the canal."

Billy simply grinned and went outside to blow life into his dead vermin!

"Ivy writes that Harold and Molly have settled in at the school and Reggie is busy working on windows for a Church at Ingoldmells. I do miss them Annie but how wonderful for those children to live so close to the coast. Their little home sounds just right, it is only a half mile from Reggie's father's workshop at Skendleby."

Davina poured another cup of tea and prompted Annie to help herself to a slice of malt loaf. Ivy and Reggie had married on 23rd February, very quietly at the local Chapel. Neither felt able to make any celebration, too many memories, too fresh in their minds would permit anything more than a simple declaration of their love through their vows of commitment.

"Yes, I had a letter too, Ivy hopes we might be able to visit one day in the summer, John and Hilda would love that," said Annie with a curious remoteness in her voice which Davina at once perceived.

"Is everything alright my dear?" She asked, aware that Charles could be temperamental, especially when under pressure. "Is the business doing as well as it should?"

Annie placed her cup carefully onto the saucer and for several seconds, seemed to stare into its depths, a stranger might have believed her to be reading the tea leaves but such 'stuff and nonsense' would have appalled aunt Bella with the consequence that Annie left make believe pursuits to those who held a desire to be charmed. Even as a child, a fairy story had not been deemed worthwhile reading matter for Annie, only the classics and books which aunt Bella described as edification could the young Annie's imagination feed on. One book however seemed less intense, closer to the life Annie knew. It was a compilation of short stories contained within a bright red cover and a picture to complement each. It had ever been Annie's favourite, one of those stories, 'Grey Friars Bobby', remained in her mind, a dog so devoted it refused to leave the grave of its master. Annie hesitated for an instant.

"I am going to have another child Davina."

"Why my dear Annie that is wonderful news, surely Charles is delighted, what a glorious outcome to all those endless months of worry and tribulation. Here was I thinking you were in some way troubled and all the time it was my insistence on your having some malt loaf, you should have said dear that you are queasy. I know that I am not qualified to speak from any personal experience but I do remember Isobel was nauseous for months when carrying Lawrence. Even the smells of food she found unbearable, she was never without the cut glass fruit bowl, it travelled with her from room to room. Isobel wouldn't countenance being sickly into a bucket. 'In my delicate condition I shall deny such vulgarity', she'd say.

Annie smiled at Davina's response to her revelation. "I have not yet told Charles, since he came back from Egypt he has been more at ease. He was very tense at first but the pleasures of Christmas spent with the children, the familiar routine of the workshops seemed to calm him. His manner has been gentle, I was surprised by the concern he showed for May when I told him the full account of her illness and by his patience with Hilda, you know how she does chatter so," said Annie.

"Then for goodness sake, why haven't you told him?" Asked Davina.

"It sounds silly but I feel the calm is fragile, as though the slightest tremor might shatter it." Annie sighed and pulled vaguely at a loose thread on the cuff of her jacket.

"Hormones my dear, why we must have them goodness knows, tonsils, adenoids, appendix all these we can manage perfectly well without, so why then must we endure the vagaries of hormones. Tell Charles this evening, put a good measure of whisky in his hand and tell him without further delay, he is a lucky man."

Davina patted Annie's hand before crossing the room to take something from the bureau.

"I have made my Will, I sense no imminent demise, however what happened to Isobel has concentrated my mind. In this envelope is the relevant document, it is a copy of the original which my solicitor holds. I want you to know where it is to be found should anything untoward occur. I'm afraid Annie, it is with you I place the trust and the responsibility to see that my wishes are upheld."

Annie looked surprised and puzzled. "Surely Lawrence is more suited to such a trust and why should your wishes not be upheld in any event?" She asked.

Davina stooped over Annie and with a pair of scissors she had taken from her sewing basket, snipped off the loose thread from her sleeve. "There I've cut it off. Perhaps hormones confuse us older women also." Davina made light of Annie's question and smiled. "Please, simply agree to my request."

"Very well, but on one condition," said Annie.

"What is that dear?"

"That you grant me a stay of time, at least a dozen years or more before I must take up my charge. With an expanding family and a business to think of I cannot, just yet, be expected to attend to your hormones as well as my own."

Both women laughed, Davina returned to the bureau, placed the envelope back inside, feeling relieved as she turned the key in the document drawer, she gestured that Annie take note of its designated place of safekeeping.

With the help of a good cleaning lady two mornings a week, Davina had insisted she was more than capable of managing. She visited Sarah each Tuesday and Sarah returned the kindness every Friday. They looked forward to their time spent together but still it left five days of loneliness.

Maggie was now walking out with Toby Hillier, a pleasant young man, not really displaying any strong traits but quiet, almost studious. He worked in the office at the lace market which is how he and Maggie came to meet.

The munitions factory closed down, it was rumoured that it was to become a glass works but as yet the site remained unoccupied. Both Maggie and Mavis had applied for work at the lace market, Maggie had been taken on but Mavis was unsuccessful. As it turned out, a position more convenient, being closer to Melton Road presented itself. Turpin's, a small grocers next to Hastilow's needed an assistant. Sadly Miss Turpin had developed St. Vitus's Dance, she had stoically continued to serve behind the counter until one day when weighing up dried peas, she had let fall the entire content of the bag. The sympathetic customer had immediately offered to help the poor woman clear the floor of the contrary little escapees but the more they brushed the more the peas spread far and wide. Miss Turpin surrendered to a flood of tears, the customer could do nothing but retreat and the shop was closed until a reliable, trustworthy assistant could be found. Mavis was entirely suited to the work and Lois Turpin, encouraged by a compassionate Mavis helped in the shop each afternoon.

'The poor soul will fast turn into a recluse, afraid to appear before anyone', had been Mavis's firm belief at seeing Lois, trembling and twitching like a frightened child, in the back room when she first began work there. Sarah had taught all her children to be tolerant of others less fortunate. 'There but for the grace o' God', an expression regularly voiced at 69, Mitchell Street.

In the new year Jean had surprised everyone by announcing that she had made up her mind to go to London. Art was important to Jean, she worked with a good heart and was well liked at Burton's but a void had existed in her life since Samuel had died, she could lose herself in painting and sketching. In London, opportunity to become noticed, ability to sell work, was very much greater than in the Midlands. London embraced expression through all forms of art, the galleries considered inspirational, forward looking as well as traditional. Amidst a torment of good wishes and tearful farewells, Jean had boarded a train to Paddington at the beginning of March. One of the tutors at Nottingham College of Art had given her the address of safe, affordable lodgings and in the immediate Jean would work for Louisa Burton's cousin, a florist at Bayswater.

Sarah missed Harold and Molly too, Maggie cared very much for her Mother but her obvious affection for Toby Hillier convinced Sarah that before long Maggie would follow Gertie and Mavis into marriage. Annie's family was a great comfort and the pending arrival of another grandchild when Gertie and Steve became parents, gave Sarah something to cling to.

Annie felt concern for those whom she loved and witnessed, month on month, showing age and weariness. Bertha still sharp as a needle in mind, struggled with failing sight and May, now so thin and withdrawn, pulled at Annie's heartstrings dreadfully. Even Robert Appleyard had become noticeably hard of hearing over the past six months. Only Catherine seemed resistant to the unkind advances of, 'Father Time'.

Margaret was back at the Convent, once more cocooned in that cloistered place of prayer. Catherine however, had reconciled her difference with the, 'Holy Mother' and called on Sister Agnes from time to time.

'I ask most graciously if I might speak with Sister Agnes for just a short while but on leaving I make a point of calling back down the echoing corridor, sending a pulse of life through those petrified generations now lost forever in those walls of stone, cheerio Margaret, your father sends his love'. Catherine had told Annie with her usual streak of defiance and a self satisfied chuckle at the mischief of it.

Davina sat down again, reassured that her wishes were in safe hands.

"When is the baby due Annie, does Sarah know?"

"I shall tell Sarah on Sunday, we are all going there for dinner. Freddy killed two cockerels last night and took them to Mitchell Street on his way to work. He described one as having a breast comparable to Rosie Potts and legs like Arthur Cropley, I think the other was less well endowed but Sarah will take delight in cooking them and will proclaim them to be a sight better than Cheetham's. Freddy could present her with an old broiler and she would still extol its virtues if Freddy had himself reared the bird. The baby is due in September, it could be close to George's birthday," said Annie with a sigh.

"Tell Charles my dear, you are fretting, that won't do at all. Mind and body need to be serenely calm for the baby's sake," said Davina authoritatively. Annie smiled, rose to her feet, picked up the tray and insisted she carry it to the kitchen. "If you don't leave those few silly dishes for me to do Annie Eddowes, I shall despair at me own futility."

Annie was quite happy to let Davina clear the tray, it occupied the solitary hours but she was not prepared to leave it for Davina to carry along the hallway. A degree of rheumatism hampered Davina's movements of late, she would laugh at her creaking joints, 'To think I once climbed the old yew tree in father's garden, shinned up it like a monkey'. Davina had reminisced one day.

Annie kissed her friend's cheek, "George will come very soon to clip the shrubs and tidy the borders."

"Oh good," Davina clapped her hands in glee, Annie knew her delight had nothing to do with restoring harmony to the garden, it was entirely created by the thought of plying young George with food and lemonade and inveigling from him any knowledge of what the family might need. Fortunately George was wise for his years and gave little enough away, allowing just the odd 'tit bit' of inside information to satisfy Davina's need to be giving.

"What do you think of this Celia girl, she strikes me as being feeble, is William really smitten, he seems to take her for granted most of the time. If I had treated Enid like that she would have fed me to the wolves," said Charles. He lay in bed, his head resting on his hands which entwined at the back of his neck.

"I believe Celia is a bright, responsible young woman, I am sure she is intensely fond of William, whether he fully appreciates her feelings I am not altogether sure, they are both very young after all." Annie took the last pin from her hair and drew the brush through her tresses, she put out the lamp and climbed into bed beside Charles. She was aware that quite irrationally, her heart pounded in her chest. "I have waited until I was sure before telling you Charles." She paused and his face turned towards her. In the dim light of the room it was difficult to define his expression but Annie sensed his unease. "We are going to have another child," she said. Annie hoped for his fingers to find her own, that his response would calm her anxiety within.

"When?" Charles' response was cold, his tone harsh.

"It will be September, probably late September," she replied. He turned away from her to face the wall, nothing more was said.

Charles did not sleep, his eyes open he stared into the gloom until so accustomed were they to what little light there was, he could make out the outline of the photograph. Askew's had developed the film which George had begun with the group photo by the dresser in the kitchen. That one had come out so clear Annie had framed it and ever since, it had stood on the chest of drawers by their bed. The photograph of Annie wearing the necklace had, as Charles predicted, come out blurred. Annie had laughed, declaring the softer image a kindness, 'My lines and wrinkles are much better veiled', she'd said. This photograph lay in a drawer of the sideboard, amongst items of miscellany.

Charles could not repel the demon now intent on commandeering his reason. Over the past few months, idle chatter, misguided gossip delivered by thoughtless individuals with too little to employ their time had taunted Charles' better sense. In The Standard, a man, rendered stupid by drink, had one night asked Charles, 'Does your missus minister to all the weird and wonderful, or is it only to Edwin Garbett she offers her mercy. Sitting together in the arboretum is nothing more than a civil pleasantry I'll grant yer but the floor of the bank, now that is unusual wouldn't yer say'?

Charles had sought an explanation from Gerald Birkett when doing business at the bank. Edwin's seizure, as described to Charles, allayed his concern almost completely but a tiny doubt niggled away. Conversely it brought an irony of comfort to Charles. His driven need to lay Clem to rest with that one act of abandon in Clem's name had ever plagued him. Annie's possible transgression served to mitigate the surety of his own. Charles' knowledge of Annie's character prevented him from truly believing her to be any other than faithful yet his contrived denial of her total loyalty granted him an assumed redemption. But a child which he must deem to have been conceived at his homecoming, when it had taken three years for John? Had Annie and Edwin really had a liaison, did they secure one last glorious union before Charles returned to deny them?

Doubts festered into the early hours and by morning Charles' emotions were so charged, he dressed and unshaven left the house before his sons stirred. Annie lay awake but with eyes closed, that sense of dormancy, of an event in waiting had suddenly become realised. The war had spared Charles and sent him back to his family, for a little while Annie had believed him to be changed, mellowed. Last night William had occupied his thoughts, now his inquiry was directed at Annie.

On the kitchen table she had found an envelope addressed to herself, within, a single line written in Charles' hand. 'Should I expect this child to look like me or to resemble Edwin Garbett?'

In the privy Annie retched from morning sickness and wept from despair.

William had grumbled his way through their meal, when Charles was still not home at seven, Annie had fed the others, suggesting their dad must be delayed at Basford.

Edna took charge of the proceedings at Winchester Street whenever Charles was absent, locking up if necessary. He had been gone from Hood Street since before six that morning and in such a disturbed frame of mind, Annie could not know where he might be. William had told Jessie Tozer he would ask Charles if he'd care to attend a special charity whist drive at the Masonic Hall and give Jessie the answer this evening when he called on Celia. William's agitation had increased with each quarter hour chime of the mantel clock, until unable to wait any longer, he had stormed out, slamming the door in his temper.

"One day he'll burst a blood vessel," said George, as he stooped to pick up from the floor Annie's jacket which had fallen off the hook behind the door. "Are you alright Mam, you look a bit peaky?"

"Your brother is impatient, whatever he sets his sights on he must have at once, his dear mother was like that too. William can't help himself, the old adage, 'the grain of the trunk will grow into the branches', can be very true sometimes." Annie avoided answering George's question, in fact she felt tired and sickly, instead she diverted his attention from herself to Freddy. "I know he said it wouldn't take him long but planting the peas and beans at the allotment after his days work at the farm, especially today when he and Arthur had to move all the sheep, would seem much less daunting if there were two of you. I think you should join him, Mrs.Cropley will have fed him a good tea, I've no doubt of that but you know how Freddy will work until he drops and never ask for help," said Annie.

George laughed, "I'll go and see what he's up to, shall I take him some lemonade?"

"Good idea," said Annie, relieved by the good humour of her son. John and Hilda would soon be in bed, if Charles returned, as he surely must before too long, then with the older boys out of the way she could speak with Charles and put an end to his mindless notion.

It was almost nine o'clock when Charles finally arrived, his uncustomary stubble hardened his appearance and Annie hesitated, her nervousness at his unpredictable mood challenged her resolve.

"Where have you been until now, what have you eaten all day?" She said, holding the laundry basket in front of herself as she prepared to set about the ironing.

Charles crossed to the scullery and poured himself a tumbler of water. Without turning to face Annie he said. "I went to see Garbett this evening in answer to your first question and I have eaten a pie which I bought from Mavis at Turpin's in response to your second."

"How could you possibly think anything so cruel, so malicious. Edwin must be convinced you have lost control of your senses," Annie's tone was sharp.

Charles now sat by the kitchen table tracing a joint in the planking with his finger. "I was away for more that two and a half years, that is a long time, two and a half years," he repeated the words emphasising such a duration of time by holding on to each, just as a piped organ holds every note, extending the sound until one drifts into the other. "You wouldn't be the only woman by any means, I wouldn't even blame you. I might not have come home, God knows thousands didn't, but a child, another man's child. I have raised George, with no misgiving or regret, that was entirely different. Harold was a friend, he died. Raising the child of another in any other circumstance I could not abide."

Annie tried to speak but he continued.

"So, it is mine, if you and Garbett both say so then it must be mine. Have you kept my tea, I shall tell Mavis when next I see her that a pie should have something contained between its two crusts."

He looked directly at Annie and positioned the cruet by his tumbler of water. She took a plate from the range, lifted the small bowl she had used as a cover for the meal and checked the potatoes for heat.

"It is hot," she said, placing it in front of him. "William wanted to speak with you before going to Celia's, I think it concerns an event at the Masonic Hall."

Annie left Charles to his food and returned to the ironing. She felt neither hurt nor anger but numb. Freddy and George would be home at any time, as she directed the iron across the linen she began to hum, 'Danny Boy', without any conscious intent. Charles fed on boiled beef and for no reason he could sensibly define, thought of Enid.

Edna locked up the workshop and waved off Sylvia and Bessie. Billy was to take Victor and the girls to The Meadows with a kite, a present from their aunty Ada, an appropriate wind had obliged the plan.

'I shall go straight to Annie's, Charles will be at Basford 'til at least 2 o'clock', Edna had told Billy earlier that morning. She had walked but a few yards, when turning the corner and heading Edna's way was Winnie Bacon.

"Cooee." Winnie's free hand waved franticly, the weight of her shopping bag suspended from the other caused the bottom of the bag to bulge alarmingly and when Edna drew closer she could see a trickle of something escaping from the Hessian.

"Your spillin' summat Winnie, look." Edna pointed at the pavement behind Winnie where a trail of purple-red spots stretched into the distance.

"Bugger!" Said Winnie, putting her bag down by the lamp-post in dismay. "I told our Elsie that Kilner jar wouldn't seal wi' out a new rubber, 'It's not like I've 'ad to cook it mam', she said, 'tis only a bit o' pickled red cabbage, keep it upright an' it'll be alright'. 'Tis all well an' good for 'er to say keep it upright, on me way back from Elsie's I've been to butcher, baker, newsagent for 'is paper an' baccy an' ironmongers for a new flat iron. The old one wer' me mam's afore I 'ad it, donkey's years old 'tis, gone bit rusty in one place an' the damn thing covered me best white tablecloth wi' iron mould. Ted tried rubbin' the bottom o' the iron wi' a file but when I went to press the bed sheets it left dark streaks, the soddin' sheet looked no better than pillow tickin'." Winnie sighed. "They'll find me cold on the floor one o' these days an' do you know what, I reckon they'll look at each other an' say, 'Well who's goin' to fetch the Sunday joint an' the race results this week then'. Dogs body that's what I am, nowt but a dogs body."

Winnie picked up the shopping bag and trundled off with it. Edna gazed down at the purple-red puddle at the base of the lamp-post then back to Winnie who was just about to turn into the entry, the trickle of dyed vinegar following on like some sinister seeping life blood. Poor Winnie, thought Edna, taken for granted much of the time. She walked on, anxious to tell Annie about the baby before Charles got home from Basford.

Annie was pegging out washing when Edna reached No.14. The two women were pleased to see one another. Hilda ran to Edna eagerly, knowing that from her pocket would appear a sweet.

"Where is John?" Asked Edna.

"He's gone with the eggs for aunty Bertha," said Hilda now intent on removing the wrapper from a butterscotch.

Annie felt surprised, "I've not seen you with those before, have you gone off sherbet lemons?"

Edna gave Annie a smug look, "I'm fancyin' summat different for a change, nowt wrong wi' that is there?" The last item pegged on the line and with Hilda singing as she skipped, Edna sized the opportunity to impart her news. "I'm expectin'."

Annie smiled, "Snap, so am I," she said.

"Bloody Hell, this is goin' to challenge 'is nibs, 'e'll 'ave to think for 'isself wi' the two of us in confinement," said Edna.

Annie looked over at Hilda, the little girl's feet leaping the rope in time to her verse. "I'm really pleased for you and Billy, perhaps it will be a boy this time."

"He'd like that, 'Got to try an' make one o' them as comes wi' a handle,' he says. You should see 'im on that allotment, God 'elp us I despair. You know 'e went to get 'is father's wheelbarro', our Annie 'elped 'im bring it 'ome 'cause 'e only got the one arm. Now the silly sod 'ave devised a way o' pushin' it. 'E ties a rope around the 'andles, stands inside wi' the rope 'round back of 'is neck an' steers it wi' 'is right 'and. I told 'im, other fellas, if they wear anythin' at all around their necks 'ave a chain wi' a St. Christopher to keep 'em safe or a picture o' their sweetheart but what does my Billy 'ave, a bloody rope 'round 'is neck wi' a soddin' wheelbarro' on it. What does your Charles want, 'e'd like another girl I suppose, if I 'ave a girl an you 'ave another boy we'll swap 'em." Edna giggled. "Your Charles 'ould 'ave a fit if your kid grew up to look like my Billy." She had no way of knowing the irony of her remark and took Annie's quietness to be concern for the business. "Sylvia an' Bessie are very good, we've plenty o' time to train up another girl, I've 'eard as Kathleen Spooner is bright. Another wage 'ould certainly 'elp in that household, poor Tommy works the tallow off 'is bones. I met Winnie today, she's lookin' old, all of a sudden. 'Ave you seen May recently?" Asked Edna

"I shall visit May next week, I promised Mabel that I would. They were sent a letter from The War Office, Alfred was commended for his bravery. Mabel said she read it to her mam but May uttered not a word. We are all to go to Sarah's for dinner tomorrow, I shall tell her about the baby then. I haven't said anything to the children yet, only Charles and now yourself know."

"I can tell Billy can't I?" Said Edna sucking on a butterscotch, Annie had declined the offer of one, confiding in her friend that sickliness was a problem at the moment.

"I'm lucky," declared Edna, "I 'aven't felt a bit sick, just bloody starvin' all the time. I ate enough porridge this mornin' to 'ave fed the night shift down pit an' wer' still ready for an eccles cake by mid mornin'."

When Edna reached home the family was back from The Meadows and Susie, having the most patience, was sat on the floor trying to untangle the kite strings.

"It wer' alright 'til the wind dropped a bit, then it come down in an elder tree, some lads got it down for us but by then it wer' all tangled up," said Billy. " We took Victor 'ome an who should we bump into but Alfie Creswell's mam. I asked after 'im, told 'er I thought I might 'ave seen Alfie about the place, in a work queue or the pub like yer do, I felt awful when the poor woman said, 'Alfie's dead'. Apparently on the boat bringin' 'im 'ome from Egypt 'e took bad just a couple o' days into the journey. Seems an infection set in the wound, turned to septicaemia, 'e died an' they still had nine more days at sea. The heat an' the boat bein' full o' people, I suppose they couldn't do no other, Alfie wer' buried at sea. Poor old 'six feet', bloody hell Edna, more like fifty fathoms now."

"I've got some news an'all," said Edna, "Annie's pregnant, she's due about the same time as me."

Billy laughed, "If Annie's appetite develops like yours the city'll be in famine. I'm pleased for 'em, might be the makin' o' Charles. The war seems to 'ave mellowed 'im a bit, another child could be just what 'e needs."

"I'm not so sure," said Edna, "summat's up I can tell, Annie says she's alright, a bit sickly that's all but I can feel it in me bones, summat's up.

Billy scoffed. "Don't you get like your grandma, she reckoned the end o' the world was nigh when your Ada got pregnant first time wi' Morley."

"When the second one come along we all thought the end o' the world was nigh," said Edna. "Ugly little begger she was an' you wer' no better, sayin' 'er nose 'ould span the widest stretch o' The Trent by the time she wer' twenty one."

" 'Ugly in the cradle pretty at the table', that's what me mam says. Full o' sayin's is me mam, comes from readin' Old Moore's Almanac I reckon," said Billy, "mam reads it from cover to cover. Me dad used to say he could tell when it wer' best to button up and let 'er alone, nothin' to do wi' time o' the month, it wer' Old Moore an' 'is soddin phases o' the moon as brought me mam's foibles to the boil."

"Done it," shouted a triumphant Susie as she pulled free the last section of tangled string.

"Let's all walk to Turpin's an' buy an ice cream off Mavis, she only makes it on a Saturday," said Billy. They were all in total accord and a very happy Dodds family left predictions of the future to those so inclined as they walked, skipped and sang their way to the shop.

Sarah stood behind a large roasting pan basting the breasts of two chickens. "You can tell by the smell that these birds are better than Cheetham's, you should set up in competition Freddy, give 'im a run for 'is money, Robert Cheetham's had it all for far too long," she said, casting a ready smile to Annie's family.

Charles was quiet, his manner subdued. Annie could not allow anything to suggest a problem to Sarah, with Jean away and Gertie due very soon Sarah must not become preoccupied with matters beyond her own immediate family. To forestall any questioning of Charles' reaction to the baby when at some point, Annie revealed her pregnancy to Sarah, she suggested he sit with his paper. "It has been a difficult week, Charles has worked long hours, I expect he will be very discourteous and nod off to sleep after dinner," said Annie.

"He can snooze away to 'is hearts content 'ere," replied Sarah. "Davina and me both dropped off last Friday afternoon, we didn't wake up 'til the Evenin' Post come through her letterbox an' clattered onto the floor. When you can be that comfortable with a friend you know 'ow lucky you are to 'ave 'em."

"What can I do to help," asked Annie.

"Nothin' dear, I've set the table, the vegetables are on. Maggie will be back presently, she's gone for a walk with Toby. On the mantelpiece in the living room you'll see an envelope, a letter came yesterday from Jean, you can sit down Annie dear and read it," said Sarah, prodding a potato with a fork and declaring they could do with another ten minutes.

Annie sat opposite Charles, he had retreated behind his newspaper. The atmosphere between them was strained yet not in any aggressive way, neither sought conflict, indeed it was the dread of argument which bound Annie's tongue and simply not knowing what to say that held Charles in a brooding silence. Annie opened the letter it was dated April 27th.

Dear Mam,

Often I wish you were here to see the people, they can be so diverse, I thought Nottingham had its share of characters but London is like one great production of drama. I imagine sometimes that a big curtain will descend to rapturous applause and everyone I have met thus far will take a curtain call, a magnificent encore, then we shall all sing the anthem and the sound shall be so loud you and Maggie will hear it at Mitchell Street!

A frightfully posh lady came into the shop yesterday, the fur on her collar was so thick it nearly obliterated her earrings, each one a large pearl set in gold, they shone through the sleek fur like a cat's eyes at dusk. She had four rings on her fingers, her nails perfectly manicured and whilst inside the shop, she lit a cigarette which she smoked in an elegant holder, if elegant is quite the right word, I thought it made her look ridiculous. She asked for a dozen Arum Lilies, it's a good job I didn't express my sympathy, I felt sure she must be attending a funeral, we've always called them funeral lilies but she said, 'Would you please attach a card with the words, For my darling husband with wishes for a full recovery'. Seems she was on her way to the hospital but last night I saw her again, arm in arm and very cosy indeed with a much younger man. I could hear dad sayin, 'She's no better than she ought to be'.

One day this week I sold a single white rose to a lovely old gent, he must be at least 85 if he's a day. He told me, 'I give my Mary a white rose every year, she used to take it from me with a kiss and put it in the spill vase which we bought at Berwick Street Market. Now I have to put it in an urn at the cemetery. I missed our second anniversary, I was at the Crimea, Mary bless her, said if you forget again I shall tell mother that I am sorely neglected', he chuckled. 'This must be the 64th bloom', he said and gave it a kiss. It made me cry, after work I went to Paddington Green Cemetery, I couldn't help myself, it seemed foolish, what likelihood of finding a single white rose on Mary? Whoever she was. But it was peaceful there, I could picture dad and remember Harold and Frank. I walked for nearly an hour and then I found it, the only white rose that I could see in the entire cemetery. Mary Irene Boniface, she died in 1898. For 21 years that dear man has continued to give her a rose on their wedding anniversary. If he comes in the shop again and I feel quite sure that he will, I shall ask if he would permit me to sketch him. His face is so wonderfully worn yet the light in his eyes shines as bright and fresh as a daisy.

I have made a friend, Avril. She has invited me to her home on Sunday, I think her husband died in Italy, they had no family. Avril paints too, some of her work is for sale in a gallery not far from the shop. I would love to exhibit and sell some work. I would come to fetch you mam and we would book into an hotel and order Dover Sole with new potatoes all of exactly the same size with Crème Brulee for pudding.

Last night I had faggots and gravy, they were alright but I do miss your pastry. I lie awake thinking about the crust on your apple pie. Avril is like a beanpole, I think she must lack appetite. One day I shall take her to the French Hen, it is a quaint little tea room, they do lovely Victoria Sponge and the pot of tea is nice and strong, I squeezed three good cups from it.

There was a thunderstorm two nights ago, the lightning was fierce, someone said that a chimney on St. Mary's Hospital was struck but the damage was slight. When the rain started the drops were so big that they knocked the flowers off Mrs. Cavanagh's laburnum, when I left for work the front path was bright yellow. She has almost completed her tapestry, where she will hang it I can't imagine, every room in the house is adorned with her framed needlework. I like her tapestry of a cottage garden the best, the hollyhocks and delphiniums are really lovely but the pale mauve Canterbury bells look just splendid. I shall look in the seed merchants for some Canterbury bell seeds and send them to George and Freddy to plant in the allotment, they could put them along the back fence and you could have a big vase filled with colour at the living room window. You could even take a nice bunch to Davina.

I hope Gertie is keeping well, you will write to me as soon as the baby comes won't you. I have a dear little matinee jacket for it, white of course, until I know boy or girl I won't get another, although I was tempted by a pale blue romper with a white stripe. Mrs. Cavanagh's daughter has just had her fifth child, a boy named Rupert, very troubled by colic I understand, don't tell Gertie but apparently he cried every night, virtually all night for the first two weeks.

Another lodger arrived yesterday, he is a little odd but not at all unpleasant. He said grace over his faggots as though he sat at the feast of the Tabernacle, then he asked Mrs. Cavanagh if he might have cheese and a fresh apple rather than sago. He put an uneaten water biscuit in his pocket and almost like an exchange of favours, left a thruppenny piece under the rim of his plate. I wonder if he will leave Mrs. Cavanagh a tip again this evening, she seemed somewhat offended, although I'm sure he genuinely intended no offence.

Anyway it is nearly time for our meal so I shall sign off with much love to you and everyone.

Jean

XXXXX

P.S. Avril has a dog, an English Bull Terrier called Sampson. It is the soppiest creature, I told Avril he is the most unlikely Sampson I have ever come across. Annie's boys would love him.

Annie smiled as she folded the paper and put the letter back on the mantelpiece.

"You should read Jean's news Charles, it seems she has made a good friend."

"Um, I'll look at it later," he replied. "I'm reading about the proposed memorial, it will be in St. Andrew's Churchyard and will bear the names of all the war dead from the Parish."

Annie gave a deep sigh. "They will number far too many and that just one Parish."

Sarah's voice called out, "It's on the table."

The open back door filled suddenly with eager young faces, including Maggie who had arrived at exactly the right time. She rushed across the room to give Annie a hug and planted a kiss on Charles' cheek.

"It was lovely by the river this morning," said Maggie, "we saw Billy and Victor, Billy was smoking a most curious pipe, Toby called him 'Old King Cole'. Toby says that Queen Elizabeth smoked a clay pipe, he is very knowledgeable."

Maggie's chatter was happy, Annie caught Sarah's gaze, they exchanged a smile of understanding, Maggie was in love.

"The chicken is delicious Sarah," said Annie.

"I like the crispy skin," said Maggie, the juice coating her lips in a fetching glossiness. They all ate heartily including Charles. Everyone had finished except Freddy who determined himself to suck the last flake of sweet meat from the neck.

"It's the best of it," he declared with a grin of satisfaction.

"I've got a wishbone, come on William, pull." Maggie held out the bone and William wrapped his finger around it, the bone snapped and Maggie gleefully took both pieces, hid them behind her back whilst she mixed them then held them across the table once more for William to take one. With a whoop of delight she cried out, "I have the longest one, mine is the wish." She thought for a moment then, as if convinced her wish had been urgently despatched to the proper destination she said. "Toby asked me a riddle this morning, it's a good one, shall I try it on you Charles. What sits in a corner, unable to move yet can be found all over the world?"

Not even the sober Charles could resist Maggie's infectious good humour. "I don't know Maggie, what does sit in a corner unable to move yet is found all over the world?" Said Charles, smiling at the young woman's excited anticipation.

"A postage stamp," she cried jubilantly.

"That is a good 'en," said George, I'll ask the fellas at work tomorrow."

"The meal was lovely Sarah, it is very true as Jean says, your pastry is so good." Annie washed while Sarah wiped, Maggie had wanted to help but Annie suggested she watch Hilda skip. 'She has brought her rope especially to show you how well she can skip now', Annie had said tactfully. The boys had gone into the street to kick a ball about with John who desperately wanted to dribble between the lamp-posts like they could.

"I am going to have a baby Sarah," said Annie.

"Bless my soul, I nearly dropped this basin, my dear Annie what wonderful news," said Sarah, dabbing her eyes with her pinafore as they filled with joyful tears. "Sometimes I think it's that Samuel up there organising things so I shan't get lonely." Now tears filled with emotion streamed down Sarah's cheeks.

Annie dried her hands and took Sarah in her arms. "I haven't told the children just yet, only Charles, but I did tell Davina when I called on her a day or two ago and Edna knows," said Annie.

"Why my dear I can't believe Charles is so composed, I would 'ave thought 'e would be full of it, in fact he seems unusually quiet today," said Sarah.

"That's not all the news, Edna is pregnant as well, both of us are due at around the same time. It puts extra pressure on Charles, the workshops must be dominating his concern. Edna has taken on more responsibility of late, to ease the situation, Charles having to spend more time at Basford. I have offered many times to shoulder more of the load but since he came back from Egypt he has insisted I leave it to him. It sounds ridiculous but I feel sometimes as if he resents my ability. I miss Edna too, we don't see nearly as much of each other as we used to." Annie's voice was weary, not wanting to upset Sarah by refusing dinner she had eaten more than her queasiness would accept, now her nausea was intense.

"Now you know that we are all here to help, Mavis, Maggie and Davina, as well as myself, between us we can see that Charles won't need to worry about you and the baby at least." Chatter approaching the back door alerted them to the boys' presence, Sarah whispered, "I won't say anything until you let me know it's alright to but you must tell them soon."

The youngsters thirsty from their activities, clamoured for cold water, Annie took advantage of the diversion and slipped out to the privy.

"Jessie Tozer is pleased that you will go to the whist drive, some of the proceeds are for the widows fund and the rest is to help finance the memorial," said William. Only he and Charles were downstairs, Annie and the others had gone up to bed. "There are sure to be one or two interesting people present, Councillor Rathbone is on the committee so he's bound to be there."

William's pursuit of the influential ever assailed Charles' ears, he rose to his feet from the armchair by the hearth.

"I have agreed to go son, let that be enough." Charles crossed the room to the hallway, turning to William he said. "You are to have another brother or sister, perhaps that will turn your head away from those dreams of yours William and back to the reality of, 'our daily bread'. Work is what fills the majority of our days, there is no instant solution, no magic formula to fulfil our desires."

Charles climbed the stairs, leaving the young man alone.

William unlocked the back door and stood outside, a fowl disturbed by the sound gave a low call from its roosting place. A snail made its way up the privy wall, William observed the silent creature's progress for several seconds then plucked it from the chink in the brickwork where it had chosen to lodge itself. He let it slip through his fingers to the ground.

"If I can't climb then neither shall you."

He trod it with his boot. William spoke the words with swingeing resentment, he reached in his pocket for a cigarette. So, a brother or sister, he held no preference, he was the eldest, the first born, he would likely be married, even have a child of his own by the time his youngest sibling began school. He wondered what Maggie might have wished for, William liked Maggie, he liked Maggie a lot, she was not so very much older than himself after all. She had sparkle, mischief in her bones. Celia never laughed with abandon like Maggie did but she was soft and sweet smelling, besides it felt improper somehow to imagine Maggie in that way when John and Hilda referred to her as aunty Maggie. He threw down the cigarette end and stubbed it out, 'best get to bed, gather strength for my demanding position at the coffin nail factory' he muttered to himself.

The house finally found peace as William crept under the covers. Outside a crushed snail and the butt of a Player's Weight were the sorry remains of William's dream, for this day at least.

The individuals who William predicted would be present now sat with their faces hidden behind a fan of playing cards. Councillor Rathbone had a persistent habit of clearing his throat before every decision he made, then with a flourish, laying down his card as though revealing his claim to the throne. He was partnered by Catherine Appleyard, who, while entering fully into the spirit of fund raising, never the less possessed no competitive spirit whatsoever.

"If you played your 3 in the second hand and saved your 8 instead of the other way about that trick would be ours," said Rathbone, his heavy jowls 'concertinaing' as though the animated sides of his handlebar moustache employed him like a set of bellows. It was almost the end of the drive and Catherine's tiredness rendered her tolerance a little thin.

"Yes, Councillor Rathbone," she said, vexated by his self importance, "and as I once overheard one very astute woman remark, 'if the dog had not stopped to shit it would have caught the rabbit'."

Jessie Tozer did his best to conceal his amusement and Charles couldn't help wondering if the astute woman to whom Catherine referred might be Edna.

Sitting seven tables away was Edwin Garbett, he had nodded acknowledgement of Charles but their paths had not crossed and Charles, now sure he would not find himself at the same table, felt a measure of relief.

Gerald Birkett had partnered Edwin at one game, he had perceived a tension between Edwin and Charles, noticed their strained glances. These were troubled times, the glorious peace so long craved for now seemed unable to satisfy. Men created friction, calm was mistrusted, some men needed a means to ignite.

At last the M.C. declared the event at an end, thanking everyone for their support. With the customary 'God Save The King', Charles found himself liberated. Jessie walked alongside him.

"Your wife didn't care to come this evening?" Said Charles.

Jessie laughed, "You must meet my Gwendolyn, her mind is set on one course, if only she could spend less time in the study of Who's Who she might then grasp the rules of a simple card game. I'm sorry William chafes so over The Lodge, he is ambitious for success and a good life, perhaps we should applaud that but the truth is I would never have joined the ranks of the influential had it not been for Gwendolyn's insistence. Bless her, I believe she was convinced I would bring home each month a detailed pedigree of all those attending for her to read avidly. I fear I must be a great disappointment to her Charles. Your son and my daughter seem mutually fond, that is reason enough for us to enjoy the blissfully uncomplicated pleasure of a pint of ale. I am not a drinking man, indeed I cannot remember when I was last in a public house but tonight Charles, there is just enough time for us to abandon briefly the regularity of our days. Who knows what the prize might be or who ultimately may take it, come, a pint it shall be."

The Standard embraced the usual devotees of social intercourse,

Charles, familiar with the seating, led Jessie to a table in one corner, their fingers wrapped around their beer glasses, each took a mouthful of the refreshing brew.

"Do you know Charles, I believe this is undoubtedly the best hand of the night," said Jessie with a chuckle.

Charles gazed down at the spent contents of a pipe and numerous cigarette ends in a well used ashtray.

"As a young man I remember asking father why he didn't join the other fellows of commerce. He sat in that back office, surveying his tiny empire, seemingly afraid to venture beyond its boundaries. I saw less intelligent than he grasp the future, men in and out of the bank where I worked, ever growing in importance and influence. Father was bright, capable, I wanted him to show this city what he was made of and in turn, make me a prodigy of his success. 'Why don't you rub shoulders father'? I asked him. I can recall his answer even now after all these years. He replied vaguely and I didn't fully understand but sensing his unwillingness to clarify his words, thereafter I left the subject alone. He said, 'I tried that way once Charles and while it gave me Hilda, your mother, for which I am ever thankful, it took away my self respect and for that I am eternally sorry'. When father died I regretted many things yet still I carried on in my own opinionated way. As I grow older I think of him more."

Charles looked up at Jessie Tozer who, possessing the wisdom of years did not speak but simply patted Charles' arm.

"Time gentleman if you please." The landlord's cry seemed to summon both men home and they went their separate ways through the gloom of the streets.

CHAPTER EIGHTEEN

The constable gave a satisfied smirk as he directed the young man through the door and into the cell.

"There you go lad, spend an hour in 'ere wi' the old Irish bender, that'll bring a touch o' colour to yer cheeks."

The door slammed shut and Brian turned to scowl at the policeman's sickening laughter as it echoed back along the corridor.

An elderly man, slight of build, sat with his head slumped forward, a tangle of fading ginger hair hung from his thin, lined neck, one hand gripped the wooden bench as if to keep his frame from falling to the worn, grey slate beneath his feet, he did not look up. Brian coughed and said.

"I'm Haynes, Brian Haynes, who are you?"

With a hesitation which produced merely a deep breath, the man cupped his other hand over one knee, his fingers followed the bony contours hidden by his trouser and in so doing, momentarily raised his turn-up sufficiently to expose an ankle that narrow of flesh the shoe below cried out to be filled.

"Nobody, that's me, plain nobody," he replied feebly.

"Got to be somebody," said Brian, "even our cat's got a name, I called it Tilly. After me dad died me mam went strange for a bit, all quiet and distant like. Then one day I come 'ome from work an' there she wer' in me dad's old chair wi' this kitten in 'er lap. 'It's a girl', she said, 'it's a little female'. Well for three days it were called 'Puss' til I said to mam, 'you've got to give it a proper name, summat it can recognise as its own'. That night when I took it outside to the yard to see if it 'ould relieve itself afore we all went to bed, I looked at me lamp, then at the cat, an' that's when I thought o' the name, Tilly. So, what's your name then?"

The man raised his face. "Mahoney, Dermot Mahoney."

Brian felt surprised at seeing the aged features, the empty eyes.

"I don't mean no offence but aren't you a bit old and skinny to be gettin' yerself into a scrap. I don't rightly understand all this republican business, me dad fought in France, 'is enemy wer' foreign but Irish fightin' wi' Irish, you've got me bloody stumped." Brian sat down beside his companion. "Our Victor don't hurt anybody, 'e minds 'is own business, what's it got to do wi' the likes o' Vernon Arkwright what our Victor looks like. I've put up wi' 'is snide remarks an' soddin' insults for years, well no more, I just couldn't take it anymore. I laid into 'im, pinned the bugger to the ground and shoved 'is miserable, ugly mouth into the brambles at the side o' canal. Yell! You should 'ave 'eard 'is squeals, like a bloody pig being strung up at Cheetham's yard. When the rozzer come an' pulled me off 'im, Arkwright's face were colour o' damson jam an' all swelled up like summat putrefyin'."

Mahoney's gaze followed a beetle which crossed from side to side the cell floor, it dragged behind it a small piece of dusty fluff which had attached to a back leg.

"What's wrong with your brother?" He asked with little expression in his voice.

Brian sniffed, not from any need of blowing his nose but from a resigned acceptance of fate.

"Victor wer' born wi' this condition, a Mongol they call it, makes 'im look a bit different an 'e don't reason like most folks do, I reckon Victor thinks the world is made o' gingerbread. Yet sometimes 'e'll come out wi' a remark as makes you wonder if it isn't us that got it all mixed up. When we buried me dad Victor stood wi' Billy Dodds. Tis dire to see a man cry an Billy wer' awful upset. They knew each other from the time they were in the hospital together, Billy an' me dad. When the Vicar said, 'We commend his soul unto The Lord', mam looked like she wer' about to collapse over me eldest brother Raymond but Victor 'as this 'abit of repeatin' words an' we 'eard 'im say, 'Sold to The Lord', just like the auctioneer 'ad knocked down me dad to the highest bidder. God must 'ave really wanted me dad, I reckon Victor wer' right. Now Albert Haynes sits proud somewhere in The Lord's house, nobody else could afford 'im, too valuable for this world. Anyroad, Victor can't help the way 'e wer' born can 'e, no man can. Well, may as well make the most o' me bit o' peace, give it a couple of hours an' the plod'll kick our arses out o' this place."

Brian lay down on the bench, curled his legs and closed his eyes. Dermot Mahoney watched as the beetle finally made its escape under the bottom of the door, leaving behind the tiresome piece of life's debris. He sank his head into his hands and wondered if there would be a single bid for him when the time came.

Edna dropped the last gooseberry into the colander, rubbed her fingers over the piece of newspaper which had collected the 'tops and tails' then popped into her mouth a large, ripe, invitingly pink one which she had put aside some ten minutes earlier.

I'm fancyin' summat sharp, yesterday it wer' 'arf a stick o' rhubarb dipped in an' out o' the sugar pot. Billy thinks for sure it's a boy, it'll be shoutin' for a titty bottle filled wi' bitter instead o' mother's milk 'e reckons an' me mam says, 'you're carryin' low our Edna, sure sign it's a boy'. Accordin' to me mam, if you can sit at table an' rest your folded arms on your belly it's a girl."

Annie, weighing up the sugar for her jam, smiled at the unlikely observation. Edna was desperate to give Billy a son and clung to every hope that it might be so.

"Sylvia 'as been sittin' at 'er machine wi' a daft grin on 'er face for days an' when I found she'd sewn a badge on a blazer the wrong way up, I knew there must be summat accountin' for that soppy look, tis not like Sylvia to make a mistake but there they were, Blackmore's three upstandin' acorns hangin' down like Wrenshaw's hops. Well low an' behold Sylvia's sweet on Victor's brother Brian, they've been to the pictures twice, an' tomorro' apparently, 'e's takin' 'er to the engine sheds at Toton to show 'er the new freight engine, poor lass'll be overcome wi' excitement. What wi' Sylvia's love lorn sighin' an' Kathleen's shoutin', I know 'er dear mam is deaf an' all them kids are used to shoutin' at 'ome but I told 'er, 'try rememberin' to talk a bit quieter when you're 'ere', I'd swear the baby kicks every time Kathleen opens 'er mouth. An' on top o' that the damn machine I'm workin' on is fast gettin' past its best, it cranks an' rattles summat chronic but no use sayin' anythin' to 'is nibs, all 'e does is sit in that back office grumblin' an' chunterin' to 'isself, tis like workin' in the loony bin. What's wrong wi' 'im anyroad, no more than 'arf a dozen words 'as 'e spoke to us all week an' that's a generous estimate."

Edna smacked her lips and before Annie had chance to tip the colander of gooseberries into the pan, she pinched another blush pink fruit.

"You'll have stomach ache if you're not careful," said Annie. "I think you best make us a cuppa and eat a slice of Madeira cake to bind those berries."

Charles' moods were becoming worse but Annie had dared to hope that at his work he might maintain a calm for the women's sake if not for his own. William's relentless pursuit of that, 'better life', supposedly reached on the back of his father, did little to relieve tensions, in fact Charles' shrinking spirit of endeavour served only to swell the young man's frustration further.

Edwin Garbett had not been spoken of since the day Charles declared he had called on him, Annie had tried desperately to put the episode to rest and not until Bertha, one afternoon, in conversation with Annie, had indirectly related news of him, did Edwin's name come up again. A strange turn of events had led, temporarily, to Edwin overseeing Isaac Jacobson's business. The rather stern, less than benevolent gentleman had taken a nasty tumble when negotiating a roughly cobbled stretch of pathway used as a shortcut through Friar Gate. Most of the businessmen on leaving their meeting would use a cab or walk along Castle Road to the tram. Jacobson could save the fare and expected gratuity if he used the shortcut and then walked the half mile to his residence on Langley Drive. A broken ankle had been the traumatic result, Edwin Garbett, of necessity, had been entrusted with the clients' accounts. Annie had felt a divine intervention must surely have prevailed, Isaac Jacobson could do no other than grant Edwin a secure position now. Unbeknown to Annie, Rachel Jacobson, Isaac's wife, a gentle, good natured soul had chivvied her husband to allow Edwin some peace of mind, acquainted as she was with Edwin's mother, who had in the past worked as a 'daily' for her own mother and having a fond regard for the elderly woman who had shown much kindness to her, growing up as she did in a very strict household, where her brothers were schooled in The Faith and moulded for academic success while Rachel, the only girl, had ever felt her own role to be much less significant.

Annie sat down by Edna at the kitchen table, choosing her words carefully and conservatively she attempted an explanation, a pardonable cause of Charles' unfortunate manner.

"When Charles first came home relief consumed us all, we wore our sense of well being like a cloak, it wrapped us about in glorious warmth, beneath it we felt entirely protected against any threatening element. Charles too for the most part seemed lighthearted, at times a little remote but he had been in Egypt for more than two years, how could we know, even begin to imagine what scenes might have lodged behind his eyes, scenes to bring back cruel reminders when just for a moment he let his sights fall from the present. I have heard other women say their men are possessed of ghosts from the war, unable to simply slot back into the positions they held prior to the fighting. I think it was the immediacy, we had been married three years before John, when I told him we were going to have another child for a while he could not accept it, foolish tongues had spread gossip, distorting the incident at the bank that time of Edwin's fit. Charles doubted his own conviction, he even went to Edwin to ask if the baby was his."

"God Almighty," exclaimed Edna, "I best 'ave a word wi' Charles Eddowes, somebody needs to sort 'im out, I know 'e wer' in a shit 'ole for all that time, but so wer' my Billy an' lots of other men but their brains are still in their 'eads, Charles must 'ave left 'is in the bloody desert, I've allus thought you wer' too good for 'im, if your aunt Bella wer' still 'ere she'd skin 'im alive."

Edna rose to her feet as if not a single minute could elapse before she sought Charles to deliver her admonishment.

"No Edna," Annie's voice was firm, she crossed to the range and stirred the pan of softening fruit. Looking directly at her friend of so many years she continued her loyal defence of Charles.

"He knows it was a nonsense, at the time I felt hurt and dismayed but when I sat down calmly to think, to reason, then I could understand."

Edna lowered herself once more to the chair, grudgingly, not out of sympathy toward Charles but for the total regard she held for Annie.

"Charles was no more than eighteen when his mother died, Saul died less than five years later and we can both recall the drama, the shock. Within twelve months of that happening his wife, the beautiful Enid passed away amid the most heartrending circumstances leaving him with two infants. Charles made a good friend whilst he was away, possibly the first real friendship he had known, the war took Clem, I never met this man but Charles' letters revealed to me the depth of feeling he had for his newly found friend and his desolation at loosing him. Is it any wonder that now, after all these tragedies, Charles has a mistrust of life."

Edna perhaps more emotional than usual in her pregnant state, could not prevent the tears welling up in her eyes, she sniffed and fumbled in her pocket for a hanky. Annie took the bowl of sugar from the table and poured it over the gooseberries.

"It will be alright Edna, the baby will come and bring its love as they all do and if your mam is right, then there will be a beautiful boy at the Dodd's household."

The two women embraced and Edna's tears flowed as she poured out all her past heartache, between sobs came the words.

"Billy could 'ave died, I could 'ave lost 'im an' be sittin' like May wi' me mind God knows where. Let it be a boy, dear God let me give Billy a son."

Annie held her dearest friend in her arms until all the stress subsided. Between short breaths of recovery Edna promised her accord.

"I won't say owt if that's what yer want, but 'ow Charles could think that your baby wer' Edwin Garbett's beggars belief. Anyroad, I best be off

292

'ome, mam gave me an old recipe book, 'Cookin' on a budget'. Soon there'll be only one wage comin' in so I'm tryin' to spread the pennies. Suet crust around some knuckle wi' a thick onion sauce an' one o' Billy's cabbages is what we're 'avin' for tea today."

Edna sighed and sniffed in that order. Annie smiled, put down her wooden spoon by the side of the bubbling pan and went to the cupboard.

"This will help finances." She handed a jar of lemon curd to Edna, "it's not as sharp as rhubarb or gooseberries but it will do you no harm at all," she said with a chuckle.

"I don't want to take your jam, I'd make some of me own but that allotment wer' so grown in Billy 'ad to prune all the fruit bushes so this year they've not produced enough for more than a pie or two," she paused for a second, "but if you're sure."

William turned from the street and walked slowly up the side of the house, he heard Edna's voice and as was his unfortunate way, ever curious of others' conversation he paused short of the window.

"William doesn't help, his persistence in badgering his dad to push forward, to rub shoulders with the influential seems to drive Charles further into retreat, your family is blessed in its contentment and I am blessed to have such a friend." Annie kissed Edna's cheek.

William's senses stung from those words he had overheard Annie speak. He turned and ran quickly to the street, back to the lamppost in the opposite direction to that which he knew Edna would take, she was obviously about to leave. To still his nerves he took a Player's Weight from his pocket, not lighting it he leant against the post, holding the cigarette in his mouth, almost like a dummy from infancy. Edna appeared at the gate of No.14, she glanced his way, her arm extended to wave, she was smiling. William waved back, his eyes followed her along the street as she made her way to the corner.

So, it's my fault, it's all my fault, well, we shall see. William's thoughts drove his temper beyond his immediate awareness, he choked and spat into the gutter. Unwittingly he had bitten the end off the cigarette releasing an unpalatable measure of tobacco shreds onto his tongue. He cursed and swore at the abiding bitter taste.

Celia laughed like a child as the ladybird crawled across the back of her hand, quickly she lifted the palm of the other and held it alongside, the tiny creature crossed to the soft pink flesh which until that moment had held tight William's fingers, it travelled over her wrist.

"Look William, it's opening its wings."

Celia raised her arm as if to launch the ladybird into the summer sky, in seconds it was gone, she kissed William's cheek.

"What are you staring at?" She asked, seeing no event before them at the embankment which might merit his deep concentration.

"See that gent over there, the one with the pale linen jacket."

William nodded toward a tall, slender, distinguished looking man standing alone but observing the congenial gathering, sharing this Saturday afternoon's relaxed ambience. The sun fell warm about the prettily frocked ladies and found every glint among the blonde locks of the children, intent on various games and childish distractions which left the adults free to pursue their conversations.

"Andrew Smithfield, he's the new owner of the old munitions factory. Textiles, that's his line, woollen mainly, made his money in Ireland, mother from Tipperary, father from London, both dead and him a single man. He'll no doubt cause a flurry of excitement among the unattached ladies, could put a useful bit of work the way of me dad, new gowns and silk under slips. Reg overheard Smithfield being discussed in the pub, rumour has it he'll be taking on workers by Michaelmas. He got out ahead of the troubles, as he predicts the nature of coming years, apparently he told someone he could feel hot Irish breath on the back of his neck."

William spoke with unsettling authority, most other young men of similar years centred their fascination on the female sex or competitive sport, matters political were given only passing, scant attention. William however, directed his growing curiosity at the 'rule makers' as he perceived them. He had played snakes and ladders many times when the dice refused to fall his way, he had drawn the conclusion that the contrary dice was inconsequential to the individual who had devised the game, the 'rule maker' assured of success whichever way the dice tumbled.

Celia tugged at William's sleeve. "Look, Mr.Mazarelli has arrived with his ice cream cart, please William, please can we have a cone?"

He rose to his feet, sighed and replied, "Come on then."

Celia threaded her arm through his, crossing the embankment took them by Andrew Smithfield who now exchanged conversation with another man, Robert Cheetham. Celia paused, smiled and speaking softly through shyness said.

"Hello cousin Robert."

"Why if it isn't my pretty young cousin Celia, tell me how is your mother, well I trust," then without allowing her any chance to answer, " let me introduce you to Mr.Andrew Smithfield, a recent acquaintance and a very welcome one at that."

An easy smile came to Smithfield's face.

"It is a pleasure to meet you Celia," he took her hand and gently kissed the spot where just a few minutes earlier a ladybird had held Celia's attention. Turning to face William, his manner entirely unassuming, he said.

"How do you do?"

William took Smithfield's hand and shook it firmly.

"William Eddowes sir, my father has the workshops."

Smithfield felt amused at the directness of the young man.

"Indeed I am pleased to meet you both."

Celia, more intent on an ice cream than her cousin hurried William away with a friendly wave back to satisfy politeness.

"He's your cousin, Robert Cheetham is your cousin," said William considerably impressed by this unexpected revelation.

"Mother is a first cousin to Robert so Edmund and I must be second cousins, is that what they mean by 'twice removed'?" Said Celia.

How many times removed was of no significance to William, only the fact that Celia was related to Robert Cheetham, proprietor of two high street butchers' shops and owner of the slaughter yard. William looked back on the two men still in conversation. The lyrical tones of Mr.Mazarelli's voice, calling those present to refresh themselves with a cooling vanilla ice meant William must transfer his attention to Celia, who was desperate the charming little Italian should not sell out before they reached him. Ever popular but with limited measure and time he often raised his upturned hands in a gesture of regret and called out.

"*Tutto perduto, tutto perduto,*" to a disappointed number, too late in joining the queue.

George and Freddy were the last to arrive home, the allotment had offered up a bounty of soft fruit. Annie had transformed all the gooseberries into an array of jam, some infused with elderflowers, some with a trace of the first redcurrants. Now sitting on the kitchen table, awaiting attention, were an enamel bowl of red and white currants and a small jug of loganberries. Every item of produce was gathered at the allotment with a deep sense of loyalty to Samuel, the boys had observed his ways, airing those same frustrations at the devious doings of caterpillars, clinging to the underside of leaves and spiteful little beetles wreaking havoc below ground. George regularly scooped quantities of woodlice from upturned plant pots into an old toffee tin, transporting them in his dinner bag back to No.14 where he shook them into the fowls' enclosure and whooped with delight at the 'free for all' which ensued.

"Come along, tea is ready."

Annie smiled at their urgency to wash and reach their place at table, hungry from an afternoon of intense activity. Freddy worked long hours with

Arthur Cropley, most of the hay was now saved and Freddy had immediately turned his efforts to helping George with the 'domestic' harvest. Hilda and John had been to see Sarah and returned with the customary bag of goodies.

"There is a chocolate bar for each of you and a stick of rock from aunty Jean, she's been to Southend-on-Sea with her friend Avril, they sat on the pier with Samson and a pot of whelks, Samson licked the ice cream off a little girl's cone while aunty Jean was being sick," declared Hilda as Annie put the last plate of food on the table in front of herself and sat down.

Charles was quiet as usual. William, sitting beside his father inwardly rebelled at the wholesome family scene. Rancour, deep resentment had festered, just below the surface all the past week, Annie's words innocently spoken, had found Williams immaturity, now he delivered his volley across the table with no regard for anyone but himself.

"Your friend Edwin Garbett hasn't been to see you lately Mam, I felt sure he would call on dad when he heard of his return. Still, now he is ensconced at Jacobson's I suppose his mind must be elsewhere. Seeing all your jam on the shelf made me think of him, picking blackberries at The Meadows for his mother whilst you and he chatted. It occurred to me that we haven't seen him in months."

Charles' eyes fixed on Annie, he put down his knife and fork, rose from the table, crossed to the back door slamming it behind himself, just like William in his moments of temper shook the household before leaving it to tremor in the aftermath. Annie's gaze sought William, he lowered his eyes, shuffling his feet he offered a pitiful apology.

"I didn't intend any upset, it was the sight of all that jam, I meant no offence," he lied with as much bluff as his determined mood could muster. A sickening satisfaction enabled him to finish his meal, clear his plate. Annie prompted the others.

"Finish your food and I shall read to you the lovely letter which came this morning from Alice Hemsley."

Freddy lay in the darkness wide awake. Sharing a bed with William tormented him, he could feel the wooden bed frame galling his side but that discomfort was minor compared to the pain William had inflicted. Distance, he needed distance between himself and his brother. Annie had shown them no less love than she had shown her own George, had tended and cared for them just as devotedly, wrapped them in family. John and little Hilda deserved better than William's spiteful outburst.

George had sat with his mother until his eyes would stay open no longer, now with all the children in bed, Annie too lay wide awake in the darkness, awaiting what she knew not. It was well into the early hours when she heard faint movement on the stairs. The door of the spare room, disturbed from its inactivity, creaked a gesture of surprise, it confirmed Charles' return. So, he would rather lie there with desperate memories than recognise the jealously in his eldest son. Annie now believed there had ever existed a resentment on William's part, not merely of Edwin Garbett or even of herself but of a cruel, heartless God who gave no thought to William Eddowes, no sanction to his plans, no glory to his schemes. Annie had taken his hand as an infant and felt wondrous love, now that same hand had struck her in malice and she felt a stinging hurt just as surely as if William had physically raised his fist to her.

In the stillness the baby kicked forcefully, as if registering its own objection to this slight on its name. Annie turned the pillow, damp from tears, willing the night to pass. First light filtered through the curtains, she dressed, pinned her hair, tiptoed down the stairs and did all she could think to do. Taking an old gazette from the shelf she spread it over the scullery table and began to top and tail the waiting currants. Only a few minutes passed before Charles stood in the doorway, Annie was the first to speak.

"If you leave the house this morning still not believing the child to be yours then you will never find peace," she paused, "Edwin Garbett came here twice, the first time was late one night. When walking home from a meeting he had come across May, wandering the streets dressed only in her nightclothes, not knowing what else to do he brought her here. He came just one other time, in fact not long before you returned from Egypt. He wished to say thank you for the help I offered at the bank that afternoon of his seizure. William, for whatever reason has set your mind on a tragic course. He is young, at times foolish and although it grieves me to say it, he is selfish. He displays a streak of avarice from which most people would retreat, those who do not will doubtless be of like mind or have the misfortune to realise his character only when he demands of them. I have told you the truth Charles, I can do no more."

He closed the kitchen door to the hall and returned to the scullery, looking across to where Annie sat with the bowl of redcurrants in her lap.

"I suppose if I go to May and ask she will justify your explanation, put all my doubts to rest, that of course, is if she could recall for a moment who I am, indeed who she herself might be and I imagine it is pure coincidence that on his second visit not one of the older boys was present. You know that not even I, the pathetic Charles Eddowes would interrogate his two youngest on a subject so vulgar."

Annie rallied, returning his delivery. "The child is ours, created by you, borne by me, I feel it move within me as we speak, I pray to God it cannot hear what we say." Annie was fighting tears.

"Admit it, Edwin Garbett aside, you would rather the child be Harold Boucher's than any man's," said Charles his voice shaking with emotion.

"No more than you would have it be Enid's."

The very instant the words left her lips Annie regretted them but Charles' accusations cut like a whip. He moved towards her and for a second she felt fear of him, the colander fell from her lap spilling the contents across the flags. Confused by the small red berries which now covered the area about his feet, Charles turned and with an unlikely attempt at avoiding the fruit, reached the back door and went outside.

Annie heard the latch on the privy, she knelt to recover the redcurrants, unsure as to whether he would come back indoors or take himself off somewhere.

In the privy Charles wept silently, only the lime washed bricks and the cobbles beneath his feet were permitted to witness his misery.

'You're a rum 'en you are Charlie boy'. Clem's voice echoed inside his head, he could picture Saul's face, tired, old, looking back at Charles with bitter disappointment. Outside, the fowls hearing movement, had begun to cluck and flap their wings against the side of the coop. When he returned to the house Annie was washing the fruit in the scullery. The kettle sat humming softly over the range, Charles took his shaving mug from the ledge.

"Sylvia's mother has to go into hospital, she was told last Wednesday that she has a growth which must be removed from her insides. Sylvia is upset, Mrs.Robinson had apparently divulged nothing of the trouble until I suppose, she had little choice."

He poured hot water into a bowl, dipped in his shaving brush and lathered his face so profusely Annie believed he hid beneath this soapy mask. A curious but redeeming stillness now occupied the room, the distress of another household Charles had used to divert the tribulation of his own, it produced no comfort but achieved to hold at bay the need of further conversation.

It was Sunday, that day of The Lord, yet this day felt utterly forsaken.

CHAPTER NINETEEN

Gertie handed her young son to his grandma, now fed and content he would soon be asleep.

"I'm sure one tastes better than the other, he always wants the left one first and never seems to suck as long on the right. Steve reckons the left must be sweet and the right one savoury. 'All kids like puddin' best', says Steve. Trouble is, one's gettin' bigger than the other. Will I stay like that when Jack's finished Mam or will they go back to normal." Gertie sighed as she fastened up her buttons.

"If you want the answer to that question you should ask a woman who's had no more that two or three," said Sarah. "By the time I'd fed all of you mine had changed their identity altogether, Samuel would say, 'You can be proud o' them lass, they've served Queen an' country well'.

Gertie laughed. "Dear dad, I sometimes think Jack has the look of his grandad, can you see it Mam?"

Little Jack Wainwright's fingers explored the crochet covered buttons on Sarah's blouse.

"This child is just like Steve," said Sarah, "look at the size of his hands and I'd swear he's a good 2lbs heavier than he was last week, you've still got plenty of milk then?"

Gertie laughed, "The more he sucks mam, the more I make, at this rate I shall overtake production at Carlton Dairy."

Sarah sighed. "Annie worries me, she's lookin' awful pale, I told her to drink some stout, I know she wer' troubled wi' sickness for months but the baby is due soon an' I reckon Annie is tired out. Whenever I call at No.14 she's busy, I know times are 'ard but surely Charles' business must be doin' well enough to give 'em a decent livin' wi'out Annie scrimpin' an' scratchin' to save a penny ha'penny. Last week she wer' sewin' sheets side to middle an' yesterday I found 'er makin' brawn, instead o' sittin' down for a bit she 'ad bowls o' pigs 'ead across the table an' windfall apples for makin' sweet pickle.

If you ask her she allus says she's alright an' I really struggled to persuade her to let me chop the onions and sterilize the jars. As for Charles, I never see him whether I go by day or night an' William is like a gust o' wind, in an' out the house wi' 'ardly a civil hello. George an' Freddy work the allotment an' I've only ever seen George cutting' kindlers. What William does I don't know but his father needs to 'ave a word wi' the lad, knock the chip off his shoulder."

Sarah looked down at her latest grandson, now fast asleep in her arms, the closeness of his chubby little body comforting her own. No longer able to lie in Samuel's warmth, all the hours spent alone, moments of such reassuring love Sarah held on to for as long as she could.

"I bumped into Dorothy Cox last Saturday," said Gertie, "she was just about to go into Cheetham's as I came out, she told me that Charles hasn't taken delivery of any cloth for some time, apparently the stock is very low. Two of the women have gone over to Winchester Street, I suppose with Edna at home now and Sylvia working shorter hours so as to look after her mam, Charles thought he must bolster the situation there. Steve says the mood at the pit isn't good, the men feel sore and let down. They've worked 'til the muscles across their shoulders are tighter than harp strings keepin' the country in fuel, every drop of sweat shed willingly for soldiers and their families, driven to back all the lads with more hours cuttin' coal from the bowels o' the earth than mortal flesh should ever have to endure. Steve's come home some nights hardly able to breathe, I lie in bed listening to 'im wheezin' in his sleep. Yet pay is poor and conditions not what they should be. One day last week, as the cage reached the top, an older man just collapsed at their feet, they carried him to the office and Eddie gave him a tot of brandy. What with the war an' everythin' nobody had given a thought to the poor devil's age and he'd carried on, 'doin' his bit'. Eddie looked up his details in the file, Tom Stoker is 73!"

Sarah sighed, the last five years through their nature of tribulation, had brought a cynical outlook to many people whose character was not naturally so.

"Your grandad worked on the railway lines," she said, wiping a milky dribble from the corner of Jack's mouth with the hanky Sarah always kept tucked inside her sleeve. "I can remember him tellin' Samuel that it was his dread, fallin' down dead at work, 'cause labour wer' that cheap he believed the boss 'ould bury 'im under a sleeper to prevent any delay an' simply fetch another man out o' the workhouse, that your grandma 'ould never know what become of him."

A knock came at the front door, Gertie lifted the sleeping child from Sarah's arms.

"Now who do you suppose that is," Sarah was vexed at having to relinquish hold of Jack and tutted her annoyance as she made her way to the front door.

"Got a parcel for you Mrs.Boucher," the postman stood at the step, a big grin on his face.

"You're lookin' pleased wi' yourself today," said Sarah as she took from him a brown paper package and two envelopes.

"Me uncle Cedric died a week or two back it wer' a shock to us all, 'e never ailed a thing. Aunty Dulcie got quite excited the day 'e come 'ome from Papplewick wi' a yella face. 'E wer' the gardener there an' a nest of hornets 'ad been drivin' 'im to distraction every time 'e had to pass to get to the tool shed, so 'e decided to smoke the little buggers out wi' sulphur. Well 'e never paid no heed to a sneeze just as 'e took the lid off the soddin' stuff but it turned 'is face the colour o' piddle. When aunty Dulcie saw 'im she thought it 'ad to be jaundice at the very least, rushed for the liver salts, but no, fit as a flea 'e wer'. We used to say it wer' 'is work as a young man, emptyin' the tubs as give 'im immunity to all ills. Never 'ad as much as a sniffle in dead o' winter, yet me dad, Cedric's brother, spent more time on 'is back than 'e did upright. Mam allus kept the invalid cup on the scullery shelf beside the 'Sal Volatile', said it were a waste o' time puttin' 'em in the cupboard, they went up an' down the stairs more times than Estelle Downing. Do you know, she's bought one o' them posh 'ouses out Wollaton, retired now they say, 'ad a fancy stained glass window put on the landin' wi' 'er initials, EWD in bright red. Apparently she's Estelle Winifred. Well some wag climbed up the wall the other night an' painted an L on the brickwork beside the window." He laughed raucously, then let out a long wistful sigh. "What was I sayin', oh yes, it seems me uncle Cedric 'as remembered me in 'is Will, don't know what I've got so I shall 'ave to go an' see me aunty Dulcie to find out. She wer' in a rare old state, carried up 'is mug o' tea that mornin', just like allus an' there 'e wer', dead as a dodo wi' 'is mouth an' eyes wide open like that gargoyle on St.Andrews Church. Parcel from your Jean is it? Bet she's 'avin' a grand time in London, I've 'eard the dance halls there can 'old as many as five hundred people, mind you wi' the shortage o' young men, poor buggers, I reckon the women can't be too choosy, still many a fine tune played on an old fiddle as they say. Best be on me way, got all Ainsley Road to do yet."

Sarah gazed down at a deposit of 'mess' left by his boot, 'dogs', she concluded after lowering her nose to identify the origin.

Gertie smiled at the sight of Sarah's post. "Good, now you've something to cheer you up when we've gone, I shall have to put him in his pram now Mam, Mavis and Eddie are coming for tea tonight so I want to make sure of four nice chump chops before Cheetham's sell out. You can tell me all the news when I come next time."

The parcel did indeed have a London postmark and one of the envelopes they recognised right away as being written in Ivy's hand.

Sarah waved to them as they crossed the yard, gathered a bucket and scrubbing brush from the privy and with a few words of annoyance set about ridding the front step of the postman's unwanted delivery.

"Good morning Sarah."

She looked up at the owner of the voice, Millicent Toft, Josiah was now so crippled by arthritis he never left the house, old and weary of spirit he spent his days in a chair, thickly padded with sheepskin to keep his joints from further pain.

"How is Josiah?" Asked Sarah with genuine concern. The poor man's desperate anguish over Harold's death had nearly turned his brain. Neither she nor Samuel had ever blamed him but Josiah had punished himself mentally and his wife's despair had led her to seek help of Sarah. It was Samuel who had sat with Josiah and tried to dissuade his troubled mind of such thoughts.

"As ever, but no worse Sarah, thank you for asking," replied Millicent. "Anything you need from Waterford's, I could drop it in for you on my way back, I'm only going for some seed for the bird. Josiah sits watching the antics of that little creature for hours at a time, I just hope this one goes on longer than the last."

Since acquiring their first canary some sixteen years ago, a depressed Josiah had become so attached that when it died it was replaced immediately, but sadly, the second bird lived for only a few months, now on their third, poor Millicent tended it like a much loved child.

"I'm goin' out meself in just a little while, when I've got rid of this." Sarah wrinkled her nose and looked down at the step.

"Postman I suppose, he did the same thing to me last week," said Millicent, "if he spent more time lookin' where he was goin' instead of nosin' everybody's post he might manage to avoid the damn stuff. Well, goodbye then Sarah."

The two women exchanged smiles, Sarah completed her task, struggled up from her knees, catching sight of Harold's smiley face on the wall as she stood. It meant more to Sarah than any stained glass window. Before tears could fall she hurried inside, word from Jean and Ivy threw her a lifeline. Hands scrubbed clean and spectacles polished clear on the corner of the antimacassar, Sarah sat to read her post. Folding back the brown paper and a layer of fine tissue paper, revealed a pretty flannelette nightgown and woollen stockings, tucked inside the neck of the nightie a letter dated September 3rd.

Dear Mam.

You are sure to be called to Annie's before too long and all babies seem determined to arrive in the middle of the night so these will help keep you warm whilst you attend your latest grandchild. I know you will stay at Hood Street for several days so write when you have chance or tell Annie to write a letter to me whilst she is resting up following the birth. I am hoping to come home, just for a long weekend, at the end of this month. If it would be alright I thought I might bring Avril and Samson, you would like her mam. I have told her that what she needs more than anything is some of your pastry, blackberry and apple pie, just the thought makes me long to see you. Send young John and Hilda to pick the blackberries, the apples on grandad's old tree at the allotment are probably ripe enough by now. I shall bring some 'treats' from the big market and we shall have a feast for George's birthday.

I have had my hair cut short, it is the style here these days. I expect you will think it too modern and dad would have declared 'you look like Joan of Arc our Jean' but it is very much easier in the mornings, no tangles and no fiddling about with combs and pins.

I think I have found the ideal man for Nora, she will never meet anybody while she hides herself away at the Hymers. Surely she could have a few days off, if she travelled with Avril and me when we returned to London and stayed at Mrs.Cavanagh's, I could introduce her to him. He arrived two weeks ago, very reserved, in fact shy, since then I have engaged him in conversation and discovered he works in the laboratories at the hospital. He is driven by a determination to discover more about Tuberculosis. He told me that many soldiers survived the war only to develop TB on their return to England. He is incredibly dedicated to his work, I would put his age at about 50, he has a splendid name, Randall Tennyson and like dear Nora is deserving of someone to appreciate his qualities.

Avril says I am too romantic to be a successful cupid, she says that the God of love would take full account of practicalities before simply firing off an arrow, otherwise in no time at all, every mythological bird would be plucked bare of feathers then, unable to replenish stocks to fulfil his task, cupid would be demoted to the lower ranks. I told Avril she has no soul!

We did the flowers for a wedding last weekend, perhaps it was that which put me in a soppy mood. When I get married I shall carry deep red roses, asparagus fern and pure white freesias. The bride last Saturday chose pink and cream carnations with gypsophila, while very lovely they didn't seem quite glorious enough to proclaim true love.

Samson is very clean and would be happy sleeping in the scullery as Eli did. The boys could take him to The Meadows, he will retrieve a ball and relishes a tug of war with some old rope.

Must close now, supper will be called at any minute. I think I can smell liver. Someone has given Mrs.Cavanagh a whole lot of plums I suspect, we have had them stewed with custard, with boiled rice and with semolina for the last three nights. I counted my stones each time, Monday it was a sailor, Tuesday it would be a rich man but last night it was to be a beggar man. I think the plums are in need of being eaten. Tonight hopefully it will be bread and butter pudding or I shall be resigned to marrying a thief!

Lots of love to all.

Jean xx

Sarah smiled, folding the letter carefully, Maggie would seize upon it the moment she espied the paper tucked behind the three brass monkeys on the mantelpiece. The nightgown smelled faintly of lavender, Sarah held it to her face, dear Jean, thinking of her mam despite living as she now did in a place so filled with life but she seldom mentioned her art work, perhaps too many distractions kept Jean from quiet concentration with simply paper and paint for company. Her daughter seemed happy, that was all Sarah needed to know and if she was to have Jean at home for a little while then Sarah would look forward to the end of the month and cheerfully bake as many pies and cakes as Avril could eat, not to mention Samson who would be welcomed with a choice marrowbone.

Ivy's letters were always accompanied by the latest pictures crayoned by Harold and Molly. At least that branch of the family persisted in their creation of imaginative works of art. Today it was an impressive drawing of a threshing machine from Harold and a charming study of sheep, two white and one black, from Molly, the countryside was evidently becoming an influence upon their lives. Ivy had written on the usual letter-card, her communications were never as long as Jean's but frequent and purposefully furnished Sarah with views of the coast and landmarks of Lincolnshire. Her news was, as ever, reassuring in its goodness. Reggie's work continued to flourish, the children spent endless hours in fresh air and Ivy met more kindly people whom she regarded as friends. There was a significant P.S. When Annie's baby arrives we shall come to visit you all. Harold and Molly are excited at the prospect of meeting their two new cousins.

Jack was almost four months old, Sarah sensed that Mavis too longed for motherhood. No doubt news of another grandchild to be would find its way to Sarah before too long.

Nora, Harold and Frank had come in quick succession, then for whatever reason, a period of several years elapsed before Gertie and Jean made their respective entrances. Samuel had maintained it was Gladstone's fault, nothing positive ever happened under a liberal government, was Samuel's belief. Then between Jean and Mavis, Sarah miscarried but to their great joy two more daughters blessed 69, Mitchell Street.

It was time to get ready for her visit to Davina, they had begun making a rug together, a gift for Maggie's bottom drawer. The young couple spent most of their free time in each other's company, Sarah had been introduced to Toby's family and the announcement, at Christmas, of their engagement was expected by everyone. Davina had declared, 'red Sarah dear, we shall use a deep burgundy red, a hearth glows with the finest heat behind a deep red rug'. Sarah looked fondly on the spot where, over the years, Samuel's feet had worn thin one end of their hearth rug when at day's end he had sat by the fire dozing, watching over his family. Now a very faded red and fraying at one corner where Eli at his puppy stage chewed a thread loose, it never the less glowed with the very finest warmth still.

As Sarah walked to the tram she pondered what the postman's uncle Cedric might have left him. Whatever it was it could come nowhere near the priceless legacy Samuel had bequeathed his children. She began to hum Danny Boy, so familiar it had become through Freddy's complete conviction that music inspired the hens, Sarah often found the tune drifting through her head as she worked or made her way to the shops. 'Daniel', or Danny as it would surely be to his brothers and sister. Yes, a good solid name for Annie's baby. The thought pleased Sarah, it created a good feeling, she was curiously confident in the notion, as though he who ordained these things had allowed her privileged information. 'Magic, magic mam', so many times Harold had replied with that mischievous grin on his face when she had asked him, 'How did you know'?

Annie's fingers trembled as she pushed the hatpin through the black felt, she had awoke that morning with a feeling of nausea and tiredness which she attributed to the funeral.

"Are you sure you'll be alright, Mabel 'ould understand if yer didn't go, she knows about these things, she is a nurse for God's sake," said Edna anxiously.

Annie picked up her gloves from the table, "You are in the same condition as myself Edna, why do you suppose I should not be alright?"

Edna huffed her disapproval. "Because I'm not married to a miserable bugger for a start and my innards 'aven't once given me bother, you've been sick on an' off all the way through, not that we should be surprised by that, what wi' Charles an' 'is bloody daft notions, an' William forever chafin' after summat 'e can't 'ave tis little wonder you look like death warmed up."

Edna was protective of Annie her closest friend, they had shared so much over the years and a significant part of their past had been May. Neither of them, even for an instant, had considered not attending her funeral though inwardly they cringed at death, if was new life they sought now and that new life felt close.

Mabel, if ever a young woman needed their support it was Mabel, Annie had lain awake remembering that pretty little girl, so devoted to her brother. The house on Peverell Street, all those times Annie had walked to that place where love dwelt amid a God forsaken corner of the world which spurned life even before it took breath. All these years on, through a hideous war at which the nation had supposedly triumphed, why then did it feel like a betrayal. Poverty which afflicted households before men took up arms held families still in its grip, was that the ghastly ethic, reduce numbers to enable an inadequate measure of sustenance to meet the need by killing off a percentage. Annie pulled on the gloves.

"Come along, we mustn't be late," she cast a smile at Edna.

"'Ere suck on one o' these, mam says barley sugar is strengthenin', our mam 'as a remedy for everythin' lately but I told 'er, them Bile Beans do nowt but fill 'er wi' wind."

A tremor of dread made the words sound curiously fragile for the normally unfaltering Edna Dodds.

The two women walked arm in arm, the sweet barley sugar achieved to silence Edna and each with their own thoughts they made their way stoically to Witford Hill.

"That smells good Mam," said George when Annie lifted the lid on a pan of stew. He and Freddy had dug the first leeks and parsnips at the weekend and now their endeavours filled the kitchen with the savoury aroma of late summer and gave them a great sense of satisfaction. They had swapped surplus seeds with Billy, a scheme devised by Freddy to eliminate any waste and bring a degree of competition to their production. Now, to Victor's pride and joy, the largest marrow by far lay at one end of Billy's allotment, tended solely by Victor it had grown to enormous proportion. Billy had promised they would wheel it in the barrow to show Florrie.

"Arthur's sow had her litter last night," said Freddy, "fifteen of 'em, Arthur said she fired 'em out like popcorn, she's still got one spare teat though."

George laughed, "Typical farmer you are Freddy, that poor sow has produced all those potential gains and you rue the waste of one spare tit. You should tell Arthur to milk that one, it would probably yield enough for

Mrs.Cropley to make junket."

"You might scoff George," said Freddy, "but it all boils down to economics, it would be the same at 'Raleigh'. If fifteen out of sixteen machines were in operation it would be the redundant one which concerned management, full production makes for......."

The sound of a spoon clattering on the flags turned their attention immediately to Annie, she sat at the far end of the table, the serving spoon by her feet.

"What is it Mam, what's the matter?" George crossed the room and stood at her side.

"Don't alarm Hilda and John, keep your voice down, let them carry on playing outside. I need one of you to go to Mitchell Street, you mustn't panic your grandma but ask if she can come, tell her I think the baby has started."

Freddy at once said, "I'll go, you stay here George," he hesitated, "shall I find dad?"

"Your dad will be home when he's finished at the workshop, best to fetch Sarah first." Annie smiled reassuringly, her discomfort was severe, all day she had fought off sickliness but now it had turned her stomach and cramp like pains gripped her as she struggled to the scullery to retch into the bucket.

"Hurry up Freddy, don't stop for anything except to tell William, if you see him, to find dad, he'll most likely be waiting for the door to open at The Standard, William will know that anyway."

George was frightened, the past weeks had been strained, the selfishness of William both he and Freddy had barely tolerated. Had it not been for Annie pleading with them to ignore William's outbursts they would doubtless have given him a good hiding, brother or not. Charles returned to No.14 so late each night, often the boys had gone to bed before their dad appeared. Annie tried in vain to excuse him saying, 'without Edna your dad will be spreading his time between both places of work, it is inevitable that he will be late home'. Not very long ago George and Freddy would have accepted such explanation as readily as did John and Hilda, their young minds believed every word Annie uttered without question, their mam didn't speak untruths. But a harsh reality could be softened by the application of carefully chosen adjectives, the two older boys now recognised Annie's attempts at protecting them from troubles and perceived the reality as it really was.

George helped Annie back to the chair, her face was white as a sheet.

"Pick up the spoon please George and wash it clean. If Freddy and Sarah aren't here within the hour we'll feed the young ones. Don't be alarmed, your grandma has likely had a bag packed in readiness for days, it is the most natural thing in the world."

Annie drew a deep breath as another spasm of pain seemed to contort her lower abdomen but for George's sake she made no sound of distress. George wanted to shout out, 'childbirth killed William and Freddy's mam', his own fears challenged his senses cruelly but his mam needed him to be confident, to be calm.

"It'll be alright, Dick Sowerby's wife had another set of twins last week, like he said, ' the more that travel along the entry the smoother the cobbles get', it's a bit like Arthur Cropley's sow I suppose, you've already had three Mam, it'll be alright, it's sure to be alright."

Annie took George's hand. "Your dad, Harold, when he first saw you said, 'he's perfect'. He was right you have always been perfect, don't let anyone ever change you George, others will try your resolve but remember who you are, what you are, Harold Boucher's son, his likeness in every way."

Her fingers tightened around George's hand as yet another surge of pain raised her groin from the chair. The back door opened, Hilda and John ran inside excitedly.

"William is here, Celia is with him," cried Hilda joyfully. The little girl especially loved Celia, taking her to the bedroom to see her dolls each time she came to the house. If ever perplexed by the child then Celia never showed it. Annie had noted the young woman's patience and understanding, considering it a blessing given William's lack of these same qualities but for

Celia to have come now at such a time only added to Annie's stress. George however clutched at the presence of another woman, even the youthful Celia.

"Hello Celia," said Annie, "I'm sorry you find us in such a state of confusion, Freddy is on his way with Sarah so every thing will be fine, until then could you lay up the table and serve up the meal for you all, if you plate up some for Charles and put it in the bottom oven of the range he will eat it when he gets in from work. I shall go upstairs now and lie down, no need for any of you to worry."

Hilda's eyes held such dread and John began to cry, never before had they seen their mam so poorly, even when she had a bad cough and cold she carried on as always, now she rose to her feet with such unsteadiness George had taken her arm and walked with her. Celia, for all her youth and inexperience took charge of the situation.

"Come along Hilda, lets get the table ready before your grandma arrives and John, as Freddy is not here yet you might see if there are any eggs in the boxes and give the chickens fresh water so that Freddy can sit for his tea when he comes, after we have eaten I shall read a story, whichever book you choose."

Celia took the large serving spoon and stirred the pan of stew, having no known tragedies to haunt her mind it was a sense of happy anticipation at the thought of a baby in the house which drove her efforts. For William who had stood transfixed by the back door it was a torturous sense of cruel fate, created by his own badness which twisted ever more tightly the knot at the pit of his stomach. Annie had looked so pale, she'd appeared feeble, weakened, as George helped her up the stairs.

'As mothers go she's a bloody good 'en'. William recalled those words so deliberately spoken by Reg Yeats. He could not stay for this, he couldn't bear to be present, he must run, somewhere, anywhere but William could not remain in the house, whatever might befall. With no explanation, he turned and sped from the yard to the street, he didn't stop running until he reached the end of Sherwood Road, past The Standard and into Forest Road. He wanted to hide, to be unseen by everyone. Out of breath, his pace slowed,

St.Andrews Church clock struck a quarter to the hour, the chime drew him, strangely beckoning through the narrow streets, by the time he reached the church gate he found comfort in the thought that at any moment seven loud chimes would wipe out the sound of his own laboured breathing, under that cover granted by the old clock he could slip inside the porch and sit out of sight. It was curious how changed in tone the last two chimes became when hearing them from within the thick stone walls. He sank down onto the seat at one side, the chimes had ceased, his own frantic breathing now eased it was as if the world had suddenly stopped, no noise even from the city, did some divine order forbid mankind's irreverent hustle and bustle any place within this house of God, what would that same order consider appropriate for William Eddowes, seated as he was within its charge. Nothing happened, he felt no stern hand of judgement grip his shoulder, no flash of lightning, no bolt of thunder rattled overhead marking the spot where retribution might find him. If anything, it was the opposite, the ancient walls, silent observers to centuries of life calmed William's torment. He lay down along the seat, took his cap from a pocket and placed it under his head. For an hour or more he dozed on and off, it was the emptiness of his belly, that ache from hunger which finally stirred him to unrest.

At first William could not see Charles, the room was full, the air clouded by smoke, then a heavy framed man stood up and walked to the bar, behind where he had sat Charles played cards, his back to William, unaware of his son's presence. The startled look on his dad's face brought back William's anxiety.

"You need to come Dad, the baby has started, mam doesn't look well," his voice trembled as he uttered the last few words.

It was an irony that at the moment Charles was about to take the hand, William should appear with urgent request. It was the first hand he had won in weeks. They never played for big stakes but it mounted up, Charles needed a winning streak. The business was not doing well, he had heard that

314

Smithfield had bought a franchise from 'Viyella' at Worksop, he had processed Merino wool when in Ireland, it was Smithfield's intention to set up a production line for the end product as well as manufacturing cloth and woollen hose. Charles' lack of purpose had lost him a chance to thrust the workshops into the feverish competition Andrew Smithfield's arrival in Nottingham had created. Money had become tight, a winning hand, however small the 'pot' felt like a turn in events.

His opponent put down his cards, "This is merely the pastime of idle men Charles, a baby must take the upper hand, we shall fold for now."

Charles nodded his withering agreement, William propelled him to the door, how many drinks his father had taken he could not know but Charles' steps were unsteady.

"Come on Dad, it's time you had something to eat, Celia has a meal waiting for you at home." Charles reached the corner and made to walk in the wrong direction, "This way Dad," said William, growing ever more anxious.

"You're right Son, I don't live there anymore do I, your mother couldn't wait to get out of that house but I liked it there, things were good there, me," he prodded his own chest, "me, Charles Eddowes was happy in that little house." He sighed.

"Please Dad, we need to hurry up." William's anguished expression seemed at last to register the urgency. Charles' feet moved just slightly behind William's as the young man directed his dad along Sherwood Road, afraid of what they might find at No.14 but even more afraid of being so exposed on the street where curious eyes surveyed the two with looks of condemnation.

When the back door opened Celia's smile showed relief.

"I knew you would fetch your dad but we've been worried, you ran off without saying."

Freddy sat by the table, staring at a bowl of eggs, Celia had crossed the room to stand before Charles, she spoke calmly but with a degree of authority which the past hour had placed in her.

"George has gone for the doctor, Mrs.Boucher is upstairs with your wife, I have settled John and Hilda and when you are ready there is food for you."

Charles seemed inert, his reactions were slow, William felt awkward, then before Charles' muddled senses found order enough to respond George arrived with Dr.Latham.

"Mother and grandma are upstairs doctor," said George, "Celia will take you to them."

His eyes cast a plea to the young woman.

"Of course, this way doctor."

George had smelled drink on Charles' breath as he walked by him, now a driven need to speak out directed a sobering charge at this man, his stepfather.

"You stand there before us a pathetic excuse of a man, my mam has given you nothing but loyalty, worked day and night to keep this family going through thick and thin, without her you'd be despairing in the workhouse but how do you repay her, by listening to the childish outbursts of a son, so jealous, so avaricious as to want any title we, his brothers and sister might have to happiness." George turned to William. "If you honestly believe that a fine hat and a superficial swagger make a man then I pity you, even more I pity Celia, who for reasons only God could know, loves you. I have stood by and tolerated the actions of you both only because mam begged me to but no more, if anything should happen to my mam........." Tears began to fall down George's face, no more words would come other than to Freddy a heartfelt, "Sorry, I'm sorry Freddy."

George ran into the yard, shut himself in the privy and shook from the sobs which near stifled his breathing. Several minutes passed before a knock came at the door, a low voice whispered.

"It's only me George."

He wiped his eyes with his sleeve, his chest was tight from fear and misery. Freddy smiled, took George in his arms and for a minute or more, neither spoke.

"Grandma has just come down to tell us that the baby is breech, feet coming first, that accounts for mam's state but doctor is confident. I am sorry too George, I feel ashamed of my own, but we did lose mother, I'm not making excuses for dad and William but I know that now, through these past hours, you can imagine how it would feel to lose your mam. Perhaps something so painful you never really get over, I used to feel bad at not even being able to remember how she looked, neither of us can. William, I think made up his own image of her and kept it somewhere in his head. I was the lucky one, I simply trusted those around me, I only ever had the vision of your mother, our mam, it was enough, it's still enough. I wish it could satisfy William and dad too, I don't know how to change things, how to find whatever it is they crave for."

George sniffed to discharge a stray sob, he lay a hand on Freddy's shoulder.

"Brothers?" He said.

"Brothers," replied Freddy.

Together they went back to the house, closer then than at any time before.

Celia was pouring tea, Charles looked up from where he sat by the range, his expression bore no malice but a weariness of spirit. William sat at the table, his gaze trained down at a half eaten plate of stew, no one uttered a single word. That was how the company remained for what seemed like an age. Upstairs Annie endured an intensity of pain like none she had previously encountered but made no sound to alarm her children. At just before 10o'clock the urgent cries of a baby broke the silence. Now it was Celia's turn to burst into tears, Freddy took her hand.

"William must walk you home now, your mother will be anxious."

Her eyes begged to know that all was well with Annie. George had reached the bottom tread of the stairs when above him on the landing Sarah appeared, a weary smile passed her lips before she said.

"The doctor is just helping me clean up your new brother, your mam is alright, exhausted, but alright. Tell the others, when the doctor is gone you will be able to come up and see the baby but try not to wake Hilda and John, so far they have slept soundly."

George rushed to the kitchen where the desperate assembly awaited his words.

"It's a boy, they are both alright but mam is done in, the doctor will be down soon then we can see them."

William clutched at Celia's hand, not to strengthen her but to cease the violent shaking of his own fingers.

"I'll hurry back."

He directed the statement nervously at George as Celia waved an emotional goodnight. Freddy stood by Charles, he spoke softly.

"Let the past go Dad, for all our sakes, let the past go."

Charles rose to his feet and answered feebly.

"I would let the past go Freddy, if only the past would let go of me."

He climbed the stairs slowly but purposefully, Sarah gave him a look of reproach. When depositing her bag in the spare room she had discovered the evidence of Charles' occupation within, Annie had offered an explanation.

"I have been so restless with cramp at night it was senseless for Charles to be disturbed too."

Sarah had lived too long and through too much to be convinced.

"Your son is early Charles, by at least two weeks or more in my opinion, therefore he is small, even allowing for his premature arrival he is slight. However, he is breathing steadily, I am happy to believe that his lungs are functioning well. Annie required stitches, the baby was breech, it is not surprising that she was feeling unwell. Rest and good nourishment, which I am quite sure Mrs.Boucher will make sure of, should bring your wife back to full strength before long. I shall call again tomorrow, in the meantime, my congratulations Charles, there is many a man would envy you."

Charles automatically shook the doctor's hand and expressed his thanks. Manners taught him by his mother had ever remained, at such a time he was suitably humbled.

The house had eventually found stillness, the young people were all in their beds, including William who had, as promised, returned from walking Celia home without delay.

Annie had fed the baby, already referred to as Danny by a quietly confident Sarah. The magic had worked, Harold's magic, he was still with them, just as Samuel stood watch over 69 Mitchell Street.

Outside on the landing Sarah whispered to Charles.

"I have moved your things back in with Annie, I am tired and shall sleep in the spare room. Your place is in there with your wife and baby, when he wakes lift him to Annie, if you need me tap lightly, I never sleep deeply these days." Sarah felt compelled to kiss his cheek. "We are all afraid sometimes Charles but if we do the very best we can then at least we have no cause to fear any inadequacy, not even God could ask more of us."

She quietly closed the door on herself, Charles had shed the vagueness brought on by too great a measure of whisky, only on card nights did he take spirits believing it influential of 'lady luck'. It achieved to take more from his pocket but as yet, good fortune in cards had not been swayed by the influence.

Inside the bedroom, if Annie was awake she chose not to speak. Charles stood by the crib, his gaze if searching for that crucial feature which was convincingly Eddowes, or a look defininly Garbett found no such assurance. Swaddled in a warm cot sheet only the face visible and that face so small it appeared no bigger than the face of Hilda's doll, it showed a deep pink, wrinkled skin like no other he had ever seen. Perhaps that was it, this baby was unfamiliar in every way, he felt no sentiment either towards it or from it but a detachment, a total indifference. Unlike that first glimpse of his other children at their birth when something inside him at once claimed their innocence, for this infant he felt nothing.

Annie was very drowsy but not asleep, she felt the counterpane move as Charles crept into bed and heard him let out a long, deep breath.

"I am not renewing the lease at Basford, I told the women this morning that at the end of the month there will be no more work for them. The two most skilled have already gone to Winchester Street. To the others I have suggested they present themselves to Smithfield at Brassington, by Christmas he should be taking on."

He turned over on his side to face the dresser, Annie was too tired to respond. September 12th had laid May to rest and delivered new life. Dear Sarah had held the baby in her arms and said, 'Daniel, don't you agree it is a fine name for him Annie'? Sarah had hummed Danny Boy to her grandson, now Annie could hear the sound of Freddy playing to the hens, it drifted through her head, inducing sleep. Charles lay wide awake, afraid to let his eyelids close, lest behind them those scenes which ever haunted his mind refused to grant him peace and his own inadequacies were undeserving any measure of pardon from a God who showed compassion, only to those who tried their best. 'A pathetic excuse of a man', George's words were true, Charles wept.

CHAPTER TWENTY

It wasn't fair, why did Annie have the boy, why was Charles, a man for whom Edna had little regard, granted the son when her Billy was so much more deserving. Edna had voiced her resentment to Billy as he'd gazed at their beautiful, bonny baby, born as daylight broke on the first morning in October. Billy had scolded her for harbouring such ungracious thoughts, his happiness and pride were not one iota diminished by the arrival of his fourth daughter, Myra Dodds, a round faced, dimpled bundle of new life, uniquely theirs, half Edna, half himself. Billy would not have swapped her for any boy, from that very first moment, little Myra had clutched at Billy's heartstrings and he'd wrapped her about in pure, unconditional love.

"E's gone off, shall I put 'im down in the pram or upstairs in 'is crib?" Asked Edna.

Annie peeled the last potato and dropping it into the pan of water replied.

"In the pram , I'll walk part of the way with you."

Myra slept soundly in her pram, just inside the scullery door where Edna had insisted on leaving her, declaring the wheels to be a threat to Annie's freshly scrubbed flags.

"What's 'e up to, I see Sylvia sometimes an' the poor lass looks harassed to death, 'er mam is still as weak as Mission tea, 'ow does 'e suppose she'd manage to get forth an' back to Brassington an' still tend 'er mam an'all. I know 'tis none o' my business anymore so you can tell me to mind me own but I might 'ave got back to a machine by next spring when Myra sits up, 'tis just too awkward for Billy wi' one arm an' our Annie needs to go to school, God 'elp us, I want 'er to 'ave more learnin' than me, when I left school I thought the world wer' flat an' that it ended t'other side o' Bestwood slagheap."

Edna suddenly stopped walking and let go the handlebar of the pram.

"These soddin' shoes are enough to drive me to drink."

She bent down and one at a time took them off to adjust the lining which had worn thin and slipped from side to side.

"Smithfield's pourin' money into that factory an' they say that 'e's sniffin' round Hannibal Burton like a lurcher at a rabbit hole, Cheetham an'all, they all scratch one another's backs, I'm surprised your Charles don't join in instead o' sellin' up to 'em, p'raps 'e's afraid o' water, can't 'e swim, it wouldn't matter anyroad 'cause come Christmas mornin' I reckon Bessie or Sylvia 'ould shove the bugger in The Trent, 'e'd swim alright, that's what our Ada did to their Jimmy. 'E wer' only just out of 'is depth , but it worked. Poor kid lost 'is knitted trunks in the baths an' come out the water naked as the day 'e wer' born but 'e done eight strokes an' got a bag o' scratchin's all to 'isself."

Edna finally drew breath and Annie was about to say that she had met Andrew Smithfield in town, when a terrier dog in pursuit of a tabby cat ran past them at such speed it made both Edna and herself jump.

"God Almighty," said Edna watching the frantic cat as it scaled a wall and disappeared over the top, leaving the dog in a mood of frenzy. Realising it was beaten it cast a glance back at the two women before trotting off in the direction of the arboretum.

"Isn't that Handley's dog," said Edna, "I 'eard they 'ad to get one to keep the rats down, they were comin' in from the bone yard at the back, what a place to 'ave a bloody bone yard, round the back o' the undertakers, puts me off glue, I mix a bit o' flour an' water if I need to stick summat."

Annie sighed. "I don't know what Charles' plans are, I know he sold the machines at Basford, but I can't imagine Andrew Smithfield paid a great deal for them, they were bankrupt stock in the first place. Winchester Street is all Charles has, he wouldn't go back to working at the bank I feel sure, even if a position were to present itself. I can understand Sylvia's concern, I'll try to speak with him over Christmas when hopefully he might be more relaxed."

Danny briefly opened his eyes but the motion of the pram as they walked lulled him back to a drowsy indifference.

"I had a letter from Jean yesterday," said Annie, "I think she wrote to me to seek a measure of assurance before writing a letter to Sarah. Dear Nora wouldn't countenance going to London to be introduced to Mr.Randall Tennyson, her face paled at the first suggestion. Now it seems Jean herself has developed an attachment to the gentleman, of course her anxiety is over the fact that he is nineteen years her senior, she wonders what her mam will say."

"Age don't matter," said Edna, " Morley allus seemed old enough to be our Ada's grandad but just look at them two, 'ouse full o' kids an' far as I know, the only real 'ding dong' they've 'ad wer' when Ada locked 'im out the night 'e come 'ome late singin' at the top of 'is voice, *Angel of my 'eart'*, drunk as a lord on Silas Bendinck's parsnip wine. They said as 'ow Silas put the soddin' stuff in Cicely's big enamel jug, the one she used to fetch the buttermilk, took all the enamel off except for the bit above the rim. Cicely poured it down the storm drain out in the road an' they reckon it cleared the blockage that used to cause the lower end o' Talbot Street to flood every time it rained. Morley wer' too far gone to argue so 'e curled up under their old pear tree wi' 'is arm around Lottie Grimshaw's old bitch, when 'e woke up next mornin' 'e 'ad them pins an' needles up the back of 'is 'ead, thought it wer' alcohol poisonin' but the daft sod 'ad an 'edgehog in the crook of 'is neck, it must 'ave crawled there for warmth." Edna began to laugh. "You tell Jean to keep Randall wotsisname away from old Silas an' she'll be alright."

"I think Sarah will be happy if Jean is happy, they say that women outnumber the men many fold, especially young men, the war took nearly an entire generation, 'the war to end all wars', please God! Sarah is an understanding woman but I feel for Jean. Nora will be overcome with relief that at Christmas she won't now be under pressure to abandon the safety of spinsterhood in the pursuit of a husband."

Annie smiled at the notion and Edna giggled roguishly, as though Annie's account had suddenly brought back to mind those forgotten but colourful campaigns of her own.

"I'll only go as far as the next corner, he'll be wanting a feed very soon, at least the colic seems to be easing, this past week his sleep has been much more restful, he needs all the sleep he can get if he is to catch up Myra, Sarah says babies grow most when fast asleep."

Annie looked across to the full cheeked younger of the two who made a much bulkier mound beneath the blankets in the pram pushed by Edna.

"Give 'im a chance, poor little sod, you've got to remember 'e wer' despatched afore 'e should 'ave been, not like 'er, lollin' around in comfort, too idle to shift 'erself."

Then, as if a twinge of guilt pricked Edna's motherliness she bent over the handlebars and sent a generous kiss into the pram with the promise.

"Mam'll get yer that little teddy from Burton's," she sighed. "I looked at the old one on the end o' Liza's bed, it wer Annie as chewed one ear off an' the scorch mark wer' from the day Susie chucked it out the pram an' onto the range, weren't 'til I smelled burnin' that I spotted it, just in time I reckon, it's 'ad a bald backside ever since. I've got to get to work as soon as I can, I don't see 'ow we could manage else. Yer know what Billy's like, allus optimistic, that daft grin on 'is face, singin' an' whistlin', an' there am I wonderin' if I can afford a six inch teddy bear wi' no bloody squeak or should I give Myra the mangy old one in case the rent goes up after Christmas."

The two women stopped at the corner of Forest Road, Annie would have liked to tell Edna just how lucky she was to have a man who sang and whistled his happiness, who cast a smile over his family but instead she kissed Edna's cheek, took a small bag of toffees from her coat pocket, placing them at the end of Myra's pram.

"For the girls," she said, "winter always feels threatening, the cold finds our marrow, don't worry Edna, I'll speak with Charles."

As Edna walked along Sherwood Road the future tormented her. The only way they could physically manage to abide at No.24 would be for Billy and herself to somehow sleep in the very small bedroom and for all four girls to occupy the other. Even though Billy worked nights he shared the marital bed on Sunday, it was his space, God knows it had been vacant long enough while he was in France. Now Edna viewed it as sacred, never to be adulterated, not even by their own daughters. Annie their eldest was fast becoming a young woman, Edna had shared a small space with her sisters and knew how frustrating that could be. On the day her youngest sister had found a sanitary towel and asked Edna what it was, Edna had given her the only answer she could, at that moment think of, such a subject would normally be taboo. 'It is for when you have a sore throat to keep out the cold air'. That evening at teatime, the young Vera had descended the stairs wearing a sanitary towel, one loop over each ear and the pad itself completely covering the child's mouth, it had caused the most alarming disturbance and poor Edna had been severely chastised for allowing an item of such an intimate nature to be found by an innocent sibling, especially as the curious Vera had insisted she needed it to cure an awful sore throat!

Annie walked in the opposite direction with her own thoughts. Christmas was but two weeks away but she could muster little enthusiasm. Since Danny's birth Charles had scarcely looked at the child. He had not raised his voice in temper or made any reference to Edwin Garbett but his manner was distant, at times almost cold. For the sake of the others Annie went about the days as cheerfully as she could but the weekend at the end of September, when Jean and Avril and Ivy and the family had converged upon No14, Hood Street, the strain of covering up any hint of trouble had near reduced her to a jelly.

Danny thrived but slowly, Annie would look at the two infants when they lay side by side on the rug, Myra so plump and her own little boy so slight and picture the advertisement which appeared in the paper, 'Before and after Virol'.

Doctor Latham however, had been satisfied with Danny's progress. 'I delivered a baby quite soon after qualifying' he told Annie, 'the infant weighed only 3lbs1oz and could fit inside a shoe box, now he works at the coal face'.

Annie took comfort from that, Danny had weighed almost 6lbs at birth and now tipped the scales at eight. His sister and brothers watched over him as though he were an emerging butterfly, waiting for those delicate wings to dry, with the exception of William, who had placed a rattle in the pram on the first occasion, then on the following weekend had presented Annie with two bottles of stout. Annie had dared to hope that these gestures might have been of his own accord and not the result of Celia's promptings. Believing it best not to pressure William towards his new brother, Annie had appeared delighted at his thoughtfulness and continued to hope he might find some release from whatever it was that confined him. Despite the fact that William was Charles' son and could display his father's moods, deep down she sensed a desire in the young man to be reconciled, whether it was pride, arrogance or simply immaturity which stood in his way she could not know but neither George nor Freddy had shown him any animosity and she herself gave him no cause to feel awkward. When Ivy had extended an open invitation to the three eldest to visit whenever they liked, William had responded perhaps a little too eagerly, declaring his intent to spend a week with them at Skendleby in October. His plan had met an obstacle when Reg Yeats had told him he couldn't just appoint himself on holiday whenever he chose. Now the plan to visit Ivy and Reggie seemed to have lost momentum.

As Annie approached the corner of Hood Street animated voices grew louder, their tone suggested a disturbance of some kind, her progress revealed a cluster of women and one man. It soon became apparent that the insurance agent, normally dispensed with as quickly as possible, this afternoon had brought with him the account of an event which proved too curious to be missed, despite any need of delayed premiums.

"They reckon 'e's been in the water for days, it wer' just lucky that the body got stuck under an old tree that fell in last month's storm or it would 'ave made it to Colwick, the weight of water goin' over that weir at this time o' year would 'ave ripped 'im into shreds like carrion."

Annie shuddered, not entirely at the drama of the man's words but over the unhealthy craving displayed by the women for ever more detail, more macabre description of a mortal's tragic demise. Annie walked hastily passed the hungry gathering and felt great relief at reaching her own back door, Danny and herself now safe from their voracious appetites.

The kitchen greeted them with warmth as Annie pulled the pram over the small step and into the room, her nose detected a faint smell of tobacco, the kettle was warm someone had recently made a hot drink. Before Danny's hesitant eyes opened to a full wakening she crossed the hall to the foot of the stairs and called out.

"William, is that you William?"

Only the ticking of the mantel clock in the living room interrupted the silence. Danny began to whimper, hastily taking off her hat and coat, Annie lifted the infant from the pram, sat in the big chair by the range and put him to suckle. It was too early for William to be home from Player's and she had not known Charles to smoke in the house, he often carried cigarettes in his jacket, presumably he lit one in the pub or as he walked but someone had been in the house since she left with Edna and they had smoked tobacco.

As Danny's eager little mouth found the all comforting milk his blissful contentment could sense no measure of his mother's anxiety, Annie felt disturbed, on the face of it there was little to suggest anything untoward yet the quietness seemed to hold a trouble. She chided herself for allowing the incident in the street to influence her mind, William had likely finished work early for whatever reason and come home to make a cup of tea before going into town or calling for Celia, it would turn out to be entirely regular. Annie began to sing, softly, gently swaying from side to side as she had done with each of her children, maternal love flowed with the milk and through its surety, her anxiety subsided.

William sat on the bus, right at the front where he stared at the driver's head through the glass screen, his concentration so deep that he failed to notice Edwin Garbett boarding the bus just a few minutes after him and settling two seats back on the other side of the aisle. William's anger festered within, who was Reg Yeats anyway, a little man with no real claim to mastery. How much 'nous' did it actually demand to create a fag. It was not William's fault that the men became vocal, somebody, somewhere pocketed handsomely, he had simply suggested it wasn't those on the factory floor.

In truth William had enjoyed the attention. Over the past weeks at dinnertimes he had idly cast a contentious remark into the gathering and while men chewed on gristly meat and stale bread, while they exchanged accounts of shallow grates and late rents, he had sat back, only re-entering their debate to give a subtle stir if the heat died down. William had convinced himself that they all listened to him, paid heed to his observations, he could persuade men to work faster, increase productivity for a modest rise in pay, enhanced accordingly for himself, William being the successful arbitrator.

In his naivety, when Reg Yeats summoned him to the office, William had anticipated some acknowledgement of his intelligence, a recognition of the fact that he, William Eddowes did not mindlessly drudge through the days but analysed, cogitated and perceived a better future for the whole of Player's.

When Reg Yeats had lashed his ego with a double barrelled volley of rebuke, William's wounded pride had mounted a stand of defiance.

'You 'aven't the brains of a louse lad'. Reg had rained down his condemnation in a blistering bombardment. 'Do you suppose it's down to me, do you imagine I go 'ome to a posh 'ouse in The Park to sup port an' count me fortune. I know what each an' every one o' them men out there needs an' if I wer' Santa bloody Claus I'd give it to 'em, wrapped up in gold leaf, shinin' like the star o' the bloody east but I can't change the way it is lad. God knows I'd send 'em to their wives an' kids wi' the answer to their problems, the grace that gave 'em sleep at night if I bloody well could. I don't need the likes o' you stirrin' their bellies to more hunger than they've already got, you're a firebrand lad, a bloody firebrand, one more word of agitation out o' you an' out that bloody gate you'll go for good. If it weren't for your mam I'd kick your arse out onto the street right now so you'd find out just 'ow rosy life is out there, you don't know you're born lad, behind all them closed doors scores are existin' in misery on bugger all'.

'My mother's dead so don't use her for your excuse', William had rounded, 'if you don't want what I could give this gutless place then have it your way, I'm off to where a man can make something of himself and you can sit in this office, waiting to greet your old age with a pint at the institute and that packet of 'Navy Cut' if that's what satisfies Reg Yeats, you might need John Player but William Eddowes needs nothing more than his own determination'. William had slammed the door on his boss and on any chance of conciliation.

Since Charles had closed the Basford workshop a desperate want had dominated William's thinking. His father was on the way down, Andrew Smithfield was on the way up. William must now impress the latter with his fortitude and capability. Reg Yeats didn't understand ambition, well William would achieve regardless. Opportunities lay at Brassington and that is where he was going, bugger the pathetic socials at the institute, William wanted to stand with the Cheethams and Burtons of this world. Through a beer mug a florin looked exactly the same, it was always a florin but through a cut glass whisky tumbler one single guinea appeared multiplied, that gleam of wealth instantly increased many times over.

The driver of the bus was suddenly overcome by a rage of coughing, his attention momentarily diverted, he saw just in time, a man and bicycle a few yards ahead. The brakes of the bus bit at the wheels so hard everyone lurched forward in their seats, one woman lost her grip on the bag which she held by her feet, now potatoes, onions and a large savoy cabbage rolled around the floor of the bus like marbles on a bagatelle board. The conductor managed to retrieve a number but it was the dexterity of a small boy who, prompted by his mother, crawled from boot to shoe, reaching beneath the seat supports, gleefully counting each item recovered 'til finally he declared a total of 20, which William automatically adjusted to 26 as the eager but mathematically limited youngster had counted 10 three times, 12 twice, 15 three times and excitedly repeated his tally as he dropped the last two onions into Edwin Garbett's lap.

Where's he going, damn the man, William's inner dismay at seeing Edwin on the bus drew his features to a scowl. Distracted by the child's innocently performed good deed, Edwin had not noticed William until raising his eyes to the woman's open bag and carefully returning the onions to their rightful place, he had caught sight of William beyond the woman's shoulder. Both now speculated as to the others destination. Edwin would not normally be travelling this route but Andrew Smithfield had submitted a business plan, for confirmation of its accuracy regarding taxation and local authority revenues to Jacobson's, prior to presenting his proposals to the bank, requesting it to be returned to him by hand as soon as possible. The documents now secure within a briefcase at Edwin's side, he was on his way to Brassington.

William had no cause to board this bus in pursuit of his usual day to day activities but this afternoon his ill temper and resentment following the altercation in Reg's office, had driven him to present himself to Smithfield before, at the table of No.14 and in front of his industrious brothers, he must declare himself unemployed.

The conductor rang the bell and called out 'Brassington gates', his voice had become more languid with each stop, William imagined that by the time the bus reached the terminus the decelerating words of the conductor would echo Robert Appleyard's gramophone when, through his advancing deafness, he neglected to wind it in time. The magnificent Caruso could sound like a dire, threatening, blasphemy from the mouth of Beelzebub as the needle travelled ever more slowly over the wondrous disc.

"Hello William, how are you and all the family?"

Edwin had remained standing by the double iron gates, politely waiting for William to alight the bus. In truth, William had purposefully permitted everyone else getting off at the stop, be it lady or gent, to do so ahead of him, hoping that Edwin's business might be elsewhere and that he would not see that William's own destination was the factory. That important looking briefcase however was surely destined to be opened in the company of Andrew Smithfield.

"We are all well, in fact everything is good, very good," lied William. Then a subconscious attempt at aiding his passage produced a courteous "thank you," Edwin was obviously soon to be in conversation with Smithfield, there could be some mention of William, he should at least be considered well mannered. Edwin must not be aware of William's purpose, not yet, William tipped his cap and walked on several yards before turning to see Edwin disappear through the door of the factory. It was a large red brick building, four chimneys in a row blackened by sooty residues, pointed up at the winter sky like grandad Boucher's sooty fingers used to reach up to wave when he saw William in the street. An open yard spanned the entire front of the building and in one corner, a small corrugated shed played host to life's vagrants, an unruly bramble which had thrived and progressed without correction almost penetrated the whole of the dilapidated roof, except for one clear patch which had somehow managed to resist the incursion but now suffered an attack of rust so severe, that jagged holes enabled noisy, squabbling sparrows to come and go constantly, like the 'down n' outs' frequenting the Salvation Army hostel on Bridge Street.

William crossed the road to where a large tree overhanging the wall offered some shelter from the cold air and a degree of concealment but nevertheless allowed him to observe the factory door and in due course, Edwin's departure. He felt in his pocket for his cigarettes, 'uhm, only three left'. Having been surrounded by them for so long, to gaze at only three with the awareness that his situation was now very changed, caused his impatience to grow even more. 'Come on Garbett, finish your damn business and get out o' the way'. Eventually, after what must have been twenty minutes or more, the door opened and Edwin appeared with Smithfield. They shook hands, Edwin walked across the yard, through the gates and down the road before crossing over to the return bus stop. While he had the chance, William ran across the road out of sight of Edwin and up to the factory door which was once more closed. He could find no bell or knocker so he tried the latch, it was unlocked. Of what William had expected to find he was unsure, there was no sound of activity yet an overpowering smell of machine oil and a strange mingle of soft soap and spent sulphur. Rows of machines, looms for weaving and others for stitching, occupied an area equal in size to the factory floor at Player's. A passageway led from the entrance, a number of doors leading off, the first of which was open, before William had time to call out Andrew Smithfield strode from within and stood before William, a look of vague recognition on his face.

"Yes young man, how may I help you?"

William cleared his throat nervously and clenched his fingers around his rolled-up cap.

"William Eddowes Sir, we met last summer at the embankment when I was walking with Celia Tozer, Robert Cheetham's young cousin. I am looking for a position, you do know my father having done some business with him at Basford. Father has not been himself since Egypt so I need to engage myself in a prospering business for all our sakes, the whole family I mean." He paused to emphasise a concern. "I am sure I could prove an asset to you, I am very capable." William concluded his appeal with a smile.

"Come into the office William, sit down for a moment, there is warmth in here." A pot bellied stove crackled life, it gave a curious air of optimism, very different from the cold emptiness of the passageway. William sat by the desk and wasted no time in scanning its surface for any evidence of Edwin's purpose there. "Tell me William, have you been working with your father in his trade?"

"No sir, father's business was never really big enough, he employs excellent seamstresses, the very best but the office side of things he was able to cover himself. I've been working at Player's but it's a dead end job, I could pack cigarettes for the next ten years and the day would still end with those same boxes, all to go up in smoke. I want to be a part of something that grows and expands, changes with the times."

Andrew Smithfield looked across the room to William from where he stood by a tall cabinet, he took a folder from the top and placed it in a drawer.

"So you want to be successful William, to achieve, tell me, how do you perceive achievement?"

William's immaturity denied him a more measured response than.

" I want one day to be like you, that is what I aim to be."

Smithfield was pensive for a few moments then he too sat, the other side of the desk.

"I understand your mother ran the workshops whilst Charles was abroad during the war, is she in good health?"

Not anticipating such a question William hesitated.

"She is much better now, at the birth of Daniel, my young brother, she was ill, we were all worried but everything is alright, fortunately she is a strong woman."

His own words surprised him, not before had William spoken aloud of Annie's strengths, now they suddenly became very real and a pang of guilt and regret caused him to swallow hard.

"How old are you?" Asked Smithfield.

"I am in my eighteenth year sir," replied William.

A smile came to Smithfield's face, not in any way belittling his young company but a relaxed, friendly smile.

"When is your eighteenth birthday William?"

There was no point in fabricating a less embarrassing answer so William lowered his eyes and said woefully.

"Next October."

"I have many things to attend and plans to confirm before I could be in a position to offer you work, however in a few months there might well be an opening for you William. Meanwhile, if you are not already proficient and I would guess that you have not yet had the opportunity, then acquire the skill of driving a motor vehicle, find a way of combining some paid work with instruction, not easy I appreciate but there are such situations. Come to see me again next spring, around May month. Give my regards to your father and do convey my good wishes to your mother."

The frustration and disappointment within William he determined himself not to show, instead he graciously offered his hand, pretending in his mind to be Robert Cheetham or Hannibal Burton, not until he was well clear of the factory gates did he allow his pent up emotion release, grabbing at a piece of rough stone which idled by his feet and hurling it over the road where it fell into a heap of spoil on a patch of waste land. A crow, disturbed by the missile, abandoned its lucky find, a well seasoned sinew from a pig's trotter and flew towards William as though it intended revenge. William cursed at the harmless creature as it passed above his head. He'd not noticed an elderly woman walking behind him, she called out.

"You, come here you."

Before William had time to decide, stay or run, the woman had reached him, she prodded his shoulder with her walking cane.

"Feral, that's what you are, feral, you'll end up baited and caged."

Then it seemed to strike her, the way William was dressed, tidily, boots polished, perhaps not so wild after all.

"You need to curb that temper young man, throwing stones at your age, you should know better, what is your name?"

She had a cultured voice and an air of authority about her.

"William." He answered, still a hint of defiance in his manner.

"William who?" She could not be ignored, that tone, her demanding stare.

"William Eddowes ma'am," his eyes lowered.

"Go home William Eddowes, go on, shoo." She waved her cane, military fashion. He ran to the next bus stop, away from the old woman who made him feel like a small child, away from Brassington Gates which reminded him he had no place there. Just a few yards short of the stop he heard the bus coming behind him, a last sprint enabled him to be there, arm extended in time to request his fare. Panting and feeling almost hostile toward the noisy clamour of passengers already on the bus, he handed his money to the conductor, crumpled his ticket and thrust it inside his pocket, seating himself alongside a woman who was industriously knitting while at the same time holding an intense conversation with two other women seated behind them. The entire assembly was animated, feverishly discussing a body which had been dragged from the canal. William was annoyed, he needed some quiet, chance to think, he'd yet to mentally prepare his explanation of unemployment which the evening would demand of him. When the conductor announced the next stop 'arboretum' William decided to abandon the warmth of the people filled bus and walk the rest of the way.

Light was fast fading, although Christmas was a mere two weeks hence there seemed to abide little festive spirit. Folk were preoccupied, temporarily with life's flotsam but that would soon lose its novelty and those pressing matters of limited funds and bleak prospects would soon return to dominate their daily chatter.

As William walked between the laurel hedges of the arboretum he felt increasingly irritable, he wanted to lash out at whatever tormented his schemes, vent his sense of resentment. He sat at the back of the bandstand and took one of the remaining two cigarettes from his pocket, he gripped it between his thumb and fingers and aimed it, like the barrel of a gun, willing either Reg Yeats or Edwin Garbett to walk by so he might wound their comfortable wellbeing.

"It's me, don't shoot, mam is expectin' me 'ome wi' five cod n' chips an' two pickled eggs."

Rosie Potts laughed with abandon at the sight of William playing 'soldier' with a cigarette. She ran into the bandstand and sat on the seat beside him, her silly grin taunting his mood. Rosie held no consuming ambition, no craving for rich living, her simple acceptance enabled her a contentment William could never understand.

A thought amused him, I don't suppose this is what Reg meant when he said I should find out how rosy it was out on the streets, the notion played tricks with his imagination. William's eyes followed the line of Rosie's ample figure, he pictured the silky soft bosom which lay beneath her camel coat, warm, malleable, falling over the fingers, pure leaven flesh. He lifted the newspaper parcels from Rosie's lap and lay them on the seat, he gazed into her eyes with a dewy look of wanting and whispered.

"Do you remember our first kiss Rosie," he took her hand, "I do, I remember." He brushed her cheek with his lips and with his other hand he stroked the fullness of her chest, covering her anxious mouth with his own, his searching tongue found warmth, heat enough to melt any conscience which might try in vain to halt his shameful lust.

A numbed Rosie sat motionless, shock and alarm bound her in silence. William felt disbelief at what he had just done, hastily gathering the parcels from the seat he thrust them into Rosie's hands.

"Take the chips home to your mam before they go cold."

He turned and walked briskly away. He had indeed lashed out but through the betrayal of his best friend, it made no sense, he bore no malice whatsoever toward Tommy, he cared about Tommy. His shaking hand delved into his pocket for the cigarette which he had not lit, having neglected to put it back into the packet and as a result of his amorous activities in the bandstand, he pulled it from the pocket, dented and crumbling. Now he reached for the last one, he twisted the Weights packet and both cigarettes between his clenched fist until the effort induced a cramp in his lower arm. He threw them to the ground in contempt, muttering an oath.

"I shall smoke no more of you, I shall smoke nothing until I can light one of the better kind, you'll see, they'll all see."

Annie was turning a knuckle pie in the oven of the range, she looked up, surprised to see William, George was almost always the first home.

"Would you fetch some coal please William, I have to feed Danny in a minute, it would save me having to scrub my hands."

"Of course."

William was grateful to have been given a task, anything to delay the necessary admission of his action at Player's that morning but before he reached the door with the bucket Annie asked.

"Did you come home for something earlier, I walked part of the way to Winchester Street with Edna and Myra, I could smell tobacco when I returned."

"Yes, only briefly, I had something to do and I needed money for bus fare."

It was a feeble explanation, Annie had noticed his change of clothes, he wore his best jacket and waistcoat. Her better judgement convinced her it was best to await his voluntary account of events, his manner was affable, William could become much less so when pressured. The moment passed as Danny began to cry and on the heels of William, who had delivered a full bucket of coal to the old mat by the range, George appeared in a haste to tell them of the talk in town about a body in the canal.

If William was to have any hope of eating his food then he must 'cough up' the obstacle in his throat which prevented him swallowing. Charles had arrived home in good time and taken himself to the living room with the Evening Post. Freddy had come straight home from the farm as Arthur had sent three cauliflowers and some kale for Annie. John and Hilda, aware that when their dad was intent on the newspaper they needed to be quiet, played hangman by the fire until Annie called them all to the table to eat. Danny now slept in his crib upstairs where Annie had lit a fire in the grate. It kept a gentle warmth in the bedroom until the early hours, when if he called for milk Annie would tiptoe downstairs with him in her arms to sit by the range, which she backed up with slack before going to bed herself.

William gripped his knife and fork like a man biting on steel to make the pain bearable.

"I've finished at Player's, Reg and I had a difference of opinion, it's alright, I shall find work tomorrow, I'll start asking first thing in the morning. I've been there almost three years, it's time for something different anyway. I'd never get to do anything but pack fags and what accolade could there be in that."

Annie dared not look at Charles, instead her attention crossed the table to John, always sensitive to any trouble, he'd already ceased eating. Annie prompted him.

"I've given you the crispiest piece of crust, I know how much you like it that way."

"What was this difference of opinion?" Asked Charles.

William, grateful that George and Freddy were more intent on their appetites than on his affairs, replied as cautiously as he could.

"I asked for more responsibility, a greater purpose than counting and stacking in the exact same sequence everyday, a man could go mad under such monotony."

Charles was quiet for a moment.

"You've granted yourself a luxury you cannot afford, we'd all like to escape the monotony."

Then his conscience ran a fleeting image before his eyes, of The Standard, a hand of cards, a whisky glass.

"You shall do just that, you'll be out the door in the morning and you'll not come back 'til you have work, honest work whatever the nature of it, 'the labourer is worthy of his hire'."

Annie felt shock, for Charles to use a biblical quotation was unusual indeed, she herself had not heard the words, that she could recall, since listening to Mr.Shawcross pounding out his guide to deliverance on the Mission pulpit. Luke, she felt sure it was from the Gospel of Luke.

George, as if recognising his mother's anxiety at William's revelation, decided the topic of conversation must be steered away from Player's and the ensuing troubles. Whilst a corpse in the canal was not the ideal accompaniment to a meal, it nevertheless felt like the lesser of the two evils.

"They think the body had been in the water for some time I wonder who it was, the general belief would confirm it to be a man but that could be just supposition, I don't imagine many women get pulled from the canal," said George.

Hilda's eyes widened as she took a forkful of potato and chewed at twice her normal rate. George had achieved his aim.

"I heard the police have identified him but are saying no more until they have informed his next of kin," said Charles.

Annie shuddered but it was William's next revelation which was to cause her the most sadness. He had put down his fork and spoken most assuredly.

"It's that little old Irishman, apparently the police identified him by the ring he always wore, a signet ring with the initials T.B. His flesh had swollen with the water so it kept the ring from falling off his finger. Folk used to ask him why T.B. when his name was Dermot Mahoney. He'd never reply so they presumed it was his maternal grandfather's or that at one time it belonged to some relative he held dear."

William had remembered the babble of voices on the bus, each one adding a piece more to the mystery of the old Irishman.

"Oh, poor Mr.Mahoney," cried Annie.

Charles looked hard at her as if demanding an explanation of her concern and furthermore, her knowledge of the man.

"I had need to go to a solicitor, many years ago, Mr.Mahoney was the clerk, I remember him vividly. I was nervous and he was very kind so I asked his name, in order to properly thank him. 'Mahoney ma'am, Dermot Mahoney' he replied."

Charles had forgotten about the ten guineas and that afternoon when Annie had left the workshop early to attend an appointment which he had known must be to see his father's solicitor, Meakin & Kirk. At his own appointments Charles had taken no notice of the clerk and had certainly not enquired as to his name, it all seemed like a lifetime ago.

It was more than William had dared hope for, all the attention had been diverted from himself to this unfortunate, drowned man. God bless Dermot Mahoney, whoever he was, he had saved William from further trial by his father, as Charles had now withdrawn to some quiet place in his own memories. It was young John who then surprised everyone.

"I expect he'd been fighting, Mr.Dunn says there's a lot of trouble amongst the Irish, I don't understand it all but I think it has something to do with a republic and Lloyd George."

For a boy of ten to have made such a political remark drove them to continue their meal in silence. Knuckle pie delivered its simple comfort to each of them.

It was still early, Annie had carried the wakeful Danny downstairs to feed and at last managed to send him to sleep in his pram be gently pushing to and fro. She had hoped his colic was completely gone, but every now and then the little boy would display spasms of pain which kept him from rest. Now dressed and the kettle boiled, Annie was about to make a pot of tea when William appeared.

" Goodness, you startled me William, it's only 6o'clock."

"Yes, I know but I said I would find work and I shall, lots of places start early."

"You haven't put on your best things today, did you go somewhere in particular yesterday?"

She tried to sound casual, a natural interest rather than an interrogation.

"I have a job lined up but I can't start until next spring so I must find work to fill in the time between now and then. It's at a factory which is still being set up but it will be a good post, with prospects." William reached up for a mug from the dresser. "I'll have some tea then I'll be off."

Annie's thoughts had immediately gone to Andrew Smithfield, William's reticence would suggest it. She could think of no other factory that was currently in the process of development and the fact that Charles had sold the Basford machines to Smithfield, that the nature of his business was textiles, would be reason for William's caginess. Annie ventured to ask.

"Where will this job be?"

William hesitated, placing the mug down on the table he lowered his voice.

"At Brassington, I went to see Smithfield, I thought it best not to tell dad, it's awkward isn't it?"

He looked intently at Annie, for all his contrariness, his obnoxious outbursts over recent months, he trusted her judgement more than that of any other.

"If your dad asks you directly then you must answer him honestly, that is all I can say to you William." She gave a smile, not to offer him pardon but to instil in him the need to be free of deception.

Annie sipped her tea, without as much as a slice of bread William had left the house. She could only hope that his search for work might be fruitful for that would almost certainly satisfy Charles and no further pursuit of William's intentions would be considered necessary.

Annie had met Andrew Smithfield briefly and totally unexpectedly one day when in town. A man she had not seen before walked towards her, as he'd drawn close he'd removed his hat and in a voice which curiously as it now seemed, reminded her of Dermot Mahoney the solicitor's clerk, he'd greeted her with, 'top o' the mornin' to you Mrs.Eddowes as my mother would say, that was always her greeting at this time of day, top of the morning, the best of it, like the top of the milk, the cream so to speak'. Annie had been puzzled and with her innate boldness had enquired as to how he knew who she was. He had explained that one day, whilst talking with Hannibal Burton, she had walked by them. Hannibal had said, 'that is Charles Eddowes' wife, she kept his business going while he was away in the war, bright woman'. Annie had felt the heat rise to her cheeks, he had laughed and carried on. 'I understand you distributed food to those most needing'. At this juncture Annie had interrupted his attempts at flattery and forcefully informed him that all credit for giving hope to those perilously close to being without any, must be given to Catherine Appleyard, she had almost gone on to tell him that Catherine's mother too was Irish but stopped herself, recalling the day she and Catherine had been to the convent, the way Catherine had revealed her past to Annie had been as a confidence she felt sure.

'I don't believe I know the good lady', Smithfield had replied.

'You will undoubtedly know her husband, Robert Appleyard, a highly respected doctor at the hospital, although now in retirement'. His answer had surprised her. 'No, I'm afraid I've not had the pleasure, indeed the honour of meeting either'.

Annie had believed his sentiment to be sincere. So this man who had caused such a ripple amid the 'establishment' had not joined Robert and those men of some standing who communed at the Lodge. Annie recalled the remark made by Edna and wondered if in fact the gossip was a misconception. Perhaps Andrew Smithfield had not adopted the habits of a lurcher, could those highly regarded men of influence, ever watchful, intrigued by the arrival of the stranger in their midst instead be intent on the comings and goings of Smithfield. Annie preferred to keep an open mind.

Footsteps on the stairs alerted her to Charles' need of breakfast, the porridge was sufficiently thickened, she lay the table and inwardly prayed that the day would provide a result to William's endeavours and compassion to Dermot Mahoney.

The day had seemed endless, William had hawked himself round the streets offering his abilities at every possible place of work he could sensibly make approach of. There had been a handful of 'try again next week lad' and a few hollow promises of 'things will pick up in the new year I'll keep your name in front of me' but despite all his conviction of securing gainful employment by teatime, he had now reached 5o'clock with no possibility of declaring to the family any redeeming success to nullify his shortcomings of the previous day.

He sat on a low wall in front of the vicarage, needing to remove his boot, all the walking had caused one sock to ruckle beneath his foot, the discomfort had become wearing. A voice called out.

"Blimey, are you off on a bare foot pilgrimage."

William recognised the voice, it was Tommy. In the light cast by the streetlamp, William could see the wide grin straddling Tommy's face as he approached, he positioned himself on the wall alongside his friend.

" 'Stranger things 'ave 'appened at sea lad', that's what Handley said but I tell yer Will, folk never cease to surprise me. We 'ad this bloke to lay out, apparently 'e wer' a keen pigeon fancier. Well some years back, when 'is favourite bird croaked, 'e 'ad it stuffed an' mounted. 'Is missus would yer believe, brought the mangy thing to the parlour an' told Handley that it wer' 'er old man's wish to 'ave it put in the coffin wi' 'im so they'd be buried together. Now the lot fell to Jonah, muggins 'ere." Tommy pointed to himself with a coal black finger from his afternoon's shift at the yard. "Handley 'anded the bloody pigeon to me to sort out. There wer' this bloke, laid out, lookin' like they all do, respectable, best suit on, real decent. Now I didn't know whether the bird ought to be lookin' down so the two of 'em could recognise each other or whether the bird needed to be face up like every corpse, to be proper, lawful like. So I asked Handley. 'Always face up lad, eyes to heaven' 'e said. Well, for a start the bloody mount made it too big to fit in the box so I 'ad to prise it apart we' out pullin' its soddin' toes off an' then when I lay it feet up on top o' the bloke's chest, the bloody thing rolled off. I tried puttin' it down by 'is side but there weren't enough room an' when I put it up by 'is shoulder where there was, it made 'im look like 'Long John bloody Silver'. All I could do wer' wrap a ribbon o' white satin around the both of 'em. I 'ad to make 'em look fitty 'cause the bloke's missus wanted to see 'em afore we screwed the soddin' lid down. I tell yer Will, they looked like they'd just come 'ome from a session at The Nelson three sheets to the wind. She wer' delighted, reckoned 'e'd go to 'is maker an 'appy man. Got me to thinkin' though, what would I want in the coffin on top o' me if I snuffed it all of a sudden." Tommy paused and chuckled. "I'd want one o' my Rosie's brassieres draped over me chest, the one 'er mam bought 'er from Drew's when she started work at the Kardoma, it's that fulsome, wholesome, I could float up to the pearly gates wi' a smile on me face sure enough wi' that to keep me company." Tommy laughed wickedly before slapping William on the back and gleefully asking. "What 'ould you want in yours?"

"I've never given a thought to such a thing," replied William in a tone which revealed his misery.

"Come on Will, don't be so glum, 'tis only a bit o' fun. Yer can surely think o' summat."

"I want them to burn me, I've read that in London folk can be cremated, that's what I want, cremation then there'd be nothin' left of me." William could not be cheered.

"Blimey, you are in a state, what's up, 'ere, you'd better 'ave one o' my fags," said Tommy, fast becoming desperate to relieve the mood.

"Given 'em up, not smoking now," said William. Then unable to keep his woes to himself any longer and feeling confident that Rosie had not said anything about his behaviour the previous evening, after all, she'd not resisted so how could she tell, out poured all William's troubles.

Tommy listened with genuine concern, all the while thinking of any way he might help his friend.

"I reckon you might be in luck's way Will, 'til Des gets back anyroad 'an that won't be too soon. Strange 'ow one man's bad luck can put chance the way of another. We're a man down at the coal yard, poor Desmond Shipley broke 'is ankle yesterday, 'e wer' rushin' to get finished so 'e could go 'ome to 'is missus, she's still gettin' over a burst appendix, been awful poorly. Desmond 'ould never 'ave 'ad the accident if 'e'd been wearin' proper stout boots. 'E caught the side of 'is foot in a bit o' broken cobble, 'is ankle went right over, we 'eard the bone crack like a bit o' kindlin' under the 'atchet. 'Is old work boots 'ad worn through beyond mendin' an' because 'er treatment cost so much, took all they 'ad, 'e'd been comin to work in the shoes 'e wer' married in, poor devil. I'll put in a good word for yer Will, come to the yard tomorrow afternoon, I'm at Handley's all mornin', I don't get to the yard 'til 2o'clock, so don't come before three, give me a bit o' time to convince 'em that you're the man they need. Yer never know, if yer play yer cards right yer might get to drive an'all. Apparently we're gettin' an ex military lorry, the boss reckons that long term it'll be cheaper than feedin' an' 'ousin' the 'orse. You'll be a right made up bloke then Will, behind the wheel of a coal lorry, wavin' to all the lasses. You just leave it to your old mate Tommy, 'e'll sort it, you'll see if 'e don't. Can't 'elp feelin' sorry for old Jupiter though, that's the 'orse, s'pose e'll be destined for the knacker yard, poor old bugger, see yer tomorrow then Will, about 3o'clock. Oh, an' just so's yer know in advance, we shall be 'avin' a whip round end o' next week, there are three kids in Desmond's 'ouse so put aside a bob or two."

Tommy went off whistling, as he always did. William felt a wave of bile rush his throat, he hung his head over the gutter, unsure if he would need to retch or if it would subside. Tommy was gone from view, William sniffed and wiped a wateriness from his eyes, he was where he deserved to be, the gutter, like all of life's undesirables, the spittle, dogs mess and discarded remnants of human kind's weaknesses.

"William, cooee, it's me."

An excited voice called to him as he sat, depressed and loath to go home. Under the lamplight William could see the radiant expression on Maggie's face, she jumped up and down with delight, her own exuberance had completely prevented her from noticing William's downcast demeanour.

"Promise you won't tell, it has to be a secret until Christmas day but I have to tell you William, I just have to or I'll explode."

Maggie reached into her handbag and produced a tiny box, she looked into William's face with utter joy, then lifted the lid to reveal a ring, it glistened under the lamp's beam, a single stone, only modest but declaring Maggie's engagement.

"I want to ask you something William, it was meant to be or I wouldn't have come upon you like this, I just know it was meant to be. I have lost dad, both Harold and Frank are gone. There's Steve and Eddie it's true but," she paused and took William's hand between her own. "I haven't known them anything like as long, we go back ages, we've known each other almost all our lives. Please, please William, when the day arrives will you give me away?"

For the first time that day William smiled, a real, heartfelt smile.

"Of course I will Maggie, nothing could give me more pleasure."

She threw her arms around him and kissed his cheek.

"Thank you, but remember you promised, you mustn't say anything to anyone until Christmas day."

The little box tucked safely down inside her bag and that now tightly closed, Maggie skipped away towards Mitchell Street, turning to wave back at William before she was lost in the dimness between the lamps.

Maggie had faith in him, in the place of her beloved father and brothers who could no longer hold Maggie in their care she had chosen himself, William. He began to walk, at first slowly, then with a brighter, lighter gait. He imagined he could feel dear Maggie's hand on his arm, a vision of loveliness in a cream satin dress as together they walked down the aisle. He was a lucky man that Toby Hillier, a very lucky man.

CHAPTER TWENTY ONE

Annie folded the letter and passed it back to Sarah.

"I'm so pleased for Jean, Mr.Tennyson does sound as though he cares for her very much and to have written to you before asking her to marry him suggests he has very traditional principles and beliefs. I know Jean loves him dearly."

Annie felt anxious, until now, Sarah had said little to her about Jean's friend Randall Tennyson and Annie had so hoped, for Jean's sake, that Sarah's quietness on the subject did not mean a disapproval.

"He's a gentleman," Sarah let out with a sigh, "I can tell by Jean's letter that she's very happy. Would you believe that last month she sold two of her paintings. She's said so little about her artwork lately that I honestly thought she'd given it up. Avril arranged for Jean to 'ave some of her pictures put in a gallery, an exhibition, along with several other people's work including Avril's. She still goes on about me goin' down there to London so she can treat me to a fancy meal an' show me the sights but I'd rather she kept her money, they'll need as much as they can get when they set up 'ome. I've 'eard that everythin' in London is expensive." Sarah poked at the grate and put a shovel of coal on the flames.

Annie smiled, Sarah had answered the question without the need of her asking. Sarah would welcome Randall into the family, his character and good nature, his ability to make Jean happy had been the priority, his age of much less importance, Annie was relieved.

"Davina's still frettin' about givin' it to you or Danny, I've told her that she's past that stage now an' besides, bronchitis isn't like an ordinary cold. The trouble is, Davina doesn't wear enough layers in winter, she says she looks fat enough as it is, shame on you Davina I said, vanity at your time o' life. The wheezin' an' coughin', especially by night, well, I've 'eard men comin' off shift at pit with better soundin' lungs. Tryin' to persuade her to use the spittoon was a right performance. I know it wer' only because she didn't want me to 'ave the job of emptyin' the thing. I finally convinced her by sayin' I didn't plan on stayin' here for months, I've got my spring cleanin' to do an' she'd get better a lot quicker if she got rid o' the phlegm."

Sarah cast her eyes at Danny, fast asleep behind two cushions on the big armchair.

"You go up an' see 'er. Bless 'is 'eart, I'll put him in his pram before I come upstairs. I'll make a pot o' tea in a bit, I just want to put a rice puddin' in the oven first."

As Annie climbed the stairs she thought of Maggie, that rosy cheeked little girl, bouncing over the cobbles in the basket of Lovatt's bicycle, now engaged to be married and soon to be Jean as well. Two weddings to look forward to. Samuel would be so proud of all his daughters, Nora may ever remain a spinster but her quiet dignity, unquestionable loyalty and loving heart would please Samuel no less. Mavis longed to start a family, her desire made deeper by the charming young Jack Wainwright, a child who never seemed to be without a smile on his face, even when asleep.

Annie had been worried over Davina's health but had been forbidden to call at The Park while such nasty germs prevailed. Sarah had insisted on taking some clothes and staying with her dear friend until she was well again, declaring Maggie to be more than capable of looking after herself and keeping house in Sarah's absence. Now much improved and considered by Sarah to be no threat to the well being of Daniel, Annie was permitted to see Davina at last. The weather had begun to lighten, frost seemed a thing of the past. At the farm, Freddy and Arthur were busy with lambing.

Annie knocked gently at the bedroom door.

"Come in if you're good looking," replied a cheerful voice from within. Davina's face beamed her pleasure. "My dear Annie, I won't give you a kiss, Sarah says I can go downstairs tomorrow and I do believe I am almost completely recovered, thanks to Sarah's wonderful care but you have that dear infant and I won't be responsible for making him poorly, goodness knows he's struggled enough with that dreadful colic. Tell me my dear, how is everyone, and the business, I do feel anxious for Charles, all I seem to read in The Post is despondency and depressing prediction. Goodness knows what happened to all those promises of reward for enduring four years of war."

Annie smiled, "We are all well, Hilda took a tumble in the school yard last week and is now sporting a magnificent scab across her knee which she proudly shows to everyone. It's the only thing that stops her picking at it, she didn't cry you see, when it happened. The scab she looks on as some sort of medal to her bravery. She lifted her skirt to reveal her wounding to Winnie Bacon when we met her in the street, 'my goodness' said Winnie, 'you are a little trooper' and took a thruppenny bit from her purse to give Hilda. I felt a bit awkward, I know Winnie and Ted don't have much. I shall take them a cake, Winnie used to bake a lot but as she's got older I don't believe she does any more." Annie sighed. "When it comes to the business, I really don't know. I think it ticks over, I tried talking to Charles about it at Christmas but it soon became apparent it was a sensitive subject so for the sake of peace, I left it. I economise as much as I can......."

"Oh my dear," Davina interrupted Annie, taking hold of her hand. "You must tell me if you have need, you must."

"It is the general situation which makes me feel that I must be thrifty. To spend without careful thought, with no concern for the fact that many households are barely existing, I just cannot do. So you see, you've no cause to fret, it is just my silly way."

Annie crossed to the dressing table to admire a bowl of hyacinths, she smelled the three large, white flower heads.

"These are lovely Davina," she said.

"A gift from Maggie for us both, Sarah and me, although Sarah would not hear of them remaining in the sitting room, 'how could they cheer you up down there', she said. I confess I have enjoyed watching them grow and open up. Your lovely little Danny must be growing, what does he weigh now?"

"Almost fifteen pounds," replied Annie, "but you should see Myra. I told Edna that if the child continues to grow at such a rate she'll make a woman the size of Billy's mam. Phyllis Dodds dwarfs some of the men in their family but she says that her size and strength come from her father, Billy's grandad Buttel. Apparently Seth Buttel used to suck milk straight from the cow. Phyllis told Edna that first he would sing to the creature, always *'Rock of Ages'*, all four verses. Then he would lie down on his back, stroke her teats and suck 'til he'd had enough. The cow would stand as quiet as could be. Phyllis reckoned Seth showed more tenderness to that old Jersey cow than he ever did to her mam, of course this information has come to me via Edna so perhaps we should allow for some exaggeration." Annie chuckled.

Davina burst into laughter which brought on a bout of coughing, between spasms she declared.

"Ooh Annie, such a tale has set me off, but it was well worth it, better than any medicine."

Wiping tears of amusement from her eyes Davina said.

"In the top drawer Annie dear, I have some more cashews, would you hand them to me, I don't want any more of that bitter linctus, just something to suck."

Annie opened up the drawer, an abundance of handkerchiefs made it necessary to look beneath them for the box of cashews. It was a photograph, only small but framed which took her eye. For a moment she'd thought it was William, then realised that the young man in the picture was dressed in much earlier fashion and was probably in his twenties. The likeness was remarkable. Annie had seen a photograph of Nathan and Davina on their wedding day, Nathan wore a moustache. She was about to ask who the young man was when Sarah came into the room with a tray of tea.

"The dear child didn't stir when I put him in his pram so I thought while 'e's still asleep we'll all 'ave a cup of tea up 'ere together."

Annie pushed the drawer closed and handed the cashews to Davina, who immediately related to Sarah the cause of her need for them.

"I remember Phyllis Buttel floorin' a man," said Sarah, "she would only 'ave been in her twenties at most. There wer' this dreadful disturbance outside the foundry gates, one big man pickin' on a little chap half 'is size. All the others stood watchin', doin' nothin' to stop it. Phyllis come along with a sack o' beet carryin' for the pig an' walloped 'im with it, sent 'im to the ground without alterin' 'er stride."

Davina popped a cashew into her mouth and rocked to and fro against her pillows, holding her sides. Annie looked at Sarah and they both erupted into gales of laughter. It was a happy moment and to bring up the subject of the photo, hidden as it seemingly was beneath the hankies, seemed inappropriate. One day she would ask Davina, it is said that everyone has a double and William's lay among the sweet smelling linen in Davina's drawer, her curiosity could wait.

Murmurs downstairs alerted Annie to Danny's waking.

"We shall call again next week, then you will be downstairs and able to see him," said Annie.

As she pushed the pram towards home Annie pondered the reality. She could not have divulged to Davina her concerns regarding Charles and the business. One day she had come home from shopping to find him in the living room rummaging through the sideboard drawers. When she had asked what it was he was looking for, after a few inaudible mutterings he had produced a envelope saying simply, 'I've found it now', and immediately left the house. William too, was unsettled and tetchy, day on day Annie felt she was walking on eggshells.

Following William's altercation with Reg Yeats, a highly charged week had passed with William unable to find paid work. He had said nothing to the family about the possibility of a job at the coal yard, just in case it proved futile. Despite Tommy's best efforts on William's behalf, the vacancy had gone to a much older man already able to drive a lorry. William's ill temper had reduced poor Celia to tears and in a moment of utter despair she had told him that she never wanted to see him again! In his arrogance, he'd dismissed Celia's words as merely a 'fit of pique' and called at the Tozer's the following evening as though nothing untoward had occurred and even wearing his bowler hat. So close to Christmas Celia couldn't bear to think of him in a state of misery so had forgiven his truculent behaviour on the night he kicked a cat into the entry and wilfully snapped a bough of a maple tree which had dared to overhang a wall and brush his shoulder as he'd walked by. She had kissed his cheek, a sort of 'semi' pardon as she viewed it, then given him his Christmas present early, a very fine leather bound diary, declaring her father would offer him some hours of work, the pay would be modest as much of the time would need to be spent instructing William in the craft of shoemaking.

With nothing better in sight and believing the arrangement would at least placate Charles, William had accepted graciously with the full intent of terminating his employment to suit his purpose when spring came and with it the awaited position at Brassington. This of course he neglected to tell Jessie Tozer, after all Celia's father did not drive. William had spoken to Celia and her mother of his eagerness to acquire the ability, not mentioning his real reason but implying it was something a young man should do if he was to keep up with progress. While her husband did not drive, her cousin, Robert Cheetham did, Gwendolyn, believing William's attitude was admirable in someone so young, pleaded with Robert to allow William to sit alongside him each Saturday morning when he made his delivery to The Majestic Hotel. A coveted account which for many years had proved highly lucrative to 'Cheetham's, Butchers and Purveyors of Quality Meat and Game', the words displayed on both sides of the sign written van.

Now at the end of March, William had a good grasp of the requirements in manoeuvring a motor vehicle but only limited skill in shoemaking and leather craft. To be fair, the latter demanded considerable study time and a degree of application. The truth was, William had paid lip service to it, his concentration lay elsewhere.

Annie turned into Hood Street just in time to see a young woman walking away from No.14. She called out.

"Hello, Mabel, we're home now."

Annie raised her arm to wave and could see the smile on Mabel's face as she turned to look back. Annie hurried forward.

"I wanted to see you before I go away," said Mabel.

Come along, lets go inside, the temperature is beginning to fall now the sun's gone in. We've been to see Davina, she's recovering from bronchitis."

"Yes, Edna told me Mrs.Wright was poorly, I bumped into her and the baby at Hastilow's. Edna was buying teething powders, gripe water, kaolin and tincture of iodine. I think the previous few nights had been a bit unsettled, if Edna yawned once she must have yawned twenty times in the minute or two we spent chatting." Mabel laughed. "Myra is on her third tooth already, two at the top and one breaking through the bottom gum."

Mabel grinned and then mischievously mimicked Edna's account of events. 'I could do wi' out it, our Annie 'ave just started, 'The Curse', an' she's waddling' about like a dyin' duck, Billy's got a boil on the back of 'is neck and now Myra's bit me soddin' tit'.

"Yes, that sounds like Edna," said Annie chuckling at the very accurate description.

"I'm moving to Leicester Annie. I've been offered the chance to train in midwifery at the maternity unit of Leicester General. I've thought about it but what's to keep me here. With mam gone now I feel I need to make a change. It's not that far away, I can come to see you on the train when I have time off and go to the cemetery."

"You shouldn't hesitate," said Annie. "May was so proud to tell Edna and me when you earned your buckle. You'll make a wonderful midwife, I know you will. Practice on Danny, he needs his nappy changing and I must go for a wee." Annie laughed as she handed the little boy to Mabel. "All his things are upstairs on the bed, the door's open.

Mabel looked at the photograph on the chest of drawers, all the family except George who presumably took the picture. Emotion welled inside her, her dad, her own dear Alfred, her mam too, all gone, all sense of family lost. Mabel turned her eyes back to Danny lying on the bed, kissed his forehead three times, gathered him in her arms as if for that moment he embodied all her need, then, almost reluctantly, she went downstairs to pass him back to his mother.

"There you are, he's all cleaned up and smelling sweet as a rose." Mabel put the child in Annie's arms once more. "I must go now, I'm on duty at 4o'clock. I catch the 11-20 train on Saturday, when I'm installed and know my full address I'll write to you and perhaps you'll write back."

Mabel's lip began to tremble, the tears to fall.

Annie put Danny in his pram and held Mabel tight. An unspoken understanding between them enabled a smile to return to Mabel's face.

In the stillness, as Danny fed and the only sound was the humming of the kettle, Annie felt a loneliness which she could not explain, a longing for those days when she'd walked along Peverell Street with cloth for May, stopped to smooth the velvety head of Shawcross and carried inside her the excitement of knowing she would see Harold when he came to aunt Bella's with his book and that special smile which soothed away all troubles. At any minute John and Hilda would be home from school, why then did she feel so beleaguered. The tears fell and not the song she sang to Danny nor her gentle swaying as he suckled could stop the tightness in her throat or ease the hurt.

Charles sat staring at the letter on his desk. The women had finished for the day, the machines lay still, the workshop drifted in his imagination to those times when Saul occupied the chair where Charles now sat. When Edna, May and Annie filled the air with sounds of industrious bobbins, clickety click, clickety click, speeding the thread along the seams and hems, each highly competent and entirely reliable. His father's quietness of spirit, total lack of self importance, dull, lifeless as Charles in his arrogance had so often judged it to be. If only he could turn back the clock.

He picked up the letter and read it again. It was dated the 22nd May 1919.

Dear Mr.Eddowes.

It is with regret we must inform you of the sudden and tragic death of Gerald Meakin.

Until such time as Mr.Meakin's affairs of estate can be proved I have been appointed by The Law Society to attend his client accounts and the business of the firm of Meakin & Kirk.

I see from your file that for many years your father, Saul Eddowes Esquire, was a valued client and that following his death this firm acted as executor to his estate.

I appreciate that due to the change of circumstance you may wish to use the offices of another solicitor, if that should be the case then would you please advise me in writing of your intention, otherwise I will assume that this firm continues to represent your very best interests.

The letter was signed, yours sincerely, Fergus Cavendish.

Charles folded the paper and placed it back in the envelope. A glance at his watch convinced him it was too late to go to London Road to request an interview with Mr.Cavendish but he could not delay, in the morning he must call at the offices of Meakin & Kirk to inform them of his intention to sell the premises at Winchester Street along with the business. Also No.14 Hood Street. Charles was overdrawn at the bank, trade had been slow, continuing bad luck at cards and his own lethargy had all combined to produce a crisis of funds. Gerald Birkett at the bank was bringing pressure to bear, so far Charles had managed to pay the women, now even that facility was critical.

Earlier in the week he had gone to Brassington. Andrew Smithfield had received him courteously and if the man had guessed the reason for Charles' visit then he certainly made no show of it.

Charles carried serious doubts as to whether Smithfield would be interested in buying the Winchester Street concern. It was a distance from the factory and very small fry in comparison but desperation drove Charles to Brassington.

Andrew Smithfield in the first instance, had wondered if William's recent visit had brought Charles to his door but with no mention of William and the revelation that Charles was offering his remaining business for sale, Smithfield was perceptive enough to realise that William had said nothing to his father of their meeting. To Charles' great surprise , Smithfield had agreed in principle to the deal but would proceed no further until his accountant had gone over the last three years trading figures for the Winchester Street workshop, requesting Charles to deliver the necessary ledgers to Jacobson's. Charles had left the workshop incensed at the thought of Edwin Garbett examining his accounts, especially as over the three years in question, it was the first two which showed healthy profit, the period over which Annie had managed the business.

A lengthy consultation with Birkett at the bank had resulted in Charles agreeing to a transaction, 'mutually beneficial to both parties', those were the very words of Gerald Birkett. A shop premises on Gregory Street, well placed for custom, sited as it was between Player's and Raleigh was for sale. A newsagent's, general grocery and tobacconist, having accommodation above, not large but adaptable, a good opportunity. The owner was retiring after many successful years and now looking to buy a property to let, having already a property at Wollaton. Birkett was confident he could broker a good deal for Charles, it would enable him to clear all his debts but retain self employment, to which he had become accustomed. Birkett however, chose not to reveal to Charles the fact that the vendor of the shop on Gregory Street, one George Sneddon was Birkett's own brother in law, his sister's husband. Highly unethical given his senior position of trust, and his assurance to Charles of a mutual benefit, as unreliable as his scruples. Even if Charles had known it would have made little difference. All Charles wanted was to be free of the worry, to climb from the trough which daily would seek to bury him deeper.

The proceeds of the sale of Winchester Street would not be its true value. The recent trading figures would determine what Smithfield was prepared to pay, especially in the current economic climate. Brassington was taking Smithfield himself into debt, much rested on his future with Vyella and the opportunities presented by new printing and design. Whatever the sales raised, it should be sufficient to establish the shop and leave a balance, albeit small on the transaction with Sneddon, the sale of No.14.

Charles would not tell Annie until the situation forced him to. He had asked Smithfield to speak of their exchange with no one and regulations of the bank, Charles felt sure, confined Birkett to silence.

Charles opened the drawer of his desk, placed the envelope within and turned the key in the lock. His fingers smoothed the arm of the chair, he spoke aloud as though Saul could hear every word.

"Well, what are you making of all this, at least I didn't sell as soon as the five years were up, which is probably what you expected I would do. You had so many more years with mother than I had with Enid. You never understood Enid, not really understood. There were times when I didn't either but those times didn't matter, they were forgotten when she looked at me that certain way. I've tried father but I can't seem to leave those times behind, I think I have, then I turn around and there they are, following, watching me from the shadows. How did you cope, you were always here, in this small office, perhaps that was it, you somehow managed to exclude mother from this room, was that your defence? Not even in Egypt could I lose the past. Perhaps if Clem had survived things would have been different. You certainly would not have understood Clem, not at all. I was your Charles but Clem's Charlie boy. It sounds silly now but back then it made me feel big. How contrary is that. You addressed me as a man and I felt like a boy. Clem addressed me as a boy and I felt like a man.

I don't mean to hurt Annie, she has strengths Enid could never find. You were lucky, I know mother was no age when she died but at least she left you with only good memories and nothing happened to torment your loyalties.

The house is only bricks and mortar after all. Mother died there and you, Enid too but life went on. Freddy, John and Hilda were born there, and Daniel." Charles rubbed his palms along his thighs and fought back tears. It hurt, it all hurt.

As Charles crossed the floor of the workshop he noticed a pin, shining beneath Sylvia's stool. "See a pin, pick it up and all your days you'll have good luck." He recited the old adage as he held the pin up to the lamp, then stuck it firmly in a bobbin of thread on Sylvia's work table, took down his coat from the hook and set off home to No.14, while he still could.

CHAPTER TWENTY TWO

Victor tugged at Billy's sleeve as they walked to the allotment.

"Billy, Tilly's had kittens again Billy. Edna might want one, ask Edna if she wants one Billy." Victor drew in a deep breath of anticipation, then at the look on Billy's face, let it go again with a sigh of disappointment.

"I told you last time Victor, she don't want one, 'tis not that she don't like cats, but Edna says me an' the girls are enough of a menagerie as it is." Billy rubbed the top of Victor's head, "don't worry about it lad, it 'appens wi' cats, nowt else for it."

Poor Victor, every time one of his brothers took down the pail from the hook and Florrie gave Victor his favourite chocolate bar, his simple view of things prevented him accepting the fact that Tilly's offspring could not remain. Billy recognised the sadness in Victor at what he believed was a heartless denial of a creature's right to a life. Twice it had been Victor who'd discovered Tilly , cuddled up to a litter of kittens. Florrie had tried to explain to him that they couldn't live in the bedroom he shared with her, even though he'd tipped all his special bits and pieces from the cherished wooden box which Albert made for him, to create a place for them to sleep. Billy tried to distract him.

"I reckon we'll grow some crysanths' this year Victor, folk can't resist 'em. The lovely big 'ens, all different colours, we can bunch 'em an' sell 'em. That 'ould make a few bob, yer could buy summat nice for your mam. Edna 'ould take yer shoppin'. Our Annie an' Susie love the shops, 'specially Burton's, there's everythin' in that place from a tin o' sardines to a pearl necklace."

Victor looked pensive. "Elbow grease, I'll buy her some o' that, mam's allus sayin' she needs elbow grease." He smiled up at Billy. "Tell Edna we'll buy elbow grease, tell her Billy." His lips puckered and blew bubbles with his spittle. Billy was satisfied that Victor's mind had moved on from Tilly's kittens, bubbles were always a sign of his contentment.

Their efforts at the allotment had transformed the plot of ground and now it sustained two households with vital fruit and veg, but times were hard and although it went against the grain to do it, Billy had felt it necessary to padlock the allotment shed. Some men had found cabbages cut and gone, their store of onions minus a string and in the worst incident, tools taken from a shed. A cabbage, a few onions, a man could turn a blind eye to, Billy had jokingly declared to Edna that in his case it would be easy, but for any man to steal the tools of another's trade, even if it were only his gardening, was considered the very lowest of the low.

There was hunger among families and bitter resentment at all the failed promises. Many men had been without paid work since their return from the Fronts. Their philosophy then had been a common belief, a united gratitude at being alive, at surviving. Now it had changed, a man could not eat his gratitude, neither could his wife and children. Men had a duty to provide, it gave them self respect. Billy had found work, the telephone exchange would seem tame employment to some but Billy was thankful. His nature prevented him from entering into the heated debates which took place in the dark corners of the pubs. Men could be like hounds, singly, harmless and affable, but as a pack, entirely altered, intent on the quarry, unwilling to deviate from their course. Men had begun to gather in agitated groups about the city, an empty belly didn't allow contentment, wakeful nights denied the mind its peace.

The shortest walk to the allotment took Billy and Victor past Waterford's and as they drew close to the shop, a number of men, eight, nine maybe, approached from the opposite direction. There was something about their demeanour which suggested trouble. Billy felt anxious, not for himself but for Victor, the lad shouldn't witness the desperation of men, decent men, driven by frustration and shame.

"Come on lad, we'll go the other way, their business, whatever it is got nowt to do wi' you an' me." Billy turned, "Just walk on Victor, keep hold o' the strap on me rucksack, Edna packed us a nice bit o' bread an' drippin' in there."

Billy wanted to put some distance between Victor and the group of men, it had taken months for Florrie to really relax when Victor was away from her, there was no way Billy would risk any harm to Victor or upset to his mam.

Even from the next street Billy could hear raised voices, shouts, general commotion. A whistle sounded in the distance, then again, coming closer. A policeman ran past the top of the street, within seconds, several men ran past the bottom of the street.

"Nothin' for you to worry about Victor, just men wi' nowt to do, come on you an' me got plenty to get on with."

Victor gripped tight the strap on Billy's rucksack. "Policeman," he said, "policeman Billy."

"You're like a bag o' ferrets lad, stop strugglin', 'tis no good, if yer get away from me now I shall only turn up on yer mam's doorstep, is that what yer want?"

The youth shouted abuse at Liza Waterford as the constable finally pinned his frantic arms behind his back.

"Yer tight fisted old cunt."

"Mind your mouth lad or I'll wash it out meself wi' carbolic, whatever would your father 'ave said , God rest his soul."

"Two soddin' candles, a bit o' soda, God help us missus, would it 'ave killed yer to let me 'ave that." The youth's tirade continued.

"Calm down lad, look around yer, all them men as egged yer on, where are they, eh, go on lad look, where are the buggers now."

Finally defeated, the youth bowed his head, Liza Waterford turned and shooed a stunned Calib inside, closing the shop door behind her, then, as if doubting the constable's abilities, opened the door again and called out.

"If you don't deal with the little 'toe-rag' I shall."

She waved her fist in a threat, which made even the constable flinch before disappearing once more. Her raised voice, delivering instructions to Calib could be heard still, when the policeman and the offender had walked several yards away.

"Bloody hell," said the constable. "Bloody hell."

The room was small, three chairs and a table. Scratched into the table top were the words, rozzers are wankers. On the wall, a picture of The King and a calendar still displaying February. Joe sat awaiting his fate.

"What yer got in there then Sid?"

Asked a fellow officer of the law, seated behind a desk, endeavouring to look busy. The constable related an account of the events outside Waterford's shop, adding his own observation.

"The lad's got pluck, you've got to hand it to 'im, 20-21 stone, she's got to be all o' that, an' she's allus got her sleeves rolled up."

"Bloody hell," said his colleague. He resumed his writing, muttering to himself, '21 stone, bloody hell'.

Joe looked up as the door opened and the constable returned to the room.

"I know you," his large hand rubbed his chin and he screwed up his mouth in concentration. "Let's 'ave your name then," he said.

"Joe."

The constable looked stern and waited.

"Spooner, Joe Spooner, 'ow is it mister that yer reckon to know who I am yet yer don't know me name?"

"Officer to you lad, an' less o' the lip. Tommy Spooner's your brother then, I thought so."

"Aye, that's right, me older brother, I'm next man down though, I'm sixteen in June. Two girls come between me an' Tommy. Our Kathleen, she works at Eddowes' an' Joyce, she dailys for a woman at The Ropewalk, the three young 'en's are still at school."

"Don't you think your Tommy could do wi' out this sort o' bother. He works himself to the bone for your lot. Good lad is Tommy, salt o' the earth," said the constable lowering himself onto a chair beside Joe with a weary sigh. "I know it's tough out there lad but what you did today, that's not the answer. It's not fair on Tommy an' if you don't curb it you'll bring real heartache to your mam."

"I work too yer know," said an indignant Joe, it's not just Tommy. Fifty hours I done last week, fifty bloody hours o' stirrin' shit. What do folk think 'appens to it, do they s'pose I go down Sherwood Forest an' chuck the whole bloody lot at fairies. Last Saturday afternoon the foreman come over an' said, 'sorry lad, they've cut the rate, nowt to do wi' me'. Twenty five bob, twenty five measly bob for fifty hours o' shitty sweat. Do you know 'tis true, after a bit, your pores sweat shitty, yer can smell it on yerself, comin' from inside yer. Even a bath o' carbolic at the end o' the week can't get rid of it. Not much chance of gettin' a girl is there when yer stink to high heaven, but when yer can give your mam enough to pay rent an' yer see 'er eat summat for a change, it keeps yer goin'. Sometimes we hear mam cryin'. Because she can't hear 'erself, deaf yer see, she thinks we can't hear 'er neither." Joe sniffed and wiped his face with his sleeve.

"I'm goin' to keep you in a cell tonight lad, for your own good. Don't worry I'll see to it that your mam knows you're alright. Don't do it to 'er lad, she'd rather go hungry than 'ave you in clink. You're young, them older men should 'ave known better but even they wouldn't 'ave spoken to a woman like you did. Yer can't say such things Joe, yer just can't speak to a woman, not any woman, like you did today." The constable rose to his feet, shaking his head from side to side he pulled the door shut behind him, muttering under his breath as he walked away, "specially not Liza Waterford, bloody hell."

Word of the incident at Waterford's had spread rapidly and with it that copy cat element of human nature which, when applied light heartedly could create new fashion, inspire a fresh game of amusement. When applied with a heavy heart however, could begin a trend of unrest. Two further such incidents had occurred and extra constables had been drafted into the area but even they could not be everywhere. It was the events at Turpin's which were to bring an end to these copy cat marches on the shops and restore a law abiding calm.

Mavis was weighing up tea, some customers still insisted that the branded packets were filled with the dusty dregs and would only purchase Assam tea from the big wooden chests, Mrs.Burtwell being one of them.

"I'll have a quarter dear please, now me dad's no longer with us, it lasts all week. He allus wanted it strong as bark, I used to tell 'im, if yer don't cut down a bit dad folk I'll start callin' you 'Sahib Henry'. I'd swear 'is skin wer' gettin' browner every day an' 'e wer' never one to be out in strong sun, allus reckoned it give 'im prickly heat. It makes sense when yer think about it, where tea comes from they're all that colour an' they must drink a lot more o' the stuff than we do 'cause it 'ould be cheaper out there. I better 'ave 'arf a pound o' sugar, I've tried drinkin' it wi' just the one spoonful but I never enjoy it so well. You've got to 'ave a bit of indulgence after all. We used to go to the flicks, but now Albert can't be bothered, once 'e gets in that chair wi' 'is paper there's no movin' 'im. I begin to think 'e only took me out to get away from me dad. I 'ad to take 'im in when me mam died, what else could I do, our Norman's wife didn't want 'im, she 'ad enough trouble wi' their Walter, he were still wettin' the bed at fifteen. I've never seen anybody jump in a chair so fast as Albert did when me dad died. I said, jump in his grave as fast would yer?

Oh an' a nice piece o' cheddar Mavis love, try an' cut me a piece wi'out the rind, you'd be surprised how much that stuff weighs an' there's nowt you can do wi' it, no good even for the mouse trap, too hard to stick on. I can't get rid o' the little buggers, cat does 'is best, 'e 'ad four last week but this mornin' when I went to the cupboard to get clean pillowslips, there they were, them miserable grey droppin's all over me linen. How's Miss Turpin, I've not seen her in a while?"

Mavis wrapped the cheese in greaseproof and put it on the counter with the tea and sugar.

"Miss Turpin is well thank you, she's busy in the store room but I'll tell her you asked. That will be 3/2½d please Mrs.Burtwell."

The bell clanged as she opened the door to leave but no sooner had she got outside than she rushed straight back in again.

"God 'elp us Mavis, there's a bunch o' men marchin' towards the shop, lock the door dear quick."

"Don't you want to leave first Mrs.Burtwell?"

"No time for that dear, I shall just 'ave to stay 'ere now. I hope it don't come to rain, I've got a line o' washin' out, I've even done me front room curtains. I'm allus anxious to get them back up as quick as I can, I've got nets but Cynthia Clayton is so damn nosy, I've seen 'er wi' 'er nose pressed to somebody's glass many times. Albert reckons that one day she'll get an eyeful o' more than she bargained for, rumour 'as it that 'im at No.32 likes to walk about the 'ouse wi' no clothes on. Takes all sorts don't it Mavis?" Minnie Burtwell had crossed the floor of the shop, taken up a safe position behind the counter, lodging her shopping bag between a stack of kindling wood and a box of firelighters which sat on the floor below the till.

Mavis bolted the door, top and bottom then peeped through the gap between the Bovril poster and the closed sign. Now more confident of the situation, Minnie shoved Mavis out of the way so she could take a look.

"Now I know 'im, the one on the left wi' the bald 'ead, that's Walter Owens. His father wer' double jointed, used to go around performing an act on the stage. Called 'isself the 'Human Knot', me aunty Elsie went to see it at the Hippodrome, she reckoned it wer' that as brought on 'er palsy. Now I am surprised to see 'im out there, the tall one at the back, that's Godfrey Whale, 'e ought to know better, I can remember 'im standin' wi' 'is little candle holdin' singin' '*Jesus bids us shine*', all on 'is own at Chapel Anniversary, there weren't a dry eye in the place when 'e finished."

Just then Lois Turpin came through from the back, twitching and jumpy as always.

"What is it Mavis?" She asked.

"Don't be alarmed Miss Turpin, I've bolted the door, I know there's been trouble at some of the shops but I've not heard of any real violence. They just demand food or whatever they can get I suppose." Mavis tried to maintain a calm.

"Don't open the door, come away from the glass." Said Lois and promptly disappeared into the back.

"Well, fat lot o' good she is," said Minnie, "she might not be hundred percent but the least she could do is stand 'ere wi' you, 'tis her shop when all's said an' done."

"There is no need for her to be here, or you Mrs.Burtwell," said Mavis, "I'm quite sure none of the men would have bothered you, they don't intend to harm us. They'll find the door bolted and simply walk away."

A pair of eyes stared into the shop from above the closed sign. Someone rattled the door, banging the frame with their fist.

"Don't you serve men at this shop, what's wrong wi' my money, 'ow do you know I 'aven't come for five bob's worth o' lentils. Open the bloody door." Again it rattled, harder this time.

There was a sudden loud crack, Minnie screamed, fearing the fist had broken through the glass but the door was intact. Voices could be heard, panic stricken, frantic voices. Mavis ran to look, the men appeared to disband, to fall into total disarray, she pulled back the bolts and ran into the street. Minnie, still frightened but too curious not to follow, grabbed a broom from behind the counter and stood menacingly in the doorway, bristles at the ready.

"What in God's name wer' that," she cried.

Mavis had seen real fear on the faces of the men, her own attention was drawn to a window above the shop where movement had caught her eye. Lois Turpin stood at the wide open window with a gun in her hands, the barrel of which flailed the air with every convulsion of her tormented muscles.

"Miss Turpin, do be careful."

Mavis could scarcely believe her own eyes, Minnie, desperate to see what Mavis was looking up at, ran to the curb and followed Mavis's gaze, just as Lois withdrew catching her elbow on the window frame, this discharged another pellet sending a loud crack through the air once more and striking the mantle of the street lamp, bringing it to the ground below in shards of splintered glass. Mavis ran inside to find Lois at the foot of the stairs, the gun in her hand by her side, mercifully pointing to the floor.

"It's only a rat gun," she said, "father taught both mother and me how to shoot. He had a fascination for it, would shoot blackbirds, starlings, pigeons anything that flew. He had several guns, we couldn't abide it, mother and me, but he insisted a woman should know how to defend herself. I don't think he would have been so obsessed had it not been for the dreadful incident which involved his own mother. She was robbed, in broad daylight, the ring from her finger and the brooch at her neck. This is the only gun I kept."

Lois crossed to the under stairs cupboard and hid the weapon away among the numerous items stored on the shelves. Mavis suddenly remembered Minnie Burtwell. The shopping bag was gone, the broom rested against the open door but there was no sign of Minnie.

Mavis gathered the broken glass onto a shovel, calling across the street to a number of mystified women who had ventured outside now the commotion seemed to be over.

"Everything is alright, just the mantle, what a loud crack it made as it shattered."

"I heard two cracks," came the reply from one woman. It required quick thinking on Mavis's part.

"Yes, it must be the echo, the street is narrow and sound reverberates."

She hoped her explanation might satisfy, not feeling at all sure if Miss Turpin's actions had been lawful.

The men were unlikely to report the incident, after all, it was their alarming approach which instigated the whole affair. If tongues became loosened by beer, then the police would be obliged to make enquires but under such circumstances, would need to allow for some distortion of facts.

Thankfully, aside from the mystery of the shattered lamp, which was replaced a few days later, no one from officialdom had called on Miss Turpin and the wrongful activities of the men ceased. Mavis felt it should be recorded in history, that an uprising had been quelled through the most unlikely means. Could man ever have dreamt that a conflict would be settled by a case of St.Vitus's Dance in charge of a rat gun.

Edna was mangling a sheet when Billy appeared at the back door, stretching his one good arm and saying.

"Why didn't yer wake me, I wer' goin' to get the runner beans in."

"If yer wer' awake enough to notice you'd see weve had a downpour. That allotment'll be wet as tripe. Didn't yer 'ear the thunder, it wer' over'ead for a good twenty minutes an' the lightnin' wer' that fierce. Ted Bacon'll be pleased, 'e reckons lightnin' sets the blossom on his fruit trees." Edna stood up to ease her back. "No need to guess who Myra takes after, she went down for her nap just 'afore it all started an' never stirred, not even when one almighty clap 'near shook the place to its foundations."

"If I'm lyin' on me good ear, 'ow am I supposed to 'ear owt," said Billy.

Just then, another flash seemed to illuminate the rooftops.

"Count the seconds," said Edna, "one, two, three, four..." she counted several before a distant rumble followed. "Moved off now, I reckon it's over Long Eaton way. Some o' the lightnin' wer' fork. Me mam allus made us stand back from the windows when it wer' fork lightnin' but Ada wer' mesmerised by it, 'tis only the fairies loadin' coal, mam 'ould say every time the thunder rumbled. It must 'ave been what mams said 'cause that wer' what a lot of us kids thought it was, fairies loadin' bloody coal." Edna laughed. "Ada 'ould stand upstairs at the window as if it somehow put 'er in a trance, 'til mam went up an' pulled the curtain across. Stick the kettle on Billy, just one more sheet then I'll do us a fried egg. Annie give me a dozen yesterday. I wish I wer' a fly on the wall in that 'ouse, she never says 'owt but I can tell things aren't right. I thought Charles must 'ave got over that daft business wi' Edwin Garbett, don't you ever say anythin' mind, I promised Annie I wouldn't tell anybody, not even you."

Myra now sat up against the cushions in her pram, sucking a crust. Edna and Billy had just begun to eat when frantic banging came at the back door.

"Who the devil is that, just as we're about to eat," said Edna, "I'll get it, 'ave your egg 'afore it goes cold."

The opened door revealed Raymond Haynes, a look of dread on his face.

"Is Billy there Mrs.Dodds, there's been an accident."

Edna's heart sank, more trouble, was there ever to be an end to trouble.

"Come in Raymond, Billy's right 'ere."

Billy was already on his feet and reaching for his jacket. Raymond's voice trembled.

"There's been a lightnin' strike at the freight yard. Brian an' another bloke 'ave been taken to hospital. Mam says can yer come Billy, Victor's all upset, she can't leave 'im on 'is own."

As they sped down the street, between gasps of air Raymond told Billy all he knew.

"A constable come to the factory, asked for me. I thought it must be our Jack in bother again, the little bugger keeps runnin' out o' school. 'E'll be leavin' this year anyroad but 'e can't wait an' twice a copper's caught 'im climbin' over wall o' scrapyard. 'It's your brother Brian', 'e said, 'accident at freight yard, yer best get yerself to the hospital'. It's Brian's leg Billy, they've got to do an operation. I'm goin' back to the hospital wi' mam, the others don't know yet, only Victor."

It was after 4o'clock when Raymond and Florrie returned. Billy had kept Victor distracted as best he could but even his own nerves were raw. Florrie's face was blotchy and swollen from crying, her hands shook as she took off her coat, sinking into the chair with a whimper of despair. As if sensing Florrie's need of comforting, Tilly rose from the mat by the hearth and jumped onto her lap, purring and nuzzling her hand. Florrie bent her head to kiss the creature, which immediately then lay down, curled up and continued to purr its pleasure as Florrie's tired hands travelled slowly along the length of its back.

Billy's compassion told him to leave Florrie be for a little while, allow her to find some peace. He took Raymond back to the scullery to ask what had actually happened, first telling Victor not to worry, his mam would be much brighter when she'd had a cup of tea. Victor sat at the table, carefully removing last years saved kidney beans from their dried out pods.

"One of the men told me how it was," said Raymond, "the storm had been circlin' round, gettin' closer. Then there wer' this sound like cannon fire. 'E said it looked like a stream o' quicksilver racin' down the bricks an' along the ground. There wer' a smell o' burnin' but no flames, then everythin' went still. It wer' the workshop, 'e could see daylight through a split that went all the way up the walls and right through the roof an'all. 'E said it looked like somebody 'ad cleaved it in two wi' an almighty axe, yet it stood, wi' a partin', like Moses an' the tribes of Israel 'ad passed through. Brian an' a bloke called Rashleigh, Steve Rashleigh, wer' the only two inside. When the others went in, it wer' the strangest spectacle, like some sort o' quake 'ad took place, apparently it's what they call a thunderbolt. All the stuff 'ad fallen off the shelves, machine parts, heavy metal sheets 'ad tumbled from their stacks an' strange smoky vapours come up from the dirt floor. Steve Rashleigh got a busted arm an' nasty cuts but our Brian wer' trapped by the foot an' ankle, it's crushed the bones real bad. They're operatin' on 'im now, doctor said we should go 'ome for a bit. Mam needs to 'ave some sweet tea an' get over the shock. I shall go back to the hospital when the others get 'ere. Has our Jack been 'ome yet Billy?"

"We 'aven't seen 'im," said an anxious Billy, "I'll speak to yer mam an'

Victor, try an' make 'em feel less afraid, Victor's best occupied. Then I shall need to go Raymond, 'cause 'o work, I daren't upset the manager at the exchange, yer know what it's like."

Billy knelt by Florrie and took her hand.

"I shall come straight 'ere in the mornin' when I come off shift. Brian's a strong lad Florrie an' young flesh heals well. Them doctors are clever blokes. I wer' a right bloody mess when I come 'ome from France but they got me sorted."

Florrie squeezed his hand and with eyes full of tears she whispered.

"I can't drive Albert from me mind, our Brian's so young, 'e's a good lad Billy, 'e don't deserve that."

Poor Florrie was tormented by visions of amputation.

"Now we don't know what the doctors 'ave done and until we do Billy Dodds is goin' to believe the best, not the worst, an' that's what you've got to believe an'all Florrie." Billy turned to Victor. "Come 'ere lad." Billy was about to tell Victor that he would walk with him to the chip shop but knowing he would make himself late, it was with relief that he looked up to see Jack Haynes coming in through the back door. Raymond, made short tempered by the anxiety of it all, rounded on his younger brother.

"Why can't you come straight 'ome instead o' wanderin' the streets an' gettin' into bother, yer never think of anybody but yerself, serves yer right if the copper locks you up on bread an' water."

Billy felt the day held enough tribulation without an argument between two of Florrie's sons, he quickly intervened.

"Just the man I need young Jack. Your Brian's 'ad a bit of an accident lad, Raymond's got a lot on 'is plate at the minute so I want you to go with Victor to the chip shop on Ainsley Road." Billy took a half crown from his pocket. "I know the chap as works there, you tell 'im that Billy Dodds'll put it right tomorrow. Ask 'im to let yer 'ave seven big portions o' chips an' a bag o' batter bits."

"I can carry them on me own," said a thoughtless Jack.

"Just do what I ask lad, for yer mam's sake. She can't be expected to think about tea today an' Victor needs to be occupied."

Billy gave Jack a wink and a smile of encouragement. Raymond 'tutted' as he carried a mug of hot sweet tea to his mam. Hoping that he would find the situation improved in the morning, Billy left them to hurry to Winchester Street. The possibility of losing his job at the telephone exchange was an unbearable thought and Edna would already be tetchy over the fact that Billy had allowed himself no time to eat before going to work. What a day, and still the runner beans had to be planted.

"Poor Sylvia," said Edna, "as if that lass 'adn't got enough to worry about, they say 'er mam is thin as a rake, an' the colour o' Fullers Earth. She's not picked up since they took that growth from 'er insides. I didn't know what to make o' Sylvia when she first started at workshop. Havin' no brothers or sisters she seemed feeble, yer know what I mean, like she needed to toughen up a bit."

"Well Annie didn't 'ave any brothers nor sisters neither but she's never seemed feeble," said Billy.

"Well p'raps feeble isn't the right word. Our 'ouse wer' never still, you couldn't claim anythin' as yer own. 'Let your sister 'ave it for a bit' or 'them little piccaninnies God love 'em, 'ould like 'arf o' what you got'. Mam wer' forever tellin' us 'ow blessed we was but there were times when I could 'ave gladly give our Vera to the gypsies an' I come close to stranglin' Ada when she nabbed the manicure set that aunty Win give me for me sixteenth birthday. Anyroad, I changed me mind about Sylvia, there's more to 'er than you think. Sylvia an' Brian 'ave been seein' quite a lot of each other, she's got the patience of a saint to listen to 'im goin' on about engines an' combustion. First time I 'eard Sylvia talkin' about steam pressure an' fire tubes I thought she'd got it bad but Brian seems keen an'all. You're goin' to the freight yard now then?" Asked Edna. Billy kissed her lovingly.

"I just need to know that everythin' will be alright, to make certain for Florrie."

Despite Brian's continuing progress and the doctors prediction that he should be home within a week or so, Florrie had become more and more tense. Brian's lower leg and foot would be in a cast for some time yet and he would need to attend the hospital fracture clinic at regular intervals. Raymond had explained to Florrie that Brian would have to sleep downstairs. Provided he had something on which to lay his legs, he could sleep in the armchair. The ottoman from Florrie's bedroom was chosen to be the 'other half' of Brian's sleeping arrangement.

When Billy had urged Florrie to 'cheer up' for the lads' sakes she had burst into floods of tears and the reason for her anxiety and moroseness finally became spilled.

'Who pays the doctors Billy, I've nothin' put by, what shall I do when they give me the bill.'

Billy had reassured her. 'The railway 'as insurance for accidents Florrie, it weren't Brian's fault, they'll pay the hospital, that's nowt for you to worry about'.

Florrie had gripped his hand and said, 'Are you sure Billy, are you really sure o' that'.

He had persuaded her to drink up her tea and think no more about it. The look of relief on Florrie's face had haunted Billy for the last two days, since their conversation on the subject. He couldn't rest until he had established the accuracy of his belief. Now Billy made his way to the manager's office at the freight yard.

"What can I do for you?" Asked the rather gruff individual whom Billy had been directed to when he'd asked for the manager.

"I've come on behalf of Brian Haynes, well his mam really. The poor woman is frettin' 'erself ill thinkin' she'll 'ave to find the money for the hospital. Now I told her that the railway insurers sort all that out, so I've just come 'ere to see you, to confirm that's the case so Brian's mam can put 'er mind to rest once and for all."

"You best sit down for a minute," said the unlikely manager, his features were familiar, Billy sensed they'd met before, at sometime in the past.

"Believe me I've tried, you're Billy Dodds aren't yer?"

"That's right," replied Billy, "ave we met before?"

"I did nineteen years at chainmakers, about as long as a man can do if 'e wants to carry on livin'. I remember you startin', you'd lost your best mate. I left soon after that an' got a job 'ere. Done alright, worked me way up to this so called manager's office." He paused in his account of events to take a packet of cigarettes from his pocket, he offered a 'smoke' to Billy.

"No ta, it's a bit difficult makin' a roll up wi' one arm, I allus made me own, liked 'em that way. After the war, it seemed sensible to give 'em up anyroad, the money wer' more useful for other things," said Billy.

"Sometimes I wonder what I'm bloody well managin'. The insurance company won't pay out. Act of God, that's what they called it. A bloody Act o' God an' apparently they don't cover the doings o' The Almighty. I argued wi' 'em, pushed 'em as 'ard as I could but the bastards won't shell out. I'm sorry but there's nowt I can do. If the lad mends well enough to get back to workin' I'll do me best to find 'im a job, I like Haynes, 'e's a good lad, keen, bright, wants to learn. Go to the hospital Billy Dodds, ask for the almoner, I reckon you've 'ad dealin's wi' an almoner before lookin' at yer. They'll tell yer what the procedure is, there must be some contingency for folks who can't pay."

Billy shook his hand with mixed feelings. He sensed a genuine regret in the man, yet part of Billy wanted to shout abuse at a rotten system that left people in despair. Act of God, why hadn't God sent the thunderbolt down on the insurers instead of Brian and Steve Rashleigh. It was sick, all of it.

Finding a degree of calm as he walked, Billy made straight away for the hospital. He remembered the almoner at Hemel Hempstead, a nice woman, gave every man hope, a fragile one perhaps but no one left there without first being reminded of their own worthiness.

"If you would take a seat in the corridor for a moment, Mrs.Pearson will see you shortly."

The nurse gave Billy a reassuring smile before bustling away. Only six or seven minutes passed before the door opened and a tall, strong looking woman extended her hand, shook Billy's hand firmly and bid him sit down by her desk. Following Billy's explanation for being there, his description of Florrie's worried state, to which she listened intently, her face broke into a warm smile.

"This hospital would cease to function were it not for those kind benefactors, those people who make donations, bequeath funds at their death, work voluntarily many hours to further the care here. Do you suppose Mr. Dodds that we permit suffering because of an individual's inability to pay for their treatment. Tell Mrs.Haynes that all of Brian's treatment will be covered by this hospital's own contingency fund and I would suggest, 'that', rather than the thunderbolt, is the true Act of God.

Whilst you are here perhaps you could speak with Mr.Colman, the surgeon who operated on Brian. I think he would welcome the opportunity to explain the long term effects of the injury. I will see if he is available. She picked up the extension phone and within seconds was talking with Mr.Colman's secretary. Placing it back on the hook she said.

"He's on his way now."

Billy turned it over in his mind as he sat on the bus back to Sherwood Road. So Brian's ankle would have no mobility, it would always be rigid. Other than that however, once the muscles had regained strength, which the physiotherapist would ensure then Brian would be ready to resume work. The disability of the ankle joint would cause him to walk a little awkwardly and steps may slow him down but the prospect of employment was bright. Billy would make sure the manager at the freight yard was as good as his word.

Suddenly he felt encouraged and he began to whistle one of his old army tunes.

Edna had pushed Myra in her pram to Cheetham's, now anxious to know if Billy had returned home with the news that all was well she turned into the back yard of No.24 to find Billy marching up and down by the clothes line, an awkward gait to his tread.

"What the dickens are yer doin' now," said Edna.

"I'm tryin' to walk wi'out bendin' one ankle, I've got to imagine it bein' rigid. That's what Brian is goin' to 'ave for the rest of 'is days, an ankle that won't bend at all. I've tried it on the stairs an' goin' up is worse than comin' down 'cause it don't 'arf pull on yer calf muscle." He turned again and walked back towards Edna with a big grin on his face. "I reckon Brian'll soon get the knack, what do you think Edna?"

Edna wanted to scream the words, 'What do you s'pose you can do Billy Dodds whether Brian gets the knack or not, yer work day an' night as it is'. She looked at him, one ear missing, almost no sight in his damaged eye and an empty sleeve where an arm should be. Edna knew no words which could adequately tell just how much she loved her Billy. His compassion, his utter loyalty and sheer determination. Edna lifted Myra from her pram and carried her inside, sitting the little girl on the rug with her teddy. She filled the kettle, set it over the heat and instead called out to Billy.

"What do yer fancy for yer tea, belly pork or liver?"

CHAPTER TWENTY THREE

Charles had picked at his meal. Annie had noticed his extended visit to the privy and the way he nervously fidgeted. Whilst the younger ones played and the older ones were out of earshot, Annie asked him if he was unwell, an upset stomach perhaps.

"I have something to tell you."

Charles rubbed his fingers along the edge of the dresser, as though he were checking for dust.

"I've sold the workshop, all of it, premises and the business."

Annie was about to ask 'to whom' when Charles deliberately, as Annie felt it to be, stifled her words and continued, to pause would have allowed Charles' resolve to weaken, already he wanted to run from the house, from the whole situation.

"I've bought a shop premises on Gregory Street. It's very well placed for trade, the men must use it to buy their smokes and a paper. Raleigh is just five or six minutes away and Player's not very much further. It's double fronted, stocks a sensible range of general grocery, some confectionary, the owner is retiring.

"But why a shop?" Asked Annie. "You have knowledge of textiles and clothing, neither of us has experience in retail. What about Sylvia and Kathleen, Edna was hoping to get back to a machine very soon. Who has bought the business?"

"Smithfield," said Charles

Annie could detect the resentment in his tone. His voice now strengthened by his growing irritability, he defended his decisions.

"There have been seventeen years since father died, I need a change, what's so bad about that. I can't know what Smithfield's plans are but why would he buy Winchester Street if he didn't intend working it. It's not for me to dictate who the man employs but if the girls ask, he might consider them, Edna as well."

Annie was quiet, reluctant to pursue her questioning for fear of what the answers might be. Charles swallowed hard and continued.

"We need to leave ourselves secure financially, I couldn't do that by selling the workshop alone. There is accommodation above the shop, not large but with some adapting and if I clear the cellar for storage it will be adequate."

Annie looked on him with disbelief. "Are you trying to tell me that we are moving to Gregory Street to live?"

"We have to be out of this house by the end of the month, we move into the shop then."

"It's the middle of May now, why haven't you said something before. You must tell the boys Charles, in fact you must tell John and Hilda too, it's not fair on them otherwise."

Charles pulled on his jacket. "You tell them, they always listen to you."

He turned to walk away but Annie called him back.

"Has Smithfield bought No.14 as well?" She asked, her own voice becoming more forceful with the need to establish facts.

"No, the house is nothing to do with Smithfield. George Sneddon, the man selling the shop, he's to be the new owner of this house and good luck to him. Now you know as much as I do. I'm going out for an hour, I've had enough of the inquisition. Not all of the furniture will fit in the rooms at Gregory Street, decide on those pieces you like the least and I'll put them through the auction room. Freddy's chickens will have to go to Cropley's, can't have the risk of rats behind a shop." He was through the door and gone before Annie had chance of reply.

Annie had dreaded telling William, she could anticipate his reaction. So to spare his feelings she took the opportunity to call him into the bedroom where she was changing Danny's nappy. The little boy smiled at his older brother, now eight months old and developing a personality, Annie found him so much company when the others were out of the house. William lowered his hand, the infant grasped a finger, wrapping his own around it and gurgling with delight at the contact. Annie wondered if even at this tender age, Danny sometimes puzzled his little head over William's ambivalence and his father's remoteness. It was as if in holding his brother's finger, Danny tried to let William know that he wanted them to be friends too. What Annie had now to tell William would do little to bring him closer to his family. Why couldn't Charles recognise all the confusion in his first born son, brought about, as Annie was often inclined to believe, by Charles' own actions and his disregard for William's troubled emotions.

"I have myself only learned from your dad this evening that he has sold the workshop. He feels the need of a fresh challenge, he's tired of the sameness of the business after all these years so he has bought a shop on Gregory Street. The transaction would have left us financially vulnerable so he decided, in order to grant us all security for the future, he would sell the house. There is accommodation above the shop, I imagine it will require some alteration but your dad says it is adequate, if this shop is double fronted, as I understand it to be, then the area above must be of some size."

Annie paused, forcing herself to turn from the innocence of Danny and look into William's face.

"So, he's lost too many hands at cards and drunk to his defeat. Why is it he does things the wrong way around," William pulled his finger away from his baby brother. "It is Smithfield who's rescued him I suppose, the man must laugh at us."

"Andrew Smithfield has bought the workshop but it is the gentleman retiring from the shop who has bought the house. Sneddon, your dad said George Sneddon."

"When does all this happen then, when are we to take up residence on the salubrious Gregory Street."

William's attitude was snide, disparaging. Annie sighed and gathered Danny in her arms.

"We must leave here to occupy the shop by the end of this month. I've not yet told the others."

"He couldn't even do that himself. Well, dad's future might lay in that pathetic shop but mine I shall find at Brassington. I was going to see Smithfield last week, he told me to come back in May but Cheetham said he has to go to Grantham this Saturday and I can take the wheel. I thought I'd use that last opportunity of driving practice. It's at least given Jessie Tozer an extra week of my assistance. I dare say he'll be surprised when I tell him I'm off. I like Jessie, he's a decent man but it was only ever to be an interlude."

"You did tell Celia's father that it could only be temporary didn't you William?" Asked Annie, now feeling concerned.

"Such things a man needs to keep close to his chest," said William, "there's always someone ready to jump into another chap's shoes." He laughed. "Perhaps if I'd stayed at Jessie's a bit longer I might have actually completed a pair."

William ran down the stairs, still chuckling, as though he found it all amusing. Annie doubted William possessed the discernment to recognise a decent man. Jessie Tozer had obliged his purpose, that was William's sad interpretation of decency. If he had truly acknowledged the goodness, the very sincere character of Celia's father, then William would have felt compelled to tell him of his intention to work for Smithfield.

When Annie had sat George, Freddy, John and Hilda about her in the kitchen and told them the news the two youngest had in unison asked the question, 'What about Byron'? The house seemed to be of little significance, their devotion to that special place in the garden, despite both being too young to remember the dear friend, was their very first concern. Freddy had looked dismayed, Annie had suggested it might be possible to fence off an area of the allotment in which to keep the hens if he wanted them to remain separate from the poultry at Bobbers Mill. 'Gregory Street is further away from the farm, it will take me longer to walk there', Freddy had woefully observed. George had seen the anxiety in his mother's eyes, of what his real thoughts might have been he gave no inkling, instead he encouraged Freddy. 'Whether they go to Arthur's or the allotment you will still be the man tending them and I dare say funds would run to a second hand bicycle wouldn't they Mam'? George had smiled ruefully. 'I bet William wishes he'd stayed at Player's now, it's only a stones throw from the shop. I've been in there myself many times. I reckon it could be a good business, the men from Raleigh get their tobacco there and I've seen women coming out with full shopping bags. It could do with a good spring clean, it looks a bit tired but with some new varieties of stock, one or two discount lines to pull folk through the door, it would soon build up a regular number of customers. I've seen at least two paper boys setting off from there with The Evening Post. Mr.Sneddon wasn't the most welcoming of shopkeepers, I don't suppose he could help it but he had an unwashed odour about him. When folk see a cleaner shop and a fresh face it'll make all the difference'. Dear George, Annie's eternal optimist, a young man with the intuition and foresight his stepbrother William would never achieve to understand.

There was so much to do, Annie had begun to empty cupboards and drawers, as methodically as she could. It was strange, although most women would have felt an urgency to see their new abode, that was not for Annie the most compelling. The need to sit with Bertha and Sarah in turn, to explain as thoughtfully as possible this new situation. To call on Catherine and Davina but without giving them any reason for concern, tell them of Charles' decision to sell the workshop. These things Annie would do first and foremost. Edna was Annie's main worry. Only a few days earlier Edna had spoken of her intention to ask Charles for work. Myra was a happy, obliging little girl who already ate a dish of food many an older child would find daunting. Billy was at home by day except for the time he spent at the allotment and as Edna had pointed out, 'She'll be 'appy sittin' in 'er pram watchin' Victor and Billy 'an playin' wi the wooden serviette rings. What aunt Win thought I'd ever do wi' a set o' bloody serviette rings I can't think. Still, they've found their usefulness at last, albeit for the first time since we got married'.

Victor had shown delight at the arrival of Myra and would happily help Billy look after her. Their eldest daughter Annie would be fourteen at the end of the year. Edna tried not to think about her leaving school and seeking work. Once school days were ended and with it childhood, life suddenly became much less carefree. Edna had observed many young girls, fresh faced, a twinkle in their eyes, after just half a dozen years, develop lines of weariness, lose that sparkle of enthusiasm which previously the innocent playing of games had kept safe and secure.

Annie had put Danny down for a nap and was about to begin emptying the sideboard of the best china and start packing it between the spare linens when a knock came at the front door.

"Hello Mrs.Eddowes, I hope I've not come at an inconvenient time."

Andrew Smithfield smiled warmly. Annie felt embarrassed by her untidiness. Several boxes sat in the hallway and the open living room door revealed further confusion.

"I'm afraid Charles isn't here, he would likely be at Winchester Street," said Annie. Aware that her fingers were dusty from her activities she let them fall into the folds of her skirt, discreetly wiping them clean.

"That is what I imagined. It is yourself I wish to speak with, for just a few minutes if you will permit."

Annie opened wide the door. "Please come in, you must forgive the disorder, I do believe the kitchen at present is the least cluttered, perhaps you would sit in there for a moment."

She was puzzled by his visit and his need to speak with her, surely Charles had attended to all aspects of the agreement between Smithfield and himself.

"You appear to be packing Mrs.Eddowes, are you moving house?"

Annie was even more taken aback by his enquiry.

"Hasn't Charles told you about the shop, I felt sure that either he or William would have said something."

"Oh yes, Charles seemed keen to tell me that he had acquired a shop premises. He didn't enlarge upon it and said nothing of your moving home."

Andrew Smithfield seemed genuinely surprised.

"Charles has sold No.14, he feels the need of a complete change. The shop has accommodation above, we move from here at the end of the month," said Annie trying to sound confident and attuned.

So, Smithfield thought to himself, the rumours were correct. He had heard speculation over Charles' finances. Some had inferred that he was strapped for cash and being squeezed by the bank. It was in fact that which had influenced Smithfield to buy the workshop, not from a shrewd business angle but because of his own memories, because of Annie.

"I wanted simply to tell you that Charles approached me with regard the sale of his business. I was anxious that you might consider Andrew Smithfield to be ruthless, intent on some sort of monopoly. Eddowes' has an excellent reputation for quality, I admired it but I did not covet it. As for William, he is young, ambitious, sometimes a little over zealous I fancy but we all of us, had to learn the ways of the world. I shall be fair, you have no cause to worry that he might be exploited. That is all I really wished to tell you."

He smiled again, an easy spontaneous smile. It gave Annie courage, she must not let the opportunity pass.

"I need to speak with you also, regarding Sylvia, Kathleen and especially Edna." Annie hesitated.

"Go on, I am listening," he said, that same expression of kindliness upon his face.

"They are skilled at what they do, you would not find women better, not only at their machines but in their total honesty and reliability. Both Sylvia and Kathleen, for two so young, have responsibilities far beyond their years, Mrs.Robinson is very poorly, Sylvia cares for her mother while maintaining the quality of her work as always. Kathleen comes from a big family, Mrs.Spooner is profoundly deaf. Just two of so many families who have lost fathers through the war. Billy, Edna's husband, thank God returned but his injuries were severe. He lost an arm, an ear and has virtually no sight in one eye. They had their fourth daughter last October. Billy works nights at the telephone exchange and by some miracle of strength, seems to be busy with his allotment most of the days too. Edna I know, was hoping to return to a machine. Would your plans be likely to include these women? Forgive my directness." Annie suddenly laughed. "I should tell you that Edna is experienced in all aspects of the workshop, except the accounts. Edna Dodds is also one of the most brutally honest in her speaking, she is no shrinking violet and she will tell you just what she thinks. On the other hand, she would work 'til she dropped if necessary and remain ever loyal."

The smile had spread across Andrew Smithfield's face 'til it finally turned to a chuckle.

"I have an aunt with whom I live, believe me, no one could be more outspoken. Aunt Alicia's principles are etched in stone, the very same stone on which she daily whets her tongue. I've always believed her direct speaking good for me and I have the highest regard for her. Mrs.Dodds, as you describe her, must be of very similar character, that augurs well I think.

I shall need someone to oversee the day to day running of Winchester Street. Your friend Edna you would consider suitable for the task?" He looked at Annie enquiringly.

"She would struggle with bookwork although Edna is more than capable of preparing a list for the suppliers, she knows the stock and its purpose. The orders would be completed on time and be of the very best standard. The girls like and trust Edna and would work with a will at whatever she set them to do. The actual accounts would be too much responsibility for her." Annie had tried her best.

He sat quietly thinking for a minute or more.

Tell Mrs.Dodds to come to the workshop on the 28th at around 12-30. Does she live close by?"

"No. 24, just a few minutes walk up Winchester Street," said Annie.

"I have asked Charles to keep the workshop running as on any other day. We have agreed that following my payment to Charles' solicitor of the asking price, which I shall make that morning, at midday I shall come to the workshop to collect the keys. I will talk to these young women of whom you speak and of course Mrs.Dodds. Hopefully we can find a way forward that will benefit everyone. I trust that you will prepare Edna for what I shall ask of her. The books are not a problem provided she can record each day's activity and let me have details of what needs to be ordered. As she lives nearby I shall ask her to lock the premises each evening and to open up in the morning. Now I must leave it to you to persuade Mrs.Dodds of my own integrity or I might be harshly interrogated on the 28th." He laughed. "I must introduce my aunt to Mrs.Dodds, I think that could prove interesting indeed."

"About William," said Annie. "He told me some time ago that he hoped to begin work at Brassington in the spring. Now that you have given him a date to start I feel I should ask what it is he will be doing."

"In due course there will be deliveries to be made, some will be outside the area. I think William might be suited to travel, in the short time I have spent with him I gathered the impression he was not the sort of chap to be confined. For now however, he is to assist in the print shop under the supervision of Robert Armistead, a master of his craft. I shall endeavour to further William's knowledge but just as it is for everyone else, he must accept the monotony of the daily grind and appreciate that not only William Eddowes has ambition, others too seek a better way and he has to learn to accommodate them in his scheme of things.

As they stood at the door, Annie felt grateful to this man. He was in business and no doubt his plans for the workshop and for William were to ultimately benefit Andrew Smithfield, yet when she said, "Thank you, thank you very much," Annie meant it sincerely.

The factory was empty, everyone had left except Smithfield. He sat at his desk casting his eyes towards a number of envelopes, all containing bills for something or other. Aunt Alicia would ask him about the day's events when he went home, his mind was not ready for that, it resisted the 'here and now' and instead chose to settle on the past, to stay with memory.

It was following his dialogue with Hannibal Burton when as he believed it to be, Burton spoke with no actual intent but simply a casual exchange, of Annie's competence during Charles' time in Egypt, and then his own brief meeting with Annie in the street that day she had been so defensive of Catherine Appleyard's deeds, that he had felt a great measure of respect for Mrs.Charles Eddowes. The past was never far away and his own constantly reminded him of how easily a man can fail, not just himself but all those about him.

His father had been in business in London, wines and spirits. As it turned out, a most unfortunate occupation for Amos Smithfield. Had he achieved to confine himself to the role of merchant he would doubtless have made a very lucrative living. However, his need to sample the goods and against all sensible practice, to swallow in such careless volume, drove his finances to exhaustion and his morals to a depth of depravity which sickened every decent being around him.

It was his choice to abide by the standard 'the devil may care'. His problem with drink was not his only failing. Andrew, as he had grown older, came to believe that his father's desire for married women was the disastrous pursuit of the unattainable precisely driven by copious amounts of alcohol. His father held an aversion to everything regular and acceptable. He took wine with the devil and lived by the devil's creed.

Andrew had watched his mother shrink from society through her embarrassment and shame. The rows which erupted between his parents had at times, reached heights of verbal abuse and violence which sent the young Smithfield running to the sanctuary of his aunt's house.

Alicia, his father's sister, was appalled, disgusted by her brother's behaviour but not even she, a woman with uncompromising beliefs and a fearless tongue to support them, could dissuade Amos from his hell bent course.

It was when in aunt Alicia's company that Andrew felt safe, decent, immune to the affliction which day on day would destroy yet more of his mother and father. The inevitable happened, Amos Smithfield was declared bankrupt with numerous creditors. Everything had to be sold and even then, some were in receipt of a mere pittance.

Andrew's mother could take no more, all she yearned for was to return to Ireland. So they left Amos to his disgrace, Andrew took his mother across the water where he discovered a place of beauty, a people blessed of music and charm. He stayed, worked hard, progressed, his only regret was the distance in miles between aunt Alicia and himself. His uncle Josh' had been a Major in the army, his aunt and uncle sadly had no children. That had seemed an irony to Andrew, he considered them far better suited to parenthood than his own father and mother. Despite such belief, Andrew cared for his mother very much, any dreams she might have had as a young woman were dashed most cruelly by the man who promised her love and loyalty yet delivered neither. Major Josh' Plowright died fighting with the British Army in the Boer Wars. Andrew had corresponded regularly with his aunt Alicia, one letter had come from England bearing the news of Amos Smithfield's death, not in battle, bravely, but self inflicted through years of contempt for life.

Sclerosis of the liver had taken Andrew's father to wherever his allegiance with the devil transported him.

Andrew had felt gratified that his mother enjoyed a good number of years in her beloved Tipperary before, one night, quietly in her sleep, she passed away.

A few years after the death of her husband, Alicia moved from London to the Midlands where lived a dear friend, recently widowed and lonely, as herself.

Andrew had ever been thankful that he could take a drink and feel no urgency for another. The demise of his father, the resultant torment and misery suffered by his mother, left Andrew with a dread of developing his father's traits. Then something happened which alarmed him, terrified his conscience. He had become drawn to a married woman. His mother no longer there as that constant reminder, he had lost sight of the past horrors. The hot, Irish breath on the back of his neck, of which he had spoken, was not in fact the breath of a militant, crusading for The Republic but the breath of a husband defending his wife. The disgrace that it was, pulled him up in his tracks, reined him in sharply, he was afraid. To have inherited his father's weakness for women already spoken for and even worse, such failing not to be the pathetic result of 'drink' was intolerable.

Ireland had become a very tense, troubled place. The music and charm were fast being replaced by politics and dogma. The beauty of the land, awesome as ever, now sadly overlooked in the pursuit of unanimity, a Republic of Ireland. Andrew knew he should get out before tensions spilled from impassioned communities which so far had contained them. He sold up his business, house and chattels, for less than their true worth but the climate had become too heated to enable cool, calm, unhurried negotiations.

With finances intact and simply personal belongings in modest baggage, he returned to England, to join once more his aunt Alicia, who having sadly lost her friend to pneumonia, seized upon her nephew's arrival with open delight. It was a reciprocal arrangement, Andrew brought company to an elderly lady and she provided that steadying hand, the certainty that his feet would remain firmly on appropriate ground. Not under Alicia's watchful eye would Andrew, ever again, tread so close to his father's way. The chance to acquire the old munitions factory had been more than he had dared to hope, he believed it providence. To be successful he must channel all his energies into the business, it would leave no time for anything beyond work, exactly what he needed.

When he'd heard rumour of Charles Eddowes' financial difficulties, it had been the memory of his mother and the thought of Charles' wife which influenced him to buy the Winchester Street workshop. In a strange way he felt it somehow redeemed his past wrong doing.

He looked at the rather 'sorry' old clock on the office wall, almost seven. He put the bills in his desk drawer with a sigh, they could wait until morning. Aunt Alicia would be listening for the door latch, she would smile her pleasure and present him with a small glass of sherry, along with the instruction to 'sip it' as herself. This apparently rendered the indulgence 'good for the heart' and proved the worth of a very modest measure. Aunt Alicia opposed excess in any area of life. He must tell mischievously, of the likely new manager at Winchester Street, one Edna Dodds whom he believed to compare impressively with herself when it came to direct speaking. He laughed aloud at the notion. His curiosity made him eager to meet Mrs.Dodds. The future suddenly seemed bright, hard work it may well be, Andrew Smithfield looked forward to it nonetheless.

"Edna you could do it standing on your head," said Annie. "So many times I relied on you when Charles was away and not once did you give it a thought. I have told Mr.Smithfield that you would not want the responsibility of the books, he is fully aware of that and is quite happy in the knowledge. Remember you will be doing it for Billy and your girls. It would allow young Sylvia and Kathleen some security too."

Annie was determined to bolster Edna's confidence. All the years Edna had worked as a seamstress, she now deserved the opportunity to show her abilities and to reap the reward.

"Well if 'e takes me on an' I mess it up, I shall tell 'im it's all your fault. Why Charles 'ad to sell up to 'im is beyond me. Charles'll 'ave you stuck behind the counter o' that shop every day, you mark my words. Won't be long afore 'e disappears somewhere an' you're left wi' the business to run between cookin', cleanin', lookin' after Danny, 'ow does 'e think yer can do so much. Charles sticks 'is 'ead in the sand like the soddin' ostrich but one o' these days somebody's goin' to come along an' put a boot right up 'is parson's bloody nose." Edna was genuinely anxious at the situation. "Why don't I serve in the shop at Gregory Street then you could be where you should be, runnin' that workshop. I'd do well organisin' 'is nibs, if I sent 'im off on the paper round that 'ould get 'im out o' me way for a few hours, 'e'd be sure to call at The Standard, spend a shillin' an' sell sixpenneth. I've listened to the barro' boys in town, I know the secret o' sellin'. 'All fresh today missus, an' ripened to perfection, yer can 'ave a little squeeze if yer don't believe me'."

Edna let out a loud huff of frustration as she resumed her efforts with the sunlight soap on Billy's shirt collar.

"If you rub any harder you'll go through the cloth," said Annie. "I don't know why Charles wanted a shop, I can only imagine that money was tight and he saw this as a way forward. For the children's sake I shall make the best of it. Charles will surely work behind the counter for much of the time. His sense must tell him that he needs to promote himself as the new owner, widen the range of stock, perhaps offer some discount lines, win custom through his friendliness and cordiality." Annie tried to convince Edna of her optimism.

"Just which bloody fairy story does that come from, you an' me 'ave allus 'ad our eyes wide open, 'tis the only way yer can 'ave any chance o' missin' what yer don't want to tread in. If Smithfield offers me the job I'll take it, I don't want our Annie leavin' school just to go skivvyin' for somebody. I want 'er to 'ave a chance at summat better. Billy needs to sit down every once in a while instead o' workin' every hour God sends. I'll run Smithfield's workshop but if Charles don't treat you right I'll ring 'is bloody neck."

Edna ran the soap along the length of the collar harshly before finally thrusting it down into the wash tub once more and stirring the contents with the 'dolly'.

"If yer want to go to Bertha an' Sarah, why don't yer leave Danny 'ere wi' me. If you're on yer own you'll likely be quicker, yer might even 'ave time to go to Davina an' Catherine an'all. I know you'll be 'ome by 'arf past three 'cause of Hilda an' John. I'll take Myra an' Danny through the arboretum for a bit o' fresh air then come along to Hood Street for when you get back. You'll 'ave to send George to collect your pram, I can't push two. Myra can sit one end an' Danny the other."

"It would help but are you sure you want the bother?" Asked Annie.

Edna watched the two infants playing together on the living room floor.

"E's no bother, it'll be a novelty changin' a lad." Edna felt envious still of Annie, a boy, a son. She loved Myra to bits but why couldn't her Billy have been granted a son. "You get off, remember me to them all an' if yer think about it, ask Catherine if she's 'eard from Donald or Eric."

"I ask every time I see her, she hears from Donald quite often but when we last spoke she had still not heard any news of Eric." Annie roguishly added, "I wonder what became of your admirer, Benjamin?"

"Probably married to the Queen O' Sheba by now," replied Edna, wiping her hands on her pinafore. "Yer don't get many like 'im in a bag of allsorts."

She waved Annie across the yard and returned to the living room where Myra shared the serviette rings and an empty candle box with Danny. Sinking into the big chair by the range, Edna felt too emotional to move. Her gaze fell on the little picture and verse which Annie had left on the shelf for Billy and herself the day they'd moved into No.24. 'A world of happy days'. There were those familiar words, still where Annie had placed them, each time Edna dusted the glass and put it back on the shelf, she remembered those long gone days. Now Edna could not stop the tears which welled in her eyes, the feeling of heartache which by its title suggested a pain deep within. It was silly, she didn't know why she was crying. Myra looked worried the little face frowned and her activity with the playthings stopped. Edna slipped from the chair to her knees on the rug, she kissed Myra and gently squeezed Danny's hand, "Uncle Billy will be 'ere soon, I can 'ere 'im upstairs, 'e's awake." It was 11o'clock. Billy would wash quickly, gobble down some bread and jam, tickle Myra 'til she became hysterical then wink at Edna before going off to collect Victor. Edna sighed, raised a smile, put the kettle over the heat and went back to the 'dolly' to wash her woes away.

Bertha sat with a large magnifying glass, scanning a page of the previous evening's newspaper.

"Hear it is, you read that."

She pointed to a small line of print. Annie read the words, 'Councillor found guilty of fraud'.

"I never liked him, his father were no good neither. Fancy, Rathbone, always so full of himself but fiddlin' money from the council's coffers all the same time. It's come out now though. No wonder she could afford that big house at Wollaton, Councillor Rathbone and Estelle Downing. It's been goin' on for years they reckon." Bertha was truly incensed.

"I have some news too Bertha," said Annie. "We shall be moving from No.14 very soon."

Annie explained as carefully as she could, reassuring her elderly friend that the distance from Gregory Street was little more than from Hood Street and Bertha would see the boys and Hilda just as before.

"Sneddon had that shop didn't he," said Bertha. "A shrewd piece of work, he married Agnes Birkett, you know who I mean, she's a sister of Birkett at the bank. She's a simple soul, wouldn't say boo to a goose but there's nothin' simple about the men, they know every little wrinkle. Why I wouldn't be surprised to hear that they were thick with Rathbone. That Downing woman has likely entertained half the city elite over the last twenty years, all of Nottingham's merry men!" Bertha chuckled, then sighed long. "I sometimes wonder what would have happened to Enid had she lived, she could so easily have been drawn into the wrong crowd." Bertha sounded so cynical that Annie could not bear to hear it.

"I really cannot imagine Bertha, that Enid and Estelle Downing could ever have shared an interest. Enid had her family, Charles, William and Freddy they meant everything to her."

Bertha smiled. "I loved that girl, but Enid was an enigma to me. So many times I felt like giving her a good spanking yet from the start, she crept under my skin. I think about her every day, I suppose I always will. So Annie dear, you will all be living on Gregory Street at Sneddon's shop. Poor Charles was never the most confident when faced with the public but I'm sure he'll adapt, you will soon establish a good trade when folk get to know you."

As Annie made her way to Mitchell Street, she pondered on Bertha's revelation. A brother in law to Birkett, presumably Charles was aware. At least the scandal surrounding Councillor Rathbone had engaged Bertha's thinking and diverted her mind from the sale of the business and No.14. It seemed curiously fortuitous, Annie had feared her news would upset Bertha but now it paled alongside greater events.

"It's a good job Maggie and Toby have decided to wait until next spring to be married, I don't think I could cope with all the excitement. Jean is determined to fetch me. I suppose she's made a nice lot of friends in London but I reckon Jean's gettin' married there so I can't go makin' too much fuss. She's promised to bring Randall home for a few days in the summer so you'll all meet him then. Maggie can 'ardly wait, the very young have a strange perception of age and I think Maggie imagines Randall to look like grandad Boucher, she's 'eard us all talkin' about how much older than Jean he is. I'm really lookin' forward to the weddin', it's to be a quiet 'do' at the registry office, Avril an' me are the witnesses. She's sold some more of her pictures. Apparently Jean's been writing to her old tutor from art school, Mr.Sands. Now 'e's asked 'er to bring one of her 'works', as she calls 'em, to Nottingham for 'im to hang in the gallery for the students to see. When I think of folk in them big posh 'ouses in London with our Jean's paintings on their walls it makes me feel quite strange."

Sarah proudly displayed a number of Jean's early attempts. The picture of Eli had always been Annie's favourite. It reminded her of those magical days when Samuel sat in his old chair, observing his family. Of Harold pulling her into their midst, the laughter, the fun created by Frank as he mimicked Mr.Lovatt's customers.

Sarah was greatly surprised when Annie told her of their changing situation but her concern seemed mainly to be for the actual, physical difficulty of moving furniture and belongings from one place to the other.

"I shall 'ave Danny 'ere wi' me. Maggie'll fetch 'im before she goes to work. You can't be expected to move 'ouse an' care for a baby at the same time. I shall cook a meal for all of you, it'll be a while before you get your kitchen organised. Tell Charles that you're all to come to Mitchell Street for your tea that day an' I shall bake a few bits to send back with you. Let the men do all the heavy liftin' don't you go strainin' yourself, 'tis only last year that you frightened us all when you let yourself get so worn out an' run down. That used to be a busy shop but Sneddon is an idle so an' so. It's been gettin' worse each year. I found a packet o' soda in there that wer' that old an' damp, it 'ad set in a solid block an' there wer' rust all round the bottom of a tin o' corned beef. It smells musty in that shop, like it needs a good scrub an' a coat o' lime wash behind the shelves."

Annie listened quietly, each passage of description sending her spirits further and further into dismay.

Jean's forthcoming marriage and Sarah's trip to the capital would keep her mind fully occupied. Annie felt relieved, Sarah spent many hours alone with her thoughts, their own great changes and the problems which might arise, would not now feature too strongly, much happier events kept Sarah from dwelling on Mr.Sneddon's left over, neglected shop fittings. Annie imagined they would become no one's problem but her own.

"Why do come in Annie, how good it is to see you," said Catherine. "Robert has discovered a new fascination, it can get a bit messy but he seems able to completely lose himself in it, quite literally, I found four stuck to his sleeve yesterday."

Catherine led Annie to the sitting room where Robert sat with his back towards them, engrossed in some activity on the table in front of him.

"Robert." Catherine spoke quite loudly but it failed to draw his attention. "You will need to speak up Annie, he's so hard of hearing these days. I confess it can feel rather lonely sometimes, he spends hours happily working on the model and scarcely uttering a word."

Annie peered over Robert's shoulder, the table was covered by newspaper and strewn with matchsticks, on a board, taking shape was a model of a church. Robert at last realised that someone was there.

"What do you think Annie, it is supposed to bc Southwell Minster. I have always been inspired by those builders of centuries ago. Mine is a humble effort but I hope it goes some way to honouring such skilled craftsmen."

"I think it is quite incredible Robert," said Annie. "You have created a masterpiece, so much fine detail, I wouldn't know where to begin."

Annie had raised her voice as much as seemed polite but the troubled expression in Robert's eyes, fleeting, but very telling suggested he had heard only some of Annie's remarks. His smile however was warm and welcoming, he took her hand and kissed it. Annie could feel the stickiness of the glue with which he worked, it amused her. Determined that he should understand, Annie decided to shout, if that was the only way then so be it.

"I think Robert that we are united in our appreciation of great works," she took his hand and clasped her own fingers to his. They momentarily bonded and both laughed heartily. Robert, this time had heard and his relief and pleasure were plain to see.

"We are going to the kitchen to make some tea," said Catherine loudly, yet carefully pronouncing each word as though encouraging her husband to read her lips. He nodded his agreement and returned to his endeavours.

Catherine prepared a tray, Annie protested saying she could not stay long as she still had to call on Davina. It was difficult to find the right moment to tell Catherine about the move when it was obvious the poor woman was concerned and distressed at Robert's deafness

"Isn't it so sad Annie, his world becomes smaller every day. I do try to make him feel more confident but he retreats noticeably. He no longer attends his Lodge, you would think, wouldn't you, that some of his associates would call, sit with him, if only for a short while but no one does. People seem to have so little patience with the deaf yet blindness earns endless compassion. Both are tragic, I don't imagine Robert hears birdsong anymore, the gramophone sits gathering dust, he can see very well I know but surely the limitations imposed by deafness are deserving of greater tolerance.

We have at least something to look forward to. Norman has invited us to Durham for the summer. We shall be away for six weeks. It will be a blessing for Robert as Norman will do everything possible to make his father happy. I am simply grateful for the prospect of a change."

"There is to be a significant change for us too."

Annie considered the topic fortunate, it made it easier to tell Catherine about the shop. Trying to give a cheerful account, Annie omitted any information which might cause concern and had forced herself to smile throughout.

"My dear, I shall purchase all of our groceries at Gregory Street in future as I am sure many others will do. I don't know the shop at all so it will be an interesting new experience." Catherine was genuinely excited at the notion. Annie felt guilty.

"You must not forsake Hannibal Burton, he was so good in donating for our deliveries."

"Hannibal does very well, very well indeed. I cannot imagine that here at The Ropewalk or at The Park, there is a single house which does not contain items, expensively priced but nevertheless purchased at Burtons. I have not the slightest doubt that my purchases at the new Eddowes' shop will cause no significant downturn in Burton's profits. The matter is settled and that's that." Catherine picked up the tray of tea, "Come along Annie, let us see if the north west tower is complete yet."

Despite Catherine's anxieties and Robert's deafness, the hour passed very quickly and Annie enjoyed their company.

Robert insisted on leaving his task to see Annie to the door. When

Annie turned to wave back, for the first time she saw two elderly people, vulnerable and lonely, she determined herself to visit them as often as she could, especially when they returned from Durham but for now at least, their thoughts were on the summer and the very real pleasure of spending time with their son.

"Where is the child what have you done with Danny?" Was Davina's immediate response when finding Annie standing alone at the door.

"He's with Edna, she's had him since mid-morning so I mustn't stay long, I've been on a round, first Bertha, then Sarah and I've just come from the Appleyard's. I have some news to tell you," said Annie as they walked to the kitchen where apparently Davina was in the process of mixing a Genoa Cake.

"Sit down dear, I've only to add the flour and then it's ready for the tin. I had a letter from Lawrence yesterday, he has to travel to Derby, would you believe it has taken all this time for the solicitor to prove Isobel's will. Some of Owen's stocks were difficult to sell and as Lawrence was in no hurry to dispose of the house he would take no less than the asking price, they eventually found a buyer willing to proceed and now he is to attend the solicitor's office as it is ready to be finalised.

If he has time, he may come here to see me, just for a flying visit, he did emphasise the 'if time' bit but a nice cake in the house is always good to have and it will get eaten whether Lawrence turns up or not." Davina put her hands on her hips and sighed. "Enough of all that anyway, now dear, what is this news you must tell me, has William proposed to Celia, it will need to be a long engagement they are both still so young."

Annie smiled, "No it's nothing quite as exciting as that. We are moving from Hood Street."

Annie went on to relate recent events, Davina listened as she smoothed the top of the cake mix with the back of the spoon.

"If there is ever anything you need Annie you must tell me. Charles I know can be insensitive and too preoccupied with his own thoughts. I doubt that he means to be, men are very different to women when it comes to emotion. We tend to put on a brave face and sally forth but men can brood, withdraw to a remote place. Perhaps this shop will be good for him, after all a shopkeeper can hardly retreat from the public, they are his living. I shall make my purchases at Gregory Street in future, alas one old woman could scarcely buy in sufficient amounts to raise the takings dramatically but as mother would often observe 'every little helps as the sailor said when he pee'd in the sea'."

"Just as I told Catherine, you really must not abandon Burton's, Hannibal was very generous during the war. So many items in our prams were there through the kindness of Burton's," said Annie anxiously.

"And what was Catherine's reply?" Asked Davina, closing the oven door on the Genoa Cake and noting the time.

"Catherine said that Hannibal would not suffer any threat of insolvency as a result of her patronizing Charles' shop for general commodities."

"Excellent," exclaimed Davina, my sentiments entirely. He is a highly respected gentleman with undeniable assets, some within his character, others deposited in the bank. I do believe my dear, that a little healthy competition even he would relish, it is a challenge and we shall all rise to it. Only last week his picture appeared in The Post, he is to officiate at the unveiling of the Memorial. I believe originally the honour was to be Councillor Rathbone's but the Councillor has fallen from grace, or perhaps that should be Estelle." Davina laughed wickedly. "My dear Annie you must be shocked at my lack of couth." Davina was chuckling still when Annie ventured to ask.

"When I called here that day you had begun to feel better from the bronchitis, you asked me to reach into the drawer for some cashews, do you remember?"

"Yes dear, laughing so much at the story you told me of Billy's family brought on my cough, but why do you mention that now?" Replied Davina.

"Speaking of Hannibal Burton's picture in the newspaper reminded me," said Annie. "That day in your bedroom, I couldn't help seeing the little framed picture, beneath the hankies. It startled me for a moment, at first I thought it was William then I realised it could not be, the image was too old, the likeness to William is remarkable and I have wondered ever since who it is."

Annie noticed the deep breath Davina took before answering.

"Nathan's mother gave the picture to me, it was taken before we were married. Nathan later grew a moustache and the hair just above each ear turned grey. It made him look very distinguished, he was an elegant man, possessed of great charm. Sadly, he was to die so young with very much more to give. I choose to remember him as he was through the years we were together. His youthful face I allow to remain in the drawer. How remarkable that you should see a likeness to our dear William, of course it is said that we all have a double," Davina chuckled, "mother would often tell me that I held a strong resemblance to Charlotte Bronte, I was wonderfully slim then you know, when we were married my waist measured a divine eighteen inches, Nathan could encircle it comfortably with his hands." She gave a deep sigh. "Whatever happened to those times Annie, where did fate hide them when it spirited them away."

Annie kissed Davina's cheek.

"I hope you enjoy Lawrence's visit, don't forget your cake. I must go now, I promised Edna to be back home by 3-30 for John and Hilda, Edna is bringing Danny back to Hood Street."

Davina waved Annie from view, scolding herself for allowing Annie to find Nathan's picture, how careless. She had taken it from her bedside cabinet, where it had sat for years, when Davina herself had noticed William's developing similarity to Nathan. It seemed strange, other than a fleeting recognition she had experienced when looking directly into Charles' eyes, never had she considered Nathan's son to bear his features at all. William however, grew to resemble his grandfather and so the little picture had been hidden beneath the linen. Davina felt that much of her life had lain hidden, waiting for someone to discover a use of it. Then Annie came to the house, that glorious day when Davina had emerged, opened her eyes to a fresh new chapter of life. Now she looked upon Annie as the daughter she never had, from that first moment, Davina had felt drawn to this young woman, strangely a part of Davina's past. When Harold was killed it made their bond even stronger and the curious fate which brought about Annie's marriage to Charles, inevitably bound Davina to Nathan's child. Charles displayed none of the qualities Davina had seen in Annie. As she aged and gave thought to her own mortality, Davina knew that while she felt a duty to Nathan, it was to Annie she must will her trust.

The news which Annie had just delivered, endorsed her belief that Charles could not be relied upon to keep safe her estate following her death. When the time came, it would be revealed that the house was to be sold, the proceeds, plus whatever money she had in the bank, were to be divided equally between Annie's children. Davina had identified them individually to ensure no confusion. Annie was the named trustee, she would hold their title until they in turn came of age. At 21 years they would each receive their share. Charles could have no reason to question it. William, Freddy, George, John, Hilda and now Danny were beneficiaries. Bella was dead, Davina herself had no intention of ever telling Charles that Saul was not his father. Indeed in every way but bloodline, Saul was his father. Only Alice Hemsley knew the truth and Davina could not imagine that after all these years, Alice would feel the need to divulge the sorry past. It was recorded in their minds but as Bella Pownall had so wisely pronounced, to tell of it could serve no useful purpose, it was far best left securely locked away in memory.

The cake would be a little while in the oven before Davina needed to attend it. She felt the need of a sherry, pouring herself a glass, her emotions led her upstairs to the bedroom. She put the sherry by the bed and opened the drawer of her dressing table. Lifting the little framed picture from within, she lowered her weary joints to the edge of the bed.

"Have I done right Nathan?" She spoke aloud, tracing with her finger the outline of his face. "What else could I do. Why Nathan, why?"

Davina took a sip of the sherry. She had cried many floods over the past yet still, all these years later, tears welled in her eyes and an ache, deep inside, drove a longing for her lost love. She took a more generous 'gulp' from the glass of sherry, placed the picture back in the drawer, catching sight of herself in the mirror as she did so. 'When that Genoa Cake comes out of the oven Davina Wright, you shall go outside and take some air, you have a pallor fit only for the deceased'. Her thoughts had moved on, she may have a visit from her young cousin Lawrence, he mustn't find her looking feeble. One last swallow emptied the glass. 'Perhaps just a few scones as well', thought Davina, as she returned to the kitchen to check the cake. The smell of baking when she opened the oven door filled the kitchen with a sense of goodness, 'Buggersham castle, all would be well'.

The days had passed so quickly, Annie's thoughts had often drifted back to Davina's explanation of the little picture but so much had to be done, cupboards and wardrobes emptied, delicate items carefully wrapped. Some pieces of furniture had gone to the auction room, now it remained only for the beds to be stripped in the morning and the bedding to be packed before the arrival of the van which was to transport everything to Gregory Street.

George had been delighted to find, after so long, Freddy's missing snail. It was affixed to the back of a drawer in the wardrobe. As George observed, 'poor little sod must have starved to death', now an empty shell the only evidence of its existence.

Annie still had not seen what was to be her new home, she had walked by the shop front many times and on a few occasions purchased items, but beyond the inner door was a complete unknown. George's earlier description and Sarah's account of her recent experience at Sneddon's had done nothing to reassure her, neither had exactly spoken of it in glowing terms. At least they faced summer in the immediate and would hopefully be well and truly installed long before the winter weather threatened.

Charles had said that there was a small area of garden at the back. Hilda and John had grieved at having to leave Byron's special place behind so Annie had promised that they could create another spot for their friend at Gregory Street.

Freddy's chickens had gone to the farm, he would tend his poultry there but Annie felt sorry for him. The enterprise in the back garden at No.14 had been Freddy's very own. Charles was not perceptive enough to notice the sadness in his son or to realise how much the situation pained John and Hilda.

Annie picked down the last load of washing from the clothes line. William had gone to visit Celia, George and Freddy were at the allotment, the three youngest were in bed and Charles was out, probably at The Standard. Annie put the basket down by the back door and looked around the yard. She recalled the day she had ventured to look inside the house, finding Saul in his chair, having died alone. That dreadful day when Evelyn Easter had come to the workshop to fetch her and Enid's last, pitiful hours.

Annie walked across the path and knelt down, her fingers followed the letters made from gravels, 'BYRON'. Aunt Bella's words came back to her as clearly as on the night she had uttered them, that last time Annie had been in No.24 before leaving the house for Edna and Billy. 'He will be wherever you and the child are'. Child! George was almost a man, indeed in his bearing and insight he was already a man. This quiet corner had given Annie peace, hope and limitless strength. To walk away from it the next day would be heart wrenching. She was still Bella Pownall's pupil, ever sensing that guidance which enriched her knowledge as a child and continued to steer her through life's tribulations.

In Annie's coat pocket she had purposefully secreted away a bag of humbugs, the coming days would be hard, she would need a tonic to see her through. Most of what lay ahead Annie could have no certainty of, but each little mint, whenever she took it, despite events round about, would surely 'do her good'.

Given William's lack of consideration Jessie Tozer had been more than accommodating. Had William been sufficiently discerning he would likely have recognised the relief in Mr.Tozer. Celia loved this young man and Jessie loved his daughter. It had been these facts only which enabled the poor man's tolerance. He didn't dislike William, however, it had become apparent quite early on that the craft of shoemaker was not one William Eddowes had any real desire to acquire. Hopefully this position at Brassington, which the self important William had described as being almost junior management, would suit his interest and focus his concentration. Celia had been most impressed by William's progress behind the wheel of cousin Robert's van and caught up in his fervour of accomplishment and future opportunity, had overlooked the very selfish manner in which he'd used her father. Gwendolyn Tozer, on discovering Charles had sold his house and business, had been receptive indeed to the rumour of his financial dilemma. She had set about her favourite occupation, research into pedigree, discovering as much as she could about the Eddowes of this world. Her casually made enquiries of any likely informants had reached a frustrating halt at Saul. She concluded that William's grandfather must have been a most colourless man with nothing about him to have warranted any note in history, no one seemed able to enlighten her beyond the current generation. So, she had ventured along Charles' mother's side. To date she had established that Hilda, nee Braithwaite had sadly died when Charles was but eighteen and that her mother and father, Constance and Jack Braithwaite, had been highly respected, Jack Braithwaite being the owner of the bank before they had moved to Lincolnshire. To have found a distinction on one side of the family at least, gratified Gwendolyn immensely. Her daughter was quite right to indulge William in his predictions of personal success at Brassington. The young man had ambition, surely some degree of mental agility had passed down from his maternal grandfather, one did not become a bank owner without confidence, intelligence and enterprise. Gwendolyn had relaxed in the knowledge whilst Jessie, harbouring some doubt, nevertheless wished only for Celia to be happy.

Edmund, his son, had left Blackmore's to go straight into the employ of a firm of solicitors, Chaucer, Caffin and Holt. Jessie's fear was that his wife would cause herself a seizure through her reluctance to accept that a rigid code of ethics did not allow their son to reveal all the legal affairs of the clients. At times, Jessie Tozer would have gladly swapped his lot with the old tramp who sat in the recess of the castle wall selling matches.

William walked Celia back home through the arboretum. His discomfort at sitting with her in the bandstand following his shameful disrespect of Rosie he had managed to shed weeks ago. Only when he met with Tommy did guilt sour his stomach.

"Can I help your mother tomorrow William, I should be quite happy to," said Celia, threading her arm through his.

The thought alarmed William, what would she think of the place. When Annie had scrubbed it and made it half decent, then Celia could be invited but until such time he could not countenance her seeing the disarray which was Sneddon's shop.

Celia had no falsehood, she genuinely offered her assistance, having a very fond regard for Annie. William more and more clad himself in pretence, although he could not yet know it, someone was soon to see through his shallow veneer. Already William had unwittingly called attention to himself in the presence of Andrew Smithfield's aunt Alicia. In the coming months he would discover that the elderly lady who had cautioned him to 'know better' that day outside the factory was none other than Alicia Plowright. William had met his match.

CHAPTER TWENTY FOUR

"Randall has been commandeered by Toby, they've gone to watch the match at Mapperley. Maggie is delighted, she can't bring herself to tell Toby that the game doesn't really inspire her that much and to tell the truth , it would bore me rigid. Now I've discovered Randall enjoys a good football match, he's never mentioned it before. He's usually so quiet and reserved, I didn't imagine him to be interested in sport, it seems that when he was younger he played rugby, it only goes to show just how much I still have to learn about him."

Jean chatted happily with Annie. As promised, she had brought her new husband home to meet all the family. Their wedding had taken place at Marylebone Registry Office on July 3rd. An occasion, which despite being modest, Sarah had enjoyed so much she had spoken of little else since. Sarah had worked herself into a state of nervous tension at the thought of travelling to a place so removed from her familiar surroundings at Mitchell Street. When she arrived in London and found Mrs.Cavanagh to be a pleasant woman, it bolstered her spirits and the elegant meal at The King's Acre Hotel, which Jean insisted was their special treat for her, took Sarah into a world not even fantasy could parallel. Although far too polite to make comment, she had wondered just what kept the men from starvation in that genteel world. Her Samuel would have been gnawing on the bedpost within a week, the portions, while very pretty to admire, could scarcely have any real hope of sustaining hours of physical labour. Even Sarah herself, by morning, had been more than ready for a good bowl of porridge at Mrs.Cavanagh's table, sprinkled liberally with brown sugar and a little single cream.

Jean had fulfilled her dream and at the ceremony, carried red roses, white freesia's and asparagus fern. She wore an off white two piece outfit, a simple dress with a bolero type jacket. The jaunty little hat with cream, silk daisies to one side had moved Sarah to declare that her daughter looked 'a real picture' like she'd lived all 'er days in that posh London place!

Jean had left her job at the florists and both Randall and herself had given up their rooms at Mrs.Cavanagh's to move into a small rented flat. Mr. and Mrs. Tennyson now resided at Bridge Street, Flat No.3a, Mayfield House. It was conveniently situated for Randall's work at the hospital and close to the small studio which Avril and Jean used for their artwork. The galleries took a good number of their pictures and the activity now engaged them full time.

Five days ago Jean and Randall had travelled on the train to Nottingham. Having now met all the family by degrees, the couple were to return to London next day to be ready for work on Monday morning.

"I'm on my way to see Mr.Sands, I promised him months ago that I would bring one of my works for the college. He's at home today so I'm invited to call on him at his house on Clumber Street," said Jean.

"Oh please, can I just have a peep, I would love to see one of your pictures, I imagine it will be somewhat advanced since your study of Eli," said Annie.

Both women laughed, Jean was about to untie the ribbons around the portfolio when the shop doorbell clanged.

"Tis gettin' hot out there, I told Cheetham, I don't want a piece o' brisket wi' as much fat on it as 'e give me last Saturday or it'll be rendered down to drippin' inside me bag afore I get 'ome."

"Hello Edna," said Jean, "I haven't seen you in ages, how is everyone?"

"Well I can give yer the full story or yer can 'ave the edited version," said Edna with a 'huff' of frustration.

"Whatever's happened now," said Annie, casting a quick smile at Jean.

"Our Liza come 'ome from school on Wednesday wi' a note from teacher to say she'd done nowt but fidget through every lesson an' I should check to see she 'adn't got worms. Now 'ow am I supposed to do that. Anyroad, I found out what wer' wrong, she'd gone to school wi' no knickers on. 'Ow could yer forget to put yer drawers on I said to 'er. I didn't forget she said but I couldn't find me clean ones an' you'd put the others to soak. She said she asked 'er dad, but she might as well 'ave asked Ted Bacon, Billy don't know which drawer to look in. So off she went 'wi'out 'em. Now the chair Liza 'as to sit on by 'er desk got splintered when Alfie Sissons climbed onto the window sill outside 'an threw his cap bomb at it. The lad can never play sensible like the rest. Miss Coomber reckons 'tis impossible to teach any o' that family, they're all inbred. She said if grandad Sissons 'ad only walked a bit further than 'is cousin's 'ouse to do 'is courtin' an' bought 'is own lads a donkey they might 'ave stood a better chance. Poor Liza, by the time she got 'ome last Wednesday 'er nether regions were red raw, she's allus been the bashful one, she were too embarrassed to tell Miss Coomber. I emptied the jar o' Vaseline tryin' to sort 'er out.

Then would yer believe Billy got a bloody thorn in 'is thumb from the allotment. Would 'e sit wi' it in a cup o' boiled salt water, no, couldn't be bothered. Last night it wer' all swelled up an' throbbin' worse than a tooth ache. It called for drastic measures so I sat 'im down in the yard, stuffed a big chunk o' nutty toffee in 'is mouth an' lanced it wi' a hot darnin' needle. Yer could 'ave started a plague wi' the stuff that shot out. What's that you got in there?" Edna's eyes had fallen on the portfolio.

"Jean is taking one of her pictures to her old tutor, to display at the College," explained Annie.

"Let's 'ave a look then," said Edna putting her bag down on the floor.

"Just a quick peep," said Jean, "I must get along or Randall will be back before me."

Annie made more space on the counter for Jean to lay open the portfolio. For several seconds no one spoke.

" 'E's stark naked," cried Edna, " 'e's not got a stitch on, does 'e 'ave to sit there like that while you draw 'im?"

The picture was of a naked male, seated on a stool, one hand laid casually across his genitalia. Jean did her best to persuade Edna of a better understanding.

"It's a nude Edna, an art form. In London they sell for considerable sums of money. The subject proves so popular that Avril and I work in this medium most of the time."

"There's nothin' medium about 'im," observed Edna. "When Morley got our Ada pregnant, aunt Win said she aught to 'ave kept 'er 'and on 'er halfpenny. Lookin' at the shoulders on 'im, I reckon 'e's lookin' after a tanner at least."

"It is a very respectable form of art Edna, the human body is a beautiful thing," said Jean.

"That's not what me man 'ould call it, she allus reckons that even a woman looks best wi' 'er bits covered but a naked man is one o' the ugliest things on earth. If that's the fashion in London I don't know why I wer' worried about our Liza goin' to school wi'out 'er drawers on. I thought the picture 'ould be a bowl o' roses or a clump o' trees, summat tasteful like that. Whatever did Sarah say when she saw it?"

Jean sighed then began to giggle before taking another sheet of paper from underneath and laying it over the nude.

"I've only shown mam this one," she said. All three women now gazed upon a very demure bowl of flowers and instantly burst into laughter.

"Quick," said Annie, someone's looking in the window.

The portfolio was once more ribboned just as the customer entered. Jean waved back to Annie.

"I'll write soon, goodbye Edna."

Still chuckling to herself Jean hurried towards Clumber Street.

"I want quite a few bits an' bobs so if you've come for somethin' quick you go first Mrs.Rashleigh," said Edna. "Is your Steve goin' on alright? Brian Haynes is back at work at last, only started last week. Must feel strange goin' back there an' seein' the place they worked in razed to the ground."

"Yes, but Steve says that the shed they're in now is only temporary, in twelve months time the railway 'as to surrender the lease. It's property o' the colliery an' they've got a use for it. Can I 'ave arf a pound o' rashers please Mrs.Eddowes an' a dozen eggs, Bill's allus enjoyed a good bit o' smoky bacon."

"Where's Danny, I suppose 'is dad's taken 'im for a nice long outin' in the fresh air seein' as 'ow 'is mam is stuck 'ere in this shop."

Annie sighed at Edna's sarcasm but could not deny the sentiment. "No, but John and Hilda have. They've gone to call on Bertha, just for a few minutes, then they'll push him to the allotment to see George. They're both sensible and the summer sunshine does them all good."

"Our Annie's pushed Myra to their grandma's, Susie an' Liza are wi' Billy an' Victor. There's summat I need to ask yer." Edna's expression became serious as the frown lines furrowed her brow. "Did yer know William ad' told Smithfield that 'e wer' livin 'in The Park wi' 'is elderly aunt Davina, apparently William is lookin' after 'er, like 'is uncle Frank used to until 'e wer' killed in France. I reckon William's out to impress, 'e knows Smithfield lives wi' an old aunt an' 'avin' The Park for an address 'ould suit William down to the ground wouldn't it. That boy needs to be taken down a peg or two."

Annie felt dismayed. "He's no longer a boy though is he Edna, he'll soon be eighteen."

"Aye, eighteen goin' on six, 'is hormones might 'ave carried on growin' but 'is brain cells 'aven't," said an admonishing Edna.

"I shall speak to him firmly. Say nothing of it to Andrew Smithfield, I think that best, William does need the job at Brassington if he is ever to offer Celia any security, I wouldn't want him dismissed for giving such a fabrication."

"I shan't say owt, that's why I've told you. I'll 'ave these few things then I'm off 'ome." Edna handed her shopping list to Annie.

Since returning to a machine at the workshop and undertaking the responsibility of organising the girls and the orders, Edna had loyally come each Saturday afternoon to shop at Gregory Street. In many ways it kept Annie's spirits alive. The chatter of her closest friend, the constant assurance which Edna's company had ever provided, kept Annie strong. She could not have imagined how run down were Sneddon's shop premises. When Annie had stepped through the inner door for the first time and smelled the damp, seen the peeling paintwork and felt the dirt of ages beneath her feet, she'd wanted to weep. George's stoic efforts, every evening and weekend had shamed Charles into action too. Annie had scrubbed until her arms ached so much, at night they could find no resting place.

Freddy had tried hard to find time to help, the early summer was a period of great activity on the farm and Annie had felt tormented by his look of tiredness when he'd determined himself to lime wash the shop walls and the privy. The one big blessing which Gregory Street had bestowed was running water. At the top of the cellar steps was a sink with cold water tap, it seemed the most unexpected privilege. Never before, apart from on her visits to Davina and Catherine, had Annie experienced such luxury. At both Winchester Street and Hood Street, all water had to be collected from a stand pipe. Many times, when she'd lived with aunt Bella, whilst waiting quietly to fill the buckets, Annie had no other option than to listen to the older women, exchanging tales of that austere life which bound them to the bare bones of a house. Feeding, washing and cleaning for more souls than their four walls were designed to hold. It was something that Martha Ingle had said which came back to Annie so sharply the day she'd stepped inside the shop. 'Me back don't know what upright is anymore an' one o' these days, me heart'll forget 'ow to tick'.

Now at August with much more still to be done upstairs, Annie nevertheless felt satisfied that the shop smelled clean and fresh, all the shelving had been scrubbed and the floor sealed with red ochre to prevent so much rising dust.

Charles had sought new suppliers and extended the range of stock. The steady flow of customers which they feared might decline once the novelty had worn off, in fact remained constant. Annie had noticed over the last two weeks, children home from school for the summer coming into the shop frequently on errands for their mams and grandmas, harassed households, finding themselves besieged and noisy, could achieve brief interludes of calm if the children were sent to fetch, one at a time, the purchases that mother would normally collect as a bagful. Aware that many existed on meagre budgets Annie had persuaded Charles that one or two staples they should price with only small mark up. Her sense worked as it had all those years ago. Folk would seize upon good value and remember where they first found it. It laid a strong foundation. Provided they always took account of just how much that foundation could bear and not be tempted to exceed it, there should be no reason for the structure to tumble.

At first Charles had seemed willing to front the business, Annie spent all her time arranging the furniture to give the most space, unpacking the linen and clothing, organising the kitchen area. Danny was still so young and needed attention. It was a relief to Annie when school closed for the holidays, enabling John and Hilda to push their baby brother in his pram, if only short distances, so that he might benefit from the air and the extra hours of company.

Over the past month Charles had begun to retreat more and more from public view, not until late afternoon would he appear to organise the paper boys and attend to the evening trade. The shop door was closed at 8pm and opened in the morning at 7am, to enable the men to buy a paper or smokes on their way to work.

William appeared sadly embarrassed at being part of it all. Edna's revelation had not really surprised Annie, he showed little interest and marked his disapproval with a sulking silence much of the time.

The doorbell caused Annie to look up from entering Edna's purchases in her book. Andrew Smithfield paid Edna and the girls monthly, explaining that the distance from Brassington made it difficult to guarantee him being able to come to the workshop on a given day every week, he was also overseeing considerable development at the factory. Fortunately both Sylvia and Kathleen were capable of managing their money and the first thing Edna did on receiving her salary, as she proudly referred to it, was to make her way to Eddowes' shop to settle her account. 'No tick', Charles had declared forcibly, he accepted a running account for Edna and one or two others of obvious reliable character but those less fortunate mortals who juggled life's needs, he showed no compassion for.

Even Annie had recognised some attempts at credit as being decidedly risky but other genuine pleas she had accepted and put her faith in their promise of 'payment on Saturday', saying nothing to Charles for the sake of peace. Thankfully her trust so far had not once been betrayed.

"Hello Annie," said a familiar voice. Edwin Garbett smiled warmly. "I feel guilty at not calling before. How are you all? I can imagine how hectic moving from Hood Street must have been. There is only mother and myself at home but I wouldn't know where to begin if I had to pack all mother's bits and pieces, plus my own hoarded clutter."

"How is your mother Edwin?" Asked Annie.

"Not so well I'm afraid, she gets around the house with difficulty, her legs and ankles are terribly swollen. Mrs.Jacobson has been very kind, she visits mother often, taking a jug of sorrel soup. Apparently it has properties which prove beneficial in cases of fluid retention. I don't see evidence of any actual improvement in the dropsy but mother is always brighter in herself following their conversations. The house I'm sure seems very quiet when I'm at work, mother can become a little melancholy some days."

"I really should make time to call on your mother Edwin, it is dif......." Before Annie could complete the words he interrupted.

"I understand the many reasons why it might be difficult Annie, please don't be troubled. Besides, you have your young son to care for, how is he progressing?"

Annie winced from her recollection of Charles' visit to Edwin, she forced herself to appear at ease.

"His brother and sister have charge of him this afternoon, I expect them back at any moment. Danny is doing very well, it will be his birthday in four weeks time," said Annie. Thinking of that, curiously calmed her nervousness.

"I see William from time to time," Edwin hesitated, "I rather think he has a low estimation of this pathetic individual, prone to fits and still picking blackberries in his middle years."

He laughed openly. Annie felt he did so to relieve her likely anxiety but that vague sadness which she'd detected in Edwin's eyes on past meetings was there still.

"I'm afraid William is far too pre-occupied with William. If he seems distant I'm sure it is simply because his thoughts are settled entirely upon himself. He is the same when at home, if I were to sprout a second head or if his father grew an enormous handlebar moustache, I'm quite sure William would notice neither."

Annie watched Edwin walk away from the shop with his purchases, she quickly completed the entry to Edna's book and was about to go to the door herself to look if John and Hilda were in sight when Charles appeared at the inner door, he made her jump.

"I didn't hear you get back," said Annie, "did you see the children on your way?"

"What did he want," Charles replied ungraciously.

"A quarter of tea, a packet of arrowroot biscuits, a bottle of vinegar and two boxes of matches. If you'd come through to speak to him you would know that without having to ask."

Annie was annoyed at Charles' manner, it was uncalled for.

I'll take over now, the boys will be here for the papers in half an hour or so. I caught a glimpse of John and Hilda in the distance as I was crossing Ainsley Road, they must be nearly here by now."

Edwin recognised the two youngsters heading towards him.

"Hello, I've just come from the shop and looking very smart it is too. I shall call again soon, no doubt my mother will have need of some more groceries."

The smile he received in return was different indeed to the sullen response given him by William. Edwin looked on the infant in the pram, blonde hair, pink cheeks, if only he were the father. He had resigned himself to the fact that Edwin Garbett would not marry, that he would never know fatherhood. Given his affliction perhaps it was for the best, yet inwardly he longed for someone to tell him otherwise. No one did, not even his mother, now his doubts were too well established and his regret along with them.

Annie had followed William upstairs on the pretext of taking clean nappies to the drawer. He sat on his bed, fingering his watch, Annie sat down beside him.

"Are you so very miserable here William?" She asked.

"I only sleep and eat here so why should I be, the rest of the time I'm at work or with Celia."

Annie chose her words carefully. "This house is different to No.14, we have less space, perhaps you feel it offers little privacy. Falsehood never works William, it can't, when you make up a situation it's outside reality, so eventually it fails. Only truth moves with us naturally. Why did you tell Mr.Smithfield that you lived at The Park with Davina?"

William arched his back, like a dogs hackles rise in defence.

"When did he tell you, now he'll think I'm a no good liar, it was only a harmless fib, what difference could it make to anything at Brassington. I suppose you couldn't wait to put him straight."

Annie persisted. "Why did you make up such an untruth William, I need you to give me an explanation."

"This place, it depresses me, it even depresses dad and he bought the bloody shop. Why else does he take himself off for hours at a time. You stand in that shop, behind the counter nearly all day. He comes home with the excuse of checking the competition, sourcing stock, anybody would think he'd bought the bloody arcade. You know as well as I do that he could describe every detail of The Standard but if someone came into that shop downstairs and asked him for a packet of ground rice, he wouldn't know where to reach for it.

Smithfield is confident, his own man. He doesn't doubt himself. That's how I want to be and I need to show him that William Eddowes means to get on in life, that I'm not just at that factory to clock on and off between sessions in the pub, then go out and piss it all up the wall."

"Mr.Smithfield doesn't know you lied to him, he spoke of it to Edna in passing conversation."

"So, Edna's the tell tale, I might have known," said William scornfully.

Annie's voice now found an authority which shook William.

"Yes, you should have known, because Edna is truly honest, she doesn't fabricate events in some silly attempt at making her lot easier. Edna takes life for what it is, no lies, no distortion of fact. Instead she applies her own strength, her conviction, you have not the slightest comprehension of what inspires confidence. It comes from within, from self respect. If you really seek to achieve anything of worth William, then you must base your days on reality and that means acknowledging your own miserable failings."

He sniffed and drew the back of his hand across his face, Annie continued.

"I went to see Davina this morning, I have sensed for some time her nervousness at being alone in that big house by night. I suggested it might ease her mind if you were to sleep there, to know that someone beside herself hears those unsettling sounds the night hours seem mysteriously to invoke." William made to speak but Annie cautioned him. "Let me finish. Davina is an elderly lady, she has been a devoted friend to this family since you were but an infant. If you go to stay at The Park, then at all times you will show her the utmost respect and give her every regard. You will put Davina's well being before your own always. You shall continue to come here straight from work for your meal and once a week you will bring me your clothes for washing and ironing. I have not done this merely to negate your falsehood but to bring some measure of comfort to a very dear and loyal friend, which Davina has most certainly been to you William, almost your entire life. If you dishonour our agreement in any way, then you can believe me when I say to you that I would go straight away to Brassington to inform Mr.Smithfield of your total lack of integrity, your disregard for mutual trust. I am quite convinced that in such a circumstance he would not hesitate in dispensing with your contribution, however significant or otherwise it might be. His business would function to its best extent only through his ability to rely on people he could trust. He knows that William, as you describe him, he is his own man. Before you become attuned to the notion however, you must ask your dad for his agreement. If he opposes your going to stay at Davina's then you should not cross him. You feel yourself entitled to abide wherever you choose I'm sure, but the fact remains that you are not yet eighteen and to vex Charles would bring down the most unpleasant atmosphere on us all."

William raised his face to look at Annie, it almost crumbled her defence. This was William, that same little boy who had clutched at her hand all those years ago, searching Annie's eyes for reassurance. Even now his expression revealed insecurity. His lips formed the words, his voice trembled the sound.

"Thank you."

Annie smiled as she had always done, in her constant desire to keep William from harm, to guide him to happiness.

"Be patient William," she said as she stood, the bundle of nappies still in her arms. Annie leant over and kissed his hair then quickly left the room and William, to ponder their accord.

CHAPTER TWENTY FIVE

Freddy had been awaiting an appropriate moment, the weeks had slipped by and his conscience would not permit him to accept his birthday gift, to listen whilst Annie wished him all good things and still not have asked.

The weather had taken a very wintry turn at the start of October, now at the threshold of November, Freddy's journeys, to and from Bobbers Mill, were cold, miserable affairs, undertaken in the dark on an old bicycle. Mrs.Cropley, a caring woman whom fate had not chosen to bless with offspring, daily asked of Freddy, 'Well, did they say yes'? It did indeed seem a sensible proposition, that Freddy should move into the farmhouse to live, sparing him that battle with the elements and enabling him to be on hand for calving and lambing, which had begun to tell on Arthur's health, he was no longer a young man.

Apart from George, there was no one else in the room but Annie and himself. The young ones slept and Charles was supposedly having a drink with Jessie Tozer. Annie sat knitting some warm woollen leggings for Danny. The rooms had a damp, coldness about them in spite of Annie's tireless efforts at keeping fire in the grates and hanging old blankets across the doors to prevent draughts. Her own toes burned with chilblains from so many hours of standing on the stone floor of the shop.

"It seems to have worked alright doesn't it, William staying at Davina's. Though it's made no difference to your workload Mam, he still comes for his tea and brings his washing, you need some relief from it all. Weeks ago now, Mrs.Cropley suggested it would be a real comfort to Arthur if I moved in with them, to be there when a calf comes in the middle of the night or if the sow has piglets at about four in the morning."

Annie had put down her needles as she listened. Although she had said nothing to Freddy, it had not escaped her notice, his quietness, his preoccupation with something beyond Gregory Street. She had even wondered if he'd overheard people talking thoughtlessly, Charles did lay himself open to the criticism of others.

"We would miss you a great deal Freddy," said Annie, "but if it helped the Cropleys, they've been so kind to us all in the past, and as it would make your mornings and evenings considerably safer, I wouldn't argue the merits of your living at Bobbers Mill. The one thing I could not bear is the thought that you might then become remote from us." A rush of emotion brought a shakiness to her last words.

"That wouldn't happen would it Freddy," said George confidently. "I bet he'd be here nabbing my shaving soap, he knows I only use it when there's an R in the month." George forced himself to laugh in an attempt at lightening the situation.

"Mrs.Cropley said if I didn't come home to you for my tea once in the week and have dinner with you on Sundays then she would not countenance the arrangement," said Freddy, looking appealingly at George.

"Well there you are then Mam, not the slightest chance of being rid of any of us," chuckled George. "I suppose it means I shall share a bed with John instead of you then Freddy. That'll be an improvement, if we have onions for tea I'm usually in danger of methane poisoning by midnight."

Annie was pensive. "Just as I told William, you must ask your dad Freddy, if he is willing and if you promise to come home often, then I suppose it will be alright." And so it was that the following evening, before his birthday, Freddy spoke with Charles.

"Please yourself lad, in truth that's exactly what I did at your age, I pleased Charles Eddowes. Perhaps you should bear in mind just where it got me but if you still want to go, then go."

Annie could have wept at Charles' indifference, she had lain awake in the darkness many hours thinking of William, no longer under their roof. Now Freddy too would be absent, it may not pain their father but for Annie, it left an ache which would not subside.

William knocked at the office door. "Come in." The affable voice of

Andrew Smithfield seemed never to deny entry. For many weeks the door had remained open but now operations were fully underway, he had explained his need to be removed from the noise of the factory floor whilst he calculated and negotiated the all vital deals which kept the machines turning.

"Mr.Amistead says the gum won't………" William's eager delivery was rendered to a fading, whispered nervousness at the sight of an elderly lady, seated opposite Smithfield.

"It's alright William, you are not interrupting, carry on with what you came to say." His boss smiled, put down the papers he'd been studying and awaited William's message from Robert Armistead.

"There won't be sufficient gum to see us through the month. We shall need more Dragon and more Senegal. There's a problem with the dyes, the Oxford blue paste has different batch numbers. Mr.Armistead says they must carry the same code or there'll be a slight variation in the run." William shuffled his feet in his desperation to be gone but he was not immediately dismissed.

"I would like to introduce you to Mrs.Plowright, my aunt. This is Willi………" Before Andrew could complete the pleasantry, she intervened with a purposeful, "Uhm, William Eddowes as I recall. Isn't that right young man, you see, ancient I may be but the grey matter still works, thank God." She had fixed her gaze on William throughout, in his dilemma he could think of nothing appropriate by way of response, he stood mute, other than to issue an awkward cough through the trembling fingers of his hand.

"I didn't realise you had met each other," said Andrew, curious and somewhat amused at the obvious discomfort aunt Alicia's presence had engendered in William. He imagined his aunts directness had, at some point previously, alarmed the comparatively unworldly young man.

"We met outside this factory, many months ago. I remember you were very disturbed, having lost something most important," said Alicia. "As you now stand before me looking quite relaxed and assured, I can only assume you recovered that, which at the time, caused you to be so agitated." Not once did she avert her gaze, William knew he must reply, at first his anxiety had prevented him grasping the rather cryptic nature of her remarks. Now he realised this elderly lady, Smithfield's aunt, made reference to that day his annoyance and frustration had driven him to throw the stone and make public display of his ill humour. The loss, most important, she obviously implied to be his temper but what would Smithfield now say.

"William is working under the instruction of Robert Armistead in the print shop, producing fabrics of the most wonderful colour and design. One day Aunt, I shall bring home a length of our best Vyella and you shall have it tailored to your own wishes. William here, will drive you to Winchester Street at Sherwood, where Mrs.Dodds will take your precise measurements and oversee the creation of your frock, suit or whatever you decide your wardrobe is in need of. Is that not correct William?"

"Yes Sir, it would be my pleasure."

The young man's relief at not having been disgraced in front of Smithfield induced the most charming smile. William could indeed be charming when he chose. Alicia Plowright offered her hand.

"Now we have been formally introduced I shall look forward to seeing you again William Eddowes."

He felt an unexpected strength to her grip, her arm had not been raised idly. William sensed everything Andrew Smithfield's aunt ever did, held genuine purpose, a clear intent. William would need to endear himself, after all, this was the aunt of whom his boss often spoke with such fondness, she could prove a key to success.

"I can't spend so much time in the shop Charles, now the weather is so wintry it becomes too cold in there for Danny so I have to run to and fro between customers to check on him. He needs me to read to him, sometimes simply to play with him. It was alright whilst John and Hilda were home in the summer but an infant must have stimulation or he'll never learn."

"For heavens sake, you read a book to him every bedtime, what do you suppose he learns from it at his age, that's what school is for. He'll be happy enough with you in the shop, he sees other children and I dare say the women make a fuss of him. I shall buy a paraffin heater from Waterford's, I need to go by there tomorrow morning. It will encourage people to use the shop, somewhere to warm their hands and feet while they stand gossiping. The boy is at least walking now, put him in extra clothing and give him Virol."

Charles' mind was set and to persist in her request that they change the routine to enable Annie more time with Danny during his waking hours would almost certainly have led to a strained atmosphere. That would not be fair on the others and Annie was desperate not to allow an unpleasant mood within the home, drive away still further Freddy and William. Annie had realised quite early on the reason Charles had chosen his current work pattern. He shied away from the older, married women who tended to make up the most custom through the morning and into mid afternoon. Charles would get up early to sort the papers and serve the factory men, then take over again with the arrival of The Evening Post until he locked the shop door at 8 o'clock. Bertha's words had come back to Annie, 'Charles was never very confident when faced with the public'.

So the days continued as before but a paraffin heater now provided some degree of warmth and Annie had folded a thick blanket and lain it on the floor behind the counter, where it created a bulk of warmth on which Danny could sit to play with his building blocks. She had dressed him in woollen leggings and two jumpers over his vest, he seemed content in himself. Danny would always get to his feet to socialise with other children if they came into the shop with their mothers.

It was particularly cold outside, no snow but an air frost, condensation formed inside the windows making it difficult to see out or in. Annie was replenishing the stock of oatmeal, she had been amazed at the amount sold, everyone must begin their day with porridge she thought. The door bell clanged and along with the rush of cold air as the door opened wider came Mrs.Glasson and her young son Arnold. Danny immediately ran from behind the counter to greet his friend. Arnold was convulsed from coughing, he had mittens made from old socks over his hands and a woollen hat, stretched from being passed down a line of offspring, pulled down around his ears, his face was pinched with cold. His coat was fastened on the wrong button and hung lopsided around his knees.

"Stand over there by that heater an' try to be a bit quieter, glory be, me nerves won't stand much more of it," said Mrs.Glasson.

Annie took Danny's hand and led him back to his blanket.

"You stay here today, there's a good boy."

Annie knelt before little Arnold and pulled up his socks, which having lost their elastic, had sunk in a bedraggled heap about his ankles, his legs felt icy cold. Annie smiled up at the little boy.

"My goodness that is a nasty cough Arnold." Again and again the spasm in his throat shook his slight frame and brought a wateriness to his eyes from the strain. "Has the doctor seen him Mrs.Glasson?" Asked Annie.

"I told 'is dad last night that we should 'ave doctor to 'im but yer know what the men are like, allus afraid they might 'ave to cough up their ale money. I've been givin' Arnold butter, sugar an' vinegar melted down, like our mam used to give us but it don't seem to be doin' much good. Anyroad I better ave' a bit o' cheese an' some more butter, the sugar should last 'til end o' the week."

The doctor had to be paid for, sometimes it was a choice between food enough for all the family or medicine for one. Annie quickly weighed up the cheese and butter, charging only for the wedge of cheddar. Mrs.Glasson, in her state of anxiety, had not questioned the cost and Annie would rather eat no butter herself for a week if it enabled poor little Arnold some relief.

Edna had finally managed to convince Victor that Ponds Cold Cream was the same thing as elbow grease. Susie waited outside Hastilow's with Myra in her pram whilst Edna accompanied a hesitant Victor inside to make his all important purchase, a birthday gift for his mam. In his pocket tied into a handkerchief, the proceeds of Billy's chrysanthemum sales.

"Ask the lady then Victor, tell her what it is you've come to buy," said

Edna. In spite of repeated attempts since leaving Florrie's house to persuade him he must say, 'Please may I 'ave a pot of Ponds Cold Cream', when he speaks to the lady behind the counter, Victor's lips bubbled his excitement and pleasure before requesting.

"A pot of elbow grease for mam's birthday please, elbow grease for mam."

Edna smiled and pointed to the actual item, the woman, possibly tired and looking forward to the following day off, muttered something tetchily before asking in a manner devoid of all grace.

"I suppose yer want it in a bag?"

Edna was glad to get out of the shop to join Susie and Myra. It was a source of frustration to Edna that her youngest had not yet walked off, as she was aware that Danny had done so three weeks ago. It was Billy's earnest belief that Myra was too heavy and lazy to make the effort. Riding in the comfort of her pram or being carried around on Edna's hip, in Billy's opinion, appealed to Myra far more than being self propelled. Edna, a little put out at the suggestion that her daughter was fat, in the first instance had rebuked Billy for even thinking such a thing. Now as the days passed with still no real effort on Myra's part to stand on her feet and advance, Edna had joined Billy in his theory and had denied her sweet biscuits since the previous weekend.

"I'm afraid it is croup Annie," said Dr.Latham. "Daniel was slight at birth but showed us all his strength then, be positive and pray that he will do so again. Keep him in a warm room but with a moist air. The kitchen is ideal, steam helps the condition. See that he remains in a sitting position, don't let him lay flat. If you hold him on your knee support his back with your upper arm. Give him, just a few drops at a time, the glycerine and lemon. It may help ease the muscle spasm in his larynx. The night hours seem always to be the worst, don't keep too bright a light, neither use an ordinary candle, a 'nightlite' is best. It gives a gentle glow which may help him rest, a larger flame would take up the oxygen." He closed his bag, sighed and briefly laid his hand on Annie's arm. "Children are surprisingly tough, I never fail to be amazed by their powers of recovery, take heart my dear."

"What of John and Hilda, should I keep them away at all times?" She asked.

"Young boys have a predilection. Croup will prevail usually between the age of birth to three years. It would be sensible not to encourage John and Hilda to spend time in this room with Daniel but it is not a likelihood that they would catch it at their age, especially Hilda. Do take adequate nourishment yourself Annie, he will need you to be strong."

"Can I push Edna? I'll push the pram," said Victor.

"Alright then, you can push Myra as far as Annie's. Be careful at the curbs, you're not pushin' that soddin' wheelbarro' now." Edna had left Billy in charge of their other two daughters. All last evening she had sat skinning pickling onions, which had soaked in a bowl of slightly salted water overnight. Now it was the task of Annie and Liza to put them in jars with the spice and vinegar. 'Don't let 'em use too much bloody spice', Edna had cautioned Billy. 'I want to 'ave some skin left on the roof of me mouth when I've 'ad one wi' a nice bit of Annie's cheddar come Christmas'.

Edna lifted Myra from the pram to take her inside the shop.

"Can we 'ave a bag o' pear drops Mam, aunty Annie always gives us more than Mavis," observed Susie.

"Just open the door will yer, come on Victor, the pram'll be alright out there wi'out you 'avin' to 'old it, I put the brake on." Edna finally ushered the two inside and had to look twice, the sight of Charles behind the counter on a Saturday afternoon was most unexpected.

"Hello Edna, let me have your list," he said with an air of impatience.

"What's up, where's Annie?" Edna sensed troubles.

"She's in the back with Daniel, he's not very well, the doctor's been, apparently it's croup."

Edna was agitated, her overwhelming desire was to go straight through that inner door to see her dearest friend, but croup. Edna knew of its severity. She had Myra in her arms, Susie and Victor were with her, before she could go to Annie and Danny she must take them home.

"I'll take these things quickly Charles an' get off 'ome but tomorrow mornin', while Billy's there for the girls, I shall come on me own. Tell Annie, I shall be 'ere in the mornin'.'"

" There's nothing you can do Edna, just take care of your own," said Charles.

Edna's tone was sharp as she said. "Annie is as good as me own, she's allus been like a sister to me. Tell 'er what I've said, in the mornin' I'll be 'ere."

Charles picked up the groceries in silence, handing them to Susie to pack into the shopping bag. Sensing the tension, Susie made no further mention of pear drops and they left. Myra was put back in the pram with the heavy bag at the foot end. Victor felt concerned, he fingered the precious pot of cold cream in his coat pocket, making sure it was still there, safe. His innocent mind was aware of something amiss, thinking of the surprise when he gave his mam her present made him feel better.

Annie listened to Charles banging about in the cellar. The situation had forced him to take over all the hours behind the counter, it had made his mood so intense, speaking to him on any subject could prove alarming. Freddy had come home for his tea in the week, only to be shouted at by his dad for choosing to work at the farm instead of a decent job. In his ill temper Charles belittled Arthur Cropley's occupation. William had floundered his way through three evenings of Charles' miserable, hard done by complaining and not surprisingly, had declared he would be taking fish and chips in for Davina and himself the following evening and having his tea with the Tozers the next.

Edna had called the previous Sunday and insisted she would come again this Sunday.

When Sarah had heard how poorly Danny was she had been firm on the matter, 'John and Hilda shall come to stay at Mitchell Street, it will keep them out of risk and be two less to feed and wash for'. Dear Sarah, she persuaded Annie that the arrangement would give herself a much needed dose of happiness at having young company plus a purpose to stir her idle bones from the chair. They would remain at No.69 until Danny improved.

Annie had despaired of cooking a substantial Sunday dinner today, William and Freddy would find it a very makeshift offering.

George was Annie's right arm, bringing in coal, stacking the grates, carrying food for Charles and himself to the small sitting room and washing up the pots after. When his day's work at Raleigh was done he'd offered help to his dad, even at this moment George was carrying stock up the cellar steps and into the shop.

A tap came at the back door before it was immediately opened and Edna's voice called out, "Only me." Annie's spirits rose to the sound, she missed John and Hilda, especially the constant chatter of her daughter, ever eager, so full of life.

"How is he now?" Asked Edna, placing what appeared a heavy basket onto the table. "Thank God for that, me arm wer' droppin' off." Edna had only to listen to Danny's breathing, the rasping eruption of coughing which tore at his tiny chest, to know that he struggled for survival. Edna flopped down onto a chair and burst into tears.

"Hush Edna, don't upset yourself so. We are in the best place, the room is always warm and we keep the kettle steaming." Edna's eyes had focused on Danny's hand, encircling Annie's finger, how it flexed with each spasm.

"I've brought a pot of knuckle stew, it'll do for the lads and Charles, I guessed you wouldn't be eatin' owt so I've baked a marble cake, yer can surely force a slice o' that down, you've got to eat summat or you'll keel over wi' weakness."

"I promise I shall have a piece of your cake Edna, George will make us all a cup of tea soon," said Annie.

"Don't worry about tea for me, I've got to go back in a minute, Billy's doin' an extra shift at the exchange. One o' the other men got took bad yesterday, fell off 'is chair at work, out cold 'e wer' for several minutes, left some poor sod in Stapleford thinkin' 'e must 'ave set off on foot to connect 'em at Melton Mowbray."

"You go home Edna, by next Saturday when you come to the shop with your list, we might be altogether improved." Annie quickly averted her gaze away from her friend, for fear of breaking down at the sight of such compassion. Edna's heart ached from her will to make everything better and all her love and devotion showed in those eyes. Edna put two fingers to her lips and transferred her kiss to Danny's forehead, squeezing Annie's hand she said, "If you need me, you know I will come, any hour of the night."

Annie nodded but could speak no more.

Charles had walked into the kitchen in search of his penknife. "I'm sure I left it on the ledge in the cellar but it's not there now. I shall need it in the morning, the light is too dim to see anything in here." He rummaged along the top of the dresser. "At last, who put the damn thing there."

He was about to leave the room when Annie said, "I feel he is fading Charles, would you like to sit with him, for just a short while, he might take strength from his dad." Annie's head felt awash with tears, awaiting their release.

Charles stared back at her. "What could he possibly draw from me. You are his mother, all children respond best to their mothers. Even Freddy and William favour you over me. You will see him through, make him better, I always make things worse don't I?" He disappeared into the shop to finish replenishing the shelves.

George seemed unwilling to leave them. Charles had retired to bed. The kitchen had found that stillness the night hours wrapped about man's dwelling place, that respite before a new day. The air hung with steam from the simmering kettle, the soft glow from the nightlite cast its watchfulness over the weary features of Danny's face.

"You should get some rest George, you have work tomorrow. I have everything I need, go to bed now."

The bedroom could become quite chill in the early hours, George awoke. He missed the warmth of John who would normally lay beside him and creep ever closer through his hours of sleep, until by morning, the two brothers had denied Jack Frost any chance of reaching their fingers and toes. The quietness seemed overbearing. George pulled on his trousers over his nightshirt, he'd not removed his socks for days. As he tiptoed downstairs to look for that faint glimmer which identified the bottom of the kitchen door, a rush of dread caused his limbs to tremble. It was pitch black. Trying not to make a sound, he carefully negotiated his way.

"Why are you sitting in the dark Mam? George felt the air to be different. He stood by Annie's side and knew her desolation before ever she spoke. He knelt and lay his hands over his mother's, hers still held Danny lifeless on her knee. Neither uttered a single word, they wept for the infant and for each other until grief was exhausted.

"What do you want me to do Mam?" Asked George.

"Light will crack soon, until then we must be patient. First you must go to Dr.Latham then to Mr.Handley. Call at the factory, ask if you might have the day off, they will understand I'm sure."

"What about William and Freddy, should I go to tell them?"

"No, there is little chance of either hearing at Brassington and Bobbers Mill. William will be here when he finishes work, that is time enough to tell him. I think he will then have need of something to occupy his mind. I shall ask William to go to the farm to tell his brother. When you have spoken with Mr.Pollard at Raleigh, go to Winchester Street, not to the workshop but to No.24. Explain to Billy and he will tell Edna in the way he feels fit."

"Do you want me to rouse dad?"

Annie drew a deep breath and sighed, her voice wavered as her chest sank back, "Charles will be up early anyway, for the papers, we'll let him sleep until then."

"What's the matter wi' mam?" Asked Liza.

Edna sat upstairs on the edge of the bed, her face drained of all colour, her fingers clutching at a hanky, so wet from tears it could absorb no more as they continued to fall from Edna's cheeks to her lap.

Billy stirred the teapot. "Look after Myra for me, there's a good girl. Annie and Susie are runnin' an errand for their dad. It'll be alright, we've 'ad some bad news, it's made your mam sad but a cup o' this tea wi' a nice bit o' sugar should make 'er feel better."

Upstairs, Billy put his arm about Edna's shoulders, "Don't persecute yourself Edna, it won't help anythin'." She snivelled her misery.

"I wer' jealous of Annie 'avin' a boy, I used to look at 'im wi' envy an' ask God why we didn't 'ave the boy instead o' them. You wanted a son, I know yer did. 'Ow could I 'ave been so mean, she's my best friend, all these years Annie's never once failed me. I can't bear the hurt Billy, I can't stand it." Edna wailed her grief and remorse, Billy's own eyes stung, he couldn't bear to witness his wife's torment.

"Annie is goin' to need you Edna, you'll be no use to 'er in this state. We 'ad out Myra an' I've not for a single second ever regretted that. Yes, to 'ave 'ad a son 'ould be grand but I've got Victor," said Billy, squeezing Edna's hand. Her cries were pitiful, she sank her head onto Billy's chest and not until Liza appeared, carrying Myra, did Edna find some calm.

"Put 'er down, you'll do yourself a damage carryin' 'er weight up them stairs," said Edna between sobs. Liza lowered Myra to sit on the floor, where she promptly stood up and walked, a little unsteadily but determinedly to where Edna sat on the bed. Edna smiled through her tears and grasping Billy's hand she whispered. "I've never regretted neither."

Billy had sent Annie and Susie to the exchange to tell them he'd be late but that he would be there as soon as he could and explain. What the coming days would hold and how they would manage everything Billy did not know. Back in France when death was all around him, Billy had closed his eyes and thought of Winchester Street. Now death invaded every place, Edna's grief brought back all that hurt, the despair which would try to crush any hope. He had endured it at Albert Haynes' funeral, now it consumed him again.

"Where do you want our son to be buried Charles, I know all your family are at Rock Cemetery," said Annie. "Mr.Handley needs to know by this afternoon."

Charles sat at the table struggling to eat a slice of bread. His irritable mood had left him only to be replaced by extended periods of silence. His manner with customers had at times been brusque, Annie imagined all those aware would make allowance and others would in time, forget any lack of courtesy as they dealt with problems and adversities of their own.

"You decide, you nursed him, it should be your decision." Charles could force down no more of his food. "I best sort the papers. It will be too cold, wherever it is, for Sarah and Davina, they would likely catch their deaths too. Tell them not to attend." He took his jacket from the back of the chair. "What time is Handley calling?"

"I said I would come to the Chapel, to spend a few minutes, and that I would let him know then. Sarah will keep John and Hilda at Mitchell Street until after the funeral, they are too young to face the ordeal and it effectively prevents Sarah a chance to venture to the cemetery in the cold. I shall try to persuade Davina she should stay at home but if I am to be successful in that aim then I know I must call on her after it is done. You must post a notice in the shop window alerting customers to the fact that the shop will be closed on that day."

Charles muttered something inaudible, she chose not to ask him to repeat it thinking she was probably better off not knowing.

As Annie walked to Handley's her thoughts gave her no peace. In those last moments with Danny in her arms, she had felt a presence of Harold and Bella. In her sorrow, she wanted her little boy to lay close to them but if she instructed James Handley to arrange for the interment to be at Witford Hill, then she was afraid Charles would convince himself that Daniel was not his. Only if their son was laid to rest at Rock Cemetery would Charles accept and mourn as he should.

Tommy had worked on the tiny coffin, his chest filled with ache as his hands smoothed the pale ash along its grain. James Handley lay a hand on Tommy's shoulder.

"Be strong lad and feel proud, you're the privileged one, your skill is creating Daniel's final resting place, the care shows, it's looking grand Tommy." His words were kind but they did nothing to stop Tommy's tears falling on to the satin lining and sympathy for his friend William, tearing at Tommy's heart like nothing he'd before experienced. His own dad died in France, lay somewhere beneath French soil. The distance had somehow enabled the hurt to be spread over the months and years, taking away that concentration of pain which now racked poor Tommy as he prepared the coffin for an infant so close to his own awareness.

Edna turned the key in the door and felt for Billy's hand. It was a biting wind, grey clouds had rolled overhead all morning with only the briefest glimpse of brightness. The funeral was at 2o'clock. Sylvia and Kathleen had been left with simple tasks, their minds would not accommodate anything intricate this afternoon. Myra was with Edna's mam, the girls would go straight from school to their grandma's and bring Myra home. Edna had cried herself to sleep the night before, still guilt at envying Annie and Charles a son tormented her cruelly. Billy had tried to console her but his own emotions beat at his chest from deep within.

The small Chapel at the entrance to Rock Cemetery was to be where a short service would take place prior to the burial. Edna and Billy sat to the side, there eyes fixed firmly to the front. A vase of lilies graced the altar table and someone had placed a posy of tiny white dianthus at the base of the vase. The people stood as the vicar led the bearer and mourners along the aisle. Charles walked with Annie, he looked curiously older than just a few days ago. George was with Freddy, and William clung to Celia. Jean and Randall had come from London, all of Sarah's family was present. At the last moment, Tommy slipped in at the back and sat alone.

Mr.Handley had secured a plot as close to Charles' mother and father as was possible, it inevitably lay close to Enid also. As they left the Chapel for the interment Charles suddenly spoke to Annie, the first word he had uttered since leaving Gregory Street.

"You go on, I'll catch up." He drew George and Freddy forward to walk at either side of her. Annie could do nothing but follow the bearer, her mind was too desolate to question any more.

At the graveside Annie heard not a single thing the vicar said, for as he spoke, so she too spoke, silently with Enid.

'I promised always to love your babies, I have and I do still. Now I ask that in your world, you take Danny, my baby and always love him. Do that for me, as I have done for you'.

She felt George's fingers tighten around her own as a small dish of earth was held out for Annie to take some and let fall onto the coffin. Billy held Edna around the waist with his one arm, neither could contain their grief. Tommy stood alone at the back of the gathering, watching his friend as William cried uncontrollably. Celia could not know, as she tried to console him, that William's despair was not just for his baby brother but for his own wretchedness. Surely his father had not paid any real heed to his selfish remarks about Edwin Garbett, but why wasn't he here at the graveside, where was his dad. William had seen Tommy standing with his cap at his side, quietly, inconspicuously at the back of the Chapel. William had betrayed so many of the people whom he loved, his immaturity denied him an understanding of why.

Andrew Smithfield too, had been a silent observer. As people moved off, he had for a moment, thought to speak to Annie but Charles' absence from the graveside had confused him. Under the circumstances he felt unable to make approach and slipped quietly away.

Edna sniffed and spoke shakily to Billy. "I can't leave Annie like this. You go 'ome to be there for when the girls get back, I'll be alright I promise, I'll come 'ome in a bit."

Billy's nerves were so raw he needed a little time alone before facing his young daughters. He was angry at Charles, concerned for Annie, filled with compassion for George, Freddy and William. So many hours he had listened to his own wife crying he could not bear to think of her pain any longer. He would walk through the arboretum. It was dull and cold, it would be quiet, very few people lingered there at this time of year.

As Billy approached the bandstand he could see a figure, sitting on the steps. It was Charles, his head slumped forward in his hands. Billy stood in front of him, aroused by this spectacle of weakness, incensed at Charles' wanting behaviour.

"For God's sake, aren't yer man enough to see your own child buried."

"Leave me alone Billy, go home, it's nothing to do with you." Charles spoke but did not look up.

"Nothin' to do wi' me yer say when I've listened to my wife breakin' 'er 'eart for hours at a time. You left your wife to stand alone, to face wi'out yer the sight o' Danny lowered into the ground, your son Charles, a son!" Billy cried out from the passion which drove his grief.

"We both know war Billy, the violent death of war. We've choked on its stench, the grotesque barbarity of it. Month upon month of death. We lived with it, through it, death was no longer sudden but constant, expected. My wife lies in Rock Cemetery, I buried her there."

"Annie is your wife," cried Billy. "Enid died sixteen years ago."

"One day she was there, fussing me about something or other, wanting something, Enid was there just as she would always be there and she was mine. The next morning, there was no Enid, she was gone. When I stood at that spot in the cemetery and watched them lower the coffin, I could not describe what I felt. Now I know it, the pain of a thousand wars ripped at my soul that day. People visit the graves of their loved ones don't they Billy? They lay flowers at birthdays and anniversaries. I would watch Annie and the children sometimes as they tidied Byron's spot but you see Billy, I couldn't. Not once did I go to Enid at Rock Cemetery after that day, I tried Billy but I couldn't and I could not go there this afternoon."

"You left Annie, your wife, the mother of your children, did yer not see the faces of William and Freddy. Yer left them to bear it while you ran away."

Charles stood and looked into Billy's eyes. "You have no right to tell me what I should do." Charles swayed from emotion. "It's so easy for you isn't it Billy, you always get it right. Billy, now he knows how to be a man, everyone loves Billy Dodds. You're the expert on life, the model of all things good. What does Charles Eddowes know, pathetic excuse of a man. I should listen to you shouldn't I, pay heed to Billy Dodds, that master of all things. Oh what I could learn from the man who's every day is spent in the company of an imbecile."

Billy's arm went out in that instant, the blow sent Charles reeling to the ground where he drew up his knees and hid his head beneath his hands.

Billy spoke over him. "One day Charles Eddowes, one day so help me, I shall show you for the miserable bastard that you are." Billy turned and strode away, his knuckles stinging from the force of his blow, tears streaming down his face from an anguish he could not understand. Now Billy wanted home, his daughters, Billy wanted his wife.

He had covered the distance from the arboretum without noting its passing. Now he turned the corner into Winchester Street, sanctuary was close. A figure stood outside No.24, it was Victor. Billy swallowed hard, he could take no more trials today.

"What's wrong lad, is your mam alright?" Billy tried not to show distress but his insides churned.

"Tilly's had kittens again Billy, Tilly's had kittens."

Billy could not endure Victor's usual entreaty, he was about to forestall the plea when Victor's face changed. It became suddenly illuminated, like the dial on the Town Hall clock at dusk.

"Mam says we can keep one this time Billy, this time we can keep one." Victor threw his arms about Billy's waist and thrust his head into Billy's chest in his sheer joy.

Billy fought to breathe beyond the dreadful hurt which near stifled him. He struggled to utter words. Wrapping his one arm around Victor's shoulders, he held him close.

"That's grand lad," said Billy, "that's just grand."